"Birthright is a tale of danger and romance, beautifully woven together into a story that will leave you wanting more."
~Elana Johnson,
author of the *Possession* series and *Elevated*

"Full of adventure, romance, and demons, *Birthright* grabbed me right off and wouldn't let go. Another fantastic read by Nichole Giles."
~ Heather Justesen,
author of *Brownies & Betrayal*

"*Birthright* will pull you in and weave a magic spell around you so you'll never want to leave the incredible world Nichole Giles has created."
~ Tristi Pinkston,
author of *Turning Pages*

"In *Birthright*, Nichole takes us on an exotic journey against Shadow Demons, true love, best friends, and choices with never-ending consequences. Hold on tight because everything you thought you knew about Abby and Kye is about to change."
~ Rachelle J. Christensen,
author of *Diamond Rings Are Deadly Things*

Published by Jelly Bean Press
PO Box 548
Osawatomie, Kansas 66064

Copyright ©2013 by Nichole Giles
Edited by Diane Dalton
Cover design by Melissa Williams Design
Interior design by Melissa Williams Design
Cover photograph by Fresh Stock via Shutterstock
Author photo by Erin Summerill

ISBN 978-1-63034-007-0

Nichole Giles's author website is http://nicholegiles.blogspot.com

BIRTHRIGHT

NICHOLE GILES

JELLY BEAN PRESS

For Brayden, who has spent the last two
years living far away from
our family.

And for Brittany, who is also about to
leave the nest.
You both grew up way too fast.

Born to lead—
Destined to fail

ONE

Sick

My cell phone buzzes as I scramble out of bed and bolt toward the bathroom to pay homage to the porcelain throne. Pain clenches my insides, leaving me moaning. I could swear I spend more time doubled over, wishing to throw up, than I spend upright–or even lying flat. And there's no telling what tomorrow will bring.

Except more of the same symptoms. Val promises me there will be lots more of this.

Joy.

The phone buzzes again, Kye's ringtone growing progressively louder until it stops altogether. He'll call back, so I stay put, afraid that if I stand too fast, I'll pass out again. My days have become an endless cycle of horrendous pain, passing out, and attempting to finish high school before I die.

Some days, dying doesn't sound like the worst option. But I would like to graduate first. Feel like I accomplished something this time around.

When my phone buzzes a third time in as many minutes, I have to answer and save Kye a trip. I need to see him like I need to breathe, but I have to force some fluids into my system first–despite the potential pain it will cause. I get up slowly, rinse my dry mouth and splash water on my face, determined to make it back before Kye calls again.

The wall is my anchor as I stumble to my room and collapse in a heap on the bed. Healing crystals dangle from each post, and pieces of other natural stones mingle among the potted herbs lining my room. Landon even drilled wires into the ceiling so Mom could hang Gram's most powerful gems. But none of it is enough.

I pull the comforter over me, shivering. Winter has passed and we're experiencing the balmiest spring in recent Jackson history, but I'm always cold. And in pain. And exhausted. Thoughts of giving up hover in the back of my mind until the phone rings again. This time, I pick it up, managing a weak smile when Kye's voice tickles my ear. "Please tell me something has changed," he pleads, a desperate edge to his voice. "That you were downstairs noshing on disgusting potato chips rather than ... you know."

"Sour cream and onion," I manage, shoving aside thoughts of any and all food and the consequential pain eating brings.

"Tell me you're getting better," he continues, his voice softening. "Make me believe this is something that will pass, something we can overcome. Convince me we're not dying."

"I was actually in the greenhouse, gardening." He knows better, but it's nice to pretend. "My herbs are thriving, and I'm going to plant tomatoes in a few weeks. You wouldn't believe what Murtagh's done with the flower beds. He's a botanical genius."

"Of course he is," Kye says. "So those delicious carrots in the soup your mother sent over yesterday came from the garden, right?"

"Yes. All the vegetables and herbs were home grown. No one does vegetable noodle soup like Marian." I lean against the wall of pillows, tucking the comforter up to my chin.

"I agree," he says. "Now tell me you ate some of that soup. Convince me there's no way you're going to the hospital for an IV this week."

Stifling a yawn, I stare out the window at the sun-lit mountains. "I finished the whole pot. Marian was angry because I didn't leave any for her and Gabe."

"That's my girl," Kye says, sounding satisfied, if unconvinced. I haven't been able to eat more than a few bites of anything for over a

2

week, but the rest is true. My mom did make soup, and Murtagh really has been hard at work caring for my plants.

"About school tomorrow ..." Kye starts.

"I know we're going to pay for it. Believe me, I'm so weak I can barely stand, and it's been three days since you kissed me in that alcove. But I can't breathe. Do you understand? Missing you is more painful than seeing you, so please don't cancel on me. Please."

"Relax, babe. I'll be there. Just making sure you've got Gabe covered."

Gabe = part Dragon, part bodyguard, part babysitter, and total tattletale. He's been assigned to guard me. All the freaking time. But he does genuinely worry, which is something I use to my advantage—frequently. "I'm going to develop a sudden, inexplicable need for a hamburger between sixth and seventh periods. A craving he couldn't possibly deny."

"Good one."

"I know. Especially since it's probably going straight in the garbage can so I don't have to smell it."

"Are you sure he'll go, rather than sending someone else?"

"I'll convince him that I don't know how long my craving will last, and I need it right away. It'll only buy us fifteen minutes or so, but ..."

Kye finishes my thought for me. "It's fifteen minutes more than we're supposed to have together."

"I'll take whatever I can get," I tell him.

His answering sigh is shaky. "I feel like there's an enormous hole in my chest when we're apart like this."

"Me too," I answer, reminding myself I should be glad for the small fragments of time we've learned how to steal. Eventually, there will be no more secret meetings behind the curtains in the auditorium, or blissful seconds in the janitor's closet during lunch. Eventually, someone will see Kye sneaking into my room to hold me in the middle of the night after a particularly hard week, and they'll send one of us away. At some point, parting will become permanent for us, and we'll have to learn how to accept it.

3

Somehow. Unfortunately, I'm afraid that point is coming very, very soon.

"Back off, Gabe." I remove the pizza he just plopped on my tray and toss it on his, shuddering. "If you're so excited about carbs and processed meat, you take this."

"Abby, you have to start eating better." Gabe follows behind me, filling his tray with everything I refuse to put on mine. "You're withering away."

I add a side of vinaigrette next to my salad. "I can't help it. You know I can't. Eating fatty foods only makes it worse."

"Maybe if you—"

"Stop." My tray clatters on the table, flatware clinking against my unopened pop can. "Just stop trying to fix me. There's nothing you can do. There's nothing *anyone* can do." The familiar burn of tears throbs behind my eyes. "I'm dying, Kye's dying, and Tynan wins. Again."

Gabe knows how weak I am—all the Dragons do. It's their job to know, just like it's their job to do everything in their power to protect me, to keep me alive as long as possible while we search for a way to break the stupid curse. The hard part is that all their effort isn't about me. Not really. It's about them. They think I'm here to save them.

They don't seem to understand that I don't even have the power to save myself.

"We're not going to let him win." Gabe leans close, speaking low so no one else will hear. "The royal lineage has been restored after all this time. We won't let our queen go without a hell of a fight."

Arguing is pointless, so I rest my forehead on the table, wondering if anyone ever listens to me. "I just want Kye—alive.

Living and breathing and next to me. And I don't care about the rest. I don't want to be your stupid queen."

Gabe's hand rubs circles on the small of my back. "You'll have to take that up with Zane and Val. Again."

"They don't care."

Another hand rests on my shoulder, and the energy around me shifts with a warm, welcoming light. I don't have to look up to know Rose and Jen are here.

"We'll figure it out, Abby," Rose murmurs. "You'll both be fine."

Jen remains silent, so I glance up. Why does she seem so distant? Maybe she doesn't know what to say. How do you comfort a friend you know is dying? My stomach burns and gurgles, doubling me over with a moan. "Has anyone seen Akers today?"

Our beloved Dragon-turned-teacher allows us to call him Landon, except at school. It's a respect thing, and I totally get it. But under the circumstances, Mr. Akers feels too formal, so we've taken to referring to him as Akers.

"His car's in the parking lot," Rose says. "So he's here somewhere."

Unable to move, I hold a shaking hand to my head. "I need him."

"Eat something first." Gabe sounds exasperated. "You know he won't help you unless you try to eat."

"I can't!" I snap. "Bring the salad if you want, but I'm not going to be able to eat until my chakras are realigned."

Gabe leans close as if he means to support me, so I shove him away and push to my feet on my own. My first step is wobbly; I accept Rose's steadying arm. "I hate this."

"Me too." She asks Jen to guard her food while she walks with me.

"What am I going to do?"

"I hate to say this—because just thinking about it hurts—but it might be time for you to leave." She pauses to clear her throat. "I love you, and I'm going to miss you something fierce, but I can't—I won't—watch you die. Not when it can be prevented."

The lump in my throat keeps me from answering as we round the corner and enter the open doorway that leads us onstage.

"Akers?" Gabe calls. "Abby needs you."

I head for the office, though the window is dark. "Check the prop room," I tell Gabe. "He's probably cataloguing or building a set piece or something." I flip on the office light. As always, the desk is clear of any clutter. There's a locked drawer on the right where Akers keeps his laptop, phone, and printer. I've watched him meticulously store everything in a very precise manner a number of times. Something about balanced Chi. Or maybe it's for my benefit, because I need somewhere to lie while he gives me the energy treatments that keep me going on days like today.

While I lie back on the oak desk, Rose retrieves a block of smoky quartz from a shelf in the corner and places it between my knees. "Where are the rest?"

"I have them." I hand her nuggets of amber and tiger's eye from my jacket pocket, and then quartz and aquamarine from the chain around my neck. She situates them along my torso, on my abdomen, ribs, and throat. As footsteps clop across the stage, she retrieves amethyst from a glass display case and balances it on my forehead.

"Looks like Rose has things under control," Akers says, his piercing blue eyes landing on me. "I'm starting to feel unneeded."

Rose clears her throat. "I may be learning where to put the crystals, but I'm no Healer. Besides, we're still missing the heart stone."

"I'm not a Healer either. I just do what Val tells me." Akers signals for Gabe to close the blinds and lifts a long chain from under his shirt, drawing it over his head. "You know the drill, kids." While others turn to face the window, I close my eyes and wait for the swish and click that means Akers has closed the hidden security safe. Then the warm pendant falls into my open hand.

Eyes still closed, I hold it suspended over my heart, urging my weakening abilities to draw power from the emeralds. Akers, Rose, and Gabe join hands, closing their eyes and channeling their positive energy toward me. Val has explained that this is the only way for a Healer to actually treat herself. At first, it was just Akers and me in this little room, but we recently discovered that having Gabe and Rose present helps me to spin the crystals faster, stronger, making the stones more potent as my friends' combined energy fills the cracks in mine and my chakras realign.

After a minute, our energy holds the pendant aloft, and a number of the smaller crystals lift into the air as well. The stones revolve together, synchronized in a clockwise formation, faster and faster. I feel a jolt. Lights flicker, dance, and warmth from the Healing stones surrounds me.

"Abby." Rose's voice breaks my concentration, and the crystals drift to rest on my body. I take a deep breath and open my eyes.

Gabe smiles down at me. "Feel better?"

I nod, accepting his help to bring me into a sitting position. As I hang my head, waiting for it to clear, Akers doubles over, clutching his middle while Rose helps him to his chair.

"Sorry, Landon!"

A bead of sweat rolls off his forehead and drips onto the floor. The hue of his skin looks the slightest shade of green. "It's fine, Abby. Part of my job. Can't imagine what it's like dealing with this all day, every day."

"I wouldn't wish it on anyone. I hate having to share it with you just so I can survive the day. It's not fair."

Rose frowns, for once in her life seeming to be at a loss for words.

Landon mops his forehead with a handkerchief he's begun carrying in his pocket. "As you have so vehemently pointed out in recent weeks, none of our circumstances are fair, least of all yours."

A guilty flush warms my cheeks when I think of the clandestine meeting I'm planning with Kye and how many people will pay for our fifteen minutes of happiness. Uncomfortable with the thought, I slide off the desk, muttering, "I just wish I knew what to do."

Always solicitous, Gabe hovers near. "You okay?"

I nod, kneeling in front of Akers. If he's going to be sick because of me, the least I can do is hold the trash can for him. But he shoves it away and sits up. "I'm fine," he says. "I'll be fine. My relief will come ten times more quickly than yours. I only need a few minutes."

Rose squeezes my arm when I turn to her. "We can't keep this up. I have to do something."

Our eyes connect, hers pleading for me to go—even as she begs me to stay.

I know she's right. I don't know how or where, but the when is now—maybe this week. If I don't do something soon—leave this place that finally feels like home, and these people I love like family—it will be too late.

And Kye and I might not be the only ones who die.

TWO

Guarded

Rose stays behind with Landon while Gabe follows me outside. My lungs fill with crisp mountain breeze, reminding me of one more thing I stand to lose by leaving. I plant myself on a bench, and Gabe sits next to me.

"You okay?"

"Depends." I turn my face toward the sky, remembering another moment on a similar bench. "The pain's better, if that's what you're asking."

"Perfect." He removes the plastic top from a salad, pours dressing over it, and hands me the fork.

"How do you stay so calm all the time?" I ask, forking a mouthful of lettuce.

Gabe drapes his elbow over the bench, relaxing. "I don't."

"Right." I chew, swallow. "I've never once seen you more than just a tiny bit ruffled. Not when you found out about the Dark Elen, or that Juri and Boone were helping Eric try to open Tynan's tomb, or when Juri stabbed Kye and tried to kill us."

"Wow." His arm drops, and his face twists in pain. "You must really think I have zero feelings."

His tone startles me into meeting his eyes. "That's not what I said."

"But that's the implication."

I take another bite, irritation building as I chew and swallow. "All I meant was that I don't understand how you stay so, aloof. So composed. My entire life is falling apart, but no matter what happens, you follow behind, carrying my books and trying to feed me. Doesn't it bother you that I might die tomorrow?"

"Of course it bothers me." A crinkle forms between his eyebrows, and the muscles in his neck tighten. "And of course I was shaken by the things that happened last month. We all were."

"It's just ... you're always so calm," I mumble. He sets my drink on the bench, so I pick it up and pop the tab. Gabe stills me with a hand on my wrist.

"I'm trained to remain calm in emergency situations, or to at least appear calm. That doesn't always make it true."

I want to reply, but he touches a finger to my lips and keeps talking.

"If you recall, you weren't awake to see my reactions—or those of anyone else—after everything went down in that cave. But I was more than 'ruffled' when I got there and found you unconscious and barely breathing." He leans closer, dropping his voice. "Just because I didn't get there sooner, don't think I wouldn't have taken that blade in Kye's place. The question is, would you have saved *me* from dying the way you saved *him*? Would you have been willing to make that sacrifice if it had been anyone other than Kye?"

This is a question to which I have no answer, and one I hope I never have to find. Before, I would have been fine with never having to use my Gift, especially to save a life. But in that moment when Kye lay dying, I couldn't just sit there and watch. If it had been anyone else, someone I don't necessarily love, or someone who isn't important to me—I don't know if I could have risked myself. Not the way I did for him.

I just don't know.

"I *was* feeling awfully generous at the time," I joke. Gabe deserves a response, whether or not I have an answer. "You know, with my new royal status and all."

10

The corners of his mouth twitch, his eyes gleaming with a hint of amusement. "I hope you'll feel similarly generous if *I'm* ever injured saving your life."

I run a finger down the curve of his nose, smiling. "Of course I would Heal you if you were injured. It's what I do." Healing, yes. It's the risking my life part I question.

His smile fades, and he lets go of my wrist so I can sip my pop, leaving me with the impression that he's not thrilled with my answer. I finish my salad and stand to throw away the container. Most of the snow has melted, leaving the school property surrounded by green pastures that give way to a thick forest. In the distance, a bird trills, and another responds.

Gabe stands, joining me on the sidewalk. "You need to get to class if you plan on graduating." As we near the building, wind tears at my hair and face, carrying with it a scent I recognize, but can't place. Goose bumps prickle my arms. I flick my head to keep the tangled locks out of my eyes, and notice movement near the trees.

"Abby?" Gabe asks, following as I start toward the forest. "What is it?"

I slow, my heart thumping as my eyes search, ears straining for any unusual sound. "Something. In the trees. Or the brush."

Gabe stays close, his long legs eating up the distance faster than mine as he does a sweep of our surroundings. "I don't see anything."

"Shh!" The forest floor squishes under my feet, releasing a pleasant, earthy musk mingled with hints of pine and oak. But there's something else—something foreign, and unnatural—that I can smell, feel, but not see. A weak ray of sunlight shimmers on the leaves, breaks up the darkness, and the feeling passes. "Whatever was here is gone now." Kicking a layer of mud off my shoes, I turn back.

"What was it?" Gabe surveys the forest once more before following me.

I sniff, trying to identify any remaining wisps of the strange smell. "I'm not sure. Something that doesn't belong here. Maybe a shadow." At my words, Gabe picks up his pace, closing the distance between us.

We sneak into class five minutes late. Luckily, the teacher is so focused on his lecture, he doesn't notice as I take my seat along the back row of the physics room. Gabe—rarely far away, since Zane decided I need an escort 24/7—sits two desks over with a book he never opens. He's not actually enrolled in school, so he doesn't have to do homework or take tests. I have no idea how Akers explains his presence in my classes, but much like with Kye and Rose, people pretty much do what he asks, when he asks.

I wish I knew how to do that.

Having a bodyguard irritates me to no end. I can take care of myself. I've proven myself more than capable, but with half an army of shadow demons on the loose, the Dragons think I need extra protection.

Also, they're doing their best to make sure Kye and me stay away from each other—which is probably the main reason for Gabe's constant presence. Because the worst of the worst has happened. The curse we thought was broken? It's not. And every time we come in contact, or near contact, or in the same building—whatever—we both get sicker.

The problem is that while being near him for a few minutes makes me weak and shaky for days, and causes nearly unbearable pain in my stomach, being apart from him makes me panic until I feel like my chest is going to cave in. Only no one knows about the panic part. Just the weakness/pain part. They don't seem to get that when my chest caves in, my heart will stop beating.

I have to see him. Today.

When the bell rings at the end of class, Gabe reaches over to pick up my books.

I shove his hands away. "I can do it."

"I know," he says. "But I can too. I could carry the books of everyone in this class without straining a muscle, so why don't you preserve your strength and let me take yours?"

BIRTHRIGHT

His smug smile makes me want to hit him. But when I stand, the energy I thought I had drains into my toes. Knowing he's right, I decide to make him pay the only way I know how. "You're right." I sway for maximum effect. "Right now, even my purse feels too heavy."

This is not your run-of-the-mill basic black purse, and there is no possible way it could double as an Indiana Jones-style European Satchel. This purse = 100 % girly. Hot pink leather, black and white zebra striped accents, and a faux-diamond studded peace symbol. Kye's dad picked it up for me in New York. A gift for his new "daughter."

"Hand it over." Gabe sighs.

Wearing a grin the size of Wyoming, I sling the strap over his shoulder and follow him out. Admittedly, even carrying a purse so inarguably feminine, Gabe's luminous gray eyes, dusty-brown, shoulder-length hair, and clearly defined muscles attract the wandering eyes of, well, every female in the county. Or at least the school.

Except mine. I remain wholly, and completely in love with Kye.

But Gabe does manage to exude pure masculinity, even while carrying a hot pink zebra purse. There's something to be said for that.

Not that I'm looking.

THREE

The Prop Closet

For seventh period, I used to have P.E., but when I started getting sick, Akers convinced the coach to transfer me into his theater tech class, where I'm supposed to help build sets and create props. Really, I sit in Landon's office and do homework or read. It's only after Gabe believes I'm in this particular "safe zone" that he would consider leaving my side—even to go on a food run.

"You promise you're going to eat it this time?" Gabe asks, looking both hopeful and skeptical at once.

Though my stomach cramps at the thought, I nod. "If you get it fast enough."

"Why don't you come with me? I'll take you home after."

A desperate knot forms in my gut. This is the part where I have to convince him. "Because I need to make up that English quiz after school."

His eyes narrow. "You made that up two days ago."

The knot moves into my throat. "Oh, yeah. Forgot. Anyway, I told Rose I would ride home with her, and I don't want to leave her hanging."

The wrinkle between his brows gets deeper. "Text her."

"She's in class. I don't want to get her in trouble."

He stares at me for a long moment, as if trying to decide if he believes me or not. "All right. Landon's on the stage. Do not leave this room."

BIRTHRIGHT

I open a book and attempt to look like I'm studying. Gabe closes the door, and I watch through the glass as he talks to Akers and then strides out through the back of the auditorium. Akers is teaching, and doesn't even glance my way as I sneak into the dusty prop room.

"Kye?" I murmur. "Are you in here?"

No answer.

"Kye?" When it becomes apparent that I'm the first one here this time—which has never happened before—I find a wooden chair and sit. Five minutes pass, then ten. My hands are clammy with nerves, wondering what has kept Kye from meeting me. The face of my cell phone illuminates when I check the time, distraught. I need to leave soon if I want to avoid getting caught. My eyes prickle with disappointment as I stand and brush off my jeans. When the knob finally twists, I slide behind a freestanding wall, not daring to hope.

"Abby?" he whispers. "Are you still here?"

My breath flows out in relief as I step into Kye's arms. "What took you so long?"

"Crystal cornered me in the hall, asking about rumors that we broke up. She followed me—I had to ditch her."

Anger turns my blood hot. How dare she steal away my extremely limited precious moments with him? "Gabe will be back any minute."

"I know," Kye says. His lips capture mine, stealing away any response I might have made and replacing it with an electric zing that fills my insides with light. My hands run up his shoulders to twine around his neck, while his end up tangled in my hair. His tongue finds mine, inviting it to dance to a rhythm only we can make, until his lips move away to burn a trail down my neck, across my shoulder. "I've missed you so much," he murmurs. "I hate being apart from you."

"Me too," I manage. "I hate it too."

My brain picks this moment to remind me that earlier today, Akers voluntarily suffered for the last time I did this exact thing. And how hours ago I resolved to leave. That resolution feels impossible to fulfill right now. When we're together, I'm safe, whole, in a way I can never be when we're apart.

I clutch Kye's collar, run my fingers under the cotton to find his warm neck, and watch my ring sparkle to life. He smiles in the soft light, and his lips crush mine again. His fingers knead the small of my back, finding the skin under the hem of my sweater and sending a line of flames into my blood.

My own hands have wandered, trailing down his shoulders, across his chest, so when he tightens his grip and lifts me off the ground, my arms are trapped between us, leaving me both helpless and out of breath.

"I love you, Abby," he says, still holding me aloft. "No matter what happens, I hope you'll always remember that. Forever."

There's a lump in my throat, but I press a kiss to the underside of his chin and murmur, "I love you, too. Always."

With a final nod and one last kiss, he sets me on my feet, keeping hold of my hand. He stops near the movable wall, his grip on my fingers loosening enough so our hands can slide apart. Just before I open the door, he touches his fingers to his lips in a silent gesture of goodbye, and I'm struck with a sense of finality that terrifies me.

The lump in my throat triples in size as I sneak out the way I came, hoping Gabe encountered a massive traffic jam or was forced to wait in a long line, or that someone picked right now to learn how to stop time. The shaky weakness caused by my nearness to Kye begins just as Gabe's infuriated voice carries across the stage.

Taking a deep breath, I pick up my pace and meet him at the office door. It's hard to achieve a nonchalant tone when I see that his smoky eyes have turned to coal. "Hey. Did you get it?"

He hands me a full sack from a nearby fast food place. "I told you not to leave the office."

A sharp pain jolts my midsection, conveniently giving me the explanation I need. "Emergency trip to the restroom. I actually thought maybe this time the sickness would come out."

His expression doesn't soften. "You used that excuse last time."

I storm into the office, guilt knotting my shoulders as I toss the food aside. "In case you haven't noticed, I spend a lot of time hoping for that these days." The pain sharpens when I sit and the heat of a fever burns under my fingernails, flushes the skin on my forehead and cheeks. It's going to be bad this time.

Gabe hands me the tincture of willow bark I keep on the shelf, looking both unrepentant and unconvinced. "There must be too much of Kye in this room. I'm going to talk to Akers about me taking you home after sixth period from now on."

Panic builds in my chest. I'm on thin ice with Gabe. "That would be a bad idea." I sound desperate, even though I'm trying really hard not to. "I have finals next week. I need to study."

"You can study at home." He stalks to the discarded sack and produces a cheeseburger, slowly unwrapping it. The scent seeps through the paper, draws a trail from his hands to my nose and down my nasal passages. When the pain erupts, I slide off the chair and onto the floor, wishing for nothing more than to rid my body of the rampaging energy that doesn't belong. Unapologetic, Gabe watches me clutch the trash can, cursing, until the weakness hits and I have to let it drop. "Feel better?" A hint of satisfaction bleeds into his voice as he hands me a napkin to mop my forehead. I want to punch him.

"You did that on purpose."

"No, *you* did it on purpose. We both know what causes you to have spells like this, and we both know the solution. But you're the only one who knows why you keep sneaking away to see him."

I shove the trash can aside and lean against the back of the desk. "There's no way to explain. I've tried a gazillion times, but no one gets it. If you did, you all wouldn't be so determined to keep us apart."

"We're trying to keep you alive." He's nearly shouting, but takes a calming breath when my hands fly to cover my ears. The waves of pain have made it to the top, and I now feel like they're trying to hammer out through my skull. Gabe opens a water bottle and crouches to hold it against my lips so I can sip. "Even if *you* have a

17

death wish, *he* should know better than to keep putting you through this. It's not worth it, Abby. Nothing is worth what this is doing to you."

"How can you say that, Gabe? You've never been in this position. You have no idea what you're asking, no idea what I'm sacrificing or not sacrificing. You don't know anything about it."

He sits next to me, hands me the bottle. "I know that someone who truly loves you would never put you through this just to get some action in the prop closet."

The fever brewing under my skin burns to the surface. I can't believe he knows. Can I have *no* secrets anymore? "It's not a closet," I murmur. "And obviously you've never loved someone the way Kye loves me."

"Right. Never. You're absolutely right." He stands and stomps to the door, then whirls to face me. "You know what, Abby? I give up. Go ahead and text Kye. Tell him you have the rest of the afternoon free. Tell him to move in with you, for all I care. You'll be dead in a week, but clearly that doesn't matter to either of you. If you want to kill each other, go for it. I'm done." The door closes behind him so hard, the glass rattles.

I don't text Kye. In fact, I don't even move except to continue sipping my water. When the bell rings, Akers comes in and finds me on his floor. He sits where Gabe sat earlier. "Rough day?"

He isn't clammy and feverish, but helping me has taken a toll on him. The dark circles under his eyes never seem to go away. His face is drawn and pale, and for the first time since I've known him, Akers looks older than forty.

"I'm sorry."

"For what?" he asks, as if he doesn't already know.

"Everything. All of it."

He drapes his arm around me until I lean my head on his shoulder. "You should never apologize for being who you are, any more than you should apologize for doing what's necessary."

My hollow insides fill with remorse. "But I ... You've been so good to me and I keep punishing you for it."

"Like I said, sweetheart, you've done nothing to deserve this burden."

I lift my head, meet his eyes. "Tell me what to do. I can't be with him, I can't be without him, and while we're in this turmoil, I can't even think about helping anyone else. I feel stuck."

The gentle shake of his head is more fatherly than any other action could be. "You are stuck. And the only way to get unstuck is to do something drastic."

"Like?"

"Well, under the circumstances, seems like you have two choices. You can stay here and die—which is exactly what we're trying to avoid—or you can do the bravest, hardest thing you'll ever do, and leave."

The very idea compounds my panic until I feel like there's a bag of bricks weighing on my ribs. "Where would I go? How? I don't have a diploma. I don't have a car or any money. I'm not even a legal adult yet." And leaving would mean saying goodbye to Kye—for real. Maybe forever.

"If you can get through finals, you'll have that diploma." He loosens a wet strand of hair off my cheek. "And I know you don't like to think about this, but we'll make sure you have plenty of money, and a car, if necessary. The rest—well. You let me and Val worry about the rest. You have options, Abby."

"Not good ones." I tuck my knees into my chest so I can hide my face in them.

"No one ever said life would be easy. And I admit, you and Kye are getting the rawest of raw deals. But think of it this way. If the two of you can bear to be apart for a while, there's a chance one of us will find a way to break this ridiculous curse someday. If not, and you both die, the cycle will start over again. You already know the outcome of your deaths—so to speak. Maybe it's time you chose the less-traveled road?"

The emptiness in my chest threatens to swallow me whole, and I can't answer.

"Give it some thought. " He pats my back, and I hear him moving around, the tin echo that tells me he's repositioned the trash can, footsteps, and then the office door clicks shut.

Minutes later, Rose finds me still there, curled in a ball. She makes me stand and leads me to her car, as she has done so many times before. Somewhere between the auditorium and the parking lot, it hits me that everyone knows I've been lying. Rose has me figured out too, but she doesn't say anything, and her silence is worse than any lecture.

FOUR

Impressions

Rose doesn't speak for the entire drive to my house, so when we get there and she follows me inside, I'm both surprised and frustrated to tears. "Would you say something already?"

She pauses in the act of hanging her jacket on the rack. "What do you want me to say? You already know what I think, and what Gabe thinks and what Akers and Val think. And you're a big girl. Whether or not I agree with your choices obviously doesn't change what those choices will be any more than my opinions will change Jen's current choice of boyfriend. So what's the point in arguing over it?"

What she means by "Jen's current choice of boyfriend": A controlling boy of questionable character who demands all of Jen's time so we hardly get to see her, even though I may be dying.

"I'm sorry." I hang the jacket for her. "I don't want to argue. Your opinion matters to me. You've been my rock since I got here, and I need you."

She stomps into the living room, clearly more wound up than she wants to admit. "I need you too, Abby. Alive. I know you and Kye are having a really hard time being separated, but have either of you considered what it'll be like for the rest of us if you die? We're all pretty much screwed. We can't fix anything. We can't undo what's been done, and we can't figure out how to break the curse. Then we're stuck finishing another level of the same cycle, while I hang out *by myself* watching Jen throw *her* future down the drain. If you mess this up, your choices are going to ripple on for another hundred years or so until we all come back and try this thing again. Only the world will be very, very different. We'll be different. We might not even be able to find each other."

She sits on the sofa, and I sit next to her with a pillow in my lap. "Of course we'll find each other. Just this afternoon, Akers reminded me how history repeats itself."

"No," she says, shaking her head. "The curse continues. Raina and Theron continue. But that doesn't mean I will. Or Jen. Last week, Val told me that since the fall of Dryden, there have never been so many of us in one place. Until now."

Val told me something similar last time I trained with him. And I know he's right. This time we might actually have a chance, if I don't blow it. "I don't know if I can do it, Rose. Being apart from him is more physically painful than Healing someone. I know it sounds selfish, and that you all think we're choosing this because we can't control ourselves, but last night I woke up at three a.m. thinking I was having a heart attack. That doesn't happen on the days when I see him."

This time, her frown is puzzled rather than disapproving. A step up. "Why haven't you told me this before?"

"Because when I tried telling Val, he acted like it was me just being a baby. But it's not, Rose. I swear, it's not. Happens to Kye, too, except on the days when we get to see each other. There's something to it. I just wish we could figure out what it is."

"Probably emotional," she muses, staring out the window. "Strong emotions sometimes affect us physically like that."

"Of course it's emotional. That's the curse in a nutshell."

We continue batting ideas back and forth, and though I know she's still frustrated, I can tell Rose is genuinely trying to understand. After a while, both our phones chime. It's Akers.

Formal council meeting tonight. Valdemar's cabin, 7:00.

Then he sends a second one to me, but not Rose.

They know.

Fear tingles in my fingers as I respond.

What do I do?

He replies:

Convince them you can be Raina, and then do the right thing.

From the look on her face, Rose is as worried as I am. I show her my conversation with Akers. "What does he mean convince them I'm Raina? I already have her face. And her ring. What more can I do?"

Her smile is faint and somewhat frightening, because Rose is usually very good at hiding fear—except right now. "I don't know, but we'll think of something." She stands abruptly, glancing at her watch. "Drink some herbs and take a nap. You look like death, and that's only going to make things worse. It's four, so I'll be back in an hour to help you get ready." She starts for the door, digging in her purse for her keys.

"Rose?" I ask, my voice timid.

"Yeah?"

"What's the right thing to do?"

She shakes her head, a tear sparkling on her lashes. "I don't know, Abby. I honestly don't know."

I wake to something warm and wet tickling my elbow, and pop open my eyes to find Erda licking me. I shove her away. "Stop. Sit." She sits, then immediately stands again and gets to work on my chin. "Go away!"

She lies down, whimpering, and stares at me with sad eyes.

"Now you're trying to make me feel guilty," I tell her. "I'm sorry. I'll see if Mom will walk you when she gets home."

Rose will be here any time, so there's no point in trying to go back to sleep. Gathering my strength, I start for my bedroom, wondering how a person is expected to dress for a formal meeting with the Dragon council.

I'm standing in my closet, panicking, when I hear Rose let herself in. "I hope you brought me something to wear," I yell to her. "Like maybe a dress. Because it has been way too long since I went shopping."

"Oh, I have something." She enters my room with her arms full. "And it's not just a dress—it's the full package." Rose unloads her burden onto my bed, surveying me head to toe. "Well. Thank goodness for makeup. Sit down. We have a lot of work to do and not much time." She clears clothes from my vanity stool and gestures for me to sit while she dumps out a bag of hair-styling tools and starts plugging things in.

"What are you planning?"

She looks me over again. "We're making you look like Princess Raina. Strip down to your underwear. I'm taking no chances with your hair."

Rose fluffs and curls and pins until most of my hair has been swept off my shoulders, with a few curls deliberately left hanging free. Then she applies makeup—a luxury I haven't bothered with for weeks. By the time she's done, an hour has passed, and I'm still not positive what she's up to. I try to peek in the mirror, but Rose has covered it with a sheet, refusing to let me see before she's finished.

Normally, this makeover-treatment is something I would enjoy. Now I just want to lie down. Probably because I know I can't. Finally, Rose helps me stand. "You might freeze to death on the way to Val's, but it'll be worth it when they see you coming." She unzips the department store bag hanging from my curtain rod and I get a glimpse of graceful, sheer white fabric, layered over the top of more white.

"Holy faeries, Rose. Tell me that's not a wedding dress."

Her laughter is answer enough.

"And you're about two weeks late for prom. We wanted to go, but ... you know."

"I know," she says, a note of sympathy in her voice. She removes the dress from the hanger and steadies me while I step into a tiny white slip, careful not to catch the silk on the diamond that hangs from a thin silver chain around my waist—my gift from the Morrigana. Though she's never seen it before, Rose doesn't comment on the jewel as she slides the straps over my shoulders and meets my eyes. "It's important that you look like a leader tonight."

I nod, because I think that is exactly what Akers meant by convincing them that I can be Raina.

"If you go there looking like a scared little girl, they're going to treat you like one. But if you walk in looking resplendent and beautiful and all grown up, if you remind them of the princess they remember, they'll think, 'Hey, maybe we should listen to her. She certainly *looks* like royalty.' Then you talk like the intelligent woman that you are, and they'll listen." Her eyes glisten with emotion. "And maybe we can all work together on finding a way to save both my cousin Kye and my best friend Abby. Because I refuse to watch either of you die."

Her last fierce words send me into her arms to hug her tight. "You're right, Rose. Absolutely right. "

She checks her watch, moaning about how little time we have left, and helps me step into the dress. I slide my arms through bell-style sleeves, feeling the fabric fall in soft layers around my ankles. Rose zips the back, tightening the bodice from waist to shoulder. A scoop of pale skin around my neck and chest is left exposed.

I'm really anxious to see in a mirror now, but before I can remove the sheet, Rose stays my hand. "One more thing." She reaches into her purse and produces the antique velvet box in which Akers now keeps the Pendant of Sadira. "Akers agreed that it might help if you show up wearing it."

This, I think, is the most brilliant part of Rose's already dazzling idea. After fastening the pendant around my neck, I dig out my emerald earrings and snap them on as well.

She holds out her hand. "Let me see the ring." And because I trust her implicitly, I do. She dips it in jewelry cleaner and rubs it with a soft cloth until it sparkles. I strap on my good silver sandals while Rose digs into the back of my closet for my white wrap—the one thing from New York I managed to salvage.

"It's a miracle you got all the blood out," she remarks, checking it over once more.

"Most of it." I don't want to think about blood right now. "Whoever invented bleach was a genius."

"You ready for this?" she asks, preparing to unveil the mirror.

I nod, and the sheet slides away. My heart leaps. The reflection in the glass can't be mine. My skin is pale, arms bony and thin, with hollow cheeks and dull eyes. The girl in the mirror has healthy coloring and regal posture that, with the design of the dress, hides the bony parts. She's ... gorgeous. "How did you do that?"

"I had a lot to work with. Your bone structure is fabulous." She looks up as the doorbell rings, and I swirl the wrap around my shoulders, already chilled. Even with my shoes on, the wrap touches the floor. I start down the stairs, wondering who even rings the bell anymore, since all my friends have become accustomed to walking right in. "That better not be one of the Dragons. I swear they think I'm in danger every time the curtains in my room twitch."

"One last thing," Rose says, gnawing on her fingernail. "You're not riding with me."

I stop on the last step, dreading the idea of riding with Gabe. "Then how am I getting there?"

She gestures at the door, mumbling something about needing to give them the full effect. Absolutely dreading who is on the other side, I peek between the blinds, and though I thought I was prepared, I still don't manage to swallow my shriek.

Looks like Rose thinks I'm riding to the meeting on Finn.

FIVE

Without Reins

Finn nuzzles my outstretched hand.

"Where did you learn to ring the doorbell?"

"The bigger question here," Rose says, her eyes wide, "is *how* did he ring the doorbell?"

Kye's moose—which doesn't technically count as a pet—has been spending a lot of time near my house lately. Kye won't admit it, but I think he's asked Finn to keep an eye on me, separate from the Dragons. Either he doesn't trust them to watch out for me, or he doesn't trust them to stay away from me. But that's just a theory.

Finn lowers his head, his freakishly-huge antlers scraping the door within inches of my face. Rose and I both scramble backward. "Easy there," she says.

I scratch a soft spot between Finn's eyes, wondering how on earth I'm going to climb on his back. Rose closes the door on Erda—who is barking like crazy—and comes out armed with a thick wool blanket and a step stool. "FYI, this is Kye's idea, so if you fall off and break yourself, you can blame him."

I raise an eyebrow. "Is he going to be at this meeting?"

She grins. "We all are." She glances at her jeans, frowning. "Obviously, I'm going to be late if I don't get my butt in gear. But I'll hurry. Make a big entrance. Huge. I can't wait to see how the council members react."

I unfold the stool and stand it next to Finn. "Rose, does anyone expect me to come looking like this?"

She shakes her head, rubbing her hands together. "Just us. Akers let me take the pendant, and Kye let me borrow Finn. He also knows I was bringing you clothes, but that's it."

"What did you tell him?"

"Just that you wanted to ride by yourself so you'd have time to think. He totally fell for it, too. I can't wait to see his face."

Me either. I exchange apprehension for anticipation. Regardless of the circumstances, I get to see Kye again tonight. Be in the same room with him. Hold his hand for a while.

Rose helps me fold the blanket over Finn's back and gives me a boost as I swing my leg over. There's a bite to the air, warning of an impending drop in temperature, so I draw the hood over my hair, ignoring the way Rose cringes, and fasten the clasps to hold it closed. "Please do not destroy that dress," she says. "I haven't even worn it yet."

"I'll do my best, but no promises. I'm riding bareback on a wild animal, with no reins." For my own safety, I bury my fingers in the long-ish fur on Finn's neck, making sure I have a grip before Finn starts trotting toward the forest.

I'm confident Finn needs no guidance to Val's cabin, so I'm left to my thoughts as we whisk through the forest. A gentle breeze rustles the trees, and I sense, rather than hear, a presence hovering nearby. I don't have to look to know it's one of the Dragons, protecting me from a distance. Whoever it is keeps out of sight, which means it's not Gabe. I guess he's still angry.

A foreign disappointment stirs in my chest. It's not that I want Gabe around all the time; mostly he drives me crazy. And he deserves a few hours off every so often. But if I have to keep a Dragon around, Gabe is the least annoying of the bunch.

Besides, I need this alone time to think. To plan. I don't know what I'm going to say to the council, or even what I should do. I can only hope a solution will come to me. Or if not a solution, a temporary alternative.

Finn grunts, his colossal head bobbing as he picks up his pace. I close my eyes to prevent motion sickness as Finn and I whiz through the trees at a speed that makes everything blur around the edges. The cool air stings my cheeks, and dark clouds slide across the nearly full moon. Thoughts swirl in my mind, questions to which I have no answers. Somehow I need to find what's written between the lines. Why was our previous sacrifice not enough? What else can be done? What details have we missed? Kye risked his life to save me, and then I risked mine to save him. We were willing to die for each other. What more could either of us possibly give?

Deep inside, I know there's something—*something*. I just wish I could figure out what that something is.

There's a crash in the foliage to my right, followed by a crunch, a groan, something swishing. Finn slows, startled. I peer into the dark, but can only see tree trunks and shadows. My pulse races as a sense of impending danger tickles my instincts. Something isn't right. "Hello?" No one answers. I have to fight to keep the nervous tremor out of my voice. "Keep going, Finn. We need to get to that meeting."

Finn lowers his rack and charges on, his hooves thundering against the ground while his antlers protect me from low-hanging branches. Cold air snakes under my wrap, presses through my dress, but the exhilaration of the ride, the speed with which we cover ground, tears the chill from my mind. Finn's muscles bunch and stretch as I crouch lower, my cloak billowing around me.

Another crash, this time ahead, compounds my anxiety. My breath catches as we near a ravine, but Finn leaps across without slowing down. When we smash through the trees and into a clearing, I turn my head and brave a look behind us.

Holy. Stars.

An involuntary scream rises in my throat as I experience a new level of terror. The creature rises over ten feet high, with wings twice that wide, black as the darkest shadow of night. It moves like a cheetah, lithe and graceful, as it eats the distance between us with jet-like speed.

"Finn! Run," I shriek. "Run, Finn. It's coming!" Finn veers back into the shelter of the trees. At least here we stand a chance. Maybe.

The creature tails us into the woods abandoning its previous stealth now that I've seen it, and looms ever closer. Finn dodges trees, shrubs, and the occasional random hot spring —he knows this forest better than I ever could.

Instinct keeps me crouched low, clinging to Finn's fur. He's large, and I'm small, and we're moving fast enough that I could easily slide off his back and be left to face the demon—or whatever it is—alone. I wish I'd driven with Rose, except if this thing wanted me badly enough, it probably would have chased us both. In a car, our escape routes would be more limited.

This knowledge gives me courage. Maybe riding Finn was a better idea than Rose could have predicted. I tuck the edges of my wrap around me and lean my cheek against his neck, eyes closed.

The wicked laugh grates Raina's nerves as she clings to the reins, squeezing the horse's flanks with her heels and urging him to go faster, faster yet. Fear churns, causing the child inside to roll and kick. Though the movement causes her pain, Raina cradles her unborn, comforted by the knowledge that the child will fight along with her in this battle for their lives. She peers over her shoulder at the band of Dark Elen galloping after her with Tynan in the lead. Two groups break away from the main body, hurtling into the woods until they've somehow circled in front of her.

He laughs again, and Raina's fear explodes. There is no escape. She'll have no choice but to face him.

A loud screech brings me back to reality—to my current frightening situation—and I blink hard to clear away the vision. It's been weeks since I've had a vision of Raina. That I'd see her now has to be significant.

I peer behind us again, my blood seizing. The creature from the clearing has been joined by two more, and they're closing in on us with inhuman speed. Drops of sweat bead on Finn's hide, catching in his mane so my hands slide around on his neck. With what little energy I have, I squeeze my knees against his ribs and clutch his mane tighter, praying we're getting close.

Soon, tiny lights flicker ahead and the foliage gives way to a path. A small, purplish light zooms in and out, around and around, approaching us. "Murtagh," I shriek. "Go back. I'm coming." But the water sprite continues as if he doesn't hear.

Before I have breath to yell again, a vast shadow drops in front of us, erecting a wall of dark clouds directly in our path. For the first time since I've known him, Finn falters. He rears, pawing at the thick blackness, shaking his antlers at our shapeless foe.

I'm holding so tight, handfuls of fur rip out of Finn's neck as I'm dumped in a heap onto muddy ground. For several long seconds, I can't breathe, nor can I move. While I lie immobile, the shadows thicken, surrounding me in a funnel of darkness that blocks out all light, all sound. I can no longer see the twinkling lights of the sprites or hear the wind whooshing in the trees. Even Finn—whose white hide usually gleams brightly through the blackest night—fades from view as the shadows separate me from everything. Spots swim in my eyes, but if I don't get up and fight back, the shadows will consume me.

"Abby." A faint voice echoes in my head, growing just slightly louder as it repeats. "Fight, Abby. You know what to do." The voice is familiar, but not one I would expect at a time like this. I've heard my dead grandma Isabelle talk to me before—mostly memories of things she once said, and which are deeply ingrained in the files of my brain. And Kye. I've heard his voice in my head before too—but we were connected in Healing at the time. This is different. This human voice speaks through the fog of shadows that threaten to smother me until I suffocate.

Warmth seeps into me, thawing my icy limbs from the inside out. I open my eyes, only just aware that I've even closed them, and find myself looking at a face. He's surrounded by the shadows that have hemmed me in. As the last of my strength drains, my eyes find Gabe, standing on the edges of the darkness, and though it makes no sense, I hear his voice.

31

"Light, Abby. Find your Light."

A burst of hot air curls around me and spears of fire kindle twigs and leaves into flames before the shadows snuff them out. Moments later, an icy wind shoots by, blowing ferociously at the shadows that refuse to budge. Next, the ground under me shakes as if trembling with anger.

None of my friends' attempts will budge the stubborn shadows, but knowing that the others are here, that they're supporting me, spreads loving warmth through my bloodstream. The stones around my neck heat to life, glowing with power as I struggle to my knees and force myself to stand, bringing with me two handfuls of damp soil.

"Yes, Abby, that's right. Get up. Fight against it." Gabe's voice motivates me to find my strength. My knees wobble and I sway, but the mist clouding my mind clears as I cup my palms together and raise my arms above my head, waiting. Waiting for the Light to build.

The tingling starts in my toes and works into my heels, climbing my calves and spreading into my thighs, swirling around my waist and settling into my core. From there, shoots of power spring up, spreading throughout my system until the heat reaches my palms. I squeeze the soil in my fists, compacting it into clumps, then pivot, flinging it around me as I release my Light.

The funnel of shadow moves, spinning, spinning, until I'm in the eye of the tornado. Glowing brightness bursts from my pours, forcing away the shadows and breaking the dark curtain into pieces that blow and twist, shrinking until they've disappeared.

In the midst of the chaos, my eyes find Gabe's again. I try to force a smile as my knees buckle and his arms come around me.

"Thanks," I mumble as the last of my energy disappears. He catches me as my world goes black.

SIX

Arguments and Options

Something soft tickles the inside of my arm as I resurface into the land of light and sound. Unable to open my eyes for more than seconds at a time, I try to sort the competing voices pounding in my head.

"How could you let this happen, Gabe?" my mother shouts. "I thought you were supposed to be protecting her from those things."

Then, from a different direction, "Val, you promised this wasn't going to be a problem."

"I don't ... I wasn't even on duty," Gabe sputters. "It was Marcus's shift." I blink and see Gabe facing Akers. "Has anyone seen or heard from Marcus? Did you send someone to find him?"

Akers lays a hand on Gabe's forearm. "Finn is taking Tobias and Gil back there now."

"What was that thing?" Jen asks, her voice trembling.

The voices blend as explanations and arguments continue. When I'm finally able to focus, I find I'm lying in a cushioned alcove, partially concealed by a privacy curtain. Kye is stretched out next to me, his back against the cool stone wall. His fingers run along the inside of my arm, but he's focused on the cluster of people gathered around the immense rock fireplace in Val's cabin. A bright fire burns, and I'm grateful for the warmth to thaw my icy limbs.

Kye still hasn't seen that I'm awake, so I take the opportunity to observe. The circles under his eyes look like bruises, deepened by the hollows in his cheeks that have sharpened the edges of his jaw. His pale skin is cast with yellow, a stark contrast to the curtain that protects us from being in full view of the rest of the room. The crackling flames dance across his pupils. The fingers stroking my arm pause, and his gaze flits to mine. "Hey there, beautiful. Where've you been all my life?"

"Hi." I know it sounds contradictory, given the curse and what it does to us, but seeing him, being this close to him, gives me the motivation to find my strength. It takes effort for me to shift onto my side, so Kye slides his arms under and rolls me into the familiar comfort of his chest. "I wish we could stay like this. Forget all the rest."

"Me too." He sighs. "Kind of makes running-away sound appealing." His heart thumps strong and steady under my cheek; his breaths set the rhythm for mine. "You doing okay? Whatever happened out there has people pretty upset."

I lift my head to meet his eyes. "You're holding me, and we didn't have to sneak away. Right now I'm better than I've been in weeks. How about you?"

His eyes darken as he leans into me, reaching up to untie the curtain and let it fall to hide us from reality. "Me too." His lips claim mine in a blazing kiss as explosive as our first. My fists bunch in his shirt, holding him close while I can. His hand runs up and down my side, along the boning in my dress, until he lets it rest on my hip. And then we seem to simultaneously remember that the Dragon council is on the other side of our curtain. He presses his lips to my forehead as I lie back on a pillow.

"What are they going to do to us?" I whisper.

He brushes a curl out of my eyes. "They're going to separate us. I don't know what the plan is, exactly, but that's the bottom line."

My chin trembles. I bury my face in his chest again and hold on tight to stifle a sob.

"Shh. Please don't cry. We can do this. Know why?" I shake my head, still hiding my face. "That's what leaders do, Abby. We make hard choices and tough sacrifices in order to protect others. You and I—we're meant to lead." He finds one of my loose curls and twists it around his little finger. "There are so many more people like us. People with Gifts they don't even recognize. They'll never know where they came from or what they can truly do if we don't find them. Help them."

"You're starting to sound like Val," I mumble into his shirt, sniffling.

"Where else would it have come from?" he says, voice rumbling in his chest. "But honestly? I don't know what else to say. You're sick. I'm sick. We obviously can't stay together. This is not something either of us can fix. You can't Heal me, and I can't Heal you, and that means we can't Heal the world together. So—"

"So now we have to try breaking everything apart." Releasing his shirt, I turn away, focusing on the glow of flames through the fabric of the curtain. "We can't put it off anymore, can we?"

He picks up my hand to play with my fingers. "Um, there's something else we should talk about. This could be a long process. And who knows if we'll ever figure out what to do about this curse. I think, under the circumstances, that we should consider—"

My mom flicks aside the curtain, and I'm surprised by the relief her interruption brings. "She's awake." She strokes a palm over my head and cheeks, brushes hair away from my eyes. "How are you doing, honey? Are you okay?"

"Yes, I'm fine." I have to look at something other than Kye. His expression, his vocal inflections, the determination swimming in his eyes, scream of impending doom. One that is less about him leaving and more about us having freedom while we're apart.

I don't want that freedom. But the fact that *he* might breaks something in me, something I didn't know could even crack. For the second time today, I can't breathe. But this time there are no shadow demons stealing my air. Our cozy alcove has become crowded and stuffy.

Kye swings his legs around and stands to join the others, leaving me there to deal with my mother's fussing and fluttering. I watch him walk away, staring at his back until the conversation carries, and I manage to focus on that.

"... not sure what they want from her," Val is saying. "The tomb can't be opened again now that it's been resealed. The only thing I can think is that they see her as a threat to their existence here in our mortal world. Perhaps there are more tombs, or more entrances."

"Perhaps," Akers muses. He sneaks a peek at my mom, frowning. "I find it hard to believe that they'd attack her in that way because they're afraid of her. It just doesn't make sense, given their history."

"On the contrary." Val talks with his hands as he paces back and forth. "It makes perfect sense if you look at it from a historical point of view. In the beginning, Tynan and his army rounded up the strongest Gifted, especially the Healers and the Sighted, and stole their powers and then destroyed them. It's why they came after Isleen, and why they took Raina in her place. Our Abby has proven herself to have the same type of powers, and that's reason enough for them to be afraid of her. After centuries of being trapped in what was essentially a safe-haven for shadow demons, they're living in a more fragile mortal world. The fact that Abby has accomplished one death Healing and is still very much in control of her power makes her a very real threat to them. And then there's her blood. She's proven herself as Raina, which means her blood can be used as a powerful tool, or even a weapon. Abby's blood alone carries loads of untested power."

Mom helps me remove my wrap and clutches it to her chest. Her face is only slightly darker than the fabric. "I don't care who wants to be enemies with whom, or why. You promised to protect my daughter as long as we stay in Jackson. If you can't do that—if you don't know how—I'll be forced to do the only thing I've ever known. She and I will pack our things and move. Tomorrow."

My sense of doom escalates. Akers focuses on Mom, eyes wide with distress.

"No, we won't," I croak. "Mom, this isn't just about you and me anymore. I have to learn how to take care of myself. If we run, these things will follow us, and they'll find us. Then what will we do?"

"We'll run again," she says, plopping onto the bed next to me.

"Then they'll find us again. What happens when there's nowhere left to run?" I murmur. "At least here we're not alone. "

She cradles my face in her hands. "But staying here is killing you, baby. And I won't watch that either."

"Which brings us back to the reason for this meeting." Val's deep voice re-directs everyone's attention. "From what we've just seen, Abby has progressed quickly in her training, and while I would like to keep working with her for another year or two, the time has come for us to rethink our strategy." He offers a hand to help me stand.

I take it, desperate to gain his faith, straightening my back, and remembering Rose's ingenious plan. My throat is raw and sore from having energy sucked through it, so I reach for the glass of water Mom offers and drain it.

Val nods at Akers, who circles the room. "Our current priority is figuring out how to deal with Kye and Abby's situation. We all know the facts. Contrary to what we hoped last month, Tynan's curse against Theron and Raina and their posterity has not been broken. Furthermore, though we've hoped the miles between their homes is distance enough to prolong the onset of curse symptoms, their progressing illness and constant weakness have proven that is not the case. This brings us to a critical point. It's time to discuss what happens next." His eyes pin first me, then Kye. "Let's keep in mind that your happiness, while important, is far less crucial than preserving the royal blood for the restoration of the throne."

Guilt. Guilt. Guilt.

Kye reaches over and squeezes my hand, acknowledging what we're both thinking. They don't understand. There's no way they can. It's not about happiness so much as survival, and there's no logic to that.

Akers continues. "Until an hour ago, we were planning to allow Kye to graduate and then send him to be with his mother in Mexico, keeping Abby here where the Dragons can protect her."

I hate, hate the idea of Kye being sent away. Hate it. But if he has to go, this would be the best-case scenario. I don't know when he last saw his mom, but it's been at least a year, and I know he misses her. From what he's told me, she lives in an Americanized colony on a gorgeous Mexican beach, and, according to Val, there are some serious power-centers near there. It could be just what Kye needs to get well.

If he survives the trip. Seeing him tonight, knowing how much weight he's lost, seeing his yellow pallor and the dullness of his eyes, my guilt multiplies by a thousand times ten. I'm not sure how he'll handle flying.

"But," Akers continues, "after tonight, after what happened to Abby in our very own forest, within reaching distance of two highly capable Dragons and footsteps away from a cabin that has been specially protected against dark forces, we find ourselves reevaluating this plan. It's time to look at other options."

Kye squeezes harder, shaking his head. "Are you saying you want to send *her* away? You can't do that to her. For the first time in her life, she actually has a home. Abby needs grounding. She needs solidarity. She needs her friends. I thought we agreed ..." His face crumples. "How can I stay here without her?"

Val sets a fatherly hand on Kye's shoulder. "The same way she would've stayed without you."

Conversations erupt all over the room. It seems everyone has an opinion, some louder than others. I latch onto Rose's familiar voice, and turn to see that she has arrived, in another magnificent dress, her long dark hair flowing freely. She would have made such a better Raina than me. She sits next to Jen and the two of them begin a hushed conversation. Kye lets go of my hand and stalks to exchange heated words with Akers.

Stark reality weighs like bricks on my shoulders as I stare into the leaping orange fire. They want to send me away? One look at the shock on Mom's face and I know this is the first she's hearing of this too. The council may not realize it, but I know Marian. And their decision doesn't mean crap without her approval. If nothing or no one else, I will always have her behind me.

Knowing this helps.

A couple hours ago, I planned to give a speech. To stand up and convince the council that I've grown up and can take care of myself, make good decisions and blah, blah, blah. But I'm no longer sure that argument is necessary. The glow of flames surrounds me, creating a halo of light along the fabric of my dress. If I'm going to speak up, the time is now.

All eyes are on me when I turn, and a hush falls over the room. "The shadows have been following me since the tomb. I haven't brought it up because I wasn't sure, but this thing that attacked tonight has been around for a while. I don't know what it wants—what any of them want—but it doesn't matter." I reach for my mother's arm, urge her to stand next to me. "I'm going to reverse my objection to the moving idea. We'll plan to leave after graduation. Kye's sick. Sicker than me. Too sick to travel all the way to Mexico."

"That's not true, Abby," Kye says. "I could make it just fine."

I can't look at him, because if I do, I'll lose my resolve, and I really, really want to do the right thing. "No, Kye," I murmur. "I don't think so. Your energetic vibrations are just too low."

The toe of his shoes kiss mine, and he tips my chin up with a single crooked finger. He looks at me for a long, drawn-out moment, then nods, as if making a decision. "You're right. You should go in my place."

I'm frozen by Kye's gaze. Confused by everything that's happened today. He loves me, but wants freedom, and now he's suggesting I move to Mexico with his mother? I can't think. As long as he's touching me, there's no way I can think straight, so I brush his hand off and inch away.

Mom finally speaks. "Aside from the fact that we know someone who lives there, why does anyone have to go to Mexico? Abby and I can just as easily pack up and head to California or Canada or Alaska."

Val and Akers exchange a look, and Val says, "Our counterparts in South America are seeing an influx of shadow demons since the incident with the tomb. Should she choose to go, Abby could exercise her new skills and help get things there under control while resetting the proverbial clock on the curse."

"Not only that," Akers chimes in, "but Christine is also a Healer. She can continue Abby's training. Sending her to Mexico could be a practical solution for everyone."

Mom glares at Akers. "A practical solution? I'm not looking for a practical solution, Landon. I'm looking for a way to protect my daughter. We can pack up and be out of here first thing in the morning." She shakes off the arm he tries to drape around her shoulders. "Don't think you could stop us. We've been outrunning Gifted people since Abby was born."

"If running was necessary, I wouldn't try to stop you," Akers says, clearly attempting to smooth her ruffles. "But in this case, sending Abby away will be temporary. Consider what it will be like for her to know you'll be here whenever she's ready to return. To know she has roots. Providing her with a stable home is possibly the most helpful thing you can do for her."

"Mom, stop," I say, stepping closer to her. "Those demons that followed me today, they're not alone. There are more. Lots more. I let them out. I didn't mean to, but I did it. I don't know what they want, but it's my fault they're free and it's up to me to fix it."

Mom's eyes travel over my face. "How do you plan to do that, Abby? You're just one girl. A strong girl, I'll admit, but still, just one person. And those things that just chased you down mean business. This isn't a movie, and you're not a super hero."

Leave it to Marian to compare my life to a movie. "Look at all these people. They're here to help me. Help us." Kye's warm fingers slide between mine and I cling to his hand, realizing that I probably won't have the opportunity for much longer. "I may not have a plan, but they do. I know I'm still not considered an adult, but I think this is a good idea. This way, I leave, which needs to happen, but you stay. You keep a place for me so that no matter where I go, I always know I have a home in Jackson. I think I want that. I've always wanted a place to call home."

Her eyes sparkle with unshed tears. "I'm not ready to send you away alone. What if you don't come back? What good will your home be then?"

Kye's intake of breath and squeezing hand make me wonder if he's actually thought this through. My ring hums to life. After swallowing a boulder of fear, it still feels like the best thing, the right thing. "I will be back. I promise."

Val nods his approval. "So it's settled. Abby will leave for Mexico the day after graduation. In the meantime," he narrows his eyes at Kye, "what's this I hear about a prop closet?"

Dammit. Busted.

SEVEN
Endings and Options

For the next week, Gabe hovers closer than ever. He sits next to me in my classes, as well as at lunch. The worst part is losing my freedom at home. Up to this point, the Dragons have kept an eye on me from a distance, never coming inside without a really good reason. But between my tryst with Kye and the shadow demon incident, they're extra protective. I now have two Dragons watching my every move. Gabe has been assigned as my personal body-guard while the others each take shifts guarding the "perimeter." Which is basically my surroundings within a hundred yards.

In reality, I should've seen this coming. But that doesn't make it suck less.

Even worse, I haven't talked to Kye since the meeting. Not only have I not seen him at school, but he doesn't answer or return my calls—though I've left him several messages. I'm submerged in the pool of sick dread I felt in Val's cabin, the foreboding I've avoided examining because I don't want to deal with it. But I know we can't keep doing this. The physical ache of separation is—by itself—more than anyone should have to deal with.

The morning of graduation, I'm awakened by bright fingers of sun reaching between the blinds to caress my clammy skin. I rise and shower, ignoring the anxiety that threatens to destroy what is supposed to be a monumental day for me.

My room looks like a thousand shadow demons crammed into my closet until it exploded. Every article of clothing I own is in one of many haphazard piles—what to pack, what to wash before packing, what to store in Rubbermaid containers, and what I might want to wear to the ceremony this afternoon.

It's the last pile that causes me stress. This might be the last time I see Kye for a really long time, and I want his memory of me to be unforgettable. By the time I decide on the right outfit, I'm nearly late. Luckily, the classy-biker-style I've got going (fitted black top, black pencil skirt, leather boots and matching jacket) calls for a wild and loose hairdo. I take a minute to retouch my makeup, grab my cap and gown, and run out the door.

Gabe's waiting on the porch, tossing his keys into the air and catching them again. "Cutting it close, don't you think?"

Ignoring him, I stride to the car and climb in. It's my big day. Kye's too. And also our last afternoon together. I'm not going to let Gabe be the raincloud that ruins it. "We'll probably go to dinner. Kye can bring me home when I'm ready." If I'm ever ready.

Unsmiling, Gabe shifts into drive.

"You're not going to leave me alone with him, are you?" I ask.

He takes a deep breath. "When the ceremony is over and I'm absolutely sure his attention is on you and not the hundreds of other people there, I'll let you have your time. But I'm not just going to drop you off at the curb. Consider me the overprotective parent who intends to walk you inside and sit next to you until I know that everything is secure. And even then, we'll see."

I have to force a smile. "As long as you're doing your job."

He scratches his chin—unsuccessfully hiding the humorous light in his eyes that softens everything about him. "Thanks for not being difficult. For once."

"For once? What are you talking about? I'm never difficult."

"Okay," he says, a hint of sarcasm in his tone.

"I'm not!"

"Okay," he says again.

The place is packed. Other seniors mill around in caps and gowns, glowing with excitement because for them, this is just the beginning. I wish I could feel that way. I wish I could feel anything besides the unease that weighs like bricks on my chest. I wish my new beginning didn't have to start with so many terrifying endings.

I know Kye's okay, because if he wasn't, someone would have told me. Val and Akers have both promised. The only reason I can think that he wouldn't return my calls is that he doesn't want to talk, and not knowing the reason is scarier to me than any shadow demon.

We keep to the edges of the crowd as my eyes roam endlessly to find the one person I'm desperate to see. Then it's time for me to take my place in the auditorium; I can't stall anymore. Obviously, Gabe's not graduating, but Akers has secured him a seat with the faculty, which—conveniently—leaves him only a few feet away.

Kye has to sit in the M section, two rows behind me, with the J and K sections between us. When I take my place, his chair is empty. To keep my hands busy, I play on my phone, trying to be discreet as I watch the empty spot.

He walks in with only seconds to spare, and my heart trembles as I drink in the sight of him—all glory and good looks in his cap and gown. Our eyes meet, and my breath catches. Tingles ripple along my body, reach into my soul, and warm me from the inside out.

And then ...

Then he frowns as his focus skitters away. He turns his head and avoids my gaze. For the first time since I realized I love him, an energetic wall goes up between us, cutting me off from him more completely than any break-up ever could.

All my happy sensations go cold. What's going on? A baseball-sized lump forms in my throat. The person next to me pats me between the shoulder blades, looking worried. I'm gasping.

Gabe sends me a text:

You all right?

I reply:

I don't know.

Something's wrong.

He shut me out. Something's wrong.

Him:

Danger? Where?

Gabe jumps to his feet as the principal strides to the podium, and I see Akers grab his arm and make him stay sitting, murmuring something in his ear. I text back:

No danger. Never mind. Just watch the ceremony.

I wait for my eyes to burn or fill, maybe a sob to bubble up, but none of that happens. Instead, a strange hollow chasm opens inside me, stretching and yawning as it grows bigger and bigger.

I can sense Gabe's eyes on the back of my head right before my phone vibrates again:

What's wrong, then?

My body is numb. Ignoring the last text, I try to swallow around the lump and turn again to look at Kye. His attention is focused elsewhere. On something–or someone–to his other side. The set of his jaw, the look in his eyes, reminds me of my own hopeless longing. Except he isn't looking at me.

He turns his head and catches me staring. The sides of his mouth move into an unnatural smile. He blinks a few times, and then deliberately looks away. Since I haven't heard from him all week, I don't even try to text Kye. But I can't hold it in, so I text Gabe:

Have you heard anything about Kye being mad at me?

Across the space separating us, Gabe frowns, shaking his head, then sends a reply:

He never even sees you. What would he be mad about?

He has a point. Still, there's definitely something going on. Something weird or wrong or just stupid.

Is not seeing me a reason for him to be mad?

I can feel Gabe's exasperation from where I sit, which is, sadly, more than I can feel from Kye. That hurts worse than the look on his face that insists he's determined not to look at me. My phone vibrates again:

Under the circumstances? Only if he's nuts.

Wish I could say he's crazy, but I don't think he's that stupid.

Plus, he has great taste in women.

My face warms with embarrassment over Gabe's thrown-in comment. I wish I could react, but I'm too overwhelmed by Kye's rejection, and can't feel much of anything other than nauseated.

Gabe must sense this, because his next text says:

Actually, maybe he is crazy.

Maybe the curse is messing with his mind.

Maybe there are side effects we haven't discovered yet.

I don't know what to say to that, so I put my phone away and attempt to focus on the speaker, but all I hear is white noise. By the time the principal begins reading graduate names, the numbness in my body has spread to my ears and I almost miss my cue. The girl next to me gives me a nudge, so I follow the line, grateful that I'm not first—or last, for that matter—and wait for my name to be called. When it is, I walk across the stage, blinded by bright lights and flashing cameras, and deafened by the cheers and whistles of my friends. Mom's voice is the loudest, so I wave, give a thumbs up to let her know that my accomplishment is hers as well. I accept the rolled-up diploma, shake some hands, and smile a lot, allowing myself to experience a moment of triumph because I did it. I actually finished school, despite the odds being against me in a hundred different ways. And for that, I'm proud.

I. Did. It.

For a moment, I can experience the happiness that comes with knowing that this one chapter of my life is over, and I succeeded in doing this really hard thing. I beat the odds.

And even though I'm hurt and angered by the way he's acting, when Kye's name is called, I jump to my feet to cheer and whistle and clap until my hands sting, because he did it too. I don't know why he's acting the way he is, but I love him, and I'm proud. So proud. We did it.

Then I look around. My voice isn't the loudest one, and I'm not the only person standing. Everyone is cheering for Kye. And a large percent of our graduating class are girls. Girls who will probably still be here when I'm gone. I finger the protective stones hanging from a chain around my neck, trying to draw strength.

Gabe's strong hands clasp my arms. "You okay?"

I shake my head, holding a hand against my burning stomach. "I need some air."

Gabe steers me outside to a bench. I lie back and prop my feet up, staring at the enormous blue sky. Gabe doesn't ask, but I know he thinks the curse is the cause. There's no point in telling him all is not well in love-land for me and Kye. If he doesn't already know, he will soon enough. And so will I.

"Anything I can do?"

"Just let me lie here for a bit." Minutes later, the ceremony ends and people stream out the doors. I sit up, digging in my bag for the little box wrapped in shiny blue paper. It's a leather wrist strap with a circle of howlite attached by twisted white-gold cords. I want Kye to always have a piece of the stone that kept him alive when Juri held him captive in the poisonous caves.

Maybe he won't wear it. Maybe he's getting tired of having to fight for his life. Having to fight for me. But I want him to have it anyway.

Gabe helps me to my feet, and we wind through an endless maze of families and well-wishers back into the building. It seems like no one can take enough pictures, or offer enough hugs, or shed enough tears for the graduates who have grown up so fast.

Mom finds me, grinning through her tears, and snaps a few hundred shots. She hugs me, takes more pictures, and tells me over and over how proud she is.

"I'm proud of you, too, Mom," I tell her.

Tears sparkle in her eyes, and her chin trembles. "You are the number one best thing I've ever done in my life."

I hug her this time, tight.

"Where's Kye?" she asks. "We need to take some pictures of you together."

Gabe and I exchange a look, and he says, "We haven't found him yet."

On the other side of the room, Akers has spotted us, and yells for Mom.

"Well," she says, "when you do, bring him and meet me out front." Looking flushed, she turns away from me, and toward my teacher—who, I guess, isn't my teacher anymore. But he waves for Gabe and me to come too, so I follow my mother, hoping to find Kye along the way.

And I do. Only, he's not desperately searching for me the way I've been hoping. He's standing next to the stage with his arms around another graduate —one with curly blonde hair and a laugh that grates on my ears like a screeching hyena. I close my eyes, telling myself it's okay that he's hugging a friend. People do it all the time. But when I open them, he's still holding her. When he leans down to whisper in her ear, the ground drops from beneath me, and I could swear my heart stops for a split second. The dizzy nausea I've been fighting rises up and threatens to drown me.

I can't move. I can't look away.

I

Want

To

Die.

He turns his head and sees me. An entire realm of emotions ride across his face, but the only two I recognize are alarm and sorrow. He—finally—lets go of Crystal and starts toward me, and I'm suddenly grateful that Gabe is here. How would I ever make it home without him?

"Hey there, beautiful." Kye's smooth voice sends tingles into me, even after what I just saw. "I thought you left." His eyes stray to Gabe, Akers, Mom, and then focus on me again.

"I can see that," I mumble, proud that I'm actually able to speak. "Unfortunately, I don't have it in me to desert you." I hand him the box. "Here. Congratulations."

Mom lifts her camera, but Gabe covers the lens with his hand, shaking his head.

"Abby ..." Kye reaches out to caress my cheek, but I turn away. "Babe," he murmurs. "It's not what you think." He glances at our audience, and tugs my elbow, as if he wants to talk in private. "Maybe it's better if—"

I yank my arm out of his grip. "Don't. Just ... don't. I can't think of an explanation that makes everything okay right now. I don't know what's going on in your head, but maybe it's probably best that way. Tomorrow morning I'm leaving the only place that ever felt like home to me, going to stay with *your* mom. To try to find a way to break a curse that's killing *us*. Me and you. Because I love you, whether we can be together or not." The numbness in my chest has reached my extremities, weighing them down. It's a miracle that I manage to back away from Kye to the safety of Gabe. "I want you to have a phenomenal life. Even if I can't be part of it." Actually, I sort of want to drown him in a pool of acid, but that will probably pass. In a century or two.

"Abby, wait." Kye reaches for me, but I swivel to avoid him.

"Be happy," I tell him. My eyes burn, but don't fill as I walk away from the love of my life.

As Gabe helps me into his SUV, I'm glad—for the very first time—that I'm being forced to leave Jackson.

EIGHT

Goodbyes

The rest of the evening flies like a blur. Rose and Jen stop by insisting that I come to the after-graduation party. When I collapse into a shaky, exhausted heap, they accept my refusal and leave with teary goodbyes and a pledge that Jackson will never be the same without me. Then Eric shows up. He kisses my cheek and hands me a long, skinny box wrapped in lined paper. "I know you don't love me the way I wish you could, but I'll never forget you. You, Abby. Not Raina. Please come back safely. When you can. When you're ready. No matter what happens, we'll *all* be waiting."

I throw my arms around his neck. "Thanks for saying that. You have no idea how much I needed to hear it today."

Eric swallows, his Adam's apple bobbing. "I have a pretty good idea what you're going through. It's not easy to walk away from everything that matters to you."

His words make my eyes prickle, though I'm still too numb for tears. "I'm sorry I can't be what you need. Be happy, okay?" The glimmer in his eyes hurts my heart, and I have to force myself to look away. "Goodbye, Eric."

"Be safe."

I close the door to block out the sight of him walking to his car, everything about him screaming misery. Upstairs in my room, I zip my suitcase and stand it near the window, then flop onto my bed to rip the paper off Eric's gift. When I remove the top and see the hilt of the now destroyed Arawn Dagger, my heart lurches. It's broken. I know that. Val made sure the crystal spear was severed from the hilt after the power-stealing, tomb-opening fiasco. But it's still a dangerous weapon.

My first instinct is to pry up the loose floorboard in my closet and dump it inside, but as I run my fingers over the embedded gemstones, I change my mind. Leaving it here could make my mom a target, so I cram the dagger in my suitcase. Another look around my room reassures me that I haven't missed any details. My possessions are all either packed or stored, and I finished cleaning and polishing an hour ago. The only thing left is for me to get some sleep.

I change into my pajamas, curl into bed, and hug a pillow to my empty chest. Maybe the contact will somehow shrink the yawning chasm that opened when Kye turned away from me.

He didn't even say goodbye.

Part of me expected him to show up and at least wish me luck or something. Have we already become so disconnected that my leaving doesn't matter to him at all?

The ache continues to spread, and every time I close my eyes, reels of memories loop around and around in my head. Sometime close to four a.m., I give up trying and tiptoe downstairs for a glass of water. I swallow some melatonin and valerian root, hoping for sleep. My body needs to rest, even if my heart aches for the rest of ... well, forever.

I'm glad Gabe left Mom and me here for the night with only our regular perimeter guard. He must know that tonight, of all nights, I need time alone.

The house seems extra cold, the floor like ice against my bare feet, but the thermostat is set at the same temperature as always. Upstairs, light shines under my bedroom door. I don't even remember turning it on.

I swing the door open and jump when a tiny purple light dives at me and lands on the edge of my nightstand. "Jeez, Murtagh, what are you doing here at four in the morning?"

"Oh, *Calin* friend, Murtagh so going to miss. With you I go?"

I snuggle into my bed and wrap the comforter around me. "Don't you like your new home? The other sprites?"

Murtagh's light blinks. "Yes, *Calin*, happy Murtagh here." He flies closer and touches the end of my nose. "But warrior hero must protect queen. Far away land danger place."

"You don't need to protect me." I offer a hand for him to perch on. "You should stay here and watch over my mom."

He babbles in his native sprite language, his light blinking. "No *Calin*, goddess send help—Murtagh to go."

The idea of taking Murtagh to Mexico warms something inside me. When I met him, I was frightened and alone. Then he showed up and helped me, and everything got better. Small as he is, Murtagh is my friend, and he cares.

"All right. I could use a friend who isn't a guy." Realizing what I've just said, I shake my head. "Sorry, I guess you're kind of a guy."

"Murtagh not guy." He flits up, blinking his excitement. "Murtagh warrior sprite. Protect queen much danger."

He probably knows better than anyone. Sometimes I wonder if Murtagh's more psychic than me. "If you really want to come, be back here by seven."

He zooms around, blinking. When he lands on my hand again, his face is solemn. "Bring friend. *Calin* talk him now. Sad, sad guy." He flies to the window where a tall shadow lurks on the other side of the glass. My heart drops into my toes. I fumble for a weapon while Murtagh unlatches the lock and the door slides open. A scream bubbles up and then dies in my throat when Kye steps in. My hands fly to my now thumping heart. "What are you doing?"

He takes a deep breath, but doesn't answer. Instead, he just stares. A few days ago, I'd be all gooey and sugar from being so near to him, but the canyon inside me has swallowed all my warmth, all my happiness.

"Abby." His voice is rough with emotion, and the thing inside me that cracked earlier breaks wide open when he moves closer, but hesitates at the edge of my bed.

Confused, I huddle against the headboard, folding my knees into my chest. "What do you want?"

He stares at his empty hands. "How can you ask me that? You know why I'm here. I love you, and you're leaving and—"

"Don't." His words hurt my ears, and my head, and my eyes and heart. But then I look at him—really look—and see how sick he is, and how miserable, and the cold thaws enough so the hot tears I've wished for all day finally manage to fill my eyes. Finally. One breaks free and burns a trail down my cheek.

With a strangled sound, Kye slides onto my bed and scoops me into his lap. I wrap my arms around him, turn my face into his shirt, hoping I don't regret it later. I need this. We both do. We don't say anything for a long, long time. An ocean of tears has broken through my dam, flowing freely while Kye holds me, while I can muffle my sobs in his chest or shoulder. Every so often, he muffles one of his own in my hair.

In the comfort of his arms, I drift in and out of sleep, plagued by dreams. Nothing specific or vision-like, just flashes of faces and voices and laughs and broken thoughts of all the people and things I'm going to miss. When the sting of hurt wakes me from sleep, wracking me with another sob, Kye tightens his arms, his hands soothing, and his lips find mine. When the pain eases, he fluffs my pillow and adjusts us into a more comfortable sleeping position, where we stay until the first rays of light turn the sky outside a soft royal blue.

Finally, I roll out of his arms and sit up to face him. "Is this really all there is for us?"

"I hope not." Still lying on his side, he reaches to tuck a lock of hair behind my ear.

The alarm clock buzzes, and I stretch my arm across him to turn it off. His hands frame my face and he gazes into my eyes. "I wasn't going to come this morning. Last night, I talked myself into staying away, convinced myself we would both be better off if I just let you go, but ..." He sits up to face me, letting one hand drift down my neck until he's playing with my un-brushed hair. "I couldn't do it. I couldn't let you leave without saying goodbye."

In the early morning light, his sleepy eyes are a startling shade of blue, and everything about him seems softer, more perfect than ever before. In what we know will be our last moments of intimacy, I drink him in, memorize the planes of his cheeks, the set of his jaw, the sweep of his forehead and curve of his nose. My fingers wind into his wavy blond locks, comb through his hair, memorizing the texture of it against my palms and fingertips. We move together in a fierce embrace that—when seen as a shadow against the wall, merges the two of us into one—and I memorize that too.

With my face buried in his neck, inhaling the woodsy musk that belongs to him alone, I can almost convince myself that everything will be okay. That somehow I'll return to him, and he'll still belong to me, and we'll find a way to break the curse and be together.

Almost.

A tremor of desperation rocks our entwined bodies, and I lift my face to his for one last, frantic kiss. His hands dive into my hair and I grip his shoulders, setting us off balance until we tumble backward, only barely managing to not fall on the floor. Someone knocks, but I ignore it, wishing it wasn't morning, wishing the night would last forever, wishing Kye could come with me and stay with me and be with me forever, happily ever after, the way love like ours is supposed to go.

"Abby?" Mom's voice comes through the wood. "Honey, I know it's early, but you need to get up if you're going to catch your plane."

Kye squeezes me tighter, whispering in my ear. "No. It's not morning yet. It's still night. Don't answer her. Don't go. Please don't go." He presses against me again, kissing me with startling ferocity.

Mom lets herself in, stopping to clear her throat when she sees that I'm not alone. "Uh ... Abby?"

I break away, refusing to be embarrassed, and sit up to straighten my tank top. Wiping moisture from my cheeks with the edge of the sheet, I tell her, "We need a minute, Mom." The salt in my mouth has a tale-tell taste of tears, and when I glance at Kye's red-rimmed eyes, I realize they're not all mine.

She takes a deep breath, focusing on Kye. "Have you been here long?"

He meets her gaze, looking more grown up than I've ever seen him look. "Not long enough to make either of us sicker than we already are."

Mom's eyes linger. Kye and me, together on my bed, the twisted blankets, and the pillows that somehow ended up on the floor. "That wasn't ..." By the wrinkle that forms between her brows, she seems to be realigning her thoughts. "Never mind. I'm making waffles."

If circumstances were different, if I wasn't leaving, and Kye wasn't staying, I would probably be worried about how this looks to her. Maybe about punishment or repercussions or at least an oncoming lecture, but I'm pretty sure there's nothing more anyone could do to punish me at this point.

She closes the door behind her, and I stand, distancing myself from Kye. "I need to take a shower. Do you want some breakfast?"

He tries to smile, but fails. "Don't think I can eat right now." The yellow of his face stands out in stark contrast to my white sheets, leaving me wondering how much sicker he'll be by the end of the day. Or maybe he'll start getting better once I'm gone?

I scoop up the clothes I left out for today. "Will you stay a while?"

"I don't know, babe, I—" a wicked, body-shaking cough interrupts his words.

"You're leaving, aren't you?" The numb cold starts again, flooding my veins trickle by trickle.

He stands, straightening his clothes. "You have to get ready, and my being here will only make it harder. But I want you to ... no, you know what? Never mind."

"What?"

He crosses the room, hugs me one last time, and kisses my forehead. "Tell my mom I love her, and that I said to take good care of you."

"I will." That's it? You love *her*. Good. What about me? "Kye, I—" His fingers on my mouth stop me from saying the words I desperately need to say, to hear. The cold fills my lips.

"I know. Me too." He backs out through the sliding glass door. I want to tell him not to go, to come with me, that I love him and want him to get better, to look after my mom and Erda and so many other things. At least that he can leave through the front door. But my voice is paralyzed as he glances down and whistles for Finn. He swings his legs over and holds his body against the railing, watching below.

Finn's footsteps thunder on the ground, and with one last look at me, Kye says, "Bye, Abby," and lets go. The moose's footsteps shake the windows as my knees give way. I sink to the floor, allowing the cold to take over and send the last of my body heat out the door to follow Kye.

I'm still lying there, numb, when Marian comes in to find out why I haven't showered. And she does the one thing I need, the thing she hasn't done since I was much younger.

She holds me.

NINE

Like Lightning

Gabe shows up an hour later. He picks up my very-heavy suitcase as if it's a pillow, and tosses it into the back of his SUV. Erda brushes against my jeans, nudging me with her head as I take a long final look at the first place I've ever truly considered my home. Next to me, my mom sniffles, mouth moving like she wants to say something, but can't form words.

Our life has never been what others would consider normal, but this time the burden of leaving weighs on me like a load I've never had to carry before.

Mom wraps her arms around me. "Just yesterday you were small enough to sit on my lap. I can't believe my baby girl is leaving me already. This house will be too empty without you." She dabs at her eyes with a tissue, but an embarrassed blush colors her cheeks. "Landon and I ... After your father, I believed I'd never love again. And the truth is, I didn't want to. I loved that man like there was no one else in the world. But it's been so many years, and a woman can only stand to be alone for so long—"

"Mom," I interrupt, dazed. "Are you in love with Landon?"

Her pink flush deepens to burgundy. "I don't know. Not sure I know what love feels like anymore. And I want you to understand that my feelings for Landon are very different from what I had with your dad. But ... there's something good between us. He makes me smile, and he seems to like coming around, and I enjoy his companionship. I'm going to take things one day at a time. But...if we were to start seeing each other, would you have very many objections?"

I squeeze her hands, now sniffling myself. "Of course not. It's a relief to know I'm not leaving you completely alone. I love Akers. He's a really great guy." How ironic is my life that the man who has been like a father to Kye has become my mother's sort-of-boyfriend? "I want you to be happy."

"I'm going to try." Her smile is watery as she brushes a lock of hair off my cheek and tucks it behind my ear. "And I think you should too. I know this is hard. Much harder than anything you've done before. But happiness is a choice, Abby. No matter where life takes you, or who gets to be a part of it, only you can decide to focus on the good things."

I don't know what to say to that, so I just nod.

"I know you're putting all your hopes in breaking this curse so you can be with Kye. And I don't have anything against that boy. You know that. But whether you break the curse or not, I want you to live the life you choose. Not the life someone else has mapped out for you, or the life you think is best for anyone else, or the life of some ill-conceived destiny. Baby, I want you to find what makes you truly, utterly happy, even if it means breaking the mold. Even if you think others will be disappointed or hurt. Your first, and most important responsibility is to yourself." She traces her fingers over my face, squeezes my shoulders. "Promise me. Promise you'll find happiness."

I lean my head on her shoulder, hug her goodbye one last time. "I promise."

Gabe knocks on the open door. "Ready to go?"

I ruffle Erda's ears, bend to scratch her belly. "Be a good guard dog for Mom, okay?" Her sad eyes fill me with guilt. I drop a kiss on her nose. "Love you pup."

Mom and Erda wave from the sidewalk as we drive away, and Erda barks when I roll down the window to wave back. I'm about to close it when a purple blur zooms in, startling me. "Murtagh! I thought you changed your mind."

"No, *Calin*. Murtagh warrior, protect queen, always. New job, no? Save you, not?" He perches on Gabe's shoulder, but Gabe swats him away. "I'm trying to drive, sprite. Find somewhere else to sit. Or better yet, go home. You're not coming with us."

"Yes he is."

"Says who?"

"Says me," I insist. "I invited him. I want him to come."

Gabe shakes his head, disgusted. "Val's not going to be happy about this."

I coax Murtagh onto my shoulder, where he blinks red in indignation. "*Calin* queen decide, not stinky, rotten Dragon guy." He mutters in the language Gabe and I could never decipher.

My lips twitch with amusement. "You tell him, Murtagh."

Gabe's about to object.

"Look, Dragon boy, this is going to be a long trip, so before we go too far, let's get something straight. I've never pointed it out before, but you work for me, not the other way around. You're here to guard me, protect me, and keep me from danger. We may be friends, but let's not forget who's calling the shots. This is my journey, my task to accomplish, and my destiny to fulfill. Just because you don't agree with everything I do doesn't mean it's wrong, or that I won't do it anyway. Just to be clear."

"You've got to be kidding me." He shakes his head, clearly exasperated. "We're taking the bug to Mexico? Why?"

Murtagh's wings flutter in righteous indignation.

"Murtagh's not a bug, he's a sprite. And he's my friend."

"So, you're bringing him along as a playmate? That's just peachy."

Gabe's distain knocks my ego down a notch, and leaves me wondering if he's upset over this assignment. He's leaving his home, too. I'm technically his job, and lately I've treated him like an annoyance. Except yesterday. At the very moment I thought my heart would flop out of my chest and squish itself into the street,

Gabe was there to take me home. He helped me into the car, then walked me to the house and upstairs to my room, where I collapsed on the bed in my skirt and boots and didn't move for more than an hour.

Gabe stayed with me until Mom came home and took over. I let him comfort me, let him pick me up and carry me up the stairs when my feet were too heavy to lift. He hugged me and kissed the top of my head as he put me down, and I hugged him back, thanking him for his help. Only after Mom kicked him out did he go home to his own life. To pack his own things, and say his own goodbyes.

Yesterday, I thought we had crossed a threshold into friendship. Today, something has changed, and I'm back to being an assignment.

He glares at me. "If you prefer, I can arrange to have the bug guard you while I stay here. Your royal brattiness."

I know I'm a brat. Know it's one of my coping mechanisms that Gabe hasn't recognized yet. But the idea of going alone to Mexico frightens me more than I want to admit. Rather than meet his insult head on, I have to force myself to speak. "Are you saying you don't want to come with me?"

"I'm saying that if you and your bug friend would rather do this on your own I'll—" he breaks off, redirecting his focus on the road. My eyes are drawn to the same thing as his.

We're heading full bore into a wall of solid black clouds. The colossal shadow is so wide it appears to have no end, and tall enough to block out the sky. The sun is still shining on us, but a dark line has formed between us and the airport.

Murtagh blinks like a techno strobe. "Danger, danger! Good, not. Safe, no." He flits around on my lap, looking distressed.

"What is that?" I don't even try to keep my voice steady.

Gabe's eyes are wide and round. "I don't know, but it can't be good."

"Danger, danger, danger!" Murtagh shouts. "Must have Light. Go through, use Light."

Behind us, the sky is clear. This storm, or shadow, or whatever it is, is like a wall, and we're barreling into it at fifty miles an hour. Gabe slams on the brakes, but we sail right into the cloud of black. "Uh, Gabe?" The mist rolls over the hood and winds around, cocooning us in the car.

"Yeah?" He pumps the brakes, and we start to slow, but the inky clouds create a layer of ice on the road that pitches us further. Strong winds buffet the sides of the SUV, threatening to topple it—and us—sideways.

"This is so not good," I say.

"You think?" Gabe replies.

The Jeep slides to a halt in the middle of the road as a torrent of rain pours sheets of icy water over the car with such pressure that little streams sneak through the cracks in the doors and sunroof, dripping on our heads and running down our backs. The wind continues to swirl, spiraling us in a frenzy until we have no idea which way to drive. At a loss, Gabe looks to me for help. "Okay, Miss Powerful Queen, what do we do now?"

I peer into the black as the rain becomes quarter-sized hail, falling so hard it leaves dents all over the hood. "We have to go through it."

Gabe raises his eyebrows, incredulous. "You don't say."

I shake my head, trying to tune my senses through the energy of the storm. "Shut up and drive. The longer we sit here, the harder the dark energy will pound on us. Hail this size can be deadly."

As if the shadows hear me, fist-sized lumps smash down on us. Gabe guns the gas, careening around to find and follow the faint yellow line.

"Light, *Calin*. Fight dark with Light." Murtagh's voice is swallowed in the noise of the pounding storm. Gabe flips on the fog lights, but they do little to cut through the wall of dark energy. As if the shadow is insulted that we would even try such a stunt, the bulbs explode, leaving us—once again—in inky darkness.

Breathing heavily, Gabe drives on, fast enough to combat the wind, but slow enough so we manage to stay on the road. As my eyes adjust, a flash of white flies past my window, making me wonder if Finn and Kye are caught in the shadow, too. Terror turns my knots of tension into anger that spreads through my blood, gunning for my fingers.

My limbs shake as I grab the roll bar near the dash and rest my head on my arms, eyes closed. I let the heat come, allow it to build and flow until I can channel it, turn it into a weapon. My ring—Raina's ring—sparks to life. I open my eyes. Gabe's lips are pressed into a thin line, his jaw set in determination as he wrestles to keep the car on the road until we reach the airport turnoff. Murtagh curls into a ball on my knee, temporarily silenced. Frustrated and determined, I fling my arms outward, hurling a lightening-burst of energy at the darkness.

The shadow recoils, rearing back until we can see part of the sky. The pelting hail lets up, shrinking until it melts into a light rain. Half a mile farther, we pass the edge of the cloud and shoot into bright, warm sunshine. Still cautious, I turn around and watch the blackness swirl into a funnel that uproots trees, still dumping a mixture of rain and hail, twirling and swirling into itself until it disappears into fine mists of dark smoke that evaporate into the air. By the time we park at the Jackson airport, there's no trace left of the storm.

Gabe gets out, instructing me not to move, so I open my purse and let Murtagh fly in and curl between my passport and wallet. My energy wanes, leaving my hands shaking as I open the door, expecting to find a shadow demon under the car. Gabe scoops me out of my seat, leaving our suitcases behind, and barrels for the entrance.

TEN

Loopy

Inside, we narrowly avoid plowing into a cloaked figure. Gabe sets me down as the man draws back his hood. I offer a weak smile to Zane, the Dragon Master—aka Gabe's boss. He takes my hand and leads me to a chair. "Good job defeating the dark storm, Abby. I can tell you've been working on your focus."

"Not enough, apparently." I collapse with exhaustion, hoping the shadows won't come back with so many Dragons here. "I didn't think we'd get through it."

Zane sits next to me, waving Gabe back to the parking lot. I assume he's going to get our things so we can check in and board the plane. "We've called an emergency council meeting. The pilots have agreed to hold takeoff for a half hour to accommodate us."

"How did you get them to agree to that?"

Ignoring my question, he motions for me to follow him to the check-in area. Once Gabe and I have checked our bags, Zane leads us to an executive conference room, where we're surrounded by Val, Akers, and a number of other Dragons I've met since moving here. I experience a flood of warmth when Eoin Murphy lays a warm hand on my shoulder. His smile—the one so like Kye's—sends a jolt of longing into my core.

"Hello, daughter." The sympathy in his eyes both comforts me, and threatens to cut apart the threads holding my emotions together.

"Hi, Dad." I hug him tight before settling into the cushy leather chair they've saved for me.

Murtagh buzzes in my purse, so I place it on my lap and open the top, giving him the freedom to fly out if he wants.

Standing at the head of the table, Zane calls the meeting to order. "Thank you all for coming to send off our young queen. Clearly we've had an influx of dark energy hovering in the area, the evidence of which manifested in the form of the shadow demon that came after Abby last week, and then again this morning in the form of a very dangerous, weather-bending storm. Luckily, Abby is learning to harness her power, and both times was able to fight off the dark forces without serious injury."

All eyes are on me. I wish I could disappear into my chair.

"These attacks will only become worse over time as the shadows grow stronger." Zane presses his palm to the table, leaning in. "Abby, this won't be an easy journey. As you develop more strength, so will they, and I believe at least some of them will attempt to follow you."

I nod, licking my dry lips. "Probably."

"Most assuredly. Now, that said, there is a way to give you a short respite. The trick, I believe, will be to temporarily shut down your energy for the journey."

Gabe and Eoin both jump out of their seats, hurling objections at Zane.

"No way." Gabe's voice is hard, but firm. "Shutting down Abby's energy could kill her."

"I agree with Gabe." Eoin's hand returns to my shoulder, and his squeeze is harder than I think he means for it to be. "Zane, what you're proposing is far too drastic, even given the circumstances."

Zane shushes both of them, motioning for them to sit back down. "Relax, gentleman. There are too many risks involved in a complete energy drain. What I propose is far less invasive, and will have the added side effect of being beneficial to Abby." His gaze falls on me again. "You've not slept much lately."

I shrug in acknowledgement. Clearly, I have no secrets from the Dragons, and Zane's the Dragon Master. Gabe grits his teeth, looking anywhere but me.

"What I propose will help with that." Zane moves around the table and squats next to my chair, his voice softening. "Sleep is critical to your strength, and we're counting on you building that strength into a usable force. You've got to get enough rest, Abby."

I stare at a spot on the table, refusing to meet Zane's eyes, as memories of lying in Kye's arms assault my heart and mind, until the wonderful numbness that has kept me going threatens to drain away and be replaced with misery. The most rest I've had in days was during that all-too short period of time while he held me. "I'll try," I mumble.

"Good." Zane removes a briefcase from under the table, pops it open and rummages around until he produces two tiny pink pills.

"What are they?"

"Energy reducers." When I just stare at him—as does everyone else—he explains. "Basically sleeping pills. Old Healing mixed with new technology. Calcium, Magnesium, Melatonin, Valerian—it's mostly herbal. Nothing that will hurt you, though you'll be disoriented. Having you sleep through your journey will be an excellent energy mask."

Haven't I already slept enough of this year away? "*Mostly* herbal? What else is in them?"

Zane fiddles with the clasps on the briefcase. "Some modern chemical aids." He looks up, probably realizing how bad that sounds. "Nothing illegal. I know you have strong opinions about prescribed medications, so I'm going to be honest and tell you that they also contain a small amount of Zolpidem. Assuming that you've never taken anything like this before, there's no way to predict how much—if any—memory you'll retain of the next day or two."

Two days? Huh. This idea just became incredibly appealing. I wouldn't mind closing down my brain for a while.

Zane must see my wheels turning, because he nods. "That's right. You'll get to sleep, and Gabe will see that you end up where you need to go, and protect you along the way. You'll have full use of your body, and will function in a fairly normal capacity—meaning you'll feed yourself when hungry, and use the restroom when that need arises—but your brain will be on a tiny vacation. In many senses of the word, you'll be like a live zombie."

Gabe asks, "Will it hurt her?"

"Not if you take care of her," Eoin says. It's the first thing he's said since arguing with Zane. He runs his hand through his hair, reminding me again of Kye. "Zane's right. This will be good for her." His eyes meet mine. "A solid block of sleep will be healthy for your body, mind, and spirit. Not to mention aid in mending your own broken energy."

"No, *Calin*. No hibernate energy—bad, bad, bad." Murtagh chimes in.

"Murtagh," Eoin says, "Abby's hurting right now, for several reasons. The most forward one being that she's leaving the people she loves. She's under tremendous stress, which I believe makes her more visible to the shadow demons. She's less able to block herself from their trackers. By allowing her to—essentially—sleep through the actual leaving, her energy field will be significantly diminished, which will in turn confuse the trackers and give her a few needed days, or even weeks, of relief." He leans on the table, his piercing eyes focused on Gabe. "You'll need to be prepared for any and all eventualities. Assume every dark thing is bad, and act accordingly. You see that she arrives to my wife's home safely."

Gabe swallows, seeming uneasy. "I'm still not sure this is a good idea. What if she sleeps for more than two days? What if her body reacts to the medications in those pills? What if her energy is so diminished that she doesn't get her powers back for a long time? There are so many things that could go wrong."

A knock sounds on the door, and an airline official pokes her head inside. "I'm sorry to interrupt, Mr. Zane. The pilots are anxious to take off. They've asked that your passengers either board now or wait for tomorrow's flight."

"Thanks for your help. Our passengers will be in their seats in ten minutes." When the door closes again, Zane turns questioning eyes on me. "Abby?"

"I'll do it." I close my eyes against Murtagh's furious blinking, and Gabe's distressed moan. "Sleep sounds incredible right now."

"But ..." Gabe sputters. "What if something happens? What if a shadow demon finds us while she's incapacitated?"

Zane drops the pills in my hand and offers me a paper cup filled with water before facing Gabe. "That's why we're sending you with her. We trust that you're fully capable of protecting our precious cargo."

A number of voices join the argument, Gabe included. While they're busy arguing over something that should be my choice, I pop one of the pills in my mouth and swallow. "Shall I take both or just that one?"

Zane closes my fist around the second pill. "Just the one for now. Hang onto this other one in case of an emergency. There may come a time when you need to hide your energy field again, maybe travel somewhere else."

I fold the pill into a gum wrapper and store it in a divided pill box, which mostly holds various crushed herbs. "Is there anything else I should know?"

"The pills will slow both your heart rate, and your breathing. This is normal, but Gabe will need to keep a close eye on you."

Gabe shakes his head, looking resigned.

Zane hands me a manila envelope. "Please deliver these to Christine. You might find them helpful in tracking down a possible second tomb entrance where the loose shadow demons can be sealed."

I straighten in my seat. "Wait, there's another tomb? Why didn't you tell me this before?"

"They did," Gabe says. "We've talked about it a number of times—hence the trip to Mexico. But you've been preoccupied."

I know I've had a lot on my mind, tons of distractions lately. Especially this past month. I suppose it's possible that I've missed a few details, but I'm certain that I haven't missed something quite as important as this. A second tomb? One without a broken entrance, and in which we may somehow find a way to corral the loose shadow demons? "No, really. I'm pretty sure no one has mentioned this to me before. It's not something I'd forget."

"Are you sure? Because—"

Zane stops Gabe's sarcastic retort with a look. "I'm afraid that's my fault, Abby. Your mother felt that you've had enough to deal with, and after seeing the effects of the curse on you, I had to agree. I chose not to divulge all the details. I'd hoped to wait until you've had a chance to rest and recoup, until a time when you're more physically able to handle the magnitude of what you're doing."

Great. Something tells me there's a lot more to this story. And what perfect timing for him to finally spill the beans, now that I'm starting to feel loopy and light. His words run together in my ears, and a layer of fog settles over my eyeballs. Knowing we need to board the plane, I try to stand, but the world is a rocking boat and I haven't gained my sea legs. Gabe catches me mid-sway, whispering in my ear. "Here we go, Princess. Let's get you on that plane, shall we?"

I tuck my head against his shoulder as he scoops me up. "Don't forget my purse. Murtagh's in there with my passport."

"I don't think Murtagh would let me forget him at this point." His chest rumbles with a chuckle, as we start moving. My eyes are weighed closed, so I don't try to look.

"Need my passport," I say.

"I've got it," he murmurs.

"Bye, guys." I attempt to wave. "Love you all."

Gabe laughs, and a few minutes later I'm being settled into a hard, straight backed seat, a pillow shoved against my cheek as I lean on Gabe's shoulder. And then the engines roar to life.

ELEVEN

Waking Up

My next coherent awareness is the sound of a feminine voice. "Abby can you hear me? Are you hungry?" I'm floating in comfort, surrounded by fabrics that glide along my skin. The air is balmy and warm, and in the distance, a sound I can't quite place—a dull roar that grows and fades in a rhythm as consistent as music.

I force my eyes open, expecting the shock of bright lights, and am relieved to find only a dim glow. It outlines the figure of a woman who strokes hair off of my forehead. Blinking away fog, I grasp the sheets. Silk. I move again, learning my surroundings by touch. Both the comforter and pillow are light, downy. Who would want to wake up and leave this?

But there's a reason I'm surfacing now, an urgent need. I sit up slowly, my head fuzzy and light. "Where's the bathroom?"

The woman sits next to me. "Do you need help?"

My voice is rough with disuse. "Think I can handle it."

"Through the door on your right. You have your own, so take all the time you need. I'll wait out here in case you need help getting back in bed."

I hold tight to the iron footboard, allowing my muscles time to remember how to work. "Have I needed a lot of help?"

"Not too much. You've been incredibly independent, considering."

My feet might as well be weighted with sand, but moving gets easier as I go. When I flip on the light, little bombs of pain explode in my head, so I flip it off with a moan.

"You okay, honey?" The woman's voice calls through the door.

"Yes," I say, hating how scratchy my voice sounds.

"Be careful. If you try to do too much too soon, you'll make yourself sick. Energy restoration is a slow process."

Moving like a snail, I do my thing, and then grope around on the counter to find a brush and pull it through my hair, remembering the torture of trying to detangle my long auburn locks after my last Healer's sleep. As soon as my head has been adequately tortured, my legs carry me back to the bed, where I collapse into the warmth again.

"So ... you aren't awake then?" She sounds disappointed.

"I think I am," I mumble. "But my head hurts something wicked, so I'm just going to lie here for a while. Might fall back to sleep. Sleep is good. Sleep is my friend."

"As you've been saying since you arrived." A small, strong hand pats my shoulder, and soft fingers stroke my forehead. "I'll check on you soon."

I sense her leaving. "Could you bring me my purse? I have some potassium and sea salt that will help my headache."

"Sure, honey. Anything else?"

I lick my dry lips. "Water?"

"I'll send Gabe up with your things." The shadowed form opens the door, allowing a pool of light to spill onto the floor. I want to tell her to please not send Gabe. I'm not feeling presentable. But it's too late; the woman is already gone.

A lock of hair falls across my face, tickles my nose, and I blow at it, lifting my heavy arms to gather the whole mass and tuck it behind my shoulder. My mouth tastes like wet chalk, and I don't even want to know what has happened to the small amount of mascara and eyeliner I applied before leaving home.

If I look as dead as I feel, I could be in a zombie movie.

A wave of embarrassment hits when I think about how Gabe had to take care of me while we traveled, and I have absolutely no memory—whatsoever—of the trip. I have no clue what humiliating things happened, or if I did anything that might require an apology, but I'm quite sure he's witnessed me at my utmost, and absolute worst.

Wondering how long I've been incoherent, I search for a clock, but if there's one here, it's covered. As are the windows. I hope there's a window.

A memory surfaces—me and Kye, trapped in a stone room with no doors and only a tiny wedge through which we could escape. I've never been claustrophobic, but the memory jolts me. I sit up, ignoring the pounding in my head, and rip off my covers. My skin erupts in goose bumps when my feet touch the cold tile floor. Using the bedpost as a guide, I fumble along the wall, and am relieved to discover it's a curtain.

A thin vein of light opens behind me, and Gabe comes in, carrying a tray. "What are you doing?"

Clutching the drape for balance, I search for an opening as panic rises in my chest. "I need to find a window. Please. I need to see outside and breathe fresh air." Frantic notes of terror, which I can neither control nor prevent, play in my voice.

Gabe sets the tray on the nightstand, calmly stepping aside and tugging a cord. The fabric slides open, revealing a wall of glass. The waning moon lights an expanse of white sand that gives way to turquoise water, which spreads across the horizon. "It's the ocean."

"It's actually the Caribbean," says the woman from earlier. "The water is warm, and in the day, so clear you can see the bottom."

I turn to introduce myself to the woman, who I assume is Kye's mom, Christine, but when I look at her my voice fails. Wavy blonde hair cascades to her trim waist, accentuating incredibly defined features, including sharp cheekbones that lift and frame a pair of bright eyes that rival the color of the sea outside. This ethereal beauty is more than stunning, more than memorable. She's absolutely familiar.

"Hi, Abby." She approaches me as Kye would a wounded animal. "It's nice to finally meet you."

I shouldn't be speechless. After everything that has happened this year, there's no reason I should be surprised about this. But I am. I really am. "Isleen?"

"Christine." She guides me gently to my bed. "You're exhausted. Let's get you tucked in again."

"You're ..."

She fluffs the feather pillow and presses me into it until I'm curled on my side.

"I'm Kye's mom." She tucks the blanket around me.

"No. You're Isleen, Theron's mom." Her hands still mid-tuck. I continue, "Doesn't Eoin have a picture of Isleen in one of his books? He has one of Raina. She looks exactly like me."

Christine sits on the edge of the bed, her fingers stroking the hair away from my face. "He does have a picture, and you're right, there is a remarkable resemblance." She glances away, seeming to struggle. "But similar appearances don't necessarily mean anything. And I have no memories that would indicate I have a connection with Isleen."

I struggle onto my elbows. "Do you have Witch Light?"

"No," she says, "that power has never manifested for me. At least, not yet."

My weak shoulders start to shake, so I lean against the headboard. "Can I ask, what is your Gift?"

"I'm a Healer, like you."

Like Isleen. But not wanting to push, I keep this knowledge to myself and stare at the tray Gabe brought in. It holds a bowl sealed with a lid, a spoon, and a fresh tortilla rolled in parchment paper, along with my pill box of herbs, and a glass of water. Someone has placed a single lily next to the glass, the pungent aroma helping to clear my head before I even open my box.

"Let's work on regenerating your strength, shall we?" Christine opens the lid on the bowl. The soup is loaded with chopped vegetables and tiny meatballs, topped with cheese, chives, and a dollop of sour cream. "You haven't eaten since arriving, so you must be hungry. If nothing else, the nutrients and protein will help your head, and you'll be better able to sleep with a full tummy."

"Thanks." I spoon a bite of the steaming liquid. A sting of spicy heat burns down my throat. Not wanting to hurt Christine's feelings, I chew and swallow, then bite into the tortilla to temper the heat. "Wow. That stuff will clear your sinuses, but it's really good."

Christine looks distressed. "Is it too spicy? I'm sorry. It's hard for me to gauge American taste buds after living here for so long. That's just the way we make it."

"Oh no." I shake my head, berating myself for mentioning it. "It's fine. Just unexpected. The last person who brought me food in bed was Gram. Bland chicken noodle soup."

Gabe picks up my spoon and stirs in the sour cream and cheese until the broth has a creamy texture. "Try it now. Won't be so hot."

With the addition of the cooling ingredients, it tastes like heaven. I finish all the soup and two tortillas, followed by a pinch of potassium powder to kill my headache. "Thank you, Christine. That was delicious. And thanks for taking care of me."

She takes my tray. "Gabe has done most of the caring. My only real contribution has been to stand outside the bathroom door in case you needed help."

"Well, thanks to Gabe then, too."

"Just doing my job." He turns to the window to stare at the ocean.

I wonder how long it's been since he slept. If I know him at all—and I think I'm starting to—he hasn't even seen his room yet. He must be exhausted. "What time is it?"

His watch lights up at the touch of a button. "Two forty-three a.m."

"I'm sorry." I adjust my tank top and pajamas, wondering when I changed, and if I'd needed help with that, too. "Did I get you out of bed?"

Christine takes the tray from me and sets it on the floor. "Of course not. Neither of us has been to bed since you arrived."

"How long ago was that?"

"Not long enough." Gabe glances at me, looking concerned, but his eyes don't meet mine. "Not quite twelve hours. I expected you to sleep all night, and then all day tomorrow as well."

Unsure if I should be glad or disappointed, I suggest, "You should both go to bed. I'll be fine. I'm awake enough to take care of myself."

"I think you're right." Christine wraps her arms around me in a motherly hug that's warm and familiar. In a way, she reminds me of a younger version of Gram. "It's good to meet you. And while I miss my son like crazy, I'm glad to have you here."

I want to tell her that I'm glad to be here, but I don't like to lie, and I'm not sure that's true yet. "It's good to meet you too."

Christine wishes us goodnight and excuses herself, leaving me alone with Gabe, whose frowning broodiness makes me wonder how he feels about being here, too.

TWELVE

Caribbean Moonlight

Gabe starts for the door. "I'll let you get back to sleep. Goodnight, Abby."

"Wait." I reach out, snag his hand. He stares at where I'm touching him as if he can't believe I would do such a thing—even though he touches me all the time—so I let go and pat the bed near my knees. "Can we talk?"

His expression makes it clear that he wants to decline, but then I cough. I've been doing it so much lately I don't even really notice, but Gabe does. "Do you need something else? An energy treatment?"

"No." I shake my head. He stays close, but deliberately avoids sitting. "I'd rather you tell me what's bothering you. You're unusually distant."

"Distant how? I'm right here."

I raise a brow at him.

"I'm fine, so you can just wrap up that guilt you're offering and serve it to someone else." He still won't look me in the eye. "It's my job to protect you, no matter what. That's why I'm here."

Now I know there's something wrong. A big something. "What are you talking about?"

His Adam's apple bobs. "Abby, don't worry about it, okay?"

"I wouldn't if you weren't acting so strange. Really, Gabe. Tell me."

"Nothing's wrong. I'm just tired." He rolls his muscular shoulders, stretching.

"Did something happen while I was asleep?"

"No. Well, yeah, sort of." He grabs the bedpost at the foot and continues stretching. "The customs people thought you were high. Kept us in a holding room for over an hour while they dug through our luggage. I assume they were looking for a stash, but it's hard to know since they wouldn't talk to us."

"Might help if you spoke the language."

"I do." Finally, he makes eye contact. "Didn't you know that? It's one of the reasons Val assigned me to go with you. I double as both bodyguard and translator."

"That's convenient," I say, relieved because I can tell he's letting go of some of his anger.

"Anyway, I tried to explain that you took something for motion sickness and it made you sleepy. You were walking on your own, and somewhat coherent—to their knowledge anyway. It's not like you were out cold." He twists at the waist, his trim abs rippling under his thin T-shirt.

My lips feel suddenly dry. "They probably just wanted a bribe, like Eoin warned us. Did you offer them money?"

He gives me the 'uh-hello' look that only Gabe can achieve. "How do you think I got you out of there? Those guys wanted to keep you—by yourself—until you sobered up. "

"Ugh," I mutter, not wanting to think about what could have happened. "I'm glad you took care of it. That would've been very bad."

"Tell me about it." When his gaze drifts out the window, his eyes reflect the moon. "I should let you get back to bed. Zane says you'll feel a lot better about life after some solid sleep." There it is again. That expression. That ... whatever thing he's hiding. It flickers in his eyes, the set of his mouth, the way he grinds his teeth, but passes too quickly for me to decipher.

"Zane's probably right," I agree. "I have been over extended lately."

Gabe starts to leave, but pauses with his hand on the knob. "Sleep well, Abby."

Before he can close the door, my brain makes another connection. "Wait. Where's Murtagh? Did he come with us?"

Gabe waves at the window glass. "We told him you'd be asleep for a while, so he's outside exploring. I haven't seen him for hours." Gabe doesn't wait for me to say goodnight, just slips past the door, closing it behind him.

Contrary to what I just told Gabe, I'm wide awake. Through the glass, glowing rolls of white-capped waves beckon to me. They crash onto the sand a short distance from the patio, urging me to touch, to go outside and dip my toes in the water, to walk along the beach by myself, if for only a few minutes.

My feet hit the floor, the hem of my cotton pajama pants brushing the smooth tiles as my fingers trail along the immense wall of glass in search of a doorknob or latch. When I find nothing, I drop onto an antique-looking vanity stool, debating how far I dare explore while the others sleep.

My makeup case sits next to the mirror, unzipped. When I open the lid, the case is empty. A flush of concern creeps up the back of my neck. Gabe didn't say if we got our luggage back intact. What if I have no clothes or toiletries? What if they took my crystals? Gram's box?

I start opening drawers, and breathe a sigh of relief when I find my makeup in the top one, my brushes and hairdryer in another. A drawer on the opposite side holds Gram's jewelry box, where I find my jewelry and crystals undisturbed. My racing heart settles.

I replace the box in the drawer, and find a remote with a number of colored buttons. I try them all, discovering how to work the lights, some in-ceiling speakers, and the drapes, before pressing a blue one. There's a quiet click, swish, and a low mechanical hum as the glass panels turn and slide together, three to one side, three to the other, until the entire wall has opened to the wide expanse of white sand and water.

Barefooted, I scurry onto the cobbled patio to breathe in the fresh, salty air. Positive energy follows, surrounding me with a sense of rightness, and lifting my spirits until I want to laugh. I jog to the edge of the water and stop to let the warm waves bathe my feet.

The waning moon emits bright blue energy that touches everything in its path. Water, sky, palm trees, foliage. Even my skin glows blue, along with my light-colored clothing. I turn my face to the moon, eyes closed, welcoming its healing power and allowing it to purge some of the damaged energy I've carried for so long. A rush of adrenaline courses into me, filling me with an intense, undeniable urge to run. Giggles bubble up my throat, and I let them out. It feels good to laugh, better than I remember.

I continue to splash through the shallow waves, enjoying how the sand squishes between my toes. Droplets of saltwater spray as high as my hips, leaving my pajamas damp, but not cold.

I pass houses and a possible resort, and come to a jungle. Thick tangles of dogwood and mahogany mingle with palm trees and vines that creep close to the shore, swallowing the beach and leaving only a small strip of sand.

After a while, I pause to look behind me and stay oriented. Getting lost on my first night here is probably not in my best interest. I don't speak the language, didn't grab my cell phone, and even if I did, don't have Christine's number, nor have I memorized Gabe's. Suddenly nervous, I veer out of the water, taking deep breaths of tropical air. My fingers trail onto a shrub bearing vibrant pink flowers that appear to be in the tulip or hibiscus family. Next to it, a rose bush bearing red blooms that somehow seem incredibly out of place in this tropical setting. Curious, I pick one, twirling it between my fingers.

From the corner of my eye, tiny lights flash, and I can hear a faint buzz. "Murtagh?" I murmur, stepping further into the vegetation. Another light, this one blue, flashes, and then disappears. "Hello?"

"Hello, señorita."

Startled, I whip around, yelping and tripping over my feet as I stumble into the roses.

"So sorry. I do not mean to scare you." I can't see his face in the shadows, but the man is about five ten, and medium build. I'm not sensing danger, but that doesn't mean I shouldn't be extremely cautious.

Hiding the rose behind my back, I manage to squeak, "Am I in your yard? I apologize. Your roses just seemed so out of place among the other flowers. I was curious."

"Is no trouble. Mi amigo planted this. He believes it will bring him love." He picks another, leaving the stem long, and offers it to me. "Are you lost?"

I squint down the stretch of beach, realizing I've gone much farther than I thought. "I hope not."

When he steps toward me, moonlight highlights his features and I see that he isn't much older than me. Stubble dusts his chin, and wild shocks of hair fall around his eyes and forehead. His milk-chocolate eyes take in my damp pants and rumpled hair. "Running away?" A note of amusement leaks into his voice.

"Sort of." The corners of my mouth turn up. "I mean, I went for a run, and by doing so, took myself away from where I'm supposed to be. But I should probably head back. I could still end up lost."

"Why the hurry?"

"I'm supposed to be in bed asleep, rather than walking in the jungle." By myself. And talking to a stranger. When Gabe finds out, he might murder me.

"I see." He leans a long-handled something against a tree, and his large, calloused hand engulfs mine. "My name is Victor."

"Nice to meet you," I tell him. "I'm Abby."

His teeth gleam in the moonlight when he smiles. "Now we are no longer strangers. May I walk with you? If you are lost, I will help you find your way."

I should say no. I really should. Knowing someone's name doesn't make them less of a stranger, or less of a danger. It must be his smile, or the warmth in his eyes, or the way he picked that flower for me, that makes me say, "Oh, um, okay. Why not?"

We've just started for the beach when the buzzing I heard earlier returns, this time louder than before. A purplish light zooms past us, pulsing like a strobe before it spirals to the ground and goes out. "Murtagh!" I bolt to the spot where he dropped, falling to my knees to search with my hands.

This close to the ground, the thick vegetation blocks out most of the moon's light, and I curse myself for not knowing how to make my ring glow without Kye's help. Victor kneels beside me, joining my search as I scrape through the grass and undergrowth. "What are we looking for, señorita?"

"Murtagh."

"Excuse?" He says, sounding baffled. "My English, it is good, but not perfect. What is a Murtagh?"

Crap. I can't leave Murtagh collapsed on the ground when he's clearly in trouble. Especially in a strange country. But how do I explain my sprite to someone who shouldn't know they exist? "It's um, my pet ..." Pet what? Murtagh doesn't pass as a hamster or a bird. "My pet ... fire-dragon-fly. He's a rare breed. A large, colorful breed, and I'd hate to lose him. Please be gentle."

A tiny glow flickers, and I scoop up a handful of leaves and dirt, disappointed when I don't find the flutter of paper thin, gossamer wings. "Murtagh? Where are you?"

His frantic buzz (which sounds to me like a scream) sets my heart racing. He blinks, once, twice. In those two blinks, I manage to see him, and also the reason for his distress. A large, scary Iguana, one with a row of spikes along its back and plenty more around its head, has a claw on one of Murtagh's delicate wings, pinning him to the ground. The thing's three feet long, and probably ten pounds.

"Do not worry, Abby, I save your Murtagh." Victor jumps to his feet, grabbing the pole, which I now realize is a shovel, and bounds to the rescue with the grace of a cheetah. He lands in the soft earth with very little sound, and attempts to scoop the iguana up, only to have it hiss and uncurl its long tongue in Murtagh's direction.

"No!" I scream. "Don't let it eat him."

Victor sends me a questioning look. "Shall I kill it?"

"No. You'll hurt Murtagh."

"I won't hurt your pet, Abby. I promise. I kill the lizard." With that, he raises the shovel and brings it down on the creature's head with a resounding crack. I squeeze my eyes shut, praying that if Murtagh is hurt, at least his heart is still beating.

THIRTEEN

Rescue

Given the sickening slurp, I'm pretty sure the lizard didn't survive. I'm afraid to open my eyes and see. "Please tell me that thing's brain isn't splattered all over the place."

"All is well and clean," Victor says, chuckling. Footsteps crunch away, followed by the scrape of a shovel. "Or will be after I move the corpse."

I open my eyes to find Murtagh lying on the ground, his usually vibrant light dimmed to a dull glow. "Are you okay?" His wings twitch as I scoop him up, but there is no other response as I cradle him in my palms.

Victor nods at my bundle. "Your Murtagh?"

I close a hand over my sprite, hoping Victor doesn't look too closely. "Thanks for your help."

"Is no problem. Those lizards have been known to bite."

A shiver passes across my shoulders. "I'll remember to avoid them." Victor sets his shovel aside and walks me to the edge of the jungle. "Well," I say, feeling awkward. "Goodnight."

He retrieves the rose I dropped and removes some bruised petals, then slides it behind my ear. "Come back and see me again, beautiful lady."

Heat burns my cheeks as I jog away. By the time I reach Christine's house, the stars are fading into a navy blue sky that has hints of gray peeking around the edges. The cobblestones brush sand off my feet as I hurry into my room. I lay Murtagh on my pillow and turn on the light.

I dig out pieces of rose quartz and smoky topaz and position one above his head and the other near his feet, then straighten his chakras using my index fingers.

Other than Erda, I've only ever tried to Heal humans, and the results of those attempts have varied between bad and disastrous. With one important exception.

Murtagh's size intimidates me into starting out slow. The tones I hum are higher than I would use for a person, instinct telling me that Murtagh is tuned to a higher energetic frequency. As I sing and work, the crystals lift off the pillow and sluggishly come to life. I change my pitch, and the crystals speed up, whirling Murtagh's violet energy into a funnel that aims for the center of my head.

Usually, having someone else's energy enter my body causes me great pain, makes me suffer in order to ease their agony. It's the job, the purpose, of a Healer. But Murtagh's energy is very different. I experience a prickle of discomfort, a wave of exhaustion, but very little pain. I open my eyes, worried that something has gone wrong. But the energy is already returning to him—clear and strong—his inner light already brighter. When the transfer is complete, I catch the crystals mid-air and set them on the nightstand.

He sits up, rubbing his eyes and fluttering his wings. "*Calin*? You awake. Happy, Murtagh. Thought you would forever sleep."

Murtagh appears to be feeling better himself. I cover a yawn, feeling the Healer's sleep beckon. "Just through the traveling. It was cool to go to sleep in one place and wake up somewhere entirely new."

"No, *Calin*. No cool. Hot this place. And danger for sprite."

"I saw that. What were you doing?"

He covers his mouth with both hands, his light blinking in merriment. "Large scary creature not much like Murtagh."

My eyebrows draw together as I speculate about what would cause the 'large scary creature' to not like my sprite. "What did you do to him?"

83

"Not do to him anything. Visit new sprite friends and wham—" He slaps his palm with a fist. "Run into monster." His wings flutter as he talks, assuring me that Murtagh will recover just fine. "Stuck in tangle web, and monster lick Murtagh legs. Yuck. Murtagh run, not like monster. Try to eat me, *Calin*. Not good, not fun."

We've only been here a day and already Murtagh is causing trouble. "Murtagh, I don't think it's a great idea for you to go looking for sprite friends until we talk to Christine about what else might live in the jungle. You were lucky I went out. What if I hadn't found you when I did? And someone saw you. How am I supposed to explain you to people who don't know about sprites?"

"Murtagh not afraid people. Fly faster than human run."

"Yes, I know, but that's not the point." My brain gets fuzzy as the sleep closes in. I plop down next to Murtagh, dimming the light. "People don't understand about you, which means they'll probably be afraid of you. And having people be scared of you—however little and spunky you may be—is dangerous to your health."

His body glows as he yawns. "Murtagh scary warrior. Protect *Calin* from danger."

I yawn too. Murtagh has overtaken my pillow, so I grab another and curl up next to him, scooting my feet under the comforter and cocooning it around me. "You won't be able to protect me if a giant lizard eats you. You have to be careful in those jungles. We don't know what's out there."

"Danger, *Calin*. Danger everywhere." Eyes drooping, Murtagh turns on his side and wraps his wings around his body.

I close my eyes too as the last of the moon's energy drains away. "Good night, my fair warrior sprite."

His light blinks, and then lowers as we both fall into peaceful slumber.

A delicious aroma brings me back to life, a savory whiff of cooking meat, vegetables sautéed in butter, and something sugary. The fragrance slithers under the door, through the cracks, teasing me from sleep. My stomach growls as I sit up to find the pillow next to me empty. I stretch, full body, well rested for the first time in months. The brightly shining sun has been up for hours, warming the floor tiles and filling my room with natural light. Breeze flutters my bedding, bringing with it more scents—these of water and salt—which adds a tropical flavor to whatever is cooking.

I throw the covers aside and swing my feet to the floor, stretching again.

"Did you sleep well?"

Squealing, I scramble back on the bed, clutching the blanket to my chest. Gabe has planted himself in the nearby chair, wearing a murderous expression.

"You scared me." I press a hand to my racing heart, take a steadying breath. "Yes, I did. I haven't slept that well in so long, I'd forgotten what good sleep is like."

"Glad you were comfortable." His eyebrows are drawn together so tightly that there's a deep groove between them.

Shoving off my covers—again—I straighten my pajamas to be sure I'm adequately covered. "Is something wrong?"

He raises an eyebrow, his gaze darting back and forth between me and the open wall of windows.

"Oh crap."

"Did you get enough fresh air?"

I force a smile, not wanting to think about the dangers to which I've carelessly subjected myself in the last few hours. "Not even close." I stroll to the patio and stand with my face in the sun. "I've never seen water that color."

He replies from right behind me. "If someone—or something—had been looking for you, not only would they have found you, but they'd have had full access to come in and grab you out of bed while I was in my room asleep." He grips my shoulder and forces me to turn around and face him. "What were you thinking? We've come a long, long way to protect you, to hide you from shadows. Why would you be stupid enough to leave your room open to the public?"

I want to respond. Be indignant that he would even suggest that I'm careless. But he's right. It was careless. And stupid. Leaving the windows open was an accident—but still stupid.

"Are you going to at least tell me where you went? Because this time I know it wasn't to see your boyfriend." There's a hint of jealousy in his voice, and I'm not sure what to do with that. My only explanation is the truth, and I'm thinking it wouldn't be wise to tell Gabe I ran a couple of miles down the beach by myself last night. And if I tell him I met a local, he'll flip.

"I opened the windows to get some air," I tell him. It's not a lie. I did need air. "That stuff Zane gave me made me sickish."

"And so ..." His gaze slides down my body to my feet, then back up. "You got all muddy from staying in your bed, inside this room all night? Sorry babe, I'm not buying it."

I stare at the tattle-tale sandy footprints on the tile. "I wanted to touch the water."

"So you went swimming?" He's obviously trying not to look amused, but his attempt isn't working well.

"Not exactly."

"Then ..." He lifts his hands as if waiting for me to fill in the middle of the story.

I suck at lying. Might as well give it up. "I went for a run on the beach. But only for a few minutes, and not far."

He eyes my legs again. My gaze follows his, and I notice two large, dark stains on my knees from kneeling on the soil. I swallow my embarrassment. "Okay, so I also took a walk in the jungle. I was looking for Murtagh, and I found him about to be eaten by a giant lizard. Got there just in time."

"Anything else?"

I shake my head, averting my gaze. Does it count as a lie if I don't tell him about Victor?

"You went into the jungle alone?" He sighs, exasperated. "Abby, use your brain. You can't go running all over the place in the middle of the night. We're in a strange country, for one thing, not that it would be any safer in our own, even without the shadow demons. Do you have any idea what could happen to you?" He picks up a rock and hurls it at the ocean. His superior strength sends it high and far, until it disappears into the air and lands with a large splash more than a football field away. "I don't even want to think about the things that live in that jungle. Not to mention drug lords and other human predators."

His words bring Victor to mind, and I have to school my features so I don't give *that* detail away. "I bet it's not as bad as you think."

"And I bet it's much worse than you think." He takes my wrist, a possessive move he's never made before. "Promise me you won't do that again."

"Gabe ..." I don't want to make promises about anything. In Jackson, I felt smothered, trapped by everyone who was keeping an eye on me. I don't want to let him restrict me now. Not here. Not yet.

"Say yes, because if you don't, I'm going to have to do something drastic, like disable the doors."

He sounds like a parent, and it ages him, reminds me that Gabe isn't my friend; he's my bodyguard. I peel his fingers off my wrist and turn into my room. "I'm going to get cleaned up, then I'll come after that yummy-smelling breakfast."

"It's down the hall and to the left—" he starts.

"I'll find my way." I close myself in the bathroom without looking at him.

He knocks. "Don't you want to know where your clothes are?"

I open the door and face him. "I'm betting in the dresser and closet, since my toiletries are unpacked into the vanity drawers."

"How long did you stay up last night?" He asks, looking incredulous. "I thought your head hurt and you wanted to go back to sleep."

"I stayed up long enough to find Murtagh." When he just stares me down, I add, "Do I need permission to take a shower?"

"No." He backs away, eyes filled with hurt. "I'm leaving."

"That would be nice." I close the door again. Gabe can be so irritating sometimes.

FOURTEEN

Zombie-fied

"I don't remember much about traveling except being sleepy." I shovel a helping of scrambled eggs into a tortilla and top them with salsa. We're circled around the polished wood table, which is laden with local dishes that smell divine. I'm full, and still eating, the first sign that my health is already improving.

Murtagh flits around, occasionally landing to pick at one platter or another, but never staying close for long, and he makes silly faces whenever Gabe's back is turned. I adore my sprite.

Christine's kitchen is bright and colorful, an eclectic mix of décor. Immaculate, but warm and homey. Light wood cabinets contrast with yards of dark marble counter tops and gleaming stainless steel appliances. The slick kitchen tile is similar to what's in my room, but deeper red.

"You don't remember changing planes in Denver?" Gabe picks up a piece of sweet bread, turning it over in his hands before taking a bite.

"No, I don't." As much as I dreaded leaving, I was happy to sleep through the travelling. "Why? Did something happen?"

Gabe seems to weigh his words. "Nothing big. But I hoped you'd remember something."

Christine pours juice in a glass and hands it to me. "If you tell her, it might help her remember."

My shoulders tighten as I sip, leaning back in my chair.

Gabe plays with his glass, twisting until it leaves a ring of moisture on the linen placemat. "You had a vision."

I press my bare feet against the tile, hoping the contact will ground me. "I did?" *How is it possible that I could have a vision and not remember it?* "Are you sure it wasn't a dream?"

He continues toying with his glass. "Not entirely. But if it was a dream, it was different from any dream I've ever experienced."

"Different how?"

He drains his glass and leans back, folding his arms across his chest as if he doesn't know where to start.

"Well, I was already unconscious, probably," I say, trying to help him out, "so that didn't happen."

"Actually, you weren't unconscious after taking the energy reducer. More like zombie-fied. You made it through the airport with only a small amount of help from me."

Knowing the difference between his idea of help and mine, I ask, "Did you carry me?"

He shakes his head. "Nope. You walked. I carried your purse, and held your hand—sometimes your arm—to prevent you from running into things. I made sure we got to our gate on time, and in the right seats on the plane." One by one, his thumb runs over his knuckles, squeezing each one. "We were about to our terminal, only had fifteen minutes before boarding, and you stopped. I nudged you, told you to come on, that we had to keep going." His gaze has been focused on his hands, but now he looks up. "Ever since you'd taken that pill, your responses had become automatic. I'd ask you a question, 'do you want a drink?' and you'd respond, 'no thanks,' or 'yes,' or whatever. And when I said, 'Abby, stand up, it's time to go,' you did it. But this time you didn't reply, and you didn't move. So, I was concerned."

It does sound like what happens when I have a vision.

Gabe continues. "Anyway, I tipped your head to make you look at me, and your eyes were glassy and kind of rolled up in your head, and you murmured something. Sounded like it was another language. Anyway, you knew what you were trying to say, and I didn't have a clue. Then you swayed on your feet. I dropped our lunch on the floor and grabbed you, but you tensed up. It seemed like you hurt, so I didn't dare carry you."

His gaze flicks away as he sits forward to drain what's left of his juice. "And then you said, 'Not Gabe, please. Why does it have to be Gabe? Please, no.'"

His eyes—gray with green flecks—find and hold mine. "Either you had a vision that involved me, or you hate me more than I thought."

Hate him? He thinks I hate him? I am annoyed by him, and frustrated with the situation. And irritated with everything he does because I wish Kye were here instead. But hate him? I could never hate him. He's too kind for that. "I don't hate you, Gabe. I promise it wasn't that."

"Thanks." He clears his throat and stands to help Christine with the dishes. "Let's hope you remember whatever it was soon."

There's something obvious about the vision, something I should know and remember. Something in the familiar way he moves and speaks and acts—but that I can't quite grasp yet. I need more fresh air. After clearing my plate and loading it in the dishwasher, I tell Christine, "Thanks for breakfast."

She drapes her arm around my shoulder. "You're very welcome, sweetie. Anything for Kye's great love." Her trill of laughter doesn't stop the tension that snakes into the room and squeezes tight around my chest.

Gabe's rinsing dishes, so I can only see his back. "I'm going for a walk," I announce, and retreat down the hall.

In the living room, a plush couch curves around the space, centering all focus on a large painting. Every wall is lined with bookshelves, which are packed-to overflowing. My sigh is one of pure pleasure.

Down the hall, I poke my head in closed doors, exploring in my nosey way. Three more bedrooms, but only the one directly across from mine appears to be occupied. Must be Gabe's room.

At the end, I find Christine's room. Sheer white silk drapes like a canopy over the bed, the soft white bedding accented with vibrant reds, purples, greens, and blues in the rugs, comforter, and pillows. An alcove on one side appears to be made entirely of glass, and houses a navy blue couch, with two cushy beach-style armchairs.

Here too, is a set of drapes like the ones in my room, but they're drawn back and tied against the wall. Christine's window overlooks the entire backyard and down the beach on either side of the house. A dark line is visible just off the horizon. It may be an island. "Wow."

"Beautiful, isn't it?"

Startled, I turn to find Christine in the doorway. She doesn't look angry that I'm in here, but if the situation were reversed, I would be. "Christine! I'm sorry, I was curious—"

"Don't be silly." She joins me near the window, where the sunlight turns her hair into spun gold and her eyes into sapphires, reminding me of Kye. "You're welcome to explore. Although, I do recommend knocking on occasion."

Angry with myself, I continue to offer apologies, but she insists that they aren't necessary. "This is your private space," I point out. "I promise this won't happen again."

"Abby," she murmurs, sweeping my hair off my shoulder in a motherly gesture that makes me ache. "If I believed you would steal from me, or go through my private possessions, I wouldn't have taken you in. You're in a new place and have a need to get oriented. This is the quickest way for you to begin adjusting."

"Thank you." I focus again on the water. Christine is both mystifying and comforting. She makes me long for my own mother. I start for the door, but Christine stops me with a hand on my arm.

"I was hoping we could talk," she says. "Woman to woman, if you don't mind."

My in-trouble-o-meter alerts. "Shh ... sure. Right now?"

She shakes her head. "Take your walk. I'm sure you need it. But soon. When you're up to it."

Unsure what she means by that, I scurry to escape to my room—my new safe haven—and grab my shoes. There are still other doors left unopened, more rooms to explore, but I've had enough of the inside. I really need some sun.

FIFTEEN

Walking

I venture onto the patio, hoping to catch up with Murtagh. The sun-warmed stones under my bare feet are hot, but rather than put on my flip flops, I skip across them and step into the sand as the palm trees sing with ocean breeze. "Murtagh? Where are you?"

For a moment, a foreign odor assaults me, putting my danger senses on high alert. I inhale again, searching, observing, but find no lingering trace. I must be ultra-paranoid.

Once I've made it to the edge of the surf, a glowing purple ball whizzes past. He zooms straight for the water, drops to dip his feet in the tip of a wave, and then rises again with a high-pitched squeal. He does this a number of times before landing on my shoulder. His wet legs drip water down my tank top.

"What are you doing?" I ask.

"Murtagh swimming. Fun game, *Calin.* You play?"

Laughing, I scoop up water in my hand and watch it run between my fingers. "Careful about getting your wings wet. You could get stuck in the water and not be able to fly."

"Why not fly? Murtagh water sprite. Made for water." His chest puffs with pride. "Good swimmer. Can tow whale."

Skeptical, I scoop another handful and sprinkle it over him until he's soaked. He flies off my shoulder making an overdramatic show of sputtering and choking. His wings flutter as he unfurls them. "Like this place, *Calin.*"

"I like it too." Laughing at his antics, I start down the beach. "I'm going for a walk. Do you want to explore with me?"

Murtagh glances at the house. "Dragon guy coming. Protect *Calin*."

"I don't think so."

He nods, an act which involves his entire body. "He follow *Calin*. Always. His job."

"You're right, he does." I shake my hands and dry them on my shorts. "Come with me anyway."

Murtagh flies closer, his wings already dry thanks to the breeze coming off the ocean. "Where going, *Calin*? Look sad. Need friend, yes?"

I nod, already walking, grateful to know that Murtagh is here because he chose to come.

The sun is warm, and the balmy air invigorates me until I feel dewy and fresh. When I return an hour later, I feel so wonderful I don't even realize I'm smiling until Christine grins from her chair on the patio. "You look like you feel much better."

Her words dim my smile, because I do feel better than I have in weeks, and I don't want it to be because I'm so far away from Kye. My stomach grumbles, reminding me what it's like to have an appetite.

Christine gestures to a picnic table spread with fruit, bread, and cheese, and a pitcher of limeade. "Why don't you grab a snack before we get to work?"

"Work?" I pour a glass of the frosty juice and drain it, wondering what I'm in for now.

"Yes, honey." Christine laughs. "You didn't expect this to be a vacation, did you?"

Part of me hoped, but I do know better. "Of course not. It's just that I'm not sure what the plan is, or where I'm supposed to start."

She joins me at the table as I load a plate with mango slices and crackers topped with spongy white cheese. "Val sent instructions. Gabe will keep you in shape, but you and I will work on focus, controlling your Light. And I'll continue your lessons on crystals and herbs. We'll start slow—let your strength build. You have a lot to learn and the more we can squeeze in while you're here, the better."

I shove a cracker in my mouth and chew to avoid having to respond. So much for coming to Mexico to rest.

Walking on the beach after breakfast becomes part of my daily routine. Neither Gabe, nor Christine seems to object, and they must be comfortable allowing me some freedom here, because they don't offer to walk with me. In some ways, this is a relief. Murtagh doesn't mind my thoughtful silence, and the salty fragrance of the sea combined with the squish of wet sand between my toes is therapeutic.

I spend my afternoons with Christine, working on focus, attempting to learn how to draw on my power of Light. Sometimes I think I'm getting better at summoning it, but those moments are rare. In many ways, Christine feels as much friend as mentor, and I appreciate that. Gabe keeps his distance emotionally, but physically is always where he should be—watching, constantly vigilant, looking on with approval when he thinks I'm actually learning something.

Even with them always around, I'm lonelier than I've ever been. My mother is far away. Gram doesn't speak to me here. I've spent my life moving, running, living without social attachments, and now that I've experienced true friendship, true love, and what it's like to be part of a community, it's difficult to let those things go. There's an empty cavity inside me that no amount of glue or thread can close, no matter how physically strong I become.

BIRTHRIGHT

We've been in Mexico over a week on the day Murtagh and I quietly slip out the front door rather than the back, looking for a change of scene. Unsure of what I'll find, and nervous to ask Christine, I tuck a small amount of cash into my front pocket. At the last minute, I also bring my camera, dangling it from a strap on my wrist.

For all the beauty I've experienced here—the beach, sunrise lighting my room with gold, sunset softening everything with a soft shade of rose, turquoise water, emerald palms rattling in a breeze, the spectacular colors of the jungle—I have yet to take any pictures. I'm afraid when I do I'll to want to send them to Kye, and whenever I think of him, I wonder what he's doing. Then I picture him hugging Crystal at graduation, and that ties my insides into a hundred-thousand knots.

We never talked about what happens next, never finished the conversation Kye tried to start in Val's cabin the night the shadow demons attacked. I was petrified he would say it's over, so I couldn't bring it up. But now ... now I wish I had, because at least then I'd know. I'd know it's over and begin the grieving process so I can try to somehow, someday, move on. Or at least move forward.

Or I'd know it's not over, and that he's waiting for me to call and tell him all about what's happening here. And I'd be sending him pictures daily, and writing him notes and making plans for ... whatever.

The way we left things hanging—it's hard to know how to act. What to think. How to feel. And it sucks rocks. I've tried calling, but he doesn't answer. Last night I left a message. He hasn't called back. I don't think I'll try again. At least, not for a while.

Maybe he wants it to be over. Maybe that last night, in my room, maybe that goodbye was supposed to be final. Maybe that's why it was so much harder than I ever imagined to crawl out of his arms. If it is final, and he's finding comfort with someone else—that idea knocks the breath out of me. So I try hard not to think about it.

Today I'm going to take pictures, and if I need to share them with someone, I'll send them to Mom and Rose. Because in this place beauty is a tangible thing, a taste in the air, a scent that permeates everything, the sound of waves crashing against sand so pure it seems unnatural. Beauty this strong, this alive, is something that must be shared.

Christine's neighborhood is nicer than I expected. The stucco houses and xeriscaped yards are well kept, and the roads are paved with dark, newly painted tar. A woman zips by on a lime green scooter, shouting something in Spanish over her shoulder.

"Maybe we should have Christine teach us some phrases in case we get lost," I tell Murtagh.

"Idea good, *Calin.*"

"Or you could bring someone with you," says a voice behind me. "Someone who speaks the language and who can keep an eye on you—you know, make sure you aren't carted off by strangers or kidnapped by a drug lord."

I whirl, and find Gabe leaning against a waist-high brick wall, staring me down with disapproval. Busted. "Just going for a walk." Guilt. Guilt. Guilt.

He waves me on. "Go ahead. Walk."

I turn away and start going, unsurprised to hear him fall into step behind me, which annoys me far beyond normal parameters. He has to have been following me.

"Were you were planning to go into town without telling anyone?" he lectures. "I don't care who you are, personal safety is a matter of common sense."

"I know, Gabe, I know." I quicken my pace, but he keeps up— his legs are longer than mine. "Maybe I left my common sense in Jackson. Maybe I trust my instincts enough to go for a walk. Or maybe I figure danger will eventually catch up to me no matter what I do, so I might as well hurry things along."

It's my last statement that makes him scoot ahead and cut me off. "Why would you say that? We've gone to a lot of trouble to bring you here and give you time to build your strength. Even I can sense the improvements in your energy since we came. Putting yourself in danger won't get you home faster, but it might get you killed. And I don't care how homesick you are, I better not hear you say something like that again, or you'll be locked in the house."

"You can't lock me in the house, Gabe. I'm an adult." Or almost, anyway. "If I want to go for a walk by myself, it's my choice. Mine."

"You're wrong." He steps closer, anger steaming off him. "It's my job—my whole, entire job—to keep you safe. And I will do whatever is necessary to follow through with that. Whether it involves locking you in the house, or throwing you over my shoulder and tossing you in a hole in the ground to hide you from shadow demons, I'm prepared to do it." His nostrils flare as he stares me down. "And Abby, I don't recommend testing me on this. If you think you hate me now, you don't want to know how I'll react if you keep pushing."

A thrill of anticipation shivers through me, though I'm not sure why. I don't know how to respond to this side of him, but he's forceful and confident and bold, and as much as I hate being bossed around, I like this side of him. So I start walking, and he does too. He seems cautious, on edge, like he's waiting for me to continue arguing. I probably should, but instead end up giggling because here we are, in this beautiful country, living in a ginormous house on the beach, and we're fighting. Over nothing.

My giggle breaks the tension, and Gabe shakes his head, his angry frown falling away as we round a corner into a tourist's paradise. Shops and restaurants cluster in a semi-organized shopping mall fashion. "Jackpot."

"Jackpot word strange Murtagh, *Calin.*"

The smile that curves my mouth feels foreign for the very fact that it has been so little used in recent weeks. "It means I'm going shopping. There are people back home who need presents."

"Shopping?" Gabe swears. "You were willing to risk life and limb to buy crap?"

"It wasn't planned," I murmur. "But since we're here, might as well."

He takes stock of our surroundings, and his eyes light up when they land on an electronics store that appears to be the equivalent of a Radio Shack. "All right. Against my better judgment, I'm going to let you do your thing." He checks his watch. "You have one hour. Meet me right here. Text me if you have any problems. Even if you're just scared." He strolls away before I have the chance to tell him I didn't bring my phone.

Murtagh dives into my hair as a couple strolls by, speaking a language that sounds like French. We wander in and out of stores, and I find myself smiling more easily as the day progresses. When I find a shop where the young employee speaks English, I buy a silver pendant on a leather cord for Kye. It's engraved with Mayan symbols for prosperity, happiness, and health. It isn't much, but would be easy to mail, should I decide to send it. And I can't pass it up because it makes me think of him.

As I'm paying, my eyes land on a familiar face. Victor has just stepped behind the counter. "What are you doing here?"

"Working at my job." He frowns quizzically at my purchases, then glances around as if wondering why I'm here alone. "Have you run away again?"

"Not this time." Nerves drive my hands to my hair, lifting it off my sticky neck. "Doing some exploring, some shopping."

His eyes narrow. "Alone?"

"Yes," I say, uneasy about my answer. "But not for long. I'm meeting a friend."

Victor's eyebrows draw together, forming an adorable crease. "You should not be walking in town alone, señorita. Is dangerous."

This guy and Gabe should be friends. Victor introduces me to Alejandro, the strong-jawed, dark-eyed boy who rang me up, and offers to walk with me to meet Gabe. Feeling like that's a bad idea, I decline, insisting that Gabe is very close.

When I step out of the shop, a sense of unease creeps up my back, growing bigger with each step. I'm a few minutes late; Gabe is probably frantic. And I've gone in and out of so many shops, I'm not positive how to get back to where I started.

This path seems wrong, so I turn a corner and try another. It doesn't seem familiar either. I backtrack and try another path which looks right at first, but as I continue, there are fewer people, and the shops become seedier. I backtrack again, and nearly smack into a group of leering men. Trying not to panic, I pick up my pace, worried that running will only provoke them. One of the men falls into step beside me. At first glance, his eyes appear violet, and I experience a flash of terror that maybe Boone is still alive. When the man blinks, I realize his eyes are dull brown, but regardless of color, he's dangerous. "Looking for a good time, señorita? I got just what you need."

My heart thunders, but I manage to shake my head and keep walking. The man keeps up, and one of his friends flanks my other side. "You want to buy a bit of happy?"

Dread colors my voice. "Leave me alone."

Both men laugh, and fear chills me to the bone, despite the Mexico heat. Murtagh moves in my hair, so I reach up to cover him, warning him to stay hidden.

"Pretty señorita." The first man clucks his tongue; his open admiration makes me feel dirty in a way I haven't felt since Jury dragged me down that New York alley. "All alone in a strange place. Let me help you find your way."

The second man's energy spikes as he grabs my shopping bag.

"Hands off!" I slap his hands away and run. The sound of footsteps on pavement follows, giving me eerie flashbacks of New York with Kye.

Murtagh wrestles free from my hair. "Murtagh get help."

"What are you going to do?"

"Find Dragon guy." He unfurls his wings. "Find sprite warriors help, too."

"Hurry, please." I slow, trying to focus, find my Light.

The first man grabs my tank top and yanks me off balance until his hand cuffs my wrist. "Let go!" I dig in with my heels, trying to break his grasp. I search deep inside myself for Light, but find only terror.

The second man clamps his arms around me, squeezing me breathless, while the first dumps the contents of my bag on the ground. The look on his face is one of disgust and anger. "No money? No papers?"

I shake my head.

The other guy chortles.

Something about his grating voice is frighteningly familiar; it stirs an ember in my core. I root it out, try to force a flame. "Leave me alone."

"Abby, there you are." I have never been so relieved to hear Gabe's exasperated annoyance. He's several yards away, but as Gabe approaches, my assailant's grip loosens as if he's afraid of the wide-shouldered man. I would be too if I were him. But before any of them can run, Gabe has the first man by the throat with one hand. The other man drops my things and backs off, but Gabe snags him too, holding both men aloft. "You okay?"

I nod, embarrassed because he had to rescue me—proving that maybe I do need him.

"Did they hurt you?"

"N-no. I'm—just shaken."

Disbelieving, he eyes me up and down. "What do you want me to do with them?"

"Excuse me?" My hands tremble as I retrieve my purchases, vowing this will never happen again.

"Well, I could squeeze their throats until their eyeballs pop out of their heads." One of the men whines like a puppy as Gabe demonstrates marginally. "Or shake them until their brains turn to mush." His biceps quiver as he rattles them slightly. "Or if you'd rather, I could bash their heads together until they share the same skull."

From the look on his face, he's prepared to do any or all of the above. The thought of blood spilling makes my stomach churn. I've been doing so well since we got here, I'm surprised at the speed with which the sick feeling catches up to me. One hand flies to my mouth, the other clutching my abdomen as my vision blurs and my head spins. "I don't know. They didn't actually–wow." Reality hits hard. How stupid I was to walk by myself in town. Gabe was right, and I'm afraid I'll never hear the end of it. "They didn't hurt me."

The look he tosses over his shoulder is loaded with bullets of heat and anger. "They tried. That's enough for me."

"Yeah. I get that." I'm sinking. This wave of sick comes on so fast and strong that it's hard to concentrate on anything else. "But we've only been here a few days. Should probably avoid killing ... anyone for a while." Needing something to hold onto, I grip his flexed bicep. The touch sends an unfamiliar tingle down my back, filling my insides with a warm sensation that may–or may not–have something to do with the nausea I mistakenly thought was gone for good. "Let them go. I think they'll stay away from me."

He lets their feet brush the ground, but doesn't set them free. "You sure?"

Because I'm touching Gabe, my head isn't quite so muddled. I draw in a stream of warm, calm energy. "I'm sure." Before Gabe frees the men, I decide to practice a technique I learned from Val. Cupping my hands together, I envision Light, digging deep to borrow warmth from that ember I felt earlier, then I open my palms and let the pulsing ball of Light float.

I hum a low peace tone and toss the Light up, blowing on it until it breaks into a million pieces that scatter like glitter in the breeze, surrounding the perpetrators in sparkles before disappearing completely.

Gabe sets the men free and they scurry away like frightened rabbits. "What was that you just did?"

"I blew Light in their faces. Wouldn't have done much good except that they were scared to death of you."

Eyebrow raised, he slicks back the dark hairs that have escaped his pony tail. "Are you really okay?"

"Yes." I say, ignoring my shaky knees. "Stupid sickness. Bad timing. What took you so long?"

103

He curls a supportive arm around my back. "If I remember correctly, we were supposed to meet by that restaurant where we came in."

I take a wobbly step. "I got lost."

"But," he says, mock surprise coloring his voice, "you could have made it home just fine on your own. Being that you're an adult, and all."

"Ha. Ha. Ha," I manage, closing my eyes in humiliation. I'm not sure I can make it all the way back to the house.

As if he knows what's happening, Gabe urges my head against his shoulder as we walk. "If you're still this sick, how have you gone so many days without collapsing away from the house?"

I'm reminded of what Murtagh told me the day I got here. "You wouldn't have let that happen."

His muscles tense. "I don't know how I could have prevented it, since you keep running off on your own."

"You've been following me. I'm pretty sure you've never been much farther from me than you were today."

"I don't know what you're talking about."

"Give it up, Gabe. I've got your number."

"I plead the fifth."

His response brings up another giggle, and I open my eyes to gauge his reaction. "Why didn't you say something? Speak up? You could've walked with me instead of sneaking around."

His brow furrows as he leads me to a bench. "I know you're dealing with stuff. And you spent so much time avoiding me in Jackson, I figured you wanted to be alone."

He has a point. I haven't invited him—I assumed telling him was invitation enough. In Jackson it always was. But things have changed since Jackson, and I think we both recognize it now. "I did. I do. Things just—"

My bag catches on a bench slat, ripping a hole in the bottom and spilling my purchases on the ground—again. I bend to pick up the pendant I bought for Kye, but Gabe beats me to it, pausing to run his thumb over the design and brush his fingers along the back.

Abruptly, he offers it to me with a look of sympathy similar to the one he wore the night of graduation and the disaster that followed. "You just need to breathe for a bit."

"How do you know what I need?" I distract myself with adjusting the bag so it will hold everything. "I don't even know that at this point."

"You've had a lot to deal with, and no freedom to be yourself. Ready?" He helps me stand, supporting me as we start walking once again. "I haven't helped matters by being bossy and demanding."

"You haven't been ..." I start, then rethink my words. "Well, maybe you have. But you're just doing your job."

The weakness is working through me, and thanks to Gabe's strengthening energy, I'll make it home. I'm beginning to gather a list of reasons to be grateful for him. "Abby, you're more than a job to me."

My mouth falls open. Uh oh. No. This is not a turn in conversation I can take right now. He calms me with a finger against my lips. "I'm not coming onto you. It's just that, at some point, when you dedicate yourself to protecting someone, and you spend all your time in her company, it becomes difficult to not actually care about that person ... personally."

I get what he's saying. I do. And I know he's telling the truth. But I don't want to hear any more. Partly because his words are warm and protective, special, and partly because they drop like ice into the chasm in my chest. Hearing Gabe say them feels wrong— like I'm cheating on Kye. Once again, I picture Crystal in Kye's arms, remember how distant he was during those last few days, and pain stabs my chest, draining the warmth I've stolen from Gabe and leaving me weak.

He deserves a response. I just don't have one that feels appropriate.

"Thanks for being here. For following me."

He grins. Not a small smile this time, but a full on Grin. "That's the first time you've ever admitted to needing me. Excellent."

"Shut up," I say, resisting the urge to whack the shoulder I'm leaning on. "And don't get cocky. We still have to get back to Christine's. Someone else might try to rob us."

"Doubt it," he says, chuckling.

We turn onto Christine's street, and a gentle breeze carries the calming scent of salt water and tropical flowers. It soothes my nerves, leaving me with only echoes of the hollowed out feeling that comes whenever I think of Kye.

"I need some lunch, and then a nap—on the beach." I pat my grumbling stomach. "Would you like to join me?"

A dimple creases one of his cheeks. "Seems necessary that you have protection. A shark might try to eat you." How have I never noticed that dimple? He ushers me into the living room. "You change, and I'll handle lunch. We'll eat outside."

I'm still thinking of Gabe's dimple as I don my swimsuit, wondering if this is a bad idea. Guilt, longing, and a ridiculous amount of homesickness rears up, so I pick up my phone and dial Kye's number. He doesn't answer, so—against my better judgment—I leave another awkward message. Maybe I'm making a total fool of myself when I say I love him, but the thing is, it's true. That hasn't changed just because we're apart.

I hold the phone to my chest. Something is happening between Kye and me. Something unidentifiable and wrong. However technology should keep us connected, the curse—along with so many other things—will continue fighting to rip us apart.

This is why I'm here. I have to find a way to not let that happen. As if defeating shadow demons isn't enough pressure.

SIXTEEN

Remnants

Christine knocks on my door as I'm pinning my hair up. "Hi, Sweetie." She sweeps in, grace and elegance personified, with only a perfunctory glance at the clothes I tossed around while looking for my suit. "Looks like you're settling in."

"I think so." Trying not to blush, I snatch up the clothes and shove them in a drawer. "Sorry about the mess. Gabe and I are going to have a beach break before training today. Hope that's all right."

"No worries." She perches on the armchair. "Can we talk for a minute?"

"Uh, sure." Outside, Gabe hauls two lounge chairs near the edge of the water, where he's already placed a cooler and stabbed an umbrella into the sand. One of those chairs is calling my name. I don't want to have "girl talk" with Kye's mom right now.

She catches me looking and I avert my gaze as guilt bubbles up. "You must be awfully confused," she says, her voice soft. "This has been a big year for you. It's a lot to handle at your age. Or any age, for that matter."

I rub my hand over the comforter, picking at invisible threads, desperate to get outside and avoid this conversation. "I love it here. You have a beautiful house, and I've never seen such an incredible beach."

My focus again lands on Gabe, who brushes sand off his hands and slides on a pair of aviator sunglasses before stretching out on his chair.

"I'm glad," Christine murmurs. "I hope you understand that when I told you to make yourself at home, I meant it."

"Thanks." *I hope she'll hurry and get to the point.*

"Your recovery is a priority. However, the other reason you've come has little to do with training or vacationing on the beach. The shadow demons have caused all kinds of trouble here, leaving the Mexican council and I concerned. We've never been so overcome with dark forces the way we are now. Two weeks ago, I witnessed a cruise ship being turned on its side by a demon, who then flew into the ocean and stirred a tropical storm that nearly became a hurricane."

"A cruise ship? Did anyone drown?"

Christine shakes her head. "No. We were able to right the ship in time to avoid fatalities, but there was some interior damage to the vessel. Fortunately, by the time the storm hit the ship had let out to sea, bound for another port."

Still picking at the comforter, I stare at the floor, the too-familiar weight of responsibility falling heavily on me. "What can I do?"

"You, Gabe, and I are going to round up those shadows and cage them in the tomb, where they belong."

"Okaaaay." *How in the world will we manage that?* "And the tomb is where?"

She straightens a non-existent wrinkle in her shorts. "We haven't located it yet. That's why we need you."

Of course they do. Me. Raina. The Ring of the Princess. The Pendant of Sadira. I already know all this, but suddenly I feel like I'm an inch tall and trying to hold up a boulder the size of the world. "I'm here."

"You certainly are." She shakes her head as if she can't believe it. "I'm glad for the opportunity to get to know you." She stands, glancing out at Gabe once more. "It's okay to go out there, you know."

"To the beach?"

She sighs, shaking back her wavy hair. "To your Dragon." She lays a gentle hand on my shoulder. "I know you love my son. You were destined to love him, and that wasn't a choice given to either of you. But you're both very young, Abby, and destiny or not, you each need to choose to do things that make you happy."

Appalled at the implication, I gasp. "Are you saying I should have a relationship with both Gabe and Kye?"

"No," she says, shaking her head. "No. I'm saying ... you and Kye are apart. The destined hold you have on each other will weaken with each day you spend apart. As I advised him, if you feel inclined to explore other options of happiness—you should. Not because I don't think you and Kye belong together, but because if you really do belong together, it needs to be your choice—Abby's choice and Kye's choice—and not the remnants of a relationship started by Theron and Raina. You and Kye don't deserve to have your lives destroyed by mistakes they made. Do you understand?"

"You said this to Kye, too?" The knots inside me grow and grow, stealing the air from my lungs. Is that what he's doing with Crystal? Exploring what life is like without me?

"Yes, honey, I did." Her words hit me like a door slammed on my face. I like Christine. Or liked. Wanted to keep her as a mother figure. But this—what she's suggesting, what she's told Kye—I can't like this. I can't like the picture she just engraved in my head—the one of Kye with someone else. If they sent me here to sabotage my relationship with Kye, it will mean they're against us. And if that's true, I won't fight for them, or with them. There's a reason the kingdom of Dryden fell. And no one has ever truly explained to me what that reason is.

I have no response for Christine, and I can't pretend to smile after she dropped such a bomb on me, so I turn away.

"Abby, I'm not saying I don't want you and Kye to be together. Not at all. I'd love that more than anything in the world. But there is nothing that will break a strong woman's spirit like having her choices taken from her. The ability to choose is what freedom is about. The destiny of a soul can be infinitely changed by a single choice. The trick, I think, is making the one that is right for you."

"I'm not sure I understand what I'm supposed to be choosing," I croak. Needing something to keep my hands busy, I undo my hair and run a brush through it, then secure it again.

"The real reason you've come here is to determine your path." A breeze blows in off the beach, fluttering the curtains, my sarong, and Christine's blouse as she backs out the bedroom door. "Whether that includes Gabe, or Kye, or someone else entirely, is something you'll have to figure out for yourself."

I whirl to glare at her, anger a vicious heat burning through me. "And in the meantime?"

She nods at Gabe. "You do everything you can to enjoy this break. Including spending time with another young person who needs a friend." She hesitates with her hand on the knob. "I get the impression that he's very alone."

By the time she closes the door and I step onto the warm sand, guilt and anger have stolen my appetite. I'm hollow, but I've felt this way for so long it's become my new normal. The sun is shining on the blue water of the Caribbean, and I'm completely numb.

Gabe smiles, revealing that dimple. I slam my flip-flops into the sand and fling my body into the chair, draping my arm over my eyes.

"Want a drink? This green soda is pretty good. Or there's a yellow one that's pineapple flavored, if you'd rather."

I lean up on my elbow and accept a bottle after he twists the metal top off, using just his fingers. "Thanks."

He slides the sunglasses down his nose to look at me. "So what did she say?"

"Lots of stuff I don't want to think about." I adjust the chair to my preferred position, then set my bottle on the cooler so I can rub sunscreen on my legs. "You realize this isn't a vacation, right?"

"Really?" His sarcasm breaks some of the tension. "Why didn't anyone warn me?"

I rub lotion on my arms and torso, then attempt to cover my back.

"Can I help?" Gabe's voice is husky.

"I got it. Thanks." I dry my hands and sip my drink, wishing there wasn't this wall of awkward silence between us. "What did you bring us to eat?"

He opens the cooler. "Sliced fruit, homemade bread, and some kind of leftover meat. I think it's pork—but could be chicken. Your bug claims the mangos and papayas came from some trees over there."

"Speaking of Murtagh, where is he?"

Gabe frowns. "Haven't seen him since your little scuffle earlier."

I start to stand, but Gabe stops me with a hand on my arm. "He can take care of himself, and he knows where to find us. Besides, don't you want to go swimming?"

When he doesn't move his hand, I draw my arm away, imagining how the cool water will counter the sweat already forming between my shoulder blades. "Yes, I do." I set my bottle on the cooler again. "Race you."

Gabe jumps up as I dash into the waves. Laughing, he catches up and dives in ahead of me.

SEVENTEEN

Healing

After the almost-mugging incident, Gabe adds an hour of self-defense to my training regime, and I accept, knowing it's necessary. He works with me on defensive maneuvers, offensive tactics, and encourages every type of physical strength training—running, swimming, lifting things, and even digging in the sand. In our downtime, we play in the water, lie on the beach, shop in open air markets, and one day borrow a scooter so we can zip up the coast road to a local seafood restaurant.

First for me: Dungeness crab, served in a basket at an outdoor picnic table.

Turns out, Gabe and I aren't so different. And it's okay to be friends, even though I still haven't heard from Kye.

My first weeks in Mexico are filled with good days. Healing ones.

One night, Christine joins Gabe and me in the living room as we finish watching a movie. "You both look rested and happy."

Still grinning from the comedy we've just finished, I hug her. She strokes my hair, pulling back to look at me, but not just "at" me, into me—as in, she dips into my energy field. Shocked that she would do such a thing, I drop an energetic wall, blocking her from seeing anything deeper than my physical appearance.

"You're well enough to get started," she says. I'm not sure how to react to what just happened. She doesn't look away, nor does she apologize. "You should both go to bed. We'll leave early tomorrow. Breakfast at eight. We'll go over the strategy and then get to work."

Hurt and confusion pool together, filling a corner of my hollow space. I'm happy to get back to work, but if Christine wants to know if I'm up to it, she should ask. Looking into a person's energy field is like going through her purse, or her underwear drawer, or reading her diary. She has no right, even if I'm staying at her house. Seething over the slight, I struggle to respond cordially, knowing that Christine feels no remorse, so arguing will be futile.

"Shall we come prepared for battle?" My words come out sounding caustic. I don't mean them to, but take my cue from Christine and don't apologize. Gabe frowns as if he's disappointed in me.

"Come prepared to walk." She turns away, unaffected. "And not in flip-flops. Also, you'll need sunscreen, sunglasses, maybe a hat, and a camera for photo documentation."

"Where are we going?" Gabe asks.

"We have some theories about where the tomb is located. There are several possible sites, but the best way for us to narrow them down is to take Abby and see if her ring triggers a reaction." Christine starts down the hall to her room. "This will be the first step of our ... task."

"What if the Keys don't work in the new tomb?" I ask. "Kye's not here to help power my ring, and the dagger's been destroyed."

Christine stands near her bedroom door, hand on the knob. "We don't know, Abby. I have to hope that we can do something with what we have available. At the very least, maybe those Keys will lead us to other Keys that will do the job."

"That's a lot of variables." Gabe says. "Sounds like we're going on a lot of hopes and maybes rather than solid knowledge."

Christine doesn't move for a long moment. "We'll see tomorrow, won't we?" She closes herself in her room.

Gabe stares after her, arms folded over his chest in that intimidating way that makes his biceps look enormous. "What was that supposed to mean?"

"No idea." I shake my head, disgusted. "But obviously she's expecting *me* to figure out the answer."

"Weren't you the one who figured it out before?" Gabe leans against his door as I back into my room. He needs to go to bed, and I need to be left alone to sort out my thoughts, but part of me—a very small part—wants him to stay.

"I had help," I concede. "Eoin, and Murtagh, you and the Dragons, and Juri forced my hand when he kidnapped Kye ..." My words trail off as a lump lodges in my throat. I miss him. No matter how wonderful this place is, Kye's absence is like a bubble surrounding me. I'm constantly looking over my shoulder, double and triple checking my purse or beach bag, and returning to my room over and over because no matter where I go, I feel like I've forgotten something important. Something crucial. Something absolutely critical to my survival—like water. Or air.

Another step into my room, and that bubble grows thicker, denser. Bigger. I don't know how to fight demons and track down bad guys without Kye. On my nightstand is a cell phone I never turn off. It rings daily, but the voice on the other end is never the one I most need to hear. He doesn't return my calls. Despair can be a living, breathing thing if I let it. It comes into my room at night and wraps around me, taunts me, whispers my name, and begs me to give in.

But when I open the windows to the power of the moon, the shadows of depression scurry into corners and under furniture, they hide in drawers and darkened crevices—they can't fight the power of lunar rays.

I learned this the hard way, so even though I know Gabe would kill me, I sleep with the curtains open. Every night.

"... better let you get some rest," Gabe is saying. "Sounds like we have a big day tomorrow." I force a smile, not wanting to wish he would hold me—just hold me—because I need so badly to be touched. "Goodnight."

Gabe crosses the hall and tips up my chin, and I take back my wish. *I want to be held, not kissed!* Not yet. Maybe not ever. Am I so transparent that he can see my thoughts? I'm too stunned to react, but Gabe only frowns. "You okay? You're looking green again."

I shake myself and begin to close the door, suddenly desperate to put a barrier between us and avoid admitting that I'm attracted to Gabe. "I'm fine. Exhausted."

Gabe's eyes fix on my ring. I never take it off. Not just because the diamonds are the most powerful crystals in the history of the Gifted, but because of the connection to Kye. When he's near, the stones light up, strengthening us both with powers we might not have otherwise. When we're apart, it's a reminder of my mission, my end goal. And that doesn't include giving into momentary temptation just because I'm lonely.

I drop my hand, and watch him tear his eyes away.

"If you say so," Gabe says, his voice gruff. "Goodnight."

I shut the door, but Gabe opens it once more and sticks his head inside. "Don't forget to close that glass. I was serious when I threatened to disable it." Then he's gone again.

My cell phone shows no missed calls, no messages. *Is it possible Kye has already moved on?*

I rationalize that he has been extraordinarily sick. Maybe he's been unable to talk. Maybe Val reduced his energy the way they did mine when I travelled here.

Maybe.

Maybe.

The clock on my nightstand reads 11:38. Needing the moon's rays, I stand on the patio, breathe in the salty-sweet air and beg it to calm my building apprehension. Deep breath in, and let it out slow.

In. Out. In. Out.

I'm in the Thai-chi position Akers taught me, centering my chi without having thought to do so. And it's working. Landon would be proud.

When I open my eyes, I catch a glimpse of purple light blinking in a nearby shrub, followed by a smaller green one, and then a pulsing bright blue. "Goodnight, Murtagh," I murmur. "Sleep well."

This time, before I climb in bed, I'm sure to close both the glass and the curtains. Tonight, the darkness isn't quite so scary.

My nose throbs as I resurface from sleep. A second throb has one eye popping open, and I immediately swat at the source. "Murtagh, stop. My nose is not a trampoline!"

"Wake up, *Calin*. Is sun-rising time of power. Come. Come with Murtagh and see."

I squeeze my eyes shut again. "Are you kidding? I'm sleeping."

He grips a handful of my eyelashes and yanks open my eyelid. "Must see *Calin*, important. Powerful for sprites, and for Princess Queen. Come. Come."

He won't leave me alone, so I throw back the covers and sit with my feet dangling above the floor. "I closed the doors. How did you get in here?"

Murtagh's light blinks when he laughs. "Sprite secret. No tell *Calin*." He grabs my tank top. "Come, come, *Calin*, hurry. Hurry."

I open the doors, awestruck. The indigo sky melts from the bottom up—black to blue, purple, red, orange, pink, and then a bright yellow ray reaches over the horizon and turns the shimmering water into diamonds.

I follow Murtagh to the edge and let the cool sea drizzle between my fingers. I tip my face to the sky and absorb the power of the rising sun.

"*Calin* like, no? Beautiful power, not?" Murtagh zips around, diving in the water and then returning to shake his wings all over me.

"It's beautiful."

"Sun rising most powerful time. Time powers of Light grow. Princess Queen need Light, need power. Fight bad demon guys."

"What do you know about sun powers?" I twirl, unable to ignore the tingling from energy running in my blood like a river of adrenaline. Something in me is changing.

"Water sprite know lot things, *Calin*. Smart, brave warriors listen. Learn. Remember." He flits to the patio and stretches out on the table, pillowing his head on his hands. His voice carries on the breeze. "Murtagh nap. Princess Queen absorb power. Wake sprite when time go."

Reveling in the beauty of sunrise, I kick around in the water for a while longer. When I turn to go inside, I bump into someone—ankle deep in the water. I yelp, immediately pressing my lips together, embarrassed.

"So sorry to startle you, señorita." Victor catches me by the shoulders, preventing me from losing my balance.

"Victor. What are you ... were you watching me?" The heat of a blush creeps up my neck. I've been dancing and twirling like an idiot.

His lips quirk, but he doesn't allow his grin to spread. "Just taking my morning walk. I did not see you until we nearly collided. Are you all right?"

I stumble again, but manage to stay upright. Barely. "Yes. I mean, I will be if I can make it back into the house without walking off a cliff."

His laugh sounds foreign and exotic, swirling around us as if carried by the breeze, and his chocolate eyes melt when he smiles.

Gabe might want to murder me for coming outside alone. "I should probably get back. I have ... things to do."

Victor's gaze follows mine to the house. "You must make breakfast for your family?"

"No." I sigh. "Well, maybe. I don't know who's making breakfast, but I promised my ... uh, I promised to be ready to go by eight."

"You are sightseeing?"

Rather than explain, I nod as I splash out of the water. "It was good running into you again."

117

"Yes, señorita. Let us do it again soon."

I wave, holding back the urge to skip. "See you!" My feet smack on the stone patio, startling a blink out of the sleeping Murtagh. I grab the remote and close the glass as I jump into bed. Seconds later, someone knocks.

Gabe pokes his head in. "Time to get moving."

I yawn, stretch like I'm just waking up, and rub my eyes. "I'll be out soon. Just let me take a shower and get dressed."

Gabe frowns at the closed glass before he leaves. When I climb out of bed and notice the sandy footprints, my heart sinks. Crap. I am so busted.

EIGHTEEN

Ruins

My life is in the hands of a beautiful, maniacal driver and her gas-guzzling SUV.

Christine cuts across four lanes of heavy traffic, not bothering to signal, and makes an illegal left—or at least, illegal in America—on a red light. From the front passenger seat, I clutch the door handle until my fingers ache, heart racing at every close call. "Where exactly are we going?" We've headed out of town on a road that runs through the jungle—with no end in sight.

In the rearview mirror, I glimpse Gabe gripping his door handle as well. At least I'm not the only one who wants out.

"To the ruins." Christine's hair sticks out from her baseball-style hat, swishing back and forth with the movement of the car. "At least you'll get to say you did some sight-seeing."

"Will we also be saying that's where we found our first demons?" Gabe asks.

"Most likely." She sends him a nervous glance in the rearview. "They're bold here, coming out in the open to scare away tourists. Rumors claim that the ruins are haunted. It's brought in a slew of paranormal junkies, some of whom have unknowingly video documented demons for us. It's been helpful to know some of what we're dealing with."

"So ... we're planning to face down these demons ... today?" Gabe leans forward, gripping the back of my seat. "You couldn't have mentioned that before we left the house?"

Christine's laugh comes out as a snort. "What did you expect? If we're going to find this tomb, we have to go where the demons are. What should I have said? Prepare yourselves, kids, we're going on a demon hunt."

Gabe squeezes my seat, and the frame groans from the pressure. "Better than 'bring hiking shoes and sunscreen.'"

"Okay, listen." Christine says, scarcely masking her aggravation. "I have no way of knowing what we'll find. It could be a demonic war party, or a habitat, or something else entirely. Maybe nothing much at all. We won't know until we arrive. But this is why you're here. The two of you have enough combined power to handle yourselves just fine." She glances at me, her eyes soft. "Abby, Eoin told me what happened at the original tomb, what you did for Kye."

I look away, once again angry at her for telling Kye he should see other people. How could she do that knowing I was willing to die for him?

"What if this is worse?" Gabe asks. "What if we get there and it's more than the three of us can handle?" His fingers graze my bare neck. "Abby's not wearing the pendant, which played a big role in her surviving the last confrontation."

"There could be a thousand what-if scenarios, Gabe. The plan is to observe."

Something rattles in my purse, so I unzip it and let Murtagh out. His light has turned a shade of angry red, and he blinks furiously. "Murtagh trapped in hard crunchy bag, *Calin.* No zip more. Zip Murtagh not."

Hand to mouth, I let out a sympathetic gasp. "Have you been trying to get out? I'm so sorry. I didn't mean to trap you."

He flies to the cargo space at the rear of the car, arms folded, pouting.

Gabe reaches out to my sprite, but Murtagh slaps his hand away. "No touch, Dragon guy. Alone leave Murtagh."

Shaking his head, Gabe returns his focus to Christine. "How far away are these ruins?"

Christine turns on the radio. "A couple hours or so."

Settling into my seat, I watch the jungle stretch into miles of lush green walls so thick we would need a machete to breech them. Eventually the repetition of green, green, green against blue, blue, blue makes my eyes heavy.

The hem of Isleen's threadbare dress catches on a sharp rock as she runs, slowing only to glance over her shoulder at the pursuing demons. She trips, tearing her delicate palms and splitting a gash in her chin, but gets back up and continues running.

She looks back once more, breathing heavily, and trips again. But this time her arms—instinctively thrown forward—don't find ground. She tumbles headfirst into an enormous crater, falling more than a hundred feet before she splashes into clear, cold water. She continues falling as the water closes over her, and the relentless pursuers close in from behind.

I jerk awake and pop my eyes open to find Gabe staring. He offers a half-smile and redirects his gaze out the window. Christine is absorbed in driving. I close my eyes again, needing to know if Isleen died in that water, but I can't conjure the vision again. This time when I doze, the only thing I find is actual sleep.

I wake to Christine's voice. "Abby, we're here."

We're in a dirt parking lot packed with cars, completed by a bustling shopping corridor and some street performers. This place is crazy busy considering that the tourists think it's haunted.

Gabe opens my door before I get it myself. He's gnawing on his lip—a sure sign he has something on his mind. "What?"

He shakes his head. "Nothing."

"It's not nothing. You have something to say. Stop being stupid and spit it out."

Christine opens the back of the car to access a cooler. Gabe keeps his voice low, "Did you go out again last night?"

I should be prepared for this. He saw my footprints. He knows I left, and I don't know why I didn't tell him in the first place. It's really not that big of a deal. But while I'm prepared to handle Gabe's anger, I'm not prepared for his hurt, and that's the dominating emotion rolling off him.

He meets my eyes. "I'm supposed to be watching out for you, protecting you from harm, and I find that increasingly difficult to do when you sneak out at night to run down the beach and play in the water."

Before I can find words to explain, Murtagh lands on my shoulder and tattles on me. "Princess-Queen sun-power rising."

Gabe rubs a spot on the side of his head—the same spot he rubs every time he's stressed. "What?"

"Murtagh woke me to see the sunrise," I tell Gabe, "because he's been led to believe that having me stand in the path of the rising sun will strengthen my Power of Light."

He's still rubbing, compiling my guilt. "So why did you get back in bed? And if that's all you did, why hide it from me?"

"I don't know." A blush creeps up my cheeks. "I guess maybe I'm embarrassed."

"Of what?"

Good question. Such a good question, in fact, that I should be asking myself the same thing. I wish I knew the answer, because lying has never been my thing. Bad karma.

Christine saves me from having to answer. "Okay, kiddos. We have some lunch here in the cooler. Anyone interested in carrying the sandwiches in a backpack so we don't have to stop?"

Gabe accepts the pack, along with four bottles of water, and we start down the path. We're nearly to the entrance when I catch a dark shimmer from the corner of my eye. I whip my head around, but not quickly enough. Whatever it was is gone.

There's a girl on the path, no older than three, wandering around with a stack of handkerchiefs on her head. "One dolla. Uno dolla." Her fingers are tangled together as if she's terrified to be by herself. My heart melts. "Maybe we should help find her mother?"

Christine frowns, nodding at the forest a few feet away. "She's not lost. See that woman near the trees? That's either her mother or an aunt, and she's exploiting that little girl. They figure tourists won't be able to resist her angelic face."

"Why?"

"To make money," Gabe says.

Disgusted, I glare at the woman. For a split second, her violet eyes remind me of Boone. I shiver, reminding myself that Boone died in Yellowstone, and deciding that maybe violet eyes aren't as rare as I once thought. Still feeling chilled, I sneak one more glance and notice two large black shadows looming behind the woman. "Gabe, do you see that?"

He nods, already on the move. The shadows are nearly upon her, but she clearly doesn't know. She steps into my path, yelling Spanish words in a voice that sounds familiar enough to break my concentration as I veer around her toward the shadows and slow to a stop. Seconds ago, the temperature was close to ninety sweltering degrees, the air thick and sticky with humidity, but now icy cold raises goose bumps along my arms and turns my breath into white fog. All sound except that of my own breathing is muted as the shadows funnel around me. I know I should be scared—I've seen what these things can do—but I'm far more annoyed.

"Fine! Go ahead and surround me you stupid black hole." As I yell, I keep moving, searching for a weak spot. "Leave these people alone. You don't belong here!"

Through the darkness, I can see Gabe's outline. He's trying to get through, but the haze has solidified. The shadow grows taller, blocking out my view of the sky, and I have a taste of genuine fright. "Do you hear me? I said go away." My voice cracks and, feeding off my fear, the shadow grows.

Light. You have Light.

Deep inside me, in that hidden place I haven't quite figured out how to unlock, a shaky ray of sun breaks free, spilling out by way of my hands, leaving me shocked and awed at how they glow. The shadows press down, stifling the air and sucking at my energy.

Palms aimed at the shadows, I funnel the small amount of Light and thrust it out. The attempt is weak, but splits a section of the wall. In that frozen moment, Gabe forces through.

"Are you trying to get yourself killed before we even get started?" He sounds exasperated, though I now know it's a cover for stress.

"Relax. This shadow's just trying to scare us away." Squaring my shoulders, I close my eyes and focus on that place inside me where the Light is kept, the place Christine has been trying so hard to help me reach. For the first time since I left Kye, the diamonds in my ring flash to life, then die again. But that one flash is enough to kindle my inner powers.

Gabe gawks at me.

I funnel the energy again—using a technique Christine suggested only days ago—and fire it with such force that the shadow shrieks and splits apart into four separate ones. Immediately, they attempt to merge again. Gabe grabs my hand and we run.

"Where are we going?" I ask, trying to yank my hand free. I still have some power left. "I need to finish it off."

"Not right now, you don't. We're here to observe and plan, remember?"

We find Christine yards away, kneeling with the little girl and her mother. "Christine," Gabe says, his voice strained. "Let's get them out of sight."

A line forms on Christine's brow. "Right." She stands, and as she does, I notice that the bustle of tourists is gone. The people, tour guides, entrepreneurs have disappeared. Besides the girl and her mother, we're utterly alone. "Right," Christine says again as the woman yells in her native tongue. Gabe calms her with a soothing voice, and scoops her up like she weighs nothing, though she's fairly large. I pick up the girl, who clutches the handkerchiefs in her hands, and the five of us run for a nearby structure with two standing walls and lots of crumbled stone. When the mother and daughter are safely hidden from the shadows, I look to Christine. "Well, we're here. Now what?"

She points at one of three large pyramids. "The most obvious choice would be the biggest—but the tomb could be located anywhere."

A shadow shoots past our eye-line, and another drifts above us. It hovers overhead as if it senses our presence, but soon moves on.

Christine and I follow Gabe across the grass to the next crumbling wall. Unfortunately, none of us is good with stealth, and we just about walk right into the biggest, scariest demon I've ever seen, waiting for us at the bottom of the stairs.

NINETEEN

The Altar

The black shadow rises high; I have to crane my neck and still can't see the top. Even as we swerve, it blows around, encircling us in a thick fog that divides us.

My lungs feel as though they're going to collapse from having the oxygen sucked out, and the sensation sends me crashing to my knees. I press my cheek against the ground, stealing air from the grass. Black spots swim in my eyes as the fog tries to overtake me.

"Abby! Where are you?" Someone calls my name, but I can't tell who.

"I'm here!"

"Abby? Come toward my voice." Unable to stand, I crawl. When my hands meet stone, I pull myself up, and up, and up on the rock.

"Keep going, Abby. You're almost there." The structure is built like a never ending staircase, and as high as I climb, there's always another step. My hands and knees burn with pain as rocks dig into them, but with—Gabe's?—encouragement, I keep moving. My shoulders and thighs burn, but I climb higher, not daring to stop for even a second. After forever, I run out of steps and reach a flat surface where I collapse, panting. "Gabe, I'm here." It's a wonder he made it so far without finding me. "Gabe?"

When he doesn't answer, I shiver. It was Gabe calling, wasn't it? "Gabe!" My voice is muted, like the sound has been stolen, cushioned between layers of fog. Didn't I just deal with this same thing ten minutes ago? Do these demons have no other scare tactics? "All right, enough of this." I manage to stand and try to focus my Light again. Only it doesn't work. Lifeless cold consumes me, leaving my ring useless.

Fear grows sharp talons that puncture a depth I never imagined the shadows could find. The demon will feed on my emotions, but I can't calm myself, can't stop the terror from rising. My mind whirls as I attempt to focus, keep fighting, keep digging, and nothing, nothing, nothing. Once again, the shadow squeezes my lungs, and spots swim in my eyes as I struggle for breath.

I've climbed high off the ground, and don't dare take more than a step or two in any direction. I can see nothing farther than the distance from my head to my feet, which are shrouded in fog.

"Abby, come on. This way." The sound of the voice both relieves and frightens me as I inch forward, not stopping until I stub my toes on a large, rough object.

I'm still swearing over my aching foot when a swarm of twinkling lights—all different colors—break the mist, their tiny, beating wings creating a familiar buzzing sound I've heard before. "Faeries?" No. Not faeries. "Sprites. Lots of sprites. Murtagh? Where are you?"

A purplish light darts at me, landing frantically on my shoulder. "*Calin* must leave! Not stay. Dangerous in place. Go, go, go!"

"I'd love to, but I think we're high off the ground." The other lights blink, bright enough that I can see them through the shadow. Maybe. "Murtagh, are there more sprites here?"

Clearly annoyed, the shadow gyrates, picking up enough speed to blow some of the sprites away, leaving behind wisps of color where they disturbed the fog. A sucking noise steals more precious oxygen and my head throbs as if it wants to explode. "Murtagh," I gasp, letting panic take over. "Find Gabe. Get help."

"*Calin?* No leave Princess-Queen."

I fall to my knees, preparing to give in. The demon might win. If not for this oddly flat rock, I'd collapse. I have to rest my head, and the smooth surface seems to be the best place.

127

"*Calin?* Down no lie. Up. Up, *Calin.* Go to got."

I want so badly to listen to Murtagh, to do what he wants, but I just don't have the strength, so I pillow my head on my hands and close my eyes to block out the fog.

"No *Calin.* Up get. Use power. Light. Rising sun Light."

Murtagh's reminder of sunrise stirs a whisper of heat in my chest. I picture the rainbow sky as the sun came up over the water, the way it stretched and curled as it woke, right before the sky exploded with bright yellow. And then I'm sitting up, mimicking a similar action. My arms spread wide as I tilt my head back, face raised, and let the light flow. And flow. And explode into the sky.

I blink, only now realizing that I'm no longer struggling to breathe, and see that the Light is not only flowing in my thoughts, but through my skin as I force the shadows back. I hold the Light, continue pushing until my arms shake and my energy is so diminished that my vision blurs. The shadows are gone. Somehow, I've won this round. Knowing this, I allow my eyes to close, and collapse onto the cool stone bench, exhausted.

"Abby? Wake up, honey. Come on, open your eyes." Christine's voice is both pleading and commanding. Next thing I know, a hand caresses my face, as I'm lifted and cradled against a familiar chest. Crazy relieved, I wrap my arms around Gabe's neck.

His voice joins Christine's. "Come on, princess. Wake up before that thing comes back."

"What thing?" I ask, confused and disoriented.

"Big ugly demon guy, *Calin.* Dark, scary demon, come after Princess-Queen."

Murtagh's words bring it back, in bits and pieces, but back it comes. My eyes pop open and I look around. We're at the top of a pyramid, just outside a stone room.

"Honey," Christine says. "You disappeared. Gabe and I searched for over an hour, and finally found you passed out over a Mayan sacrificial altar.

"The question is," Gabe says, a hint of strain in his voice, "what were you doing there?"

I let go of Gabe's neck. "What do you mean, what was I doing there? The shadow separated us, and then you kept calling my name, and I was trying to find you. I followed your voice." Maybe the voice I followed wasn't Gabe's? I gulp. "You *were* calling me?"

He shakes his head, alarm widening his eyes. "I didn't dare. You just disappeared, and there are demons everywhere."

I glance at Christine. "You? Did *you* call me?"

She shakes her head too. "No, sweetie, I didn't. I couldn't either. But I did see you climbing the pyramid, and I couldn't get through the shadow that had hold of you." She folds her arms together, rubbing her shoulders as if she's cold, though it's close to a hundred degrees out. "Clearly, these demons are capable of more than I thought."

"You have no idea," I tell her, my voice weak.

"But you did a phenomenal job of fighting back." Christine stares out at the rocky paths and grassy patches. "I could see your Light across the way. And now we know the tomb is not in or around this particular pyramid."

Not understanding her logic, I ask. "How do you know? It's heavily guarded."

"It is," Gabe agrees. "We've been here for over an hour, and spent all but about two minutes of that time trying to free Abby from the shadows. I'd think we're getting close."

"Call it instinct then," Christine says. "Finding the tomb here, in the first pyramid, on the first day, at the first set of ruins we try, would be too good to be true. Besides, if the tomb was here, that demon—however powerful—wouldn't have brought you right to it. That's the very thing they're trying to avoid. That would be like working at cross purposes."

I struggle out of Gabe's grasp, and he sets me on the ground, still wobbly and lightheaded. "I guess."

Christine looks like she wants to say more, but exchanges a look with Gabe and shakes her head. "Let's break for lunch."

By the time we've descended the pyramid, my legs and feet ache. We follow a dirt path to more ruins, keeping our eyes open for a good spot to picnic. Christine is extremely cautious about our every step, which tells me she's more shaken about what we've just experienced than she wants me to know. I find this both ironic and amusing after her argument with Gabe earlier.

I meander, allowing my energy to regenerate. Through the forest on one side of the path, I notice a depression in the ground that can only be a large, deep crater. "Christine, what is that—"

"Oomph." I smack into something solid and end up on my backside in the dirt. A sun-browned palm offers me a hand up, and I take it, only realizing afterward that I know the person attached.

"So sorry," Victor says. "I must watch better where I am walking. Are you all right?" He helps me to my feet, holding on longer than should be appropriate.

"Yes, thank you. I'm fine." I draw my hand away and work on brushing the dust off my shorts, noticing that Alejandro—the guy from the store—is also here. "I guess I wasn't watching where I was going either."

He waves off my apology. "You were on the path—and I was not. My fault."

"Abby?" Gabe backtracks, jogging to my side and eyeing Victor and Alejandro warily. "Everything okay?"

I nod and make introductions, relieved when Murtagh flies out of sight. Both boys offer hands for Gabe to shake, but he stares at them as if they carry a deadly disease. "How do you know each other?"

"I met her on the beach near my home." Victor sounds hesitant. "How is your—"

"What are you doing here?" I interrupt, not wanting Gabe to find out how much I haven't told him yet. He's already met his freak-out limit for the day. "You're awfully far from home."

"Oh hey, Victor. Alejandro." Christine joins us, seeming pleased. "I didn't know your group would be here today. Have the Elders reconsidered?"

Alejandro swallows, shifting his weight. "Our group is not here, Señora Murphy. Only we have come. Victor and I do not agree with the Elders. This situation requires the help of many, and we hope to join those who are here to make things better. If we can. Pedro means well, but he does not speak for all of us."

"Many hands, many eyes," Victor adds. "Each of us is strong alone. Together, we can do much more."

Christine squeezes his shoulder affectionately. "Thank you."

Apparently, there's no need for Murtagh to hide, because from what I'm hearing, these guys are ... Dragons? Maybe. "Have you known who I am all along?"

"Only after saving your sprite friend," Victor says.

"And I knew because Victor told me," Alejandro adds.

"Why didn't you say something?" This situation is starting to remind me of how things went when I first moved to Jackson.

"I did not want to frighten you on your first night in our country."

"The last person who kept something from Abby," Gabe says, his frown deepening, "tried to kill her. Forgive us if we withhold trust until you prove yourselves." He turns to Christine. "Who are the Elders and why haven't we heard about them before now?"

"The Council of the Elders is sort of like Mexico's version of our Dragons." She settles herself on a short, vine-covered wall of stone. "They declined to help track down the tomb or deal with the demons, so there was no need to mention them. These two are members, and though not technically Elders, their remarkable talents will be an asset to us." She sends Gabe a warning glance, which raises my defensive hackles. To Victor and Alejandro, she says, "Are you sure you're ready to go against the council on this?"

A spark of fire lights Victor's eyes. "Señora, I do not agree that creatures such as this should be allowed to torment our people and destroy our tourist economy. Our country has much to lose already, and the dark forces are growing."

Since Gabe's non-subtle rebuff, Victor has spoken mainly to Christine, but Alejandro's focus remains on me. "Is not your country in a similar state of chaos? Is that not why you are here?"

"Among other reasons, yes." It bothers me that they know things about me, and yet I know zero about them, including exactly what they've been told or by whom.

"If you're so gung-ho to help," Gabe says, a note of skepticism in his voice, "what are you doing hiding in the woods? Why not just announce your presence? And what do you—or your Council— know about the very large shadow demons that just attacked Abby?"

Victor's russet skin pales. "That was Abby on the pyramid? Ay ay ay. I saw a person climbing, and noticed the funneled shadow, but did not realize ..." He takes my hand again, and lifts it to his lips like he's going to kiss my knuckles, but I yank it away before he can. "I apologize for my Council, Abby. They do not understand your sacrifice in coming here."

"Yep. There you go." Gabe sweeps Victor aside, placing himself between them and me in a protective, and somewhat possessive gesture. "She's here to save your asses, and your council decides to sit back and enjoy the show while we're out here risking our lives. One more reason why we shouldn't trust you."

"This is why we've come," Alejandro argues. "To help. We are not Elders, but we are part of the council. We are offering our assistance as a gesture of friendship."

I know Gabe well enough to understand that he's standing on a ledge, and the rope keeping him from hurling himself off is frayed to the last thread, so I slide my hand into the crook of his elbow to draw him back in case he loses it.

Christine must also realize this, because she steps in front of Gabe, a physical barrier between the two sides of any possible battle. "We accept," she says. "We need all the help we can get."

TWENTY

Ghosts

While we eat, Victor and Alejandro regale us with legends about the Mayans who built the ruins—freakishly brilliant, industrious people who were big into bloody sacrifice.

The stories they tell aren't horribly graphic, but between my imagination and some of the things I've seen in visions, my stomach dances a weird little jig. Gabe urges me to eat, but Victor's talking about blood, and lopping off limbs and heads, and other revolting things. I rub a hand across my burning forehead, trying unsuccessfully to swallow the stale salt in my throat. Sipping on my water bottle, I will the sick away, beg my body to calm. I haven't felt this sick since I left Jackson.

Finally, Gabe stands to collect our garbage. "We don't have all day to listen to stories. There's work to do, and I'd like to get Abby home safely tonight so I can report to Val that I'm actually doing my job. However difficult she makes it."

I grab the hem of Gabe's shirt before he can walk away. "You're going to talk to Val?"

"Yes." He wrestles his shirt from my grip.

"Sorry," I mumble, distracted. "Have you talked to him a lot since we left? Have you heard ... talked to ... anyone else?" *Kye? Have you talked to Kye?*

"I talk to Val every night. Just Val. Why?" His eyes dart away, but in the seconds before they leave my face, I can see that he knows something. "What aren't you telling me, Gabe?"

He raises a brow as he helps me stand and drags me out of earshot from the others. "What aren't you telling me, Abby?"

Denial forms on my tongue, but I don't let it fall out. I *am* keeping things from him. Unimportant things that don't matter. And I'm keeping them on purpose, for no real reason other than maybe to have control of this one part of my life, let it belong to just me. Wandering on the beach, playing in the waves—not something dangerous. Just personal. I can—and probably should—easily tell him. But I don't. I cling to my privacy the only way I can.

"That's what I thought," he says. "When you tell me what you're hiding, I'll tell you what I know."

My hand vibrates with longing to slap the smirk off his face. Instead, I press my lips together and stalk back to the others. They're discussing theories about the tomb. "It is difficult to know," Victor says, "There has always been unrest near the ruins. Dark spirits have lived here since the first sacrifice. Perhaps the demons chose this place because there is much evil energy."

We continue along the path and soon come to the remains of a structure lined with tall, carved-stone pillars. I'm struck by the workmanship that has kept them standing for more than a millennium. "Such a fascinating society. Sacrifices aside, the Mayan people couldn't have *all* been evil."

"Nor were the Elen evil," Alejandro counters. "They were an interesting society too. Both civilizations are nearly extinct."

"Touché," I murmur.

"And yet," he continues, "after a time, good has an opportunity to restore what's been lost. We are provided a chosen one who will restore balance. Fix the thing that once caused the scales to tip."

I spin, catching a hint of earnest hero worship in his eyes. "And ... you think that person is me?"

He doesn't need to answer; it's evident in his expression.

"Great. Just what I need."

Christine laughs. "You sound like your calling is pure torture."

"Believe me, she thinks it is." Gabe says, clearly still annoyed. "The thing Abby wants most is to get rid of her power. To be a regular teenager whose worst problem is wondering who to go out with on the weekends."

His words cut deep, leaving my eyes stinging with anger. "How would you know what I want, Gabe? You never ask about personal things, you just assume. You watch from the outside and see how my life appears and pass judgment on situations you know nothing about. You have no idea what I've been through, and why would I tell you when you'll just twist it around and make it into something else?" Unable to look at him, I stalk away.

"Wait. That's not—" he stutters.

Finding I do have something left, I turn and yell back to him. "You want to know why I keep things from you? Stupid things that don't even matter? Take a look in the mirror and give it some thought."

Victor follows as I dodge ropes meant to keep tourists off the pyramids. "Abby, you cannot climb there."

I ignore him and keep going.

"Don't you want to hear the rest of the story?" He calls.

I don't answer.

"Let her go." Christine's words to Victor fade as I scurry away, grateful I'm in good enough shape to tackle another ridiculous set of stairs. Three-fourths of the way up, the sound of footsteps makes me glance back. Gabe is taking two steps at a time. I reach the top and whirl on him, hand hauled back with a slap at the ready. Before I can swing, he grabs my wrist and yanks me away from the edge.

"Don't do that." He returns my glare until we both know my urge to hit has passed, and then he lets go. "I probably deserve to be punched, but I know you. You'll regret it, and then spend the next week punishing yourself. Be mad all you want, but you've lost your mind if you think I'm letting you get more than twenty feet away from me in this place. Especially after what happened the last time we got separated."

He always knows just how to let the hot air out of my balloon. "Right. Because if something bad happens to me, Val might demote you."

He lets go of my wrist and leans against a pillar. "You really don't know, do you?"

"Know what?" I lean against the opposite pillar, facing him.

"Guarding you has never been just a job to me, Abby. I volunteered to come here with you because I didn't trust anyone else to keep you safe. Not even your self-absorbed boyfriend."

"Kye couldn't come anyway. He's sick, remember?"

Gabe blows out a frustrated breath, pushing away from the pillar to pace. "How could I forget? Your middle name might as well be misery."

I tip my head against the cold stone and close my eyes. "I can't help it, Gabe. I love him. I've loved him for, like, a million years."

"Are you sure?" His clothes rustle as he moves closer. I open my eyes to find him towering over me, one hand braced above my head. It's intimate—this nearness that has nothing to do with protecting me from danger—and I want it to be uncomfortable, but it's not. Not really. There's a part of me that longs to be held by anyone who can fill the empty spaces inside me, even for just a few seconds, and I'm tempted to grab his T-shirt and see how it would feel to have Gabe be that person.

But I don't.

He continues, "How do you know your feelings for him belong to you at all? You aren't Raina anymore, and he isn't Theron. How does either of you know how you feel for the other as Abby and Kye—without interference from the past? All the pasts?"

He leans closer, and I can't move, even though I know I should. His face is very close to mine. "How do you know there isn't someone here, living today, who would be an even better match for you? Who would make you happy, and protect you better than Kye can? Someone who won't make you sick and miserable? Someone who can stay with you, always?"

137

A confusing swirl of emotions muddies our energy—both his and mine. I swallow, frozen in place. How have I missed this side of him? I wonder what he would taste like. If his lips would be soft or firm or demanding on mine. In the moment, I wonder if he's right. If someday I'll choose to try being with someone who is not Kye.

I trust Gabe, and know he won't push me. If I want to sate my curiosity, this is his invitation—that much is clear. But I can't. Not yet. Maybe not ever. However Gabe's words, his nearness, muddles my brain and leaves my heart hammering, one solid truth remains. I love Kye.

Don't I?

I squeeze my eyes shut, trying to breathe. Of course I do. Kye is everything. The boy I've dreamed about for years. The guy who consumes my thoughts. The man who fills in my cracks.

Gabe doesn't move until I open my eyes, pleading with him to give me space. A slew of emotions flicker in his expression as he swears and shoves away from the pillar. He storms across the platform until he's standing on the other side, grumbling. "Sorry. That was out of line."

Still speechless, I shake my head. It was out of line, and yet—somehow, completely appropriate. When the tension becomes too much, I mumble, "We should look for a door or something."

"Yes," Gabe agrees, snapping into action. "Let's do what we came for and get out of this place." The next time he looks at me, his eyes are shuttered. "Too many ghosts here."

We don't find more signs of a tomb in these ruins, other than the presence of the shadows, and to my relief, they mostly leave us alone for the remainder of the day.

By the time we've done a thorough search, the sun hangs low, and the number of tourists has grown. Locals sell handmade goods from blankets along the path. We're on our way to the car, moving slowly enough to browse the wares, when I notice another path, one semi-obscured by trees.

I turn to Christine. "Where does that lead?"

Frowning, she sets down the pottery she's been contemplating. "I'm not sure. Let's take a look."

Gabe, Victor, and Alejandro are perusing paintings a few feet away, so I wave them over and show them the road we've missed. "Might as well be thorough."

Not far into the woods, we come to a gigantic sink-hole as big around as a football field is long.

The thing is so deep it's hard to tell if there's water at the bottom or just a deep, dark pit. I step closer, peering down past tree roots and shrubs that grow out of the dirt walls. A shiver crawls up my neck. There's water, but it's dark and murky, black like oil. Victor joins me in gazing from the edge. "What is it?" I ask him.

"That, señorita, is a sacrificial cenote."

TWENTY-ONE

Homesick

Victor explains that a cenote is a natural sinkhole, and that there are lots of them sprinkled throughout the jungle. The water comes from underground, rather than the sea, so it's fresh, not saltwater. From here it looks black as oil, but Victor assures us that were the sun at a better angle, we'd be able to see that it's actually very clean and clear.

"Some cenotes were used as a source of fresh water. But others were dedicated to the gods." Victor's gaze skitters away from mine. "It is believed that this is a place where virgins were sacrificed."

I stare into the depths, wondering if there could be an escape, some way to swim to safety. Dark emotion presses against me, raising chills on my arms and neck as the gloom presses in. Gabe grabs my shoulders and drags me away from the edge, reminding me to breathe. In. Out. In. Out. Until the panic passes.

"We should go," I murmur. "This is a bad place."

"Agreed." Christine wraps her arms around herself, squinting in the dying light. "We have a long drive home, and another long day tomorrow."

We part ways with Victor and Alejandro in the parking lot, and I climb in the front, closing the door as thick gray clouds thrust against our windows.

"Okay, okay. We're leaving." Christine turns over the engine and cranks up the stereo, blowing hair out of her eyes. "I think it's been a productive day."

Gabe's noncommittal sound is more polite response than agreement. He tips his head against his seat, eyes closed.

I can't agree with Christine either. I let the shadows take over—let them lead me somewhere freakishly scary, and highly dangerous. Unless we're trying to find quick ways for Abby to die, I don't find that productive at all, regardless of the fact that I somehow managed to fight them off.

By the time we make it home, the jitters in my hands are more about checking my phone than for need of dinner. I know he hasn't called, but when I find that I'm right, the events of the day crash down around me.

What am I doing here? With my life? What makes me think I'm qualified to deal with shadow demons whose goal is to kill me? How could it be so easy for Kye to move on, and why am I obsessing about him? A hundred insane questions run through my mind, coagulating into one solid thought: I want to go home.

I haul my suitcase off the shelf in the closet and start throwing things inside. Murtagh buzzes in. He looks from the suitcase to me, and back to the suitcase. "*Calin*? Run away, you not?"

"I'm not running away." I tell him. "I'm going home."

"Why?"

"Because ..." My breath hitches. "Because ..." Because if I was home, I could scream and yell at Kye for hurting me. If I was home, I could curl up with Erda and always have a friend who loves me no matter what. Because I miss my mom, and my room, and everything familiar. Because I don't want to grow up.

The suitcase crashes to the floor as I flop on the bed, arm over my eyes to cover up the ache welling inside me. "I'm homesick."

He pats my elbow. "Oh *Calin*. Mother you miss. Need love and guidance."

"I know."

"Ringie ding on the phone, your mother, Princess-Queen. Mother miss *Calin* too."

Wondering if it will help, I dial my mom's number, trying not to be disappointed when it goes to voicemail. "Guess I'm on my own."

He blinks his happy light. "No, *Calin*. Own only for one. Murtagh friend. Always here with Princess Queen."

"Thanks." The goddesses were more than kind the day they sent Murtagh to rescue me.

I lie on the bed, willing myself to stand up, do something. Go outside, or in the kitchen to help Christine with dinner. Anything. But I don't. Can't. Whether it's exhaustion or depression that keeps me there, I'm not sure. Maybe a combination of both.

When my phone rings, I spring up, fumbling to answer. Hearing my mother's voice is the ultimate relief. "Hey baby girl. How are things in paradise?"

It takes everything in me not to fall apart sobbing. "Good, I guess."

"You guess? What do you mean you guess?"

I tell her about my first weeks in Mexico, how it was relaxing and wonderful, and how much I've learned from Christine. How I'm only sick occasionally now. Then I tell her about everything that happened today.

"What?" She sounds angry. "I was told you're being protected there, not dragged into the heart of demon central."

Time to change the subject. "Have you heard from Kye?"

It takes her way too long to answer. "No, honey. I haven't. He's gone to stay with Val for a while, and I haven't seen either of them."

"Can I ask you something Momma?" I tuck my pillow into my chest, holding it tight like a hug. "Do you think Kye really loves me?" Or *loved*. "Real, true love?"

"I know he does. It's clear in the way he looks at you."

"No, I mean, do you think Kye loves *me*, not Theron loving Raina. If Theron and Raina never existed, would Kye still love me—Abby? And would I still love him?"

Silence stretches across the line until finally she says, "I don't know. But now is a really good time to figure it out."

I'm not sure I want to know the answer, one way or another.

"I have good news," she says, changing the subject again. "I'm sending you a surprise."

"What kind?"

In the background, another voice. Probably Akers.

"One that will make you happy and help alleviate some of your homesickness. You'll have to be patient, though. It won't arrive for a while."

"I love surprises." I open the glass and have a seat on a patio chair. "Can I have a hint?"

"Not this time. Don't want to ruin it." More background noise, and Mom giggles.

"Hey, is that Landon?" I ask, propping my feet on a stool. "Can I talk to him?"

"I ... sure."

Landon's soothing voice carries over the miles. "How's Mexico?"

"Hey Akers," I say, my smile growing. "Mexico is beautiful. Well, you know, except for the cray-cray shadow demons."

He laughs at my cray-cray comment. "Glad you're enjoying parts of it. Is Christine taking care of you?"

"She's great. You wouldn't believe my room here. It has a glass wall that opens onto the beach. I'm actually sitting on the patio staring at the ocean right now."

"Good. That's good." I can hear Mom murmuring in the background. "Are you ... how's my mom?" Not exactly what I mean, but I hope he gets what I'm truly asking.

His voice softens with tenderness. "I'm taking care of her."

"Okay. So, she's ... is she happy?"

"Well, she misses you something terrible, but other than that, I think ... I hope so." There's something else in his voice. Love? Maybe. Maybe. "What about ..." I can't even say his name without choking up today. The silence on the other end forces me to do it anyway. "How's Kye doing?"

"Uh ... I think he's doing better."

I have to blink away tears. "Good. That's good."

"I haven't talked to him or Val for a while though."

143

"Why not?"

He sighs, long and hard, like whatever he's thinking hurts. "Listen, Abby. While you're away, there's something important you should do. Try to break away and let go of Kye. A little bit at a time is always easiest. The thing is, honey, there's a strong possibility that this curse is unbreakable, and if that's true, you might have to live without each other—or not at all. And we need you both. So this should be a learning experience. I know he's trying ..."

Panic. Sheer panic. He's trying to what? Get over me? Live without me? Whatwhatwhat? My insides crack, burn. "Trying what?" When Akers doesn't answer right away, I ask again. "Trying what, Akers? What's he doing?"

"He's trying to let go of you, Abby. Trying really hard, and so should you." The rest of his words are lost in my roaring ears. What does he mean Kye's trying hard? How does a person let go of someone you love the way I love him? The way he loves me? Unless. Unless it's not the same for him. Maybe that's the problem. I would never have believed it before, but now, after not talking to him for so long, doubts creep in and grow and grow.

I hang up and drop the phone on my bed as I sprawl, unable to move. When did my life become so devastatingly complicated?

Obviously, the day I met Kye.

Moments later, there's a knock on my door. I ignore it, but Christine says through the wood. "Abby? Gabe and I are eating. Are you hungry?"

I don't respond. Maybe she'll think I'm asleep and leave me alone. Not so much. She peeks in. "Are you okay?"

My head is heavy as I sit up, and my eyes are sticky. I haven't realized I'm crying until I taste the salt in my mouth and feel the wet tracks on my cheeks.

"Oh honey, what's wrong?" Her arms encircle me as she sits, offering motherly comfort as I bury my face in her neck and cry. She strokes my hair and speaks in soothing tones about everything being okay, and her taking care of me, and other things I don't hear, but that help just because she says them.

Eventually, I've drained my emotional build-up, and scrounge for something other than Christine's blouse to wipe my eyes on.

"Better now?" she asks.

"Yes." I sniffle. "I'm sorry."

She rubs my shoulders, her bright blue eyes burning into mine. She understands. "You've been through a lot lately. I'm not sure what's happening with you and Kye, but I notice that there's been little or no communication between you—" She breaks off at my astonished stare. "I haven't been spying, if that's what you think. It's just—if you'd spoken to him, I'd know. Instead, you check for messages every five minutes, and then come back looking like you've been hollowed out. He hasn't called. I don't understand why any more than you do, Abby, but I want you to know that I consider you a daughter of my heart regardless of what happens between you and Kye."

"Thanks." I wipe my remaining tears.

"Just remember that you're here for a reason, and the faster we get the job done, the quicker you can get back home to your real mother." She stands. "You need your strength. Wash your face and come eat. Then you can go to bed. We're starting early again tomorrow, and the next day, and the one after that, until we find this tomb." She pads out, leaving the door ajar so I can watch her head down the hall.

Christine really is, above all, a mother.

Good to know.

I don't go outside for what I've come to consider my nightly moon worshiping. Not only do I hurt everywhere, but my well of energy is spent. I want nothing more than to lie in bed and cry until the anger portion of my grief cycle kicks in. Instead, I run a bubble bath and slide into the steaming water, covering my eyes with a cold, wet washcloth to soothe the swelling. And I stay there, for a long, long time.

After a while, a faint knock sounds on the bedroom door. I don't respond. I know it's Gabe—Christine would walk in—and I don't have words for him right now. I don't have words for anyone. I climb out of the tub and dry off, slather on coconut lotion, and slide into my pajamas. When I snuggle under the comforter, I notice a shadow under the door and know Gabe's hovering. It's a relief to have him watching out for me.

I press the button to close the curtains, and turn on my side to face the wall. By morning, my anger will know no limits. But tonight, I'm going to mourn what was—and what can never be.

TWENTY-TWO

Thirsty

Murtagh wakes me up while the sky is still pre-sunrise gray, claiming Christine sent him. We've spent weeks exploring ruins and looking for the tomb, and have managed to avoid another serious confrontation with the shadow demons. Between the walking, the climbing, and some incredibly long days, I'm exhausted. But hard work is a great way to expend angry energy, so it's exactly what I need. Because I am angry, and in some ways anger has set my Light free.

I plunk onto a kitchen chair in front of a full Mexican-style breakfast, covering a yawn. "Please tell me why I'm awake before the sun." Gabe passes me the pitcher of mango juice without looking up from the morning paper.

"I want to get back early this afternoon." Christine sprinkles salt and pepper over the eggs she's scrambling. "Maybe we'll go out to dinner later. For fun."

Gabe glances up, his lips quirking like he's fighting off a smile, and the two of them exchange a glance. I glare at Gabe, but he goes back to reading the paper as Christine brings the eggs to the table and sits to eat with us.

"What are you not telling me?" I ask, filling a tortilla.

Gabe shakes his head, still reading the paper—which is written in Spanish. "It's a secret."

"What's a secret?"

Christine glares at Gabe. "Nothing. We're getting an extra early start so we can have some downtime later, that's all."

I don't believe her, but let it go and finish my breakfast. In the ensuing silence, my mind wanders to the dangerous place I've spent my days avoiding. That place where my imagination nurtures pain, and where I allow anger and hurt to burn like acid in my stomach. That place where I imagine crazy awful things I would never really do, out of hate, or lust, or plain stupidity.

Because whatever he's doing, Kye has deserted me as surely as anyone ever could. The memory of him holding Crystal is embedded in my brain, where nothing can eradicate it. I try to dismiss the thought, try to ignore the way my stomach churns and twists when I think of him, but today the churning turns into cramps that persist until I can't eat anymore. Then the smell of peppers multiplies the bubbles pushing against my abdominal walls until my hands shake.

I'm about to be sick. Sick in a way I never was at home. Covering my mouth, I leap off the chair, leaving my half-empty plate, and bolt to the bathroom where I promptly throw up.

It's about time.

Been waiting for this since before I left Jackson. Maybe now I'll be able to forgive Kye and move on. When there's nothing left, I flush it down and rest my cheek on the cool tile floor.

Behind me, Christine asks, "Are you okay?"

"I'll be fine." I snag a clean hand-towel off the rack and wipe my face. "Give me a few minutes to clean up, then we can go."

The door opens farther. "I know you've been doing well these last weeks, but the curse ... We could put this off if necessary."

"No." If I stay, I'll have time to think, and that's not a healthy thing these days. I struggle up from the ground, desperation clawing at my raw throat. "I don't want to put it off. I'm fine. I'll be fine."

She touches my hair. "I know."

I meet her eyes in the mirror. She understands what it's like. She's been doing this for years.

Today's drive is shorter, and these ruins clearly less popular among tourists. There are people, but nothing like what we've seen elsewhere. We spend our morning climbing, exploring, and deflecting patches of dark energy, and by the time we break for lunch, I know.

This isn't the place.

Gabe hands me a tamale wrapped in a napkin, and I peel off the corn husk and nibble, grateful for the sustenance after working on an empty stomach.

Christine checks her watch. "Let's call it for the day."

"Hallelujah." I lie on the grass, grateful. "We should do some beach-time later. Salt water therapy."

Gabe takes my empty corn husk, eyeing me warily. "You aren't going to be sick again, are you?"

"Right now?" My stomach is still raw after this morning, but the tamale seems to be staying in place. "I don't think so."

He offers a bottle of water. "Wash it down, just in case. I don't want you hurling in Christine's car."

I ignore him, closing my eyes and fantasizing about taking a nap on the warm, white sand.

"You wouldn't be so tired if you'd actually go to bed at night," Gabe says, irritation evident in his tone.

I open my eyes, meeting his. "I went to bed early last night. This is a case of being awakened before dawn."

He looks away without a word and gathers the rest of our garbage. I stand and brush grass off my shorts while Christine steps away to make a phone call.

We have one last section to check—just to make sure we've been thorough. The heat of the mid-day sun beats down on us, the air thick with humidity that forces beads of sweat to trickle between my shoulder blades as I traverse the uneven ground. My mouth is dry, chalky. I wonder what happened to my water bottle? Gabe has more, but looks to be in a foul mood. I don't want to talk to him. I'll make it to the car just fine.

149

We clear the last of the ruins by the time Christine rejoins us. "All done?" she asks.

I nod, too exhausted to respond further.

"Well then. Let's head home, shall we?"

Gabe brushes past me. "Yes. Let's go." His long legs eat the path as he strides to the parking lot. Christine keeps up with him, but my feet weigh like bricks in my shoes. Lightheaded, I pause to rest in the shade of a tree, and half a minute later, I've lost sight of Gabe and Christine.

My mouth is bone dry. After I catch my breath, I continue on, wondering why today is so much hotter than yesterday. It's got to be a hundred and twenty degrees. Rounding the last bend in the path, I catch the glint of sun on windshields, and squint, blinking away gray spots.

"Hurry up, Abby," Gabe hollers. "What's keeping you?"

I shake my head, realizing too late that it has started to hammer. I pause again, squeezing the bridge of my nose and blinking more rapidly to keep up with all the spots. Another step, one more, and then my shoe catches on something and I'm falling, falling, falling.

He takes my hand and draws me up from where I've hidden on the spongy ground beneath the rosebushes. I'm relieved to have his cool palm against mine for the first time in months. He plucks a petal out of my hair and wraps his arms around me, squeezes tight, whispering in my ear, "Let's go. Before the sun comes up and the others start to stir. A few hours is all we need to disappear."

Fear and excitement are at war inside me. "But the curse ... Our child—"

"Will know both his parents. Trust me," he says.

He asked me to trust him before. Loving him has been the most difficult trial of my life, but trusting him comes easily. There is no time to prepare. I accept what he has offered, and take nothing, save the wooden box and the few supplies he has already packed.

And then we flee.

TWENTY-THREE

Surprise

"Abby? Honey, wake up. Come on now." Christine tilts my head and pours water into my mouth. I breathe it in, choke, and my eyes pop open. "There you go. Come on back around. Why didn't you tell us you were dehydrated?"

I shake my head, confused. "Kye …"

"All right, let's get her home." Another voice. Familiar, but not the one I expected.

Christine moves, and I'm lifted off the ground into gentle arms. I blink, focusing on Gabe. "Thanks," I tell him. And then, "Sorry."

He slows. "Why?"

"Whatever I did to make you mad. For constantly falling apart so you have to come to my rescue."

His chest expands as he takes a pained breath. "I don't mind rescuing you. I never mind that."

"Then why are you always so annoyed with me?"

Christine opens the car door and Gabe deposits me in the front passenger seat. "I'm not—"

"Yes you are. You're mad over something. Don't deny it. I can read your angry energy." The air conditioning is going full-blast, and the cool air helps further clear my head.

"It's not you, Abby." He sighs, bracing his arms on top of the still open door. "Why do you do this to yourself?"

"Why do I do what?"

"Gabe. Let her be." Christine gets in and buckles up. "I should've known she wasn't up to this today. Especially after this morning. It's my fault."

"No, it isn't." I lean my head back. "I knew I needed water, but I was trying to let the Hulk here have his space."

She glares at us until Gabe closes my door and gets in the back seat.

"I think," Christine says, "I've been taking your recovery for granted."

I adjust a vent so it's blowing cold air in my face. "I guess halfway around the world isn't far enough."

"We'll figure it out." She pulls onto the road.

How does she know? How could anyone know what will happen to me and Kye? I don't know myself, and I'm half of the equation. If we manage to break the curse, do I still even want to be with him?

It's hard to know when I'm so angry at him for deserting me. So confused about why. About how he could do such a thing. *I love him.* I do. So much I was willing to die for him. And that will never change. Being apart from him is like missing an organ, or a limb. But the distance, his absence, makes me wonder if what's between us—if love—is enough to make a life together.

Life with Mom and Gram has taught me to look at a bigger picture, and I can't help but water my doubts. *Is love really all that matters? Is it enough to see us through all the opposition being thrown at us?*

I glance at Gabe. Steady, solid. Always there when I most need him—even on his grumpiest days. I'm not sure what he has given up to be here because he changes the subject whenever I ask, but I think it must be a lot. At the very least, a day-job career he enjoyed. Gabe is here for *me*. For the Dragons too, but mainly for me. And he doesn't even love me—not the way Kye once claimed to. Gabe is here out of duty.

But duty isn't enough either.

Gabe hands me a water bottle. "Sip slowly."

BIRTHRIGHT

I ignore him and gulp, desperate to hydrate quickly, but then my stomach freaks out. I sit forward, covering my mouth while the water—along with the tamale I ate for lunch—threatens to make a second appearance.

"Chris, stop the car." Gabe says, his voice urgent.

She stops at the side of the road, and I jump out, doubling over. The churning eases, tricking me into believing my lunch will stay in, but then I straighten, and the heat of the sun throbs in my head, and I'm on my knees for real this time, leaving the tamale for the lizards.

Eyes closed, I brace my hands on the dirt, afraid to move, and too weak to try. Gabe brushes the hair out of my eyes. "Are you finished or is there more?"

"I think I'm done." My muscles shake with exertion. "I don't know. I just want to go home."

He helps me stand, so gentle as I sit in the car with the door open. "Do you think you can try sipping? You really need to keep some water down."

I nod, accepting a bottle.

"Slowly," Christine says. "We'll idle here until you're ready."

Gabe reaches over and levers my seat so I'm lying back, then closes my door and gets in. I curl onto my side, holding the capped bottle against my cheek, and thinking about how bad it sucks that I've come all this way—left my home, left my heart—and am still suffering. Granted, these symptoms are very different from the ones I had before, but I can think of no other explanation for them. "Chris, if we don't figure this out, if I don't start getting better soon, I want to go home before ..." *one of us dies.*

"Yes. I'll make sure of it."

Gabe's voice is rough. "We're going to figure this out. You'll see. We won't let the curse, or anything else destroy you."

A wave of shivers hits, and I have to close my eyes to fight tears. What I don't say, can't say to Gabe, is that I'm afraid it already has.

The cleaning lady has been here. My bedding is fresh and clean as I collapse on top of it. Considering the jumble in my brain, it's a small miracle I'm able to fall asleep. But I'm so exhausted that as soon as I hit the mattress, darkness takes over, and this time, I don't dream.

I awake to a loud bang and a squeal, and shoot up in bed—way too fast. Bracing myself against a wave of dizziness, I start across the room to investigate, but only manage a few steps before the door flies open.

"Abby!" Rose hops across the room to wrap her arms around me. "Surprise! I can't believe I'm here. Look at this place, isn't it fantastic?"

"Rose!" I sputter in shock. "What are you ...? How did you get here?"

"Your mom and Akers sent me." She holds me still, staring into my face. "Why do you look so shocked? They said they told you."

"They told me they were sending a surprise. I was thinking a new outfit, or a care package with pictures. I had no clue they were sending you!" I squeeze Rose tight. "Best surprise ever! I'm so glad you're here."

"How are you doing?" she asks, frowning as she looks me over.

I shrug, focus on the floor. "I'm great."

She drops on my bed with a sigh. "That bad, huh?"

Still trembling from lack of food, I sit next to her. "No, it's not horrible. This place is beautiful, and Christine is so kind."

"You must really be struggling, because beautiful and kind don't even touch the surface of this place, or my aunt."

"A little," I admit. "Who wouldn't?"

"We all would." Rose tips her head to the side, her eyes boring into me, much in the way they did when we first met. "I've missed you."

"I've missed you too." My voice cracks, because even missing everyone else, having my best friend here makes everything better—easier.

She drapes her arm around my shoulders. "Aunt Chris told me you've had a bad day. What can I do?"

Grinning, I shake my head. "You're here. That's all I need."

"Good." She stands to rummage in the vanity drawer for the remote and opens the blinds, then the glass. "Because that beach is calling my name, and we have lots of catching up to do."

Half an hour later, the two of us lie camped on the lounge chairs I usually occupy with Gabe. "Tell me everything. What's going on back home?"

"Not a lot." She rubs strong sunscreen on her pale skin, frowning because mine is already a dusky shade of gold. "The summer tourist season has your mom working tons of hours, but it keeps her occupied. Akers still checks on her every day." She winks, indicating that there's more than just "checking" going on.

I sip a bottle of water. "Good for them."

She slides on her sunglasses and leans back, dark hair waving around her shoulders. "Things appear to be going well. She acts happy."

"She never seemed lonely as I was growing up, but I know she must have been."

A breeze lifts our hair and cools our skin, bringing with it the smell of brine and water. Rose inhales. "She probably didn't realize it before she met Akers. Anyway, what else? Oh, um. Jen has a new boyfriend." She frowns, turning her head toward me. "I can't stand him. You'll hate him too."

"Probably." I stretch my arms over my head, allowing the sun to bathe me again, but this time, it's healing and wonderful. "Have you seen Eric?"

"Quite a lot, actually. I think he's trying to play body guard or something. Every time I go somewhere, I run into him. At first, I thought it was funny, but then it got annoying. And Jen mentioned that he was doing something similar to her, so I confronted him."

"I bet he's feeling lost."

"Or guilty. I asked him—politely—to please back off."

"Did he?"

"Not really. He just started being more careful about getting caught. But I'm trying to go easy on him. We're all struggling with demons—" Rose's hand flies to her mouth and her eyes go wide. "Okay, that's not a good analogy, because I didn't mean it literally. You really are struggling with demons. Real ones. And that was totally insensitive of me to say. So, strike that statement. What I meant was we're all dealing with life-altering upheavals. Yes. And I think Eric feels left out, since he's only included in council meetings when the Dragons want something from him."

I know better than to interrupt Rose when she's thinking out loud, so I just listen.

"But who can blame them, right?" she continues. "He did betray us last time. So, yeah. He needs to prove himself to the Dragons, which is what I suspect he's trying to do."

"I hope he gets a chance to redeem himself." For all that Eric has done, I believe he has a good heart. He must, or he would have gone through with killing me.

Up the beach, two figures are walking. I lean forward, blocking the sun with a hand above my face.

"Ay ay ay. Welcome to Mexico." Rose whistles under her breath. "Look at those abs! Would it be totally tacky if I run my hand over one of those washboards?"

"Yeah. Let's not do that. *They* might not object, but Gabe's watching." I glance behind us. He isn't visible in the window, but I know he's there. Always. "I think he'd lay an egg."

"So? Dragon boy's not my boss. Yours either, for that matter." She pops up, straightening her bikini. "I am a totally unattached

156

American babe. Those guys will never know what hit them. Come on."

"Wait. Rose."

She grabs my hand and drags me off the chair. "I won't tell my cousin. Let's just enjoy ourselves while we have the chance, all right? It's not every day you see muscles like those."

I let her tow me across the sand. Strangely, I have the urge to tell her about Gabe—whose abs are every bit as washboard, and who has biceps twice the size of the boys coming our way— and the fact that I actually do see him, muscles and all, every day. But for the sake of simplicity, I keep my mouth shut as we close the distance between our house and Victor's.

TWENTY-FOUR

Tension

"Hola, Abby." Both Victor and Alejandro are shirtless, and as they approach, I agree with Rose. They do have very nice abs. These two could be poster boys for a *Visit Mexico!* ad. Victor acknowledges Rose, and then focuses his attention on me. "How are you feeling? Señora Murphy told the council you are suffering today." He brushes his lips over my knuckles, leaving my cheeks flaming.

As politely as I'm able, I remove my hand from his and step back. "I'm a lot better now, thanks."

"Bueno. I am glad to hear this. I was worried when I heard."

"Ahem." Rose clears her throat, eyeing me pointedly.

I take the cue. "Victor, Alejandro, this is my friend Rose. She just arrived from America."

Victor lifts Rose's outstretched hand, repeating the gesture he used on me. "Your name suits you, American flower."

Rose giggles. "Aren't you the flatterer."

"An observation, only."

Alejandro's gaze travels Rose's length, openly admiring her curves as he also kisses her knuckles. Muscles ripple along Alejandro's shoulders and up his arms, and like Victor, his abs are well defined. And golden. And miraculous. Dark hair waves around his ears, framing the largest, darkest eyes I've seen on a guy—the kind that make a girl's heart pitter-patter.

As we make small talk, Rose turns her flirt-o-meter to full watt, managing to "accidentally" graze Alejandro's bare torso with both hands before Victor asks, "May we accompany you home? We have business to discuss with Señora Murphy."

Rose loops her arm through Alejandro's, and starts back the way we came. Victor slows his pace, allowing us to fall behind. "You're looking pale today, Abby. I hope you are being cautious. Are you sure you're okay?"

"Yes, I'm fine." I angle closer to the water and dig my toes in the damp sand as we walk. "I'm always cautious, Victor."

"Except when you are walking alone at night."

Warmth spreads into my cheeks. "That probably doesn't fall into the cautious category, does it?"

"Afraid not." Victor bends, scooping a smooth, curved shell out of the water. He rubs the pink surface clean with his thumb and offers it to me. "I am not complaining. You may visit my garden anytime."

"Thanks." Uncomfortable with the way he's looking at me, I pick up the pace to close the distance between us and the others. "I doubt that'll happen again soon. At least not at night."

He bends again, this time scooping up two smooth, flat rocks and rotating them in his hand. "That is wise."

Upon reaching our beach camp, Rose plops onto her chair, laughing up at Alejandro. Victor continues, "It might please your guard to know that after our experience at the ruins, I convinced the council to send two of our Dragons to help protect you."

"I'm sure Gabe will be thrilled. He could probably use a day off." I don't know how long he waited outside my room the other night, but I wouldn't be shocked to learn he stayed until sunrise. Sometimes I think the man never sleeps.

"I am happy to take over his duties for a day, if he needs."

"I'll let him know." I turn into the surf to cool off.

"Christine told my council about the curse between you and her son." Victor follows me into the water. "I am sorry for your illness."

Needing space, I wade until the water reaches my chest, then squat to submerge up to my neck. "You and everyone else I know."

"Do you want to talk about it?" Victor has waded in only far enough for the water to touch the bottom of his swim trunks.

"Nope." My hair swirls around my shoulders as I emerge, and I twist it, squeezing the water out. "We can talk about something else, though."

"This is painful for you."

I sidestep him. "Yep."

Rose giggles as I snag my towel off the end of the chair on which Alejandro has made himself comfortable. "Having fun?" I ask.

Rose grins, reminding me of what true joy looks like. "Always. Did you know there's a dance club in town?"

"No, I hadn't heard that." Leave it to Rose to find all the hotspots within an hour of arrival.

"Alex invited us to come with them tonight." Rose runs her toe up Alejandro's forearm. "Right Alex?"

Alejandro fixes her with an intense look that tells me he will pursue her until he catches her. "Sí. We will enjoy introducing you to true Mexican dancing."

"Abby has not been feeling well," Victor says. "Perhaps tonight is not good for her?"

"I ... uh." Before I can decide how best to respond, another lounge chair plunks into the sand, and Gabe shoves a cold glass of juice in my hand. "Sit down before you pass out. You're looking green again."

"Thanks." Until he showed up, I didn't consider that I've been missing his presence. What I haven't missed, though, is the anger I sense rolling off him in waves. Wondering what set him off this time, I stretch out in the chair, sipping the fruit juice.

Rose leans closer to me. "Do you always let him order you around like that?"

I shake my head, "Actually, I was—"

"—do you always push her past her limits?" Gabe glares at Rose.

"No, I—"

"Past her limits? The only thing I'm pushing on her is some fun. A break. Maybe freedom from the muscle-boy who tries so hard to keep her on a leash."

"I do not keep her on a leash. Abby does what she wants. I'm only here to keep her safe."

"He's r—" I try.

"If that's true, then why was she afraid to walk down the beach with me just now? She's constantly looking over her shoulder, like she's afraid you're going to catch her."

"Or maybe you've forgotten that she has another reason to look over her shoulder. One that has nothing to do with me."

"Well, you do—" Clearly, they aren't listening to me.

"Believe what you want, Dragon-boy. I'm willing to bet everything I brought with me that other than exploring the ruins, she hasn't left this house to do a single fun thing. There's a club a mile away, and she didn't even know about it."

"Well, that's because—" I try again, knowing this argument will only escalate.

"Maybe she hasn't been up to it. You know, since she's been working nonstop while sick with a curse that's killing her."

"Or perhaps you're using the curse as an excuse to keep her from living while she's here. From enjoying life while she can."

"Stop. Just stop."

They continue bickering back and forth as if I'm not here. As if Victor and Alejandro aren't gaping and hearing every heated word. I set my empty glass on the cooler and lie back, shielding my eyes against the glare of the sun. As I do, a movement over the water catches my attention. A bank of dark, heavy clouds barrels straight for us with unearthly speed, rallying the wind and causing the turquoise water to roll and churn, stirring mud from the bottom and shoving it forward with breathtaking force. While Rose and Gabe argue, a wave, no more than a mile offshore and taller than Christine's house, rears up and curls toward us.

"—can't believe you're so ignorant," Gabe is saying. "You haven't even seen her for weeks."

"Gabe," I say.

"Not my fault. I volunteered to go with her the first day, and Val would've let me if you hadn't been opposed to it."

"Rose," I say, louder. The wave rises higher, leaving my heart thundering.

"Because I needed to be able to focus on protecting Abby without you sabotaging everything I'm trying to do."

"Gabe!" I grab his arm and squeeze.

"What?"

I point out to sea. "Look."

He swears as his eyes widen with alarm. "They've found us."

Rose sees the wave too. "What is that?"

Gabe scoops me off the chair, towel and all, and starts for the house. "That, dear Rose, is the real reason Abby is constantly looking over her shoulder."

Victor breaks his silence. "Would you like us to bring your things inside?" Alejandro jumps to help as the wind howls. I wrap my arms around Gabe's neck and bury my face to protect my eyes from the swirling sand.

"Leave it. Everyone get inside." Gabe's long stride carries us to the kitchen. He deposits me on a chair, yelling, "Christine! They're here."

I wipe my sand-coated eyes with a towel as Rose and the others hurry in and close the doors.

"Will that even hold?" Rose asks, now looking ill herself.

"It should." Christine bustles in, arms laden with large pieces of quartz, amethyst, and obsidian, and leans them in a row along the door frame. "But it won't hurt to reinforce it."

I glance around again. "Where did Gabe go?"

"He's taking care of your room. We need to secure all possible entrances." She turns, meets my eyes. "It's just a precaution. There are multiple layers of protection around this house. The wave probably won't even make it to the patio."

I tuck the towel tighter around my shoulders, shivering. Christine doesn't know—couldn't—what those demons will do to get to me. Victor says, "Do not worry, Abby. We will protect you."

"Don't make promises you can't keep. None of us knows everything those demons can do, but I've faced them, and I don't know if we can defeat them. Even together."

Rose sits in the chair next to mine. "You can, Abby. Last time—"

"Was a fluke. I had Kye there with me, plus two really powerful pieces of jewelry, and Eric."

"Who was in league with the bad guys and tried to kill you."

"But saved my life instead. And anyway, even he had no idea what would happen when we opened that tomb."

Everyone tries to talk at once, but their voices are drowned by the howl of the wind. I glance outside, just in time to watch the wave crash against the shore, pick up our chairs, and hurl them at the house.

TWENTY-FIVE

Making Waves

The water picks up our cooler, rolling it over until it smashes against the rock wall at the property's edge. Our chairs clatter onto the patio, only to be picked up again and whipped around by the wind. One chair dances in a funnel, whirling until it tangles in a palm-tree's fronds, while the other hurls straight for the glass doors.

"It's going to shatter," Rose says.

"No, it isn't." Christine grips the table until her knuckles turn white.

"Señora, I am not so sure." Victor's eyes lock on the flying chair. "I have never seen things like this." The chair curves, spiraling out of control until it rams the glass so hard the entire house shakes. The doors hold, but there is now a golf-ball sized crack midway up. A weakness.

"Get used to uncertainty," Gabe tells Victor, finally returning from securing the rest of the house. "With Abby around, anything is possible."

He takes position behind me, so I crane my neck to see his face. "Thanks a lot."

The skin around his eyes and in his neck pulls taught with strain as he stares through the glass. "Just stating the facts."

The wind doubles back and picks up Christine's barbeque grill, the bent chair, and also the third chair, while filling the air with landscape rocks and sand. We can no longer see what's happening.

"Holy margaritas. We're going to die!" Rose squeezes closer to Alejandro, visibly shaking. He slides an arm around her shoulders. I tear my eyes away, feeling an inappropriate twinge of envy.

Victor inches closer, his hand grazing my shoulder as if he expects me to cling and flirt as easily as Rose. Maybe it's a culture thing. But while Rose is free to let Alejandro be hands-on friendly, I'm not. Even if Kye and me are on hold, or over, or whatever—my heart is nowhere near ready for a fling.

I stand and inch closer to Gabe. He's holding something in one hand—it looks like a circle of jade. Another rock crashes into the glass, startling me, and he rests his free hand on the small of my back, drawing me closer. He's so focused on our surroundings, I'm sure he's done this out of instinct more than anything else, but the possessive intimacy in the gesture forms a knot of confusion in my throat.

More debris hits the glass, crash after crash, leaving dings and chips in a hundred different places, further weakening the thick panes. And then the barbecue grill slams into the original crack and thin lines spider-web, growing larger and longer with each hit and ding.

"I repeat," Rose says, her voice nearing hysteria, "that door is not going to hold."

"You're right." Abruptly, Christine stands, taking charge. "It's not. We need a backup plan."

Rose snaps. "I propose we pack up what we need and get the hell out of Dodge."

Gabe opens his mouth like he's going to argue, then snaps it shut. "Agreed."

"What about Christine's house?" Panic rises in my chest. "What about our stuff?"

"Rose is right." Christine says, grabbing a folder of papers from a drawer near the phone. "The house doesn't matter. We should grab essential items while we still can."

"How much time do you think we have?" Gabe asks, guiding me to my room.

"Minutes, if we're lucky," Christine says, hauling tail down the hall.

The house is a flurry of movement and yelled reminders as we frantically try to gather our important items that can't be replaced. For Christine, it's a file-box of documents. For me, it's the dagger, Gram's crystals, and my cell phone. At the last minute, I grab a pair of sandals, and then Gabe is in my room, grabbing my arm and ushering me to the garage. "Any idea where we're going?" I ask.

"Higher ground."

"Like that'll fix anything. We both know we can't keep running."

He pauses, hand on the doorknob. "We're not prepared. You're not at your strongest today, and there are no other options."

In my peripheral vision, I catch sight of a tiny purple flash, but when I whip my head around, it's gone. Worried, I squint into the gray muck until I see the flash again. My heart plummets into my toes. "Murtagh!" I shove my things into Gabe's arms and run for the door, scrambling to find the remote so I can let him in.

"What are you doing?" Gabe snatches the remote from my hand.

"Murtagh's out there," I sob. "I have to save him."

"You can't open the door! That's exactly what they want. Even an inch will give those demons full access to all of us. Do you want to be responsible for that?"

"I can't just leave him! Murtagh's my friend. He's like my only friend, and he'll die out there."

"And if you let the demons in, you might die in here, and take the rest of us with you."

Christine honks the car horn, clearly anxious to get going. I know Gabe's right. I know it, but the third purple flash is faint, much weaker than the previous two. And I can't. Let. Murtagh. Die.

"I have to do something, Gabe. It's my fault he's here." Terror clogs my throat, thickening my voice and stinging my eyes.

Gabe slams my bag onto the marble countertop. "What do you want me to do, Abby? Get killed trying to save your pet bug?"

My eyes narrow into slits. "Nothing, Gabe. I don't need you to do anything. I'll do it."

"No you won't." He grabs my arm as I try to stalk back to my room. "Don't be stupid, Abby. I know you love Murtagh, and I don't want to see him die either, but we can't risk opening that door. You know we can't risk it. There's too much at stake."

Hot anger burns in my eyes, and I wrench my arm away. He's right. I know he's right. But the thought of losing Murtagh roots me to the floor.

"Come on. We have to go." Gabe grabs me around the waist and lifts me off the ground, hauling me out. I can no longer see Murtagh's light flashing outside. He might already be dead. He's such a small creature, it would be a miracle for him to survive the raw power of this demon storm. A sob bubbles in my chest, so I bury my face in my hands. "Please. Please, let him be okay."

"We'll come back," Gabe says, desperation evident in his voice as he hauls me into the garage. "When this is over—when it's safe—we'll come find him." He sets me on my feet and opens the car door. "Get in."

My chest rises and falls, every breath heavy and thick. I glance at Gabe and notice that he's still holding his circle of jade, but not my bag. "Gabe—my purse. The dagger."

His face goes white.

Christine leans over. "It's too late, honey. We need to go. Now."

"I can't leave the dagger—it's too dangerous. We can't let them get it."

Gabe's hard gray eyes darken to flint. "I'll go. I'm the one who left it."

I shake my head. "No. It's my responsibility. I shouldn't have brought it here with me." I start back inside, but Gabe grabs my arm.

"Please just leave it. It's not worth the risk."

I know better. I'm the only person here who knows how dangerous that dagger truly is.

I wrench my arm free and run. "I'm sorry."

Christine gets out of the car. "Abby, what are you doing?"

Gulping down fear, I croak, "We can't let them get the dagger."

I open the door just as a loud shatter shakes the house, and the stressed section of window gives. Water floods over the tile, soaking my shoes and rising to my ankles. Wind rages into the house, now unimpeded, picking up random items and tossing them dangerously close to me.

Shielding my face with my arm, I scramble to the counter and grab my purse. Among the flying things, I manage to catch sight of a faint flash of purple. "Murtagh!" I scream. "Murtagh, where are you? Murtagh come here."

I reach out, blinded by sand and debris, swiping the air, opening and closing my fists around anything with which they came in contact. On the sixth try, I grasp something semi-warm, and soft. Pinching the thing between my fingers as gently as I dare, I open my fist and sigh with first relief. Murtagh's not dead, but neither is he conscious.

Gabe seizes me by the waist and hauls me none-too-gently over his shoulder. This time, I let him deposit me into a seat and slam the car door. He then takes the front passenger seat and tells Christine, "Drive."

TWENTY-SIX

Team Effort

We make it fifty yards before Christine is forced to slam the brakes. A portion of the shadow surrounding the house breaks away and envelops the car in a dark, cold cloud of mist.

Gabe glares at Rose. "Brilliant plan."

"Shut up, Dragon boy," Rose snaps. "At least I made a decision to act. Unlike the rest of you."

"And it was so well thought out."

A headache forms at the base of my neck. "Stop it. Both of you just shut up. Rose is right. We had to do something." I open my fist and lay Murtagh on my lap, rubbing his head with my finger. "I'm done sitting around waiting for them to come for us. We need a plan that doesn't include running away." I've spent my life running, and I'm exhausted. Beyond exhausted. I don't want to run anymore. Maybe the best way to face the demons is head on. I prop Murtagh on my purse, taking a deep breath while I gather my courage.

Gabe turns in his seat as I hop out of the car and slam the door. "What are you doing now? Abby?"

"Buying some time."

He gets out too, angry, shouting over the wind. "Get back in the car."

"No."

"Abby, you don't have the strength to do this today."

"I'll find it. We have to do something—right now."

The roar of thunder eats his words as the rest of the doors open and the others join us. "We will help," Victor shouts, squeezing my shoulder. "You are not alone in this fight."

The shadows converge into a column, pulsing dark, darker, and then bursting with red light. They swirl and yank until my hair feels like it will rip out of my head, and keeping my feet on the ground requires all my strength. A form emerges, surrounded by the light, and takes the shape of a man—a man who looks an awful lot like Boone. He materializes from shadows like a supreme being of the dark, black eyes alight with electricity, sparks zapping around him. He opens his mouth, and a swarm of black-shelled beetles spews out. They're everywhere, and I have to fight the instinct to jump back in the car, screaming.

Bolstered by the presence of my friends, I close my eyes and search for a hint of the Light I know I have inside. A beetle lands on my arm, and another on my shoulder, joining the three or four in my hair. I shudder, hating that the shadows know my fears, and then ... I find it. A minuscule hint of heat in the pit of my core. I reach for it, grab hold, and tug with everything I have. The effort takes more energy than usual, leaving me winded.

"You're okay," Gabe murmurs in my ear. "I'm right here with you."

He draws out his jade, and I notice that it's glowing, pulsing.

I try again to summon my Light, drawing the energy up, into my heart, out through my fingertips. My head swims with dizziness, but I keep going, trying to pull the Light up, send it out. Up and out. Up and out. Soon, my arms grow warm, and I think maybe I can do it. Maybe I'll find the power and banish the demons, but when I try to propel the energy, it flashes and dies.

Swamped with dizziness, I sag against Christine. "It's not working. I don't know why, but I can't do it."

"Try, Abby," Rose says, her voice coated with persuasion. "You have to try."

I close my eyes again, but no matter what I do, I can't find the thread of heat again. The stifling cold of the demons squeezes in on us, and the fear I've suppressed blossoms. I gasp, try again as cold works through my toes and threads into my body like a trickling river of ice.

"Stop." Gabe tosses his stone on the ground at my feet. I feel him behind me, imagine his arms are there, ready to catch me if I collapse. But I'm not sure if he's talking to me or the demons, and any other words are eaten up in the violent wind.

There's nothing left for me to give. My energy is too taxed, drained, leaving me unable to fight back, helpless to protect myself or the people I care about. I close my eyes, searching for the smallest hint of energy. Nothing.

I don't know what this demon has done, but I feel like it has drained the life out of me.

Then the cold gives way to a balmy breeze, warming me with the strength of the sun. When I'm able to open my eyes, I find that a pillar of sunlight has broken through the shadows, rising up from Gabe's Jade circle, which, I notice belatedly, is in the shape of the Dragon symbol.

The Boone look-alike demon appears perplexed. He opens his mouth again, but this time the bugs circle his head, turning on him and pelting his face. The shadows shrink in on themselves, swirling backward until they suck up the demon man, twisting him at impossible angles until he dissolves and dissipates, along with the rest of the shadows.

The breeze swirls us in a protective bubble, bending and swaying to caress my cheeks, flutter my eyelashes, and brush the hair out of my face. It catches my sarong and billows it behind me. And then, as quickly as it came, the wind switches directions and disappears.

"What was that?" I breathe. "What happened?"

"You like my trick?" Victor's expression is smug. "As I said, you are not in this fight alone. I ask help from the wind—the wind answers."

My lips turn up. "Yes, I like your trick. A lot. Tell the wind thanks for me." I glance at Gabe, and then pointedly at his jade, eyebrows raised. He ducks his head. "Just a thing I've been working on. It's an energy neutralizer. Empowered jade. Looks like this could be a useful tool."

"Absolutely," I tell him. "Because that's a fight I would definitely have lost."

Smiling, Gabe moves closer behind me, his body heat radiating onto my bare back and shoulders. "We need to get Abby somewhere safe so she can rest."

Rose loops her arm through Alejandro's. "Let's go back inside. It's all kinds of creepy out here."

"No, that won't do," Christine says. "The house has been compromised. The demons know we're here."

Rose's mouth drops open in protest. "But ... I just got here. What about the beach? And the club? And ... and ... my tropical vacation."

Gabe claps her on the shoulder, grinning. "Looks like the vacation's over, Rosie. Now it's time to work."

Since the demons have left—for now—we return to the house to pack necessities. Gabe takes some convincing, but when I point out that I refuse to run around in my bikini for an undetermined amount of time, he relents.

He does not, however, leave my side. At all.

"I guess that's it." I zip the last of my belongings into my suitcase and stand it upright. Gabe tries to take it, but I swat him away. "I'm fine. It's not that heavy."

"Let me get it," he says through clenched teeth.

I ignore him and maneuver the wheels over the tile floor and down the hall until I get caught on a grout-line and he wrestles the handle from my grasp. "Obviously it's heavier than you should be lifting."

What the what? I blink. "It's no heavier than the stuff I lift when we work out."

"That was before," he says, tossing my suitcase into the back of the SUV. "You should at least *try* to be cautious."

Rather than ask him to explain, I climb into the rear of the car and sit next to Victor while Gabe goes inside to retrieve his belongings. My hands clench and unclench on my lap as the adrenaline drains. Victor takes one of my fists and pries open my fingers to gently lay the sleeping Murtagh in my palm. "He is all right, yes?"

I check his energy and nod, as relief flows. "Yes. He's just exhausted." Like me.

When the last of the luggage fills the cargo-space and everyone is buckled in, Christine starts the car for the second time. Gabe ends up in the front passenger seat, and catches my eye in the rearview as I lean my head back.

There's something foreign in his gaze. Could it be hurt? Victor drapes his arm behind me, and I ignore my discomfort, closing my eyes as the vibrations of the moving car calm my troubled thoughts.

TWENTY-SEVEN

Displaced

I wake with my cheek on Victor's shoulder and jerk upright, embarrassed. "Sorry."

He flips back the dark hair falling in his eyes. "I do not mind. You need the rest."

"Thanks." A sliver of sun remains on the horizon, and I can see nothing but jungle and sky. We've been on the road for over an hour. "Where are we going?"

"Back to the ruins," Christine says. "Those shadows at the house damaged a heavily populated tourist area, which put the local economy at risk. They're calling it a freak storm, but the Mexican Council has finally taken notice and deployed a company of Dragons to help us find the tomb. They're going to meet us there."

"About time," Gabe grumbles. "We've only been warning them for months."

"We're here now." Alejandro says, an edge to his words and a defensive bite in his voice. "We've come this far with you, and will stay until Enrique changes our assignment."

"Let's hope that's soon," Gabe mumbles.

"But where are we going tonight?" My heart sinks as I realize that my time at Christine's beautiful house has likely come to an end.

"A hotel." Christine adjusts the rearview and catches my eye. "We'll get some sleep, meet with the Dragons, and make a plan of action. Now that we have help, this search will go much faster, and that's important, since the situation has clearly become severe."

"Do you have a place in mind, or are we flying blind?" Rose adjusts the rear air conditioner vent so the cool air spreads.

"There's a resort near Chichén Itzá. I hear it's nice, but I've never stayed there."

"As long as they have a shower and a bed, I'm good," I mumble. A few months ago, I spent a night with Kye in a New York hotel room, where we learned the hard way that even nice hotels aren't always safe. But it was just him and me that time. Alone.

His knuckles graze my cheek. My pulse thundering when his fingers knot with mine. The attraction burning inside me when he came out of the bathroom with wet hair, smelling like lavender sage hotel soap.

Where would we be now if things had happened differently? If we had made different choices? Stop thinking about it. Stop thinking about him.

"I hope you still feel that way when we get there." Christine's voice brings me out of the memory. The look on her face indicates that in this case "nice" could have a wide range of interpretation.

"That bad?" Rose groans. "I didn't even get to sleep one night in that house. Why did the demons have to show up on the same day as me?"

Alejandro reaches forward and pats her shoulder. "Don't you worry, Rosarita. I won't allow the rats to eat you."

"That's comforting."

His hand slips from her shoulder to the top of her arm. "Do not be sad, mi flor. There are many clubs in Mexico. I will still teach you to dance the Salsa."

Rose turns hopeful eyes on him. "You promise?"

He leans closer, murmuring, "Even the shadows could not keep me from it."

I swallow the ache rising in my throat, and distract myself by checking on Murtagh. He hasn't awakened since I rescued him, but his light flickers while he sleeps. I double check his regenerating energy, relieved because I know he'll recover.

A while later, we park in a small pitted lot and emerge from the car. The last streaks of light have disappeared, and stars twinkle to life in the navy sky. The hotel is a charming white building, four stories high, with a red-tiled roof and large iron gate. Latticework balconies dot the upper front, and to our left, an outdoor market—which appears to be winding down for the evening—welcomes visitors and passersby along a redbrick path.

Gabe unloads our suitcases, but keeps hold of mine. He won't even allow me to wheel it to the steps. "Have a nice ride?"

I detect the hint of a sneer in his voice and raise my brow at it. "Yes, it was all right. Victor's a decent travel companion."

"Maybe you'd prefer to have him assigned to you from now on."

Not in the mood to argue, I ignore Gabe's hostility and follow the others. Street lights cast a dull glow on the road, but don't quite reach the concrete stairs that lead to where the sidewalk levels off. Still groggy, I stumble on the uneven ground and barely avoid face-planting on the sidewalk. Gabe drops his suitcase and grabs my elbow. "You okay?"

I wrench out of his grasp, hating that he can yo-yo between caustic and solicitous in the span of two minutes. "Fine."

He gestures for me to lead the way. We've crossed the street and started up the entrance stairs. I'm a step ahead of Gabe, and several behind the others when I can't take it anymore. I round on him, fury flaming high. "What is wrong with you? I can't decide if you're blaming *me* for the demon incident, or if you're mad because I rode in the back with Victor, or if I've committed some other grievous offense."

He waves at Christine, indicating that we'll join them in a minute. "What were you thinking going back in after Murtagh? There is too much at risk for you to be doing stuff like that."

I'm shaking my head as he talks. "I didn't go back for Murtagh. I told you, I went back for the dagger. I couldn't leave it and risk having it fall into the wrong hands. But sure. Fine. Be mad that I saved Murtagh. I'd do it again if given the chance. He may be small, but I love him Gabe. When I thought we had to leave him to die—that was one of the hardest moments of my life. Not that you would understand, but give me a break."

His eyes narrow, and the handle on his suitcase cracks from being squeezed hard. "Understand? I wouldn't understand what? Terror? Helplessness? Like how I felt watching you go into that cave with Eric? Or when we found you unconscious after you'd tried to Heal Kye? What about when the demons had you trapped in that cloud outside Val's cabin and I couldn't get past them? Or that thing at the pyramid when I knew you were in trouble but couldn't find you? You're right, Abby. I couldn't possibly understand what it's like to feel helpless while someone I love is in danger." He stalks away and leaves me standing there, stunned.

Did he just use the "L" word? In reference to me?

My shoulders knot with tension. He's probably referring to friendship love. Or love in a general sense, person to person, because Gabe's good like that. He's the guy who takes care of everyone; I know that of him. He couldn't mean love in a romantic sense. Not he's-in-love-with-me love. Because of Kye. Gabe knows most everything about me and Kye. He knows how we're bound, destined, cursed. He knows I can't love him back.

Having it worked out in my mind, I take a cleansing breath and get my bearings. By the time I meet the others in the lobby, Christine is handing out room keys and assignments. "We have two bungalows. Rose, Abby and I will share one." She darts a glance at Victor and Alejandro, then at Gabe. "I hope the three of you don't mind sharing. There are two bedrooms in each."

"Bueno," Victor says. "That is no problem."

Gabe glowers and says nothing.

Christine's face brightens. "Good. Let's get settled, then we'll find some dinner and call it a night. I've scheduled an early morning meeting with the Council."

I avoid the scorch of Gabe's eyes as we traipse outside and down the path. As soon as Christine opens the door, Gabe sets my suitcase inside, murmurs his goodnights, and leaves.

He'll get over it, I tell myself, because I don't have the energy to consider the alternative.

The bungalow is separated into two bedrooms and a small living area. It's nothing like Christine's house, but charming and quaint. Christine claims the master suite, and Rose and I each claim a bed in the other room.

Rose opens her suitcase, digging out a sweatshirt and some shorts. "You want to tell me about that stunt you pulled back at the house?"

"What stunt? I went inside to get the dagger and the door broke." The breeze from the air conditioner raises goose bumps as I riffle through my hastily packed clothes.

Rose slides the shirt over her head. "You sure? Because it looked an awful lot like you went back for Murtagh. Even though it meant risking all of our lives."

"I may be crazy, but I'm not suicidal." Stung by the accusation, I open my purse and toss the dagger on her bed. "Saving Murtagh was an added benefit."

She brushes her hair and secures it with an elastic. "I'm not saying I would blame you if you had—I love the guy too—but don't you ever put me in that situation. Because when it comes to deciding who gets to live or die at any given time, I will always choose me getting to live. *Comprende?*"

"Yes." I do get it. Rose, in her not-so-gentle way, is warning me about her boundaries—and that I've come awfully close to overstepping them. But I'm not sorry. I have the dagger, Murtagh is safe, and so are the rest of my friends. For now.

I open my purse and scoop up my still-sleeping sprite, worried because it's been hours and he still hasn't stirred. He blinks purple, then blue when I touch him. I sigh, once again relieved. As long as that light works, he'll be fine.

Christine knocks on the doorframe as I lay Murtagh on my pillow. I glance up, expecting to get a lecture from her as well, but instead, she comes to stroke his downy head, looking concerned. "How is he?"

"Okay, I think. He hasn't moved much, but he glows."

"Poor guy's exhausted." She runs a gentle finger over Murtagh's iridescent wings. "It's a miracle someone so small survived such a huge adversary. He's a fighter."

Rose drops onto her bed. "Out of curiosity, what is the average life expectancy for a sprite?"

"Depends on the sprite." Christine pockets her room key and gestures for us to follow her outside. "Murtagh is at least five hundred."

Her statement shocks me. "Years? Are you serious?"

"No way." Rose closes the door behind us and we start down the path. "He's like a kid. He can't be five centuries old."

"Of course I'm serious," Christine says. "You've never asked him?"

My mind reels. I've seen a sprite in my visions. Specifically the ones involving Isleen. Could Murtagh be that very same sprite? Why hasn't he told me?

We're soon joined by Alejandro and Victor, who tells us, "Señor Gabe will not be joining us. He had some business to take care of, and has entrusted you to our care."

Guilt sinks like a rock. Was Gabe serious when he threatened to get reassigned? "What kind of business?"

Victor tilts his head, eyebrow raised. "The private kind. But not to worry. You'll be safe with us."

I hesitate, my gaze swinging between the main building of the hotel and Gabe's bungalow. Going to dinner without Gabe makes me insecure and shaky.

"Earth to Abby." Rose waves a hand in front of my face. "Are you coming? I'm starving."

"Yes." I blink and turn away from Gabe's door, strangely hollow.

We meet the Mexican Dragon Council in a conference room in the main building. I expect them to dress in cloaks like the Yellowstone Dragons, but this group is more casual. They wear street clothes, and their only binding similarity is a leather wristband burned with symbols. Each band is slightly different from the others, but all the Dragons wear them, including Gabe.

He still hasn't said so much as good morning to me.

We're seated around a large table while Enrique, the head of the Council, addresses us. In Spanish.

He brings out an apparatus that looks like a mini-tennis racket made of copper, which apparently expels energy—I think. Anyway, the Dragons act super excited to try out their new toy, which prompts Gabe to show off his jade circle, which creates more enthusiasm, and results in a discussion about how to make more of each. Then Enrique moves onto another subject.

I discern all this by reading body language and hand gestures, because I don't understand a single word of what Enrique says. Gabe does—not that he's in any mood to translate—and Christine, too. Rose and I shrug it off, knowing Christine will highlight the important points later, but still feeling utterly useless. I'm contemplating sneaking out and going to the pool when all eyes focus on me, and Enrique switches to broken English. Unfortunately, his thick accent makes him difficult to understand, so Gabe says, "He wants to know if you can swim."

"Swim?" *What the what?* "Not competitively, but I can keep my head above water."

Gabe translates my words for them, and then translates the response for me and Rose. "It doesn't sound like keeping your head above water is the point. Have you ever done any snorkeling or scuba diving?"

An annoyed crease forms between Rose's eyes. "Yes. Abby and I scuba dive in Jackson regularly. Our favorite place is Yellowstone, in a beautiful pool of acid."

Gabe ignores Rose. "Abby?"

I shake my head. "Not unless you count sticking a piece of plastic in my mouth and diving to the bottom of a public pool. Thirty seconds, tops."

After the message is relayed, Enrique confers with Alejandro, who winks at Rose.

"If you're talking about me," Rose interrupts, "you better translate word for word."

"Yes, Rose," Gabe says, disgusted. "They're talking about you, because you are the center of the whole meeting."

"Shut it, Gabe. Must be nice to understand what's being said. And it would be oh-so-much-nicer to have someone translate certain details so that the *most important* people—Abby and me—aren't left completely in the dark."

"Abby will know everything she needs to know. I'll tell her."

"But I'm just chopped liver, right? Here for moral support, and to risk my life for the benefit of others. Yeah. Thanks. Makes me feel fan-freaking-tastic."

"Shut up," I hiss, tired of their constant bickering. "Shut up. Both of you, knock it off. I have enough stress without being sandwiched in your sexual tension. Why don't you just hook up and get it over with?"

Rose bursts out laughing. "Are you kidding?"

Gabe's face turns the same shade of pink as the purse I once made him carry. "Is that what you think this is?"

"Isn't it? You two fight worse than toddlers."

He clears his throat, moving close so he can respond to just me. "I admit, Rose and I have tension, but it's of a completely different variety. Promise."

"I second Gabe." Rose wags a finger between the two of them. "Whatever *this* is, it's not *that*."

"Definitely not." Gabe's expression softens, and the warmth returns to his eyes for the first time since yesterday. "No offense, Rose."

"None taken," she says, her eyes on Alejandro. "I can tolerate you here and there, Dragon boy, but you're really not my type."

Enrique redirects the conversation by clearing his throat. "Señor Gabe."

The conversation resumes, ping-ponging around the room, while Rose and I lean back in our chairs, making faces and silly gestures at each other now that the tension has lightened. Every so often someone translates questions and answers, and after a while, a map is spread on the table. Gabe takes my hand, tugging until I'm standing next to him to look at it. He keeps holding on, and for some reason, I don't pull my hand away.

Enrique jabs the map. "The tomb must be here. It is the only explanation."

"It makes sense," Christine agrees. "No one would look there, and it explains why we haven't been able to find it on the surface."

Gabe's frown deepens, his fingers tightening on mine. "No. That can't be right. Absolutely not."

Rose scrunches her nose, tilting her head at the map. "That looks like water."

And then the map makes sense. Pyramids. Ruins. Sinkholes. They're focused on the sinkhole—the cenote we saw the first day. "No way." A shiver rattles me as I stare at the map. "I am not searching for that tomb underwater."

TWENTY-EIGHT

Devastations

Voices escalate as everyone tries to speak at once, and my mind reels, spiraling into a headache that leaves my legs quivering. Gabe squeezes my hand, the muscles in his neck tight.

I get the feeling that the Council is hell-bent on sending me into this cenote, which currently seems like a fancy word for death trap. Dizziness drops me into a chair, eyes closed, as I fight burning, bubbling nausea similar to what I felt yesterday before we left for the ruins. This sick thing is getting old. More than being old, it's bizarre. Kye's not here, but the last few days I've felt as bad as I ever did in Jackson. Worse even, because I now have new symptoms. It's possible I've picked up a virus or parasite; but whatever it is leaves me with one priority. I've *got* to get out of this room.

A few Spanish words—Gabe's voice—and then Christine presses a hand to my forehead, murmuring. "Let's get you some air."

I want to answer, but am afraid that if I open my mouth, everything I've eaten for breakfast will reappear. *Not the impression I'm going for.* I press my lips together and breathe through my nose.

"Abby?" Rose says, sounding concerned. "You okay?"

Another breath.

In, out.

In, out.

Do not lose it now.

Black clouds boil overhead, crashing with light and sound as the mob gathers at the edge. I clutch the baby to my chest, a sob building in my throat.

It might be my last act, but I will not submit.

I glance across the distance to Liam, offering silent forgiveness, and pleading for him to protect my infant who is about to become an orphan. The midwife rips her from my arms and fades into the crowd as Tynan approaches, grasping a long silver weapon. I long to turn around, kiss my daughter, offer last words of love, but that will only draw attention to her as she is whisked into hiding. The crowd falls silent as the demon king raises his sword and thunder crashes above.

"Behold, the witch who has caused your crops to fail. Who has turned the weather against you, and brought plagues upon your houses!" At Tynan's words, the crowd roars again. "Tonight, we end our suffering by offering this woman—a former queen—as a sacrifice to the gods. If there be anyone here who objects to this punishment, let him speak now."

Liam steps forward.

Horror. Sheer horror. He cannot take my place. It won't save me. It won't solve anything. I catch his eye, shaking my head viciously, refusing to allow it, begging that he remain silent. Tynan doesn't need a reason to kill him too. Liam speaks anyway. "The queen, the Healer, is not a witch. It is your own sins, your iniquities that bring plagues and famine upon you! Only the Healer can right the world, and you would sacrifice her? You would throw her in a hole to drown?"

Tynan barely acknowledges Liam's brave words. He flicks his wrist, and two huge guards, fully armed with shiny weapons, take Liam down, binding his hands and feet. He struggles, but is no match for the demons as they toss him over the edge. "Raina!" Liam screams, his eyes wide with regret. "I'm sorry." And then he's falling, deep, deeper into the hole, until he slides under the water, leaving me with only the echo of his splash.

Movement draws me back to the present. Gabe helps me stand, supporting me against his warm chest. "She's fine," he tells Enrique. Then something else in the man's native tongue. The

Dragons must be satisfied, because Rose is the only person to follow us outside.

The sun is high and bright, breaking past clouds, reaching around buildings. It sneaks through vivid green vines, bathing flowers of lemon, blush, and ruby and landing softly on my cheeks. For the first time in hours, I'm warm enough.

"How bad was it?" Rose asks, referring to my vision. "Are you okay?"

"I'll live." Mortified, I press my face into Gabe's shirt, never so grateful to have him around as I am in this moment. "Thanks for rescuing me from certain humiliation."

He shifts so my head falls on his shoulder, and I leave it, surprised by the amount of comfort I find in the casual contact. "Thank you for giving me an excuse to leave," he says. "For the record, I disagree with them. I don't care where they think the tomb is, there is no way in hell I'm letting them dump you in that creepy sinkhole. Zane would never go for it, and Val would strip me of my leather. If the Mexican Council is certain the tomb is down there, they can find it themselves. I'll take you home before I'll let them send you."

Rose runs a hand along the iron fence surrounding the pool. "I hate to point out the obvious, because I don't like the idea either, but isn't that why we're here? Because they *can't* do it themselves?"

"No one can do what they're suggesting," Gabe says. "It's a suicide mission, and Abby's having a hard enough time as it is. She's still sick, and there are other things at stake. Things they haven't considered."

"What things?" Rose fishes a room key out of her pocket and opens our door.

"Abby's life, for one. The most important reason she's here is to keep her alive. I don't think Zane or Val or … Kye, would have sent her here knowing that the people she was coming to help are planning to sacrifice her."

He leans over, helping me settle on the sofa in our sitting area, and I wrap an arm around his neck in an awkward hug. "Thanks."

"It's nice that we can finally agree on something." Rose snatches the ice bucket. "I'm going to find some bottled water. Abby needs to stay hydrated."

"You don't have to ..." I start.

Rose glances at me on her way out, her smile fading. "Abby, you're green. Yesterday you had a mild heat stroke from dehydration. Now, I'm not a Healer, but I'm pretty sure the best cure for dehydration is water."

Once Rose leaves, Gabe urges me to lie back as he tucks a woven blanket around me.

"I'm sorry about yesterday," I tell him. "I know you care about me. Just like you care about Christine, and Rose, and your job. Even Murtagh. It wasn't fair for me to insinuate otherwise. You were trying to protect me, like you always do. I'm sorry I've made it hard for you to be here. It's not intentional. I've been taking out my issues on you, and that's wrong. I know none of this is your fault, and I'm just ... sorry."

Gabe doesn't respond, so I open my eyes, hoping that the dizziness will pass. He's standing there looking like I've punched him. *What did I do now?*

When he sees that my eyes are open, he sits on the floor near my head, bracing his arms on his knees. "I'm sorry, too. I haven't been easy to be around either, but I'm working on it, I promise."

I want to ask him why. *Why are you so moody? And miserable? And angry at me over stupid things?* But after yesterday, I'm afraid of his answer. Because now that he's said the words, I can't get them out of my head. And it leaves me questioning his motivation for ... everything. Everything he's done, and why he's here, and how far he plans to go to keep me safe. If I ask, and his answer is anywhere near the answer he gave yesterday, I won't know how to react. What to say. How to soothe him and still remind him that I can never be his. Not really. Because I belong to Kye.

Even if he doesn't belong to me.

Maybe things have changed. Maybe Gabe knows. Maybe he's frustrated because he's waiting for me to let go and start moving forward. But even if all those things are true, there's something else, too. Something Gabe's not saying. And I don't think it has anything to do with how he feels—or doesn't.

Whatever that thing is, it's honestly, truly bothering him. But I know Gabe, and he won't let it out until he's ready.

"I'm glad you're here," I say, stroking his hair as my eyes fall closed again.

He leans forward, resting his forehead against my shoulder. "Me too."

Christine and the Dragons decide that before we can even consider planning dangerous things, we'll need more training. They send others to scout the remaining ruins, inspect them thoroughly, and make sure that we're not heading in the wrong direction with our search.

No use taking risks unless they're necessary.

Some of the Dragons have opportunities to test different prototype Energy Wands—which are a hybrid of the original copper thing and Gabe's jade circle. They return excited and bursting with feedback and ideas for improvements, and then scurry away for more training with their new toys.

On our third day at the hotel, Gabe watches from the side of the pool as Rose and I have our first scuba lesson. When the instructor brings out the heavy air tanks and shoves one into my arms, Gabe lunges forward like he doesn't think I should pick it up, but the instructor cuts him off. "If she cannot carry and control her tank, she shouldn't be using one."

So Gabe steps aside as I strap the thing on. "See? I'm not a complete wimp."

"I never thought you were." He takes residence in a lounge chair, watching from a distance.

The instructor goes through the basics, starting with equipment, drilling us over and over again on which valve does what, and where is the regulator, and when should we consider doing something drastic, such as buddy breathing.

Most of the Dragons are wise enough to keep their distance with Gabe around. He spends the afternoon with his nose in a sci-fi novel, and when we're finished, meets Rose and me at the edge.

"Hey, Rosarita," Alejandro jogs up, tugging on Rose's towel. "Good news. Tonight ... we Salsa."

"Really?" Rose lets her towel slip to the ground, throwing her arms around Alejandro and pressing her wet body against him. "Where?"

Alejandro picks her up and twirls her around. "We can stay here at the resort and dance at tourist fiesta. Or ..."

Rose bats her eyes, excitement pouring off her. "Or?"

"Or we could join some of the locals at a club." His eyes flicker to Gabe, then me. "It is only a few miles away, and we're all invited."

"We're in. We're so in." Rose lets go of Alejandro, clasping my forearms. "You can handle some dancing, right? You're okay today?"

"I'm good today." After all these weeks of working to find the tomb, I wouldn't turn down a party, even if I was dying. "I'd love to learn to Salsa." I risk a glance at Gabe, and am surprised to find him smiling. "You wanna?"

Something akin to pleasure lights his eyes. "Are you inviting *me*, or just looking for a bodyguard?"

I squeeze the last of the water from my hair and send him an impish grin. "If a bodyguard was all I needed, I'm sure Victor or Alejandro could handle the task." He hands me my sarong, gripping the sheer fabric longer than necessary. "Come Salsa with me," I beg. "Drink tequila, blow off steam."

"I don't dance," he murmurs. "But I'll come because you want me to."

Nothing has changed. I'm still in love with Kye, still more confused than I've ever been in my life, but Gabe's words—the look in his eyes when he leaves me at my bungalow—touches one of the deep down cold places I've been protecting and fills it with warmth.

When I open the bungalow door, my phone is buzzing. I hurry, but can't get to it before it stops. Afraid to know, I flip it open. For the first time since I left Jackson, I have seven missed calls and four messages. All from Kye.

Twin waves of dread and relief break, swirling around me until, dizzy, I slide into a puddle on the floor, phone clutched to my chest. It's been two months, and in that time, Kye hasn't communicated with me once. I don't know anything that's happened in his life since I left. I don't know if I'm still important to him, or if he loves me, or if he's still sick. All those uncertainties terrify me.

If he's sick—getting worse—I'll do whatever it takes to get home to him as quickly as possible. If he's well ... I'm not sure I can handle a long-distance break up. But I need to hear his voice. Need it like water.

"Abby?" Rose comes out of the bathroom, looking concerned. "What is it? What's wrong?"

"Kye called. Seven times."

She grins, as if she has no doubts at all. "That's my cousin. Zero patience."

I blink rapidly, trying to gather the courage to listen to the messages. "But why now?"

"Bet he misses you." Rose dumps her makeup bag on the bed.

I shake my head, feeling like I'm stuck to the floor. "We haven't talked since I left, and Akers said he ..." Just the thought sends a knife of pain into my chest.

She freezes with a tube of mascara in one hand and a compact in the other. "You're kidding? I thought you talked all the time? For hours."

She isn't helping my nerves. "No. Not even close."

Understanding dawning, she sets her makeup aside and sits next to me on the floor. "Why?"

"I don't know. At first, I called several times a day, left messages, but he never answered, and never called me back. So."

The sound she makes is a cross between a growl and a whimper. It's the I-can't-believe-how-stupid-my-cousin-is noise I've heard her make before. "No wonder you're such a mess. I'm going to murder that guy." She brushes a strand of hair away from my eye. "What did the messages say? Does he at least have a good excuse?"

"I don't know," I whisper. "I'm afraid to listen. Don't think I can take ... bad news. Right now." My chest is heavy, like my lungs are filling with water, so I sit up, my fingers still clamped around the phone.

Rose's hands on my shoulders keep me steady. "You won't be able to concentrate on anything else until you do."

Knowing she's right, I dial my voicemail with trembling fingers.

Message one:
"Abby, where are you? I—we need to talk. Call me." He sounds worried.

Message two:
Growling noise of frustration. "Abby, please. It's important. I need—just call me back. Please." A string of curses follows before the message cuts off.

Message three (a horrible connection; only some of his words come through):
Sounding distracted, but resigned. "I—we—I can't do this anymore. I just ... I can't. I'm sorry."

Rose is saying something, but my ears feel stuffed with cotton. I don't even want to listen to message four, but I try anyway. It's nothing but a jumbled screech of sound, and cuts off after only eleven seconds. The phone slides out of my hand and clatters onto the tile floor, but I don't hear that either. Numb, I stand, my movements slow and automatic. I perch on the edge of the bathtub, waiting for the sick to come. But it doesn't. Not this time.

My stomach—which has been tender and unpredictable all week—doesn't clench or bubble. Blades of agony don't pierce my chest, and my eyes don't flood with tears or burn with anger. I'm floating outside my body; the Abby of before has ceased to exist. From where I sit, I can see my reflection in the mirror. Something's different. My aura is now overcast with a layer of muddiness. An energy blockage.

Well good. I'm okay with being numb for a while.

Rose knocks on the door. "Abby? Can I come in? Got a surprise for you." I don't answer, but that's never stopped Rose before. She enters. "We're going to that club tonight. You need it more than ever. I'll help you get ready."

She's right. My fingers grip the edge of the tub. I know I should respond, say something, but I can't. Rose pries one of my hands free and wraps my fingers around a tiny glass. "Drink this in one swallow. I know it's nasty, but it'll help, I promise."

I do as she says, barely tasting the bitter liquid as it burns down my throat. Then I sit, waiting.

For something.

For anything.

For nothing.

TWENTY-NINE

All the Drinking

"**Y**ou sure you're okay?" Gabe asks again.

"Yep, I'm great." I stumble over my feet, falsely happy, wondering what maniac stapled four-inch heels to my favorite sandals. Alejandro waits at the club entrance, allowing us to skip the line, and the bouncers wave us through like VIPs. The fast-paced live music is heavy on the bass and shakes the windows and the glasses on the bar, the tables, chairs, and wood floor. Even the people. I clutch Gabe's hand for balance as we thread to our reserved table.

Gabe shoots another concerned glance at me.

"Don't you dare say I don't look so good, because I haven't made this much effort to get ready since we left Jackson." It took a few minutes, but Rose's drink—which turned out to be tequila—loosened the tightness in my chest enough so I could breathe. After a shower and a second shot, the sting of Kye's messages dulled until the black devastation lightened to gray. With Rose's help, I managed to get dressed. And she is a genius with makeup. Again.

As everyone crams into the booth, Gabe maneuvers me so I'm between him and the table. "You look more than good. You're stunning."

"That's better."

"Go ahead." He gestures at the teeny-tiny amount of space left on the semi-circular bench. The others are packed so close together,

Rose is practically in Alejandro's lap. There's definitely not enough room for me and Gabe. But sitting = thinking, and thinking = remembering.

I don't feel like sitting.

I grab Gabe's hand. "Rose, order me something. We're going to dance."

Gabe's eyebrows shoot up, but for perhaps the first time since I've met him, he lets me give the orders, and follows me onto the dance floor. The music has a distinct Spanish vibe, and the singer manages to infuse enough passion into her voice that I feel the meaning without understanding the words. Under her spell, I let go of everything else and just dance. Eventually, Alejandro and Rose join us, and Alejandro attempts to teach us how to "dance like a Mexican." We all fail, miserably.

Victor works the room, dancing with a different girl for every song, until he taps Gabe's shoulder. "May I?"

Gabe hesitates, but then drops his hands from my hips (we've been practicing our hip-shaking Salsa). "Sure." He heads for our booth. "I need a drink anyway."

Not to criticize Gabe, but Victor can dance. *Dance*, dance. And with his help, I can too. We whirl and twirl around the club until I'm is sticky with sweat and my throat burns with thirst. Laughing, I head back to the table. Gabe's the only one sitting, but rather than have a seat across from him, I perch on his lap and grab the closest drink.

He reaches around and takes the glass from my hand. "You don't want to drink that one." Carefully, he shifts me off his lap so I'm sitting next to him.

"Why not?" I take back the drink and lick flecks of salt off the rim as I fill my mouth with the tart liquid.

He takes it back again, looking both concerned and confused. "Abby, I mean it. That's a margarita. It has tequila in it."

"So?" Giving up on that glass, I reach across the table for another. "We're in Mexico, Gabe. They're not going to arrest me for being underage. I've never been drunk in my life, and today, I deserve to get smashed."

His expression reminds me of the time my mom accidentally swallowed a fly. "You being underage has nothing to do with it. It's not good for you."

Finishing off the contents of the second glass, I nod. "Yes it is. It's delicious and makes me feel better. Don't you want me to be happy?"

Gabe grabs my wrists before I get my hands on another drink—there are five more, and I want to try them all. "If you're not going to take care of yourself, you should at least consider your ... the ..." He makes a vague gesture that I couldn't understand if I tried.

"I don't know what your sign language is supposed to mean. Just say it, Gabe. Say it. I'm a terrible person because I'm seventeen-years-old and just had my heart shattered and I want nothing more than to get absolutely sloshed and forget everything about my life. Okay?"

His grip loosens, but he doesn't let go, so I dislodge one hand and snag another drink. Gabe takes it before I taste it.

I'm on the verge of hitting him. "Lay off! I'm thirsty, and we're not allowed to drink water that's not bottled, remember?"

"I'll get you a water bottle. What do you mean you just had your heart shattered?"

I shake my head, not wanting to explain. "Let go and let me get a drink, before I slap you."

He watches, frowning, as I guzzle a second margarita—this one strawberry. Warmth slides into my belly. My fingers and toes tingle with numbness, but I want to dance again. "Okay, that's enough." Gabe slams his hand on the table. "You're going to do some serious damage. Please let me get you a water bottle."

"Why are you so worried? It's not like I haven't thrown up on you before."

"I've never seen you be so selfish. Your child could be born with a serious birth defect."

What is he talking about? A hysterical giggle bubbles out of my mouth. "I think you've had a few too many drinks. Or maybe I have. You're not making sense." When the strawberry drink is gone, I grab Gabe's hand. "Let's dance."

He comes without complaint. As we find a spot on the dance floor, the song changes to a slow tempo. Gabe holds me in his arms. "You're going to be the death of me, you know."

I close my eyes, pressing my cheek to his chest, because Gabe is solid and steady, the only thing in the club—the only part of my life—that isn't twisting in wild, crazy circles. "No I'm not. I'm going to be the death of *me.*"

"That doesn't even make sense."

"Aren't you glad you're not the only one who's drunk?"

"I'm not drunk," he says, defensive.

"I think I am. Getting there anyway." I twine my arms around his shoulders, my cheek still pressed against him.

He brushes a hand over my bare neck, tugging at a few loose tendrils. "You want me to take you home so you can sleep it off?"

"No. I want to stay here and dance. This is nice. We should go dancing every day."

He hitches me higher in his grip so my feet barely touch the floor. "I wish we could, but I'm thinking tonight's going to have to hold you for the next seven months or so."

It takes some blinking and squinting before I can actually focus enough to look him in the eye. "Why seven months?"

He squeezes his eyes shut, then opens them again. There's a load of guilt there. "It's bad enough that I allowed this tonight. Selfish, really, because I wanted to dance with you. But Abby, it's completely irresponsible for me to allow a pregnant woman to get drunk, no matter how miserable you are. The baby you're carrying is as much a part of my job as you."

Blinking, I shove him away. "What baby? Who do you think is pregnant?"

He scrubs a hand over his face. "Look, it's okay. I know you haven't told anyone, but you can't hide it forever, so you might as well face it, let us help you."

There are no words. I don't even know how to respond. Dancers move around us, bumping into me and tripping over my feet as I stand rooted to the floor. *What? What the what?*

He's going into protector mode, waiting for me to break down. Because I'm so delightfully buzzed, I burst out laughing. I have no idea where he got this idea, but I'm sure I'm about to find out. He grabs my hand and yanks me toward the door. Intrigued, I follow, shouting to Victor that we're going out for some air. I wobble to the car, my heels making it extra difficult to walk. Gabe whirls to face me, his cheeks pink—in anger or embarrassment, I'm not sure. "Are you ready to tell me the truth?"

I blink, giggling again. "Gabe, what makes you think I'm pregnant?"

"I'm not stupid, Abby, okay?" he says, and I decide the pink in his cheeks is definitely an embarrassed blush. "It doesn't take a rocket scientist to recognize the classic symptoms. You suffer from random bouts of nausea, which are especially bad in the mornings. You pass out when you overwork. You cry a lot. You're moody ... shall I go on?"

"If you tell me I have a pudgy belly, I'll have to punch you. Hard."

"You don't. But some women don't show until four or five months."

The cool evening air goes a long way to clearing my head, but it's still foggy, so I press a hand to my temple. "I'm not pregnant, Gabe."

He opens his arms like he wants to hug me. "Sweetheart, you're in denial. But it's okay. Maybe you didn't realize it until now. I should take you to Christine, have her get you one of those stick test things."

He tries to hug me again, but I swat his arms away. "Gabe. Listen to me. I. Am. Not. Pregnant. This is an absolute fact. Nothing to do with denial."

One of his hands rests on my shoulder, but I shake it off, annoyed.

"You have to know it's a possibility," he says. "It's what happened with Theron and Raina. You and Kye ..." he clears his throat, and I can see that this is the part he finds embarrassing. "I know you've been together. I saw him stay with you. The night before we left, I was guarding your house, and saw him go in through your window and stay. For hours. Abby, I saw."

That was our last goodbye, and probably the most painful experience of my life—until today. Gabe has no right to assume, he had no right to see, no right to think about what was happening in my room while he was outside. The fact that he has done all three makes me feel stripped bare, violated. Wrapping my arms around myself, I turn away from Gabe's accusing eyes. "That night is none of your business. But I assure you—it's physically impossible that I could be pregnant. Kye and I didn't ... haven't. Ever. End of story. So you can stop worrying about me drinking, or carrying heavy objects, or taking care of myself." I start back, needing to use the restroom, and then drink enough margaritas to make me pass out and forget this entire day.

"But ... you didn't? You aren't?"

"No." The music from the club gets louder as I approach the door, and once again, the bouncer steps aside. *Pregnant teen, coming through. Not.* I find Rose looking flushed and giddy and wrapped around Alejandro like clothes. When I wave her over, she extracts herself from him and follows me to the restroom.

"What's up?" She sets to work fixing her hair in the filthy mirror while I close myself in a grungy stall. "Is this a great night, or what?"

"Or what. Have you seen Victor? I want to dance and need a new partner."

"Did you and the fire-breather have a fight? You looked cozy for a while there."

197

I meet her at the sink, scrubbing my hands under the lukewarm water. "He accused me of being pregnant."

Rose's mouth drops open. "Is he right?"

I want to scream. "No! If that were even a possibility, you'd have known a long time ago."

She sighs, relieved. "Hope so. But I had to make sure I wasn't missing a huge item on the list of reasons I'm going to murder Kye."

Leaning my forehead on her shoulder, I press my fingers against my eyes. "It can't be over. I miss him. So much."

She pats my head, awkwardly, both of us knowing there's nothing she can say to make anything better. "You need another drink. Did you try the Mojito yet?"

After another hour of dancing with Victor and some of the other Dragons, and having stopped at the table to quench my thirst between songs, exhaustion—and alcohol—catches up with me. I collapse into our booth, resting my head on the table, eyes closed. I can actually feel Earth's constant motion.

Gabe is still here, but I've done my best to ignore his presence. Looking at him fills me with ire. All this time, he's believed I'm pregnant. *That's why he's been so angry.*

The whole conversation brings me back to wondering if that's the way this was supposed to go with me and Kye—the same way it went with Theron and Raina. Recent visions have made me wonder, and Gabe's accusation only adds to that doubt. But Kye and I consciously made the decision to do things differently, and now it's too late. Kye's moving on.

I wish I could too.

"You ready to go yet?" Gabe's voice is soft, close to my ear.

Wanting to nod, but afraid to move, I murmur, "Yes."

"You going to be sick first?"

"Probably."

"Should I gather the gang now, or wait?"

I moan. "I don't care, just let me pass out."

He brushes strands of hair off my cheeks and out of my eyes. "You're *so* going to regret this tomorrow."

"No more than everything else I've done wrong lately."

"You haven't done anything wrong. It's me who screwed up, and I'm so sorry for accusing you of that. For thinking it. I should've known better."

I hear footsteps approaching. My voice shakes, cracks, when I tell him, "I wish you were right." But I don't think Gabe hears me. When everyone is ready to go, I stand, forcing myself steady so Gabe won't try to come to my rescue as he always does. But I lean on Rose. The ground is so wobbly.

Back at the resort, Alejandro invites Rose to walk in the gardens, and she accepts with a hasty goodnight to the rest of us. Victor kisses my knuckles, thanking me for a good time dancing, then enters the hotel bar with the other Dragons, leaving me alone with Gabe. He tries to take my elbow, steady me, but I shake him off. "Stop. Stop it. I don't need you to help me walk, okay? I'm not the frail pregnant teen you think I am."

"How many times will I have to apologize? If you saw it from my point of view, you'd admit there appeared to be concrete evidence."

My brain chugs along, trying to process his words, his argument, but I'm still so blessedly numb, I can't make any sense of them. "Okay."

He pauses near the pool. "That was too easy. Are you going to remember this tomorrow?"

"Probably. I'm a bit toasty, not blathering with idiocy."

"Well, good." He follows me to the patio outside our door and leans against the wall. "Despite our—uh, misunderstanding—I had a good time tonight. Enjoyed seeing this new side of you."

I lean against the door jamb for stability, grateful that at least the building isn't swaying. "That's me, the whole new Abby. Single.

Boyfriend free. Ready to jump in a sinkhole and kick some demon ass, since I no longer care if I die."

Breath explodes from his mouth. "He broke up with you? When?"

I close my eyes, not wanting to think about it, but unable to think about anything else. "This afternoon. Via voicemail."

"No wonder." He inches along the wall, closer to me. "You've never been drunk before, have you?"

"I have." Not. "Okay, not drunk, per se, but I can tell you I will never be a beer drinker. However, I've decided I really like tequila when it's mixed in a margarita. Shots work faster, but leave a nasty aftertaste."

"When did you do a shot?" His forehead wrinkles with incredulity. "I didn't see a shot glass on the table."

"Before we left. Rose brought me two." I hold up some fingers, and narrowly avoid poking him in the eye. "She didn't want to leave an Abby puddle on the floor of the villa while she went dancing. Helped though. A lot. Nasty as they were."

He scrubs his hands over his face. "What am I going to do with you? I get that your heart is broken, but there are so many other ways to deal with it."

I blink, noticing the softness in his gray eyes, and the pliable lines of his pale, pink lips. He's closer now, much closer than he was a second ago. I wonder what it would be like to kiss him, to sink into his embrace the way I did with Kye that first time—the time when we learned we'd each found the person who could make us whole. I wonder if kissing Gabe might take away the sting of loss, or at least help me temporarily forget in a way alcohol never will.

When his gaze drifts to my mouth, I know he's wondering too, and before I can question my reasoning, I grab the back of his neck and crush him against me in a fierce clash of lips and tongues and wandering hands. He hauls me up so I'm standing on my toes, his heart racing against mine. Blood runs hot in my veins, plunging into places I thought would never again have a pulse, and bringing alive thoughts I've reserved only for Kye.

As if he can read my mind, Gabe softens his kiss, disentangling my arms from his neck, and shoves me away. "Sorry. That was out of line."

"I kissed you first."

"I know. Dammit, I know. But you're drunk, and depressed, and not in a good frame of mind to be starting something like this. And if I don't do it now, I won't have the strength to tell you no—regardless of circumstances."

"But ..." My already foggy brain fills with murky confusion. All I can think is how long it's been since I was kissed like that.

Gabe drops a last peck on my lips, soft and warm. "We'll talk about this in the morning. When you're sober." He walks away, with a murmured, "Goodnight, Abby."

I bang the back of my head on the door as Gabe disappears into the shadows. The ensuing pain is just punishment. What am I doing? Like my life isn't complicated enough.

Wobbling precariously, I unzip my shoulder bag to search for my room key, and am startled when the door swings open. "Abby."

My heart leaps into my throat, and the fuzziness in my brain congeals as familiar arms wrap around me and urge me inside, allowing the door to slam behind us.

"Kye?"

And then his lips crush mine in a surge of heat, longing, possession—effectively overwhelming everything else inside me until the tilt-a-whirl I've been calling my life for the last two months finally rights.

In this moment, nothing else matters, except that Kye is here, and I'm finally back in his arms.

THIRTY

Second Chances

"**I** thought I heard your voice out there," Kye murmurs against my lips. "Where's Rose?"

We're positioned halfway between the sofa and the bedroom, and I suspect he's trying to make a decision between them. "Went for a walk. I don't know where Christine is, though. Haven't seen her since this morning."

"She's asleep." Decision made, he draws me to the bedroom.

"Rose will be back soon," I warn, unresisting.

"I know. We'll have to hurry."

I pause, separating from him to see his face. "Hurry and what?"

His answering smile is amused. "Not. That. I mean, I want to. I definitely want to. But not with my parents in the next room, and my cousin in the next bed." He takes my hands, tugging me further in. "When we finally make love, there will be nothing rushed about it. But I'm supposed to be sleeping on the couch, and I'd really rather not. I haven't seen you for months, and I've spent the last few days so worried about you I couldn't eat. I'm jet-lagged, my brain's exhausted from an information dump—courtesy of my mom—and every muscle on me aches with fatigue. I just need to hold you for a while, okay? I'll stay on top of the covers, keep it legit."

I'm so confused. He acts like we're still together—like today never happened. When my only response is to stare at the floor, he moves closer, tipping my chin up with his finger. "Abby?" He sniffs, only now catching a hint that something isn't right. "Have you been drinking?"

"I thought—your messages this afternoon. You said you were done. You ... you broke up with me." Saying the words, seeing his face crumple in confusion, brings the anguish back in waves. "The first time I've heard from you since I left, and you said you couldn't do this anymore."

His mouth falls open as I separate from him, shaking my head in confusion. "Abby, I couldn't call you before. There's a reason. A good one. But it's a long story and I'd really rather not get into it tonight." He approaches me now the way he would an injured animal. "And then today," he glances at his watch. "Well, I guess yesterday, I called to tell you I was sick of doing what everyone else says, and that I missed you, and I'd rather die a horrible death than live another day apart from you. Screw the curse." He takes my hands and brings them to his lips. "I called to tell you I was on my way."

Tears sparkle in my eyes. "Why didn't you just say that?"

"I did. Did you even listen to my messages?"

I nod—then shake my head, unsure. There might have been one more that didn't come through? "I don't remember. I think so." His fingers caress my jaw, and this is so familiar, so utterly right, that I lean my cheek into his palm. "I thought it was over between us. I thought you didn't love me anymore." A tear falls, burning a trail down my cheek as he envelops me in his embrace. Everything I bottled up earlier breaks free, and Kye cradles me while I sob.

"Shh. I'm sorry. I'm so sorry, babe. I never meant for you to feel that way. Couldn't do that to you."

I hiccup again as drunken nausea hits and a dull burn coats my throat. Covering my mouth, I pull out of his arms. "Oh no."

He raises an eyebrow. "You okay?"

Unable to answer, I bolt to the bathroom and grip the sides of the toilet, waiting. *Why? Why did I have to choose tonight—of all nights—to come home drunk and disorderly?*

"Babe?" Kye sweeps my hair back, holding it out of the way. "What did you drink and how much?"

"Whatever I could find, and a lot. Mostly tequila. I think."

"Are you numb anywhere?"

"My toes." I wiggle my hands, lifting my heavy head cautiously. "And my fingers." I sneeze. "Maybe my nose." The nausea seems to have passed, so I grasp the edge of the counter and close my eyes, hoping that will steady me. Worst. Idea. Ever.

As I lean over the toilet again, Kye's there again, wrapping his arms around my waist and turning me into his chest. He picks me up off the ground, chuckling. "Okay, time for bed. You'll feel better lying down."

"I need to brush my teeth."

"Give your stomach time to settle first," he says.

My arms wind around his neck, and my head rests on his shoulder as he carries me to my bed. When he tries to let go, I tighten my grip, bringing him down with me. "Please don't leave me again. I can't do it anymore either."

"Never." He kisses the tip of my nose. "Ever, ever, ever."

While I'm looking into Kye's face, everything about the world becomes clearer, sharper, brighter. And I admit that I'll always love him, regardless of our past—or future—lives. "Stay here tonight. I don't want you to let go of me until morning. Maybe not even then."

He nods, running his knuckles over my jaw. "Okay. We'll make sure the light's off before Rose comes in. I hope she's nice enough to not turn it on." He sits up. "But first I've got to brush my teeth and change out of these clothes. I traveled nineteen hours to get to you, and now that I'm here, and you're here, and we're together, I just want to crash."

I trail my fingers over his forearm, wondering how long I'll have to be still before I can stand up. "I should probably change out of my dress, take the pins out of my hair."

He helps me up, slowly, and directs me into the bathroom again until I'm leaning against the counter. "You sure you're okay?"

My hands are shaky, but I nod. "I just need a minute." I brush vigorously, needing to erase every trace of evidence. Kye's kisses cover any reminder of Gabe that could have lingered, but I can't forget what I've done. What happened with Gabe was a mistake. I was drunk and in pain and ... lost my judgment. And eventually I'll tell Kye about it.

Just not tonight.

When I come out of the bathroom, fresh-faced, fresh-breathed, wearing my tank pajama set, Kye's already changed. He squeezes my hand as he brushes by, sending a shiver of warmth up my arm. I slip in bed to wait, grateful that the room is steadier when I'm horizontal. When Kye's here and the light is out, I curl in his arms with my head on his chest and let the rhythm of his breathing lull me to sleep, whole once again.

Incessant knocking echoes in my throbbing head, and my stomach is on fire. My eyes refuse to open, so I dig at them with my fists and try again. Kye's breathing hitches when I move, and he jerks awake, leaning down to kiss the top of my head. "Morning sunshine."

"Hi." I nestle my face in his neck, so relieved that his presence isn't a dream. But each movement causes an explosion of pain behind my eyes. I whimper. "Ow." Kye makes a sound of sympathy, his hand massaging my neck.

In the other room the knock sounds again, followed by Gabe's voice. "Christine? Rose? Abby? Anyone awake? I have food."

From the other bed, Rose groans, burrowing under her covers.

I whimper again, wanting nothing more than to stop the noise so I can slide back into the heaven of sleeping in Kye's arms.

"You okay, babe?" He strokes my arm with his fingertips, sending tingles all the way to my toes.

"Head hurts," I mumble against his chest. "So bad."

"Want me to send him away so you can sleep?"

"Mm Hm."

"Okay. While I'm up, can I get you something for your head?"

I cover my eyes with a hand. "Yes please. And my stomach—it's on fire."

Gently, he slides out from under me and tucks the blankets around my shoulders. "Be right back."

The knock comes again, louder and more insistent, but this time it cuts off abruptly, followed by the exchange of low male voices. Hard as I try, I can't hear what Kye says to Gabe. Part of me experiences a smidgen of guilt. Having Kye appear out of nowhere is bound to be difficult for Gabe—especially after last night.

Oh. My. Stars and moon. Last night. I kissed Gabe! What if he tells Kye? I have to do something, get out of bed and keep them apart until I figure this out. My attempt to sit up is feeble. My arms shake, and the rock song playing behind my eyes is not one I like. Groaning, I pinch the bridge of my nose, relieved when the door creeps open and Kye tiptoes in and perches on the edge of the bed.

He hands me an aspirin and a glass of orange juice. "Here you go. Drink this, and then go back to sleep for a while."

I swallow the pill. "What time is it?"

"Nine." He rubs comforting circles across my shoulders.

"Supposed to be at a council meeting right now," I mumble, sipping my juice. "Then scuba lessons, followed by training with Christine and then the Dragons."

Kye takes the glass as I lie back. "Full schedule. I'll take care of it." He brushes the hair off my cheek and kisses it.

"Don't go," I murmur, reaching for him. "You said you wouldn't leave."

He brushes his lips over mine. "I'm not going far. Gotta make the couch look slept on before my parents wake up. Then I'll run by the meeting and let them know you're not up to coming today. Gabe brought fruit and muffins. They're on the table if you need food. I'll be back in half an hour."

"Promise?"

"Yes." He moves to stand, but doesn't. "You know, right now, you could pretty much ask me for anything and the answer would be yes. You should capitalize on that—get me back for yesterday."

I let my eyes drift closed again, snuggling my face into the pillow that's still warm from his head. "Mmkay. Maybe in a bit. Can I go back to sleep now?"

"Yes. Dream of me, and I'll be here when you wake up." His feet shuffle across the tile, and then I hear the dividing door close.

"I thought you broke up?" Rose's voice is muffled. I open my eyes to confirm that she's speaking from underneath her blankets.

"Misunderstanding." The familiar earthy scent belonging solely to Kye floats off the pillow, inviting me to snuggle deeper.

She flicks her bedding down so her face is exposed, groaning when a shaft of light peeks between the curtains and hits her in the face. "You sure forgave him fast. And speaking of speed, what's he doing here and how did he end up in your bed during the hour I was gone? Isn't he supposed to be in Jackson, dying?"

I snuggle my bedding more tightly around me. "I don't know. He was here when I got back from the club."

"And you showed up on the arm of Mr. Muscle. Bet that was awkward."

I tap my finger against my lips. "He didn't see. But only because I was lucky. If Kye had opened the door thirty seconds earlier, he'd have caught me kissing Gabe."

Rose's eyes widen. "Uh, very awkward. He kissed you?"

Squeezing my eyes shut, I finger my crystal necklace. "I kissed him, actually. But only because I was lonely, and heartbroken, and drunk, and—"

"I get it. No explanation needed here." She holds up a hand as if to say enough. "What are you going to do about it?"

"I don't know. Probably tell Kye and hope he can forgive me for being so weak."

Rose rises onto her elbows. "And Gabe?"

"Will have to understand. I'm in love with Kye. I've been in love with him all along. He's everything I need."

She stares at me, her eyes full of sadness and sympathy. "But what about the curse, Abby? That hasn't changed. What if you and Kye can't stay together? It's all good and fine that he's shown up long enough to share your bed for a few hours, but what comes after that? The whole pregnancy thing Gabe accused you of last night? That could be a very real scenario in your future. What will you do if Kye can't be around to help raise his kid? And what happens when Gabe gets sick of being your second choice and walks away from his job guarding you? Will you fill in the gaps between Kye's visits with Victor? Alejandro?"

I roll over and meet her eyes, prepared to argue. But she doesn't look mad, she looks stricken, worried. "I don't know what you want me to say."

"You can't have everything," Rose continues. "At some point you have to figure out what's realistic and what needs to be done in order for you both to stay alive, and maybe be happy someday—even if it hurts. And while you're figuring it out, do yourself a favor and don't complicate things more by taking chances."

"Chances?"

"Sex, Abby. I'm talking about you and Kye sharing that bed. I don't know what happened last night, and I'm not going to ask yet. I won't tell on you, either, by the way. What the two of you do is your business. But I know the history of Theron and Raina too. They had a kid together, and it really screwed things up for them."

My mouth falls open as I sit up all the way, turning to face Rose for real. "That kid was one of my ancestors. She survived. That's why *I'm* here. There's nothing screwed up about it. And since we're on the subject, who are you to lecture me about chastity? You're not exactly innocent."

She sits up fully, sighing. "No, I'm not. But you know what? If I end up pregnant, I have three choices. Adoption, abortion, or teenage motherhood. And that would completely suck for me, but the rest of the world would mostly remain unaffected. It's different for you. There's a whole race of people waiting to see if you have what it takes to restore order and lead them. We both know what a huge thing that is, what high expectations. And I know you. If you have another little person to protect—a person who is part of both you and Kye—you'll do whatever it takes to protect that kid, and to hell with the rest of us."

Hugging Kye's pillow to my chest, I consider her words. "You're right. I would do that."

She leans forward, drilling her finger into the mattress. "Here's the thing. Theron and Raina couldn't do what needed to be done to stop Tynan's demons because they had to protect their offspring. They didn't have a choice, and I don't blame them. All I'm saying is that if you end up in the same position, the cycle can't end."

Having never considered this angle, I'm surprised to hear it coming from Rose. "You've thought a lot about this, haven't you?"

She rakes her fingers through her disheveled hair. "More than I care to admit. I love Mexico, but at some point I intend to go home. I'd like to think you'll get to come with me."

"Me too. Rose, I promise you, we'll be careful—"

"Don't say that. We're all careful. Just do us all a favor and don't allow the fate of the world to be decided by a faulty piece of latex or an ineffective pill."

Moving slowly, I cross the space between beds and sit next to her. "You're a smart woman, you know."

"So I hear." She drapes her arm around my shoulders. "Lecture over. I won't say another thing about it. Now. Do I get the deets of what happened last night, or is that top secret between you and lover boy?"

"Lover boy?" I giggle. "Which one?"

Laughing, she swats me with a pillow. "Now you're starting to sound like me."

THIRTY-ONE

Un-trustworthy

Rose leaves to meet Alejandro for breakfast, and though she's hung-over too, she practically dances out the door. Since I'm fully awake, I decide it's important to get to my scuba lesson. I pin up my hair and layer a sundress over my swimsuit, more conscious of what I'm wearing because Kye is here. Since my head is still throbbing, I swallow a few drops of aspen from my herbal first-aid kit and pad into the living area looking for food. The housekeeping lady is here, arms loaded with towels and extra bedding, and lets off a startled squeak when she turns and sees me.

She mutters in Spanish, setting her bundle on the couch, and waits. I'm not sure why she's waiting. "Thanks for the towels."

"Sí," she says, still standing there.

Frowning, I help myself to a muffin and some sliced mango. Uncomfortable to have the lady watching me eat, I rap lightly on Christine's door. "Christine? Sorry to disturb you, but did you need something from housekeeping? There's a lady here and I'm not sure—"

The door swings open, and for the second time in the past twelve hours I'm both shocked and pleased. "Eoin! I didn't know you were here."

"How you doing honey?" He sweeps me up in a fatherly hug.

"I'm better. So much better now that you and Kye are here."

"Guess he found you then." The look in his eyes tells me he knows Kye didn't sleep on the couch. "Maybe now I won't have such a need to strangle him." At my arch look, he adds, "He missed you. A lot."

Happiness flutters into my chest.

"What did you need, sweetie?" Christine meets her husband at the door, winding her arm around his waist. I wonder how long it's been since they saw each other, and then I'm relieved that they're both showered and dressed, and I haven't disturbed them still sleeping.

"Housekeeping's here. I have no clue what she wants."

Christine extricates herself from Eoin, but when I turn around, the housekeeper is gone. "Weird. She was just there. Why would she leave now?"

"She probably hoped you'd give her a tip," Christine says. "But that could get her in trouble. Gratuity is included in our package."

"Sorry for disturbing you over nothing." I hold up my muffin and move aside so they can see the food. "Breakfast?" They join me at the table, Christine telling Eoin about the most recent meeting with the Dragons.

When Kye comes in, the three of us are giggling over the story of how I originally met Victor. Kye draws a trail across my shoulders and down my arm, planting a kiss on the nape of my neck, his very presence sending heat all the way to my toes. "Feeling better?" he asks.

"Yes. Tons."

"Good." He sits next to me, reaching for the juice. "I ran into a friend of yours while I was out."

My heart ka-thuds. *Here it comes. The confrontation about Gabe I was hoping to put off—maybe forever.* My face burns with shame. "I can—"

He opens his hand, producing my favorite sprite. "*Mo chara!* Love this place, I do." Murtagh buzzes around my head. "*Neme-to*, sacred place, full of power. Many sprites welcome Murtagh."

I grin at my smallest, fiercest friend. "I'm glad. Is that where you've been since you woke up? I was starting to get worried."

"No worry. Murtagh smart. Survivor."

"I sent him on a scouting mission," Christine says. "I didn't want him to go crazy being locked in the villa while we've been meeting and planning. Did some spying, didn't you, Murtagh?"

Murtagh's light glows with pride. "Helping."

Kye reaches across the table to pat Christine's hand. "I could've done that for you, Mom."

She raises an eyebrow, amused. "I might have asked if I'd known you were coming before you got on the plane."

"That's why it's called a surprise." Kye leans close, swiping a crumb from the corner of my lip.

Eoin tangles his fingers in his wife's hair until his palms cradle her face. "You know us. Spontaneous to a fault." His hand glides across her neck as he leans to kiss her shoulder the way Kye did to me only minutes ago. *Like father like son.* "You ladies should know," he continues, "my son and I have decided we're done leaving our women behind—or rather—allowing them to leave us behind. The goddesses gave us this amazing gift of love, and circumstances be damned, we're going to take all we can get and pay the consequences later."

"Don't tell me you've quit your day job to come live here?" Christine asks, her eyes widening. "I'm not even sure the house is habitable after the demon attack."

"Ah ... I, uh."

He glances at Kye for help, but Kye stands, taking my hand and starting for the door. "Don't look at me. I have my own explaining to do." He picks up the beach bag I set on a table near the door. "Let's go for a walk. You can show me around before scuba."

After the door closes, I ask, "Did he quit his job?"

"It's complicated."

I shake my head. "No, it's not. It's a yes or no answer. One that doesn't matter to me either way, so I'm confused about why you're avoiding it."

The late morning air is sticky with humidity and sweet with the green scent of vines and hibiscus nectar. Needing to find my balance and come out of the clouds, I try to remember what yesterday felt like, so desolate and empty, but I can't. Not while Kye's holding my hand and jungle birds sing in the trees.

"Yeah." He lets out a breath, his face twisting in that way that tells me he's done something he shouldn't. "We're both sort of AWOL at the moment."

"What do you mean, AWOL?"

"I mean we aren't supposed to be here, and as soon as Val and Zane figure out what we've done, they'll be right behind us."

Our clasped hands swing between us, and our flip-flops snap on the cobblestones, giving me a momentary flash of memory that makes me wonder if this garden is similar to the one where Theron and Raina first met. "I understand why they want to keep track of you, but your father's a grown man. He can go where he wants whenever he chooses. Why would he have to answer to Val or Zane?"

"I never realized he did, until recently. After you left, my health started getting better, but otherwise, I was a wreck. It got bad enough that I had to leave Jackson, so I went to stay with Dad in New York for a while."

Just off the path, we find a bench peeking out from behind an overhanging tree limb, leaving it mostly hidden from view. Kye sits, propping his arm across the back. I lay my head on his knees and stare up at the sky. "What was it like to be in New York and not constantly on the run?"

"It sucked. Spent a lot of time wandering the city, thinking of how amazing it would be if you were there with me. Again." He reaches up and picks a pink flower, tickling my face with the petals and tucking it behind my ear. "One day I came home and overheard my dad arguing with Zane on the phone. Zane was trying to force Dad to bring me back to Jackson. Of course, Dad refused, telling them I was doing better there, that they wanted too much control, and that the stunt with my cell phone was over the line."

"What stunt with your cell phone?"

His hand trails down my arm to my waist, splaying over my abdomen. "I didn't know at the time, but I found out later that they blocked us—you and me—from calling each other. Did you know cell phone companies have parental controls that will actually reject calls and texts from certain phone numbers?"

I grab his fingers, squeezing, and sit up slowly to avoid aggravating my headache again. "What?" My breaths come short, shallow, as anger shoves through my contentment. "They did what?"

"They blocked us, Abby. From each other. Intentionally."

Rage, like I've never felt in my life, courses through me until my fists vibrate with it. "Why?"

"Calm down for a second, there's more." His hands cover mine, manually smoothing my fingers so my nails cease digging into my palms. "Are you calm?"

"No." I shake my head. "Why would they do that?"

"Babe, take a deep breath. I need you to remember that I didn't know any of this until two days ago, okay? Any of it. It's very important to me that you understand that before I go on."

I do as he says.

One.

Two.

Three deep breaths. "Okay. Okay, tell me the rest."

He knots our fingers together, holding tight enough so I can't run away. "Zane wanted me back in Jackson, and even though my dad was adamantly opposed, we went. Dad came with me, told me a story about having business to do in Yellowstone, and suggested that I spend time with my friends while he took care of it. Made no sense after the conversation I'd overheard. So when we got there, I started snooping, eavesdropping, whatever I could.

"I wasn't allowed in meetings with my dad and the Dragons, even though before I left, I was included in everything. I knew something was up, but whenever I asked about it, they blew me off.
"

"That's messed up." I have to swallow the expletives that come to mind.

He leans his forehead on mine. "I know, right? You know what I did? I went to your house while Marian was working and snuck into your room so I could lie in your bed, trying to feel you. I couldn't figure out why you wouldn't call me back. I was so lost."

Lumps of sadness and anger form in my throat, and I can't tell which one is bigger. "I was too. Lost without you. I thought you'd moved on. Akers told me you were trying."

"I did try, at first. Why do you think I went to New York? Anyway, we'd only been back in Jackson for a few days when I started getting sick again. Really, really sick. I thought that was it. I was going to die without ever hearing your voice again."

Kye's holding my hands, but they're still trembling with anger. "Why didn't anyone tell me?"

"Because they knew you'd come back. I didn't, but they did. And they needed you to stay. So Val mixed me some herbs, hung some crystals around my neck, and sent me to bed for a few days. It's the weirdest thing, too. Because I've never had any distinct memories from our past lives together—but I swear I dreamed about us. In the past. Has a guy named Liam ever shown up in your visions? Because I think he might have been my best friend or something."

"Yes," I whisper, confused. *How could he know this?* "Liam was a guard. A captain, I think."

"And I called you a ghrá. And Abby, I know it means my love, without Googling it."

"How did you ...?"

Kye frowns, his eyes stormy. "One day, I woke up, and I was better. They didn't know I was awake, so it was easy to sneak around, listen in. I caught Val using the pendant to siphon my sick energy to you, so that even with the miles between us, you were Healing me. And because you didn't know what was happening, or when, you were in a constant state of vulnerability that could've gotten you, my mother, and Gabe all killed." He squeezes my hands like he expects me to be as angry as him, but I'm confused.

"I can't Heal your symptoms from the curse. That's been the biggest problem all along. If I could, I would have done it willingly. They didn't have to do it in secret, so why would they? And how?"

"I don't know. But something is seriously wrong with this situation. I've trusted Val, looked up to him my whole life, and I was stunned to find out he isn't who I've always thought he is, to know he would do something like that behind my back. At this point, I don't know who we can trust, but I do know one thing. When they separated us, it wasn't to save our lives. When I was sick and asleep and dreaming about our past, I saw us, Abby. As Theron and Raina. And we were both there—both still alive—when our daughter was born."

My sudden intake of breath startles him. "What? What's wrong?"

"I had a vision of that. Last week. The day the demons found us. I collapsed from heat exhaustion, and Gabe was mad at me for not drinking enough water."

His jaw tightens. "You collapsed?"

I nod, puzzling it all out.

"Why didn't anyone call me?"

"They probably didn't want to freak you out."

His "Yeah" comes out as more of an explosion of breath than a word. "Too late. Are you still sick then?"

I start to tell him yes, but that isn't the right answer. "I don't know. When I first came, I got better for a while. A lot better. Your mom started working with me on Healing, and Gabe became a sort-of personal trainer. I was doing fine until last week."

He rakes his hands through his hair until it stands up in the stressed spikes I've always loved. "That's when I started getting bad again."

"Makes sense. The question is what caused us to get worse? That's why we were split up—to prevent the sickness from progressing."

216

"I don't know yet, but I'm determined to figure it out. They're trying to keep us apart, Abby, and I don't think it has as much to do with our health as they claim. My dad had to pretend to be Val so he could unblock our phones yesterday." He stands to pace. "Besides my parents, who else can we trust here?"

"Please don't take this the wrong way, because I love them like they're my own. But after everything—with Val and Zane and all the arguing, and then your dad taking you back to Jackson even though he didn't want to—are you sure we can trust them?"

"Yes," he says, without hesitation. "I'm sure. After Gabe called me, I confronted my dad with what I knew. He was as shocked and enraged as me. He took a few days to do some digging and set up a distraction to buy us some time, and then we hopped a plane and came here." He spreads his hands. "You can't know how relieved I am to find that you're okay." He pauses. "Or, well, you seem okay. Are you?"

"I'm fine. For now." Letting go of the tension, I lean against the bench. "Gabe called you? When? Why?"

"Couple days ago." He grins, a mischievous glint in his eyes. "Do you know he's convinced that you're pregnant? Chewed me out royally—not hearing anything I said to the contrary—and then started in on how I had to make you listen to reason before you got yourself and your baby killed. Scared me to death. He wouldn't talk about whatever happened that day, and I already knew about Val's energy-transferring trick, so I asked about your symptoms, how you were holding up.

"I tried to get him to let me talk to you, but he was on a landline, and you weren't with him. His words were slurred. Pretty sure he'd been drinking. And I've never heard him swear before, but he threw a lot of four letter words at me. I knew I had to come, because Gabe doesn't get scared, but something had him really shaken up."

The demons. The wave. The dagger. The house. I stand and stop Kye's pacing with my arms around his waist, because something has to keep me grounded. "So we trust your parents, and Gabe. And Rose."

"Yes," Kye murmurs. "I've always trusted Rose. That was never a question."

I consider Victor, Alejandro, Miguel—the rest of the Mexican Dragon contingent. And though I believe Victor's a good guy, there's no way to know for sure. I trusted Val too. Neither Val, nor Zane has ever carried a dirty aura, yet if Kye's right, they've both betrayed us. "That's all. I don't know anyone else well enough to make that judgment."

"Okay, five's a start."

A shiver prickles my shoulders. "What are we going to do, Kye? We have to find the truth."

He strokes my hair, leaning his cheek on my head. "First we're going to kick some demon ass. Because regardless of what's happening at home, there really is a problem here, and we can help. So we go about our business and speed this tomb thing into hyper-drive, because Akers and your mom can only stall Zane and Val for so long before they figure out Dad and I skipped town. And when *they* get here, we'll be fighting a whole different type of battle."

I draw a shaky breath, nerves pulsing in all my intuitive places. "There's no way we can win any kind of battle with Zane and his Dragons."

His fingers tangle in the hair at my neck as he tips my head back so I can look at him. "I know. And I don't intend to try. But they have information we need, and it's important that we have a few answers before we run."

THIRTY-TWO

Secret Plans

"Run?" My heart hammers. We've discussed it before, a long time ago. "You want to run now? Why? How?"

"Because they're trying to keep us apart, and I refuse to live the way my parents have for all these years. It's not what I want for us. I need you. Not far away, living in another country and sneaking in a phone conversation every few days. You belong in my arms, and I belong in yours—and I don't care where we go, as long as we stay together.

"I have about twenty thousand dollars in a college savings account—it's mine, and has no ties to Theron and Raina. Only my parents. Between that and any money I make when Dad sells my Jeep, we can get by until I can find work somewhere. We'll survive and be together."

Rose's words echo in my head. *The cycle may never be broken.* "What about the curse?"

A shared tremor. "That's why we need answers. We have to find out what they're not telling us. There has to be more than sickness and death in our future. I know it."

My emotions spiral in every possible direction, but I grasp onto the most important one. Hope. We leave the garden with our hands clasped, filled with determination to never let go. Even if it kills us.

While I'm learning scuba, Kye and Eoin join the Dragons in the conference room for a briefing. Before he goes, I cling to Kye, worried that the Dragons will turn informant and take him away before I've had him back for a full day. But he needs to know what's happening, and that means going through the Dragons.

We have to hope Akers can field calls between the groups for a few days.

When I arrive at the pool, Gabe is waiting in his chair with a book in his lap. No one else is here yet. I approach, apprehension in every step because I know I owe him an apology. I drop onto the chair next to him. "Hey."

It takes him extra long to look up at me, even though I know he's not reading. "I guess you and Kye are back together?"

My lips still tingle from kissing Kye before we separated, minutes ago. "Misunderstanding."

He sets his book down, not bothering to mark the page. "When did he get here?"

"Late last night."

His eyes search mine as if looking for signs of heartache or happiness. He probably sees both. "Are you ... are you happy he's here?"

"Of course. I love him." My gut clenches at the pain I can tell he's trying to hide. "He came because you called him, you know."

"I do." He tries for a smile and fails. "Wasn't sure he'd actually come—especially after I thought he broke up with you—but when he answered your door this morning, I knew."

"Thank you." I cover his hand with mine, weepy.

"I was worried about you. Figured if you wouldn't listen to me, maybe you'd listen to him." He sandwiches my hand between both of his. "And don't thank me yet. The rules have changed since I talked to him on the phone. You're not his in the way I thought. And after last night ..." His eyes linger on my mouth. "I know you were drunk, but you knew what you were doing. I can't just let it go."

I draw my hand away, standing as Rose comes around the big building. "You have to. I *am* his. That's not going to change. "

"I know there's more between us than friendship." He lowers his voice as Rose comes through the gate. "Does he know you kissed me?"

"No. But I'm going to tell him. Soon." I meet Rose halfway, needing distance from Gabe. "Where have you been all day?" I ask.

The look on her face reminds me of how I must have looked after waking up in Kye's arms this morning. She's smitten. "Brunch—with Alejandro." She grins, and I decide she's not smitten, she's full-on twitterpated. "I know it's crazy, because I've only known him for a few days, but we have something, Abby. Something good. I couldn't explain it if I tried."

"You don't have to explain. I know." I only wish I could add Alejandro to the list of people we can trust. He seems to be good for Rose. Maybe that alone is reason enough to risk it?

Scuba lessons usually zoom by, but today I continually remind myself to pay attention to the instructor and stop watching for Kye to return. When he finally does, he thunders across the courtyard, clearly agitated. I scramble out of the pool, leaving my gear on the concrete, and hurry to him, still dripping. "What's wrong? What happened?"

His eyes sweep over me, pausing only briefly on the diamond hanging around my bare waist, and his mouth twitches. "This is what I've been missing? I should've hopped a plane a long time ago." He snags a pool towel off a nearby stack and hands it to me. "Dry off, a ghrá. We need to go pack."

I glance at Rose, flirting with our instructor, and Gabe, who's trying not to be obvious about eves-dropping. "Pack? Why? What's happened?"

"They want to throw you in a hole."

I dry off and wrap the towel around me. "I know, that's why the scuba lessons. So we can breathe when we're underwater. In the hole."

He shakes his head, adamantly. "No. No way. Not happening. I'm sorry, but no. Just. No." From the corner of my eye, I catch Gabe nodding in agreement. "Have you seen it?" Kye asks Gabe.

"It's worse than it sounds." Gabe stands, offering a hand for Kye to shake. "I agree. No way Zane would go for this."

"I don't know," Kye mutters. "Zane's been known to do things none of us could understand."

Gabe raises an eyebrow. "What do you mean?"

Kye shakes his head. "If you agree that it's insane for them to send Abby down there, why haven't you voiced your objection to the council?"

"I have. On a number of occasions." He gestures at me. "Yesterday she decided she didn't care if she died, and told Enrique she was in."

Kye scowls. "Why didn't you stop her? She wasn't in a clear frame of mind, even without being half-drunk."

Gabe backs up a step, looking incredulous. "Have *you* ever tried to tell her she couldn't do something? In case you haven't noticed, when Abby makes up her mind, there's no point in trying to stop her. But I would never let her go alone, which is why I was planning to go with her."

"So was I." Rose is now standing behind me, drying off.

"If that's true, why aren't you taking scuba lessons too?" Kye winds a possessive arm around my waist as if to remind Gabe how things are.

"Already certified," Gabe says, refusing to look away from Kye's face as if he doesn't accept me being labeled as Kye's property. "I don't need lessons."

Rose hums an uh-oh, and steps in to serve as a barrier between warring hulks. "Hey, Gabe, could you explain more about what's going to happen when we go down?" She takes his arm, leading him to where she's left her shoes. He follows somewhat reluctantly.

Seizing the opportunity, I tug Kye toward our villa. "I'm starving. Let's go get some lunch."

"Abby, you can't do it." He wraps his arm around me while we walk, and I lean on his shoulder, sighing.

"It's the only way to reign in the demons that have been terrorizing this place."

"Don't you see? Even the Dragons don't expect you to make it out alive." He digs a key out of his pocket and opens the door. "I don't *want* you to do it."

I step inside and stifle a gasp. Our room has been ransacked, in the same way our Las Vegas apartment looked the night Gram died. I stumble against Kye as panic tries to knock me over. He holds me up, swearing. "Yeah. It's definitely time to go."

Kye sends his dad an emergency text, and by the time Eoin and Christine come, followed by Gabe and Rose, I've ventured into my room to see what damage has been done. We sort through my clothes and jewelry, and I'm grateful that I never take off my antique diamond ring. I'm digging through a pile of clothes on the floor when I realize what's happened. "Kye, the dagger. It's missing."

Within an hour, the Dragons swarm our villa, leaving nothing unturned. Sick dread settles over me, because I know we won't find it. Whoever broke in has what they came for and is long gone. I collapse into a chair, head in my hands, trying to force my Sight to give me a clue. What would someone want with a powerless, broken dagger?

While Kye's engaged in conversation with his parents, Gabe crouches next to my chair. "You all right?"

I shake my head. "Why would someone steal the Dagger? It's broken, disassembled. Unusable. Isn't it?"

"As far as we know." He purses his lips, looking thoughtful. "But maybe the person who took it doesn't understand that. Or maybe they know something we don't."

"Maybe."

"At any rate, we're not safe here anymore." He nods at Christine and Eoin. "Whatever they decide about the living arrangements, it's time to tighten security around you."

"Oh goodie." I blow out a breath. "Just what I wanted—less privacy, more Dragon power."

Gabe pats my shoulder. "You love it and you know it. And look on the bright side. This will force us to move on the tomb soon. Get it over with."

And then I can run away with Kye. "Maybe."

Gabe moves his hand as Kye glares territorially and crosses to me. He crouches and meets my eyes, concern evident in his. "Sick?"

I swallow, trembling. "No. Well, yes, but only because someone broke in and stole a very dangerous weapon. One of the Arawn Keys. From me. I was supposed to be protecting it."

"Babe, it's going to be okay." Kye wipes my stray tear with his thumb.

"Abby, no one blames you," Gabe says. "You can't keep every valuable item with you all the time. Everyone knows that."

But when I look up, all I can see is our apartment in Vegas, and Gram dying on the kitchen floor, and I know that this, too, is my fault. And I have to fix it.

THIRTY-THREE

Playing House

We spend the afternoon packing—just as Kye had planned. Only rather than running away, we're relocating to another section of the resort. By silent, mutual consent, our plans to run are on hold. We both know I can't leave while the dagger is missing.

There are no more large villas available, so the five of us opt to split into two smaller ones. This creates a dilemma with the sleeping arrangements. Grudgingly, Kye agrees to room with Alejandro (who has been assigned a night shift guarding the ruins) and Gabe moves in with Victor. Security aside, I'm relieved that Gabe and Kye aren't sharing—that would be ten shades of awkward for all of us.

I'm jumpy and insecure, and Kye is extra cautious too, so I don't object when some of Kye's toiletries and clothes mysteriously land in my suitcase.

Dinner is a somber occasion, even with Mariachis playing next to the restaurant buffet. Plate laden with desserts, I return to our table where the Dragons are deep in discussion about the logistics of entering the cenote. Kye's lips are pressed into a grim line. "Tell me about the time frame."

"Four days," Alejandro says. "Maybe a week."

"Why not tomorrow?" Kye taps his foot as if anxious to move right now.

"We need to prepare," Alejandro continues. "Also, we need equipment and supplies." He reaches for Rose's hand and cradles her fist against his chest in a sign of possession. Rose is engaged in a conversation with one of the other Dragons, but her eyes flit to Alejandro's and go soft. *She's a goner.*

"We're going to need more scuba gear," Kye says, tapping a list Gabe's looking over. "And that shouldn't take four days."

Gabe shoots Alejandro a glance. "In case of faulty equipment?"

"Because," Kye's voice holds a hint of impatience, "if Abby's going into that hole, I'm going, too." He focuses on Gabe. "Also, if Val or Zane ask, you haven't seen me or my dad."

Gabe clears his throat, eyebrows raised in silent question.

"We're supposed to be in Jackson."

"Then why are you here?"

"Our phone conversation knocked me straight." Kye sits back, resting a hand on my knee. "I realized this is where I should have been all along. Abby needed me. I'm here for her—to keep her safe. Same as you."

The two exchange a look of silent agreement. "All right," Gabe says.

Kye glances at my empty plate. "You ready to call it a night?"

I nod, too stunned by his new plan to say anything. That he wants to go in the cenote with us brings me to a new level of distress. We can't afford a repeat of our last tomb experience. I doubt the Morrigana will be as forgiving should I visit them a second time.

Christine and Eoin have chosen a private table. We pause there to say goodnight.

"Listen you two." Christine takes one of each of our hands. "Just because we're in separate villas doesn't mean house rules don't apply."

My face burns with embarrassment, but Kye shoot his mother an amused grin. "What rules, ma?"

"You know exactly what I'm talking about. You're assigned separate rooms for a reason."

His eyes don't leave Christine's, but his forced smile has a defiant edge. "We're both adults. Old enough to get married if we want."

"Abby's not legal for another week," she points out.

"Details." Kye wraps his free arm around my waist.

Eoin barks a laugh. "He has a point."

"Nevertheless," Christine continues, squeezing our hands harder, "you *aren't* married. And there are so many unknown variables and risks regarding your relationship. We have a job to do, and it requires your full attention. Please remember that. We're trusting you to behave."

Kye kisses his mother's cheek. "I always behave. Besides, you saw me move my stuff into Alejandro's room. I'm just going to walk Abby back." He exchanges a look with his father that screams, *quick, distract her so you can both deny you know the truth.*

Christine's eyes narrow. "I'll send Rose as soon as she's finished eating."

The moon hangs low, a bright lopsided ball in the inky sky. Billions of stars wink to life, so close I can smell their electricity mingling with the cloying scent of the jungle. My ears ring with chirping and hooting, a slither and snap. This afternoon I was enchanted by the sounds, but tonight the smallest rustling puts me on edge. As we approach the door, I hand Kye a room key. "Rose got three. So we'd have a spare."

Chuckling at the irony, he opens the door, and we do a thorough check to make sure no one's lurking behind the shower curtain or under the beds. When I unzip my suitcase and hand Kye his clothes, he's shaking. Apprehension tightens my neck muscles. "You okay? Starting to get sick already?"

"I haven't felt this well in a long time." He accepts his belongings and sets them aside in favor of holding my hands. He clears his throat. "I meant what I said back there. To my mom."

Confused, I search his face, trying to decipher the emotions. "About us being adults?"

He nods, looking vulnerable. "Well, yeah. That. But also the other part. We *could* get married. If we wanted. Do you?"

My heart races with a mixture of excitement and fear, and his face grows brighter through the sheen in my eyes. "Are you asking?"

"Yes. I am." His hand cups my cheek, then slides behind and under my hair. Ignoring the warning bells and sirens going off in my subconscious, I shove aside any doubts and wind my arms around his neck. My lips give way to his as our bodies press together. His hands roam my back, coming to rest on the exposed skin between my shoulder blades. The contact sears heat all the way to my toes, melting me so I'm pliable and soft. Despite our rocky past, in this moment of togetherness we're more than either of us has ever been alone.

Arms wrapped around my waist, he picks me up and drapes me over the coverlet, then settles next to me. His fingers toy with my hair on the pillow, his breathing ragged when our lips part. "Is that a yes?" he asks, grinning.

I nod, my cheek rubbing the fine stubble on his chin. "Yes." And even though I know this dream can't last, I mean it with everything in me.

"I love you," he murmurs, his lips catching mine again. I want to reply that I love him too, but as his hands roam, and his lips work their magic, the words never reach my mouth. Fortunately, all things considered, I'm pretty sure he knows.

As Christine promised, Rose is only a few minutes behind us. She makes a point of rattling the knob and being overly loud about telling Alejandro goodnight. When she comes in, we're propped against the headboard, on top of the covers and still fully clothed, watching Spanish TV.

"Either you're actually being good, or you were naughty way too quickly. Christine will be so happy."

"Don't even think about telling her—"

"Oh shut it. I won't." Rose waves aside Kye's objection as she kicks her shoes off. "Although she was rather insistent that I hurry back to supervise. You do understand you're dealing with some of the smartest, most observant people in the world, right? You're not fooling anyone."

Kye shrugs.

She flops onto the bed opposite us. "You could at least try to be discreet." She turns her back on us and rubs her hands on her shoulders making kissy noises.

I lob a pillow at her. "We're not *that* bad. What do people expect? We haven't seen each other for two months."

Rose opens her mouth as if to say something, then closes it, shaking her head. *She was about to mention Gabe.* I close my eyes, swallowing my guilt. I'm sure he knows Kye's here now, and he'll know when Kye leaves—even if it's not until morning.

"Let them talk." Kye gets up to retrieve his belongings, running a hand down my calf and over my foot en route to the bathroom. "It's not like we live in the stone ages. It's actually common for a man to spend the night in his fiancée's room."

Fiancée. The word makes my heart flutter.

Rose gasps, and her hands fly to cover her eyes. "Oh ew. Let's all just remember that Rose is present, okay? In the room. All night long. And I really don't want to witness your ... consummation, or whatever. Just. TMI, people." She peeks out from behind her hands as the bathroom door closes. "Fiancée? When did this happen?"

I hug a pillow to my chest, grinning until my cheeks hurt. "Few minutes ago. I said yes."

She rolls her eyes, moving over to sit closer so she can lower her voice. "Hence Kye's fiancée comment. Did you not hear *anything* I said this morning?"

"For the record, you didn't say anything about marriage. But yes, I heard you. We're trying to be good, Rose. It's just—" I take a shaky

229

breath, and the rest of my sentence comes out as a whisper. "We don't know how long we have. Makes it really difficult to be apart. I need him." *More than I ever understood before.*

"And yet you were doing fine while he was gone." She crosses her legs under her, propping her elbow on her knee and leaning her chin on her hand.

"It was an act." I squeeze the pillow tighter, recalling our reprieve at Christine's house. The nights when I ran on the beach, the afternoons spent working out with Gabe and training with Christine. Riding around on a scooter and eating crab off a napkin. And laughter. Lots of laughter. I was content spending my days with Gabe. Tonight, those days feel like the dream of another life entirely. One in which I was almost—almost happy.

Almost being the key word. Because the chasm inside me couldn't close while we were apart, and though I've begun to accept living with empty spaces, having those holes filled makes everything so much clearer, brighter. Better.

Rose blows hair out of her eyes. "Just don't let the love-fest distract you from what we're doing here. And you might consider keeping the wedding plans quiet until after we attack the tomb. That way, no one *else* will be distracted either."

I assume that when she says no one else, she means Gabe. Rose gives better guilt trips than any mother on the planet. I take a turn in the bathroom, and Rose is last, allowing Kye and me a chance to talk privately. "Did she give you a hard time about my fiancée comment?" He searches the closet for an extra blanket.

"She thinks we shouldn't tell anyone yet. Too much distraction." I wiggle into my covers, letting them pool around my waist as I lean against the headboard. "She has a point, I guess."

He doesn't say anything as he tosses the blanket at the foot of the bed and glances at the couch as if just now realizing how short it is. He's quiet long enough that I wonder what he's thinking. Finally, he sighs, lying opposite me, on top of the covers. "We should at least tell my parents. Maybe it'll make Mom feel better." He pulls me close. "Although, if people are gossiping anyway, it would be nice to give them a real reason." He nibbles softly on my neck.

"We can't," I murmur, rapidly losing my resolve. "Rose has to live here, too. And we still don't know what to do about the curse. We have to break the pattern. What if being together like that makes us sicker, faster? What if we ruin everything?"

"It won't. We won't." He nibbles again on my earlobe as he leans across me to turn off the lamp and settles on the pillow. I snuggle into the crook of his arm. "I was thinking," he says. "I want to buy you a ring—but I could never compete with the one you already have. And you always wear that one. Then that pink thing around your waist, and the pendant—yeah. I've never met a girl who owns so many valuable gems. I don't know what to give that you can actually wear."

"Don't buy me anything, Kye. I don't need it. I just want you. That's all. Just you."

"You're not helping." He hikes me up until my head settles on his chest the way it did last night. "If I get you something, will you wear it?"

"Depends on how ugly it is." The bark of his laugh is a relief. Regardless of where we are or what we've left behind, here in his arms, I'm truly home. "I'm kidding. Of course I'd wear it. But I don't need a symbol to remember I love you."

His fingers draw lazy circles up and down my arm that's resting on his chest. "It's a symbol to remind you that *I* love *you*. And I need to give you that. To make it official. As soon as we're able, I want to shout it from the rooftops so everyone knows."

He knows about Gabe. Why else would he have such a need to stake his claim? I consider telling him, right now, but it's not a conversation to have with Rose nearby. It's a conversation meant for privacy and seriousness. And I'm so warm, so comfortable in his arms. Now isn't the right time.

The knob on the bathroom door rattles loudly. "I'm coming out—you better not be sucking face, or I'm going to puke." A shaft of light illuminates the room. Rose scowls when she sees us cuddled together and turns off the lights, stumbling in the dark to her bed. "Can I just make it known that this arrangement sucks? No offense, but I don't want to share a room with you two. I should blow the whistle and end the torture for my own sanity."

"Come on, Rosie," Kye wheedles. "We're not doing anything and we're not going to. If you really want, I'll sleep on the couch. It's short, but I'd survive."

"Sorry, Rose." I say. "I know it's not ideal."

Across the room, the sheets rustle, the bed creaks, and then all is still. "You *should* be sleeping on the couch." she says, ignoring my apology. "I don't know any other eighteen-year-old whose parents would turn a blind eye on their son's bedroom escapades while we're in the middle of an international multi-species crisis."

"Don't be so dramatic. Are you kicking me to the couch or not?"

Her exaggerated sigh is stage-worthy. "No. Because then Abby will have to suffer in that big bed all alone, and you'll both wake up cranky because I kept you a whole ten feet apart for a few hours, and I'll have no one to blame but myself. And then if I ever sneak out to stay in Alejandro's room, I'll never hear the end of it."

"You're right," I agree. "You won't. Better if you shut up and let us get some sleep. I have a feeling the Dragons aren't going to let us skip tomorrow's morning meetings the way we did today."

"Fine," she snaps, being very loud as she flips onto her other side. "Just remember you both owe me. Big time. Huge. Like you've never owed me before."

"And we'll pay up, promise." Kye's arms around me tighten, and I relax against him as once again, his heartbeat becomes my lullaby.

THIRTY-FOUR

Lies

I've heard it said that you don't really know a person until you've lived with them. After a week of living with Kye, I decide that theory is true. As much as he claims he's fine, Kye's still sick. When I wake up one night to the sounds of him losing his dinner in the bathroom, I decide Akers has trained him to be a phenomenal actor.

The next morning while he showers, blatant snooping enlightens me further. I stumble upon several bottles of custom blended herbal tinctures, made specifically to combat the effects of a disease similar to a cancer. In the daylight, he acts fine. He eats, and swims, jokes, and plays. He romances me into the garden for long, lingering kisses, and every time we have a few minutes alone, we talk about the future—all the possibilities. Except I'm no longer sure a future is really possible for us.

If we get married, will one of us be dead in a year? Two? Less? Could we be lucky enough to manage ten? I doubt it.

I try to not constantly think about the curse and what it's doing to him—will eventually do to me. There's a long list of other scary things in our more immediate future, but it's difficult to think about anything else. My dreams become nightmares of Kye collapsing, tumbling into the cenote, or the ocean, or a deep, dark hole from which he will never escape, and where he will die alone because I couldn't find him.

Imagination mixed with experiences like ours can be a really bad thing.

He's first out of bed each day, showered and gone looking for breakfast so Rose and I can take over the bathroom. He makes every effort to act the solicitous fiancée, attentive, patient, protective, strong—especially strong.

I don't understand why he tries so hard to pretend he's okay, how it's possible for him to be so convincing, when clearly he's not.

The only thing I can think is that he truly believes one of us is going to die soon—and I pray every minute that it isn't him. This is not a disease I can Heal, and having him die as a result of loving me isn't something from which I'll ever recover.

I try to confront him about it, but something—or someone—always interrupts, or it isn't the right time, or I lose my nerve. And at night when I lie curled in his arms, feeling loved, and whole, and altogether too happy, it's easy to postpone the discussion for one more day. But I know we'll have to talk about it eventually, the same way I'll have to tell him about kissing Gabe.

In the meantime, the Dragons continue planning. After hundreds of laps and numerous trial runs with the scuba gear, my muscles are toned and strong, my lungs prepared to take oxygen from the tank, and my mind focused enough to use my Gift of Light if necessary—and I'm pretty sure it will be necessary.

Gabe keeps his distance, and though I was worried the first day, he doesn't bring up our kiss—to me or to Kye—a fact for which I'm grateful. I still have Dragons guarding me, but Gabe has other assignments and stays busy enough that we rarely see him. When he does join us for dinner, he acts like everything is fine between us. I know better. But again, bad timing. So I let that go, too.

The morning of my eighteenth birthday, we wake to the rumble of thunder, and rain pounding heavily on the roof. Wind whistles outside, making me think of demons. Maybe they're here. The thought quickens my pulse, gets my nerves quaking.

"You cold?" Kye draws his blanket over both of us and holds me close.

I nod, not wanting to admit to being afraid of the storm.

"Happy birthday," he murmurs into my hair. "Looks like we get the morning off. If there's lightning, they'll close the pool."

"Never thought I'd be so grateful for a rainy day." Sighing contentedly, I stretch, sneaking my leg out of the covers to run a toe across the bottom of Kye's foot—a ticklish spot I recently discovered.

He jerks his foot away, grinning at me in the gray light of morning. "Behave, or I'll sic Rose on you."

It's become a running joke between the three of us that Rose is the mediator of fights (which have yet to occur) as well as the supervisor who ensures that we keep things legit. Some days I'm grateful to have her here. Others—like this morning—not so much. Gabe showed up in my dreams, and I'm uncomfortable enough to be more reckless than usual with Kye.

I press my lips to his neck, distracting him as my fingers tease another spot near his waist, prodding until he grabs my wrist. "I mean it. You'll be sorry."

My lips burn a trail across his jaw. "What are you going to do? Wake her up and make her hold me down?"

"I'm already awake," she moans, half-heartedly punching one of her pillows. "And I think I'm going to have to hurt you both. Do you not know how to be quiet so a girl can sleep in?"

"Sorry." My apology ends in a squeal when Kye flips me on my back, holding both my wrists with one hand, while the other digs into my side, making me laugh uncontrollably.

"So glad to know you care," Rose says, sliding out of bed and heading for the bathroom. "Don't mind me. Third wheel walking through."

I want to respond, but Kye's relentless; I can't catch my breath. When the bathroom door closes behind Rose, he lets go of my wrists, his playful touch turning tender as he presses his lips to my shoulder. "I love you. You—Abby. Not because of Raina and Theron—because of you and me. You make me invincible and strong. Together we can conquer anything. I can't wait to get this tomb thing over with so we can start our life together. I want to give you everything."

It's the perfect opportunity. And I think I'm going to bring up his sickness, but all that comes out is, "I love you too. You, Kye. Only you. Always. Forever."

Unlike his playful teasing, the kiss he presses on my lips is pure, heavenly, similar to our first kiss in the way it reaches down and turns me inside out.

Rose slams out of the bathroom, fully dressed in shorts and a tank top, with her hair pinned up and lips slicked with gloss. She grabs a zip-up sweatshirt off the couch and tugs it on with her back to us. "I'm done with babysitting duties. Kye, if you're not going to use the extra bed in Alejandro's room, I might. In case either of you cares. Not that you'll miss me." She storms to the door. "Happy birthday, Abby."

Then she's gone. And we're alone. Really, truly alone, for the first time since New York.

The cycle may never be broken.

"Did she just move out?" Kye falls to his side and props his head on his hand, playful all over again. "This could be a very dangerous situation indeed." Locks of tousled hair fall over his smooth forehead, and his lips—already plump from kissing me—curl into a hungry smile. My heart slams into my chest. If he were to kiss me now, I would give in—give him everything. But he draws me up to sit next to him on the edge of the bed, where he holds out fisted hands. "Pick one."

I pick the fist he can't close all the way, and find in it a hammered silver cuff bracelet, inlayed with multi-colored stones. Turquoise, onyx, amethyst, tiger's eye, agate. It's beautiful and perfect. Kye bends the silver around my wrist until it's snug. "It reminded me of you."

The thick silver feels warm—the bracelet pulses with positive energy. It keeps me so distracted, I don't see that he has opened his other hand and revealed a delicate platinum band, studded with multi-colored sapphires. It has a cutout in the top that will allow it to be worn with my other ring. I can't breathe.

"The bracelet is for your birthday." His voice softens. "But this ... I know you don't need a symbol, but I do." He slides the ring on my finger, and I'm surprised that it fits. He's chosen well. "Let's get married. Today. Right now."

I freeze, shocked. "Now? You want to elope? But ... my mom's not even here."

"Let's not invite anyone. Just you and me. I'll borrow the car for a couple hours so we can go into town, we'll find someone to officiate and get hitched. No one else has to know until we decide to tell them."

"I ... wow." I want to do it. Every part of me wants to be his, in every way possible. But there are too many secrets between us, too many things left unsaid. Kye still doesn't know I kissed Gabe. And we haven't figured out what's happening with the curse. He doesn't realize I know he's still sick. All the giddy happiness evaporates with the stark realization that I can't marry Kye. Not today. Not while the curse is still consuming us. Maybe not ever.

He's still holding my fingers, staring at the ring, and can't seem to meet my eyes. "Please."

I look up, staring at the top of his head, wondering if what I'm about to say will destroy us. "I can't."

His head snaps up, his fingers tightening, squeezing around mine while his eyes search my face, tormented. "Why?"

He knows. He has to know. But I know his secret too.

"Because you're still sick and I can't be the reason you die before you turn twenty." I swallow a lump in my throat. "Why would you try to hide it from me? Did you think I wouldn't notice when you're up all night puking? Or that the only thing keeping you going is the pharmacy of herbs you got from Val? Your chakras are practically running backwards." Okay, so the last part isn't entirely true—I still have a really hard time reading his energy when he hides it.

"It's not as bad as you—"

Ignoring him, I continue, "Don't you think I deserve to know I might lose you? What would happen if we got married, had a baby, and then you died? I'd be left alone, destroyed without you. A single teenage mom who might be too sick to take care of herself, let alone a kid."

He lets out a pained breath, loosening his grip on my fingers, but he doesn't let go. "We'll be careful. Extra careful. We'll use triple birth control. Just marry me. Please, Abby. " He trails a finger up my arm, over my shoulder, leaning closer.

I back away, needing space, air. "I can't. I won't watch you wither away and die—because of me."

"I'm going to die anyway, eventually. At least I'll die happy." He leans in to persuade me with his lips.

"I kissed Gabe," I blurt, removing my hand from his and crossing the room.

He looks like I've punched a hole through is chest. The color drains out of his face. "I ... when?"

My stomach clenches. "Does it matter?"

"Yes, Abby, it matters," he croaks. "Just like it matters how many times, and what it meant. What it means."

"Just once. The night I got drunk, right before you got here." Or actually, he was already here. I just didn't know.

He squeezes his eyes closed, perching on the edge of the bed, head in his hands. "I knew Val made Akers tell you the same things he told me ..." he swears. A lot. "Was that the only time? Tell me it was the only time. Tell me it was just a kiss."

It was the only time. "What did Akers tell you?"

"That you needed some space to try to move on with your life. To leave you alone so you could get over me, and that I should try to do the same." His voice is muffled while he scrubs his hands over his face and into his hair.

"And did you? Try?" My voice sounds tinny, hollow through the blood roaring in my ears, because this part—this is the part I need to know, and also the thing I've been dreading since he got here. Since before that, even.

He nods, looking defeated. "Before New York. Crystal came over a few times. I wasn't in good shape. I needed something, someone, and she was decent company." He looks up, his eyes glassy with unshed tears. "I kissed her. And she was willing to do a lot more than just kissing–but I didn't. I didn't, Abby, because she wasn't you, and I knew she never would be, and it just made missing you so much harder. I missed you so much I couldn't breathe–so I left to be with my dad."

Kye kissed Crystal. A few times. Thought about doing more ... He considered ... My thoughts swirl, body shaking with emotions, the most prevalent being pain. I kissed Gabe, yes, but only once, and only after I believed Kye was already with Crystal. Which, obviously, wasn't completely wrong. I sway on my feet, eyes glazed and unfocused. Kye jumps up, grabs me like he thinks I might collapse. I shove him away. "When? When did Akers ... When did you and Crystal ...?"

Saying her name leaves a scorch mark on my tongue, and I have to swallow.

He shakes his head. "It didn't mean anything, Abby. That's the only thing that matters, okay? I'm here. I came because I love you, and I will always love you forever. Only you. Crys ... she only clarified what I already knew."

"Nine days, Kye. Nine whole days we've been living together. How many more secrets have we kept? How many lies by omission?"

"None, Abby. None. And I swear I'll never keep anything from you again. I'll never lie again. I'll never ... can you just look at me?"

I can't. I can't look anywhere but the floor. He tries to wrap me in his arms, tries to soothe me, but I shove him away again, numb. "You wanted me to marry you. Today. You weren't going to tell me, were you? Don't you think this is something I deserve to know?"

"Of course. Of course you deserve it. I just ..." He's flustered, shaky, fidgeting. "What do you want me to do, Abby? Yes, okay. I should've told you some stuff, and you should've told me some stuff, but we didn't because we needed time to be together without tension. It happens. I wouldn't change it, because for nine days, yours was the first face I saw when I woke up, and the last before I fell asleep. Nine days of sleeping with you in my arms, without any other expectations, because I know you're scared for a hundred different legitimate reasons. I've never pushed you for anything more than what you were willing—what you're able—to give, and it's been a lot harder on me than you know. But it's worth it, because your well-being is more important to me than anything else in the world. More important than the safety of the world. I need you—"

"If my well-being is so important to you, how could you risk me dying from the curse, knowing you yourself are still sick?"

"I ..." He snaps his mouth shut, shaking his head. "Because it's different than before. Different symptoms, different energy. Everything. I don't know what's happening. I ... we don't know who to trust except each other, and I don't think the curse is the problem."

I do. There might be more, but underneath the surface, I know that one fact still remains. We can't be together without killing each other. And I would rather live a life of misery than watch him die a slow, torturous death. "How can I trust you after you lied? You ran to Crystal the minute I left. Before I left, even. And how can you trust me after I kissed Gabe? If we can't trust anyone else, and we're lying to each other—how does that work?"

His chest heaves, his hands shaking like he might explode, but he stands his ground, rooted. "We love each other. Nothing else matters. You're everything to me. Everything. I do trust you. And it's okay if you don't trust me, because I'm willing to spend the rest of forever doing whatever I can to earn that back. I'm so sorry about Crystal. It didn't mean anything. I swear, Abby. It didn't. That's why I'm here."

Finally, I'm able to meet his eyes, but only because I've found my nerve, my resolve. "I want you to move in with Alejandro for real. Today. Now."

Eyes wide with shock, fists clenched to his sides, Kye stumbles toward me. "What? No. Abby, I need you. I need you more than I need air. You can't kick me out. Not now."

Swallowing everything I really want to say—which is that I love him too, need him too, and want to marry him immediately—I lift my chin. "I am. I'm getting in the shower, and I want you gone by the time I come out."

"A ghrá. Babe. Please. Please don't do this." He runs a hand down my arm, and I let him, closing my eyes and allowing a few hot tears to fall, because I can do nothing to stop them. "I'd rather die than live without you. That's why I came—it's why I'm here. Please."

The raw ache in his voice rips me apart inside, threatening to destroy everything I'm attempting to do. "Please just go." I turn away, closing myself in the bathroom, wondering how I'll ever be able to breathe again.

THIRTY-FIVE

Inevitable

I spend an hour in the bathroom, terrified that when I come out Kye will still be there, and even more terrified that he won't.

When I find the courage to look, I see that he did as I asked. His shoes and sweatshirt are gone, and so is he. There's a note on the bed, scrawled hastily on hotel paper.

You are my life. I love you. Please forgive me.

Kye's words start my tears flowing again. No amount of aloe or ice or vitamin C cream is going to diminish the swelling in my eyes, or fade the brightness of my Rudolf-red nose, but I don't care. I pick up my cell phone and dial my mom, but the call won't go through. I hold up the phone, wandering as I search for just one little coverage bar, but it's no use. *Must be the storm.*

Desperate to have her tell me that everything will be okay, I try the phone on the desk, not caring that it will cost a small fortune. But dialing out is—apparently—complicated, and no one at the front desk speaks much English. There's a pay phone in the lobby. I dress in shorts and a hoodie, and grab the calling card Mom sent for emergencies.

The downpour has settled into a misty drizzle. Wisps of steam float in the garden and roll off the cobblestones, filling the air with pungent scents of green leaves, damp earth, and exotic flowers. I trudge across the grass until my feet are pink with cold, the front of my head throbbing with each step as I clomp into the building. A handful of Dragons linger in the restaurant, so I duck behind a pillar and pick up the receiver. She answers, sounding sleepy.

"Mommy." I burst into gut-wracking sobs. It's several minutes before I can talk, and by then, she's wide awake, yelling at Erda to stop bellowing so she can hear. Even with the distance between us, my faithful pup can sense my pain. "Mom, I miss you. Can you come here? Please?"

"I miss you, too, sweetheart. Tell me what's going on."

So I do. All of it, even though it's only been a few days since we last talked, and she already knows some. I explain how I met Victor and Alejandro, and the time I spent with Gabe, how I saved Murtagh's life—twice. How Rose came, and right behind her the demons who destroyed Christine's house, and then how we came to this place, and went dancing, and I got drunk and kissed Gabe (she gasps) and then Kye showed up and I've been happy—happier than ever before.

I'm careful to gloss over the part about Kye moving in with me, but she's not stupid, and hints that she knows. I tell her about his proposal. Our fight. How much I need her because she's my mommy, and I don't want to be a grownup anymore. "I'm booking a flight right now," she says. "Okay? I'm coming. I'll be there as soon as I can, but it might be tomorrow."

Relief pours through me. "Thanks, Mommy."

"Listen to me," she says, in her no-nonsense-mother voice. "I want you to go back to bed until Rose comes to check on you, okay? I'll see you as soon as I can."

Because I know she's coming, and because she told me to, I manage to trudge back to my villa without collapsing face-first on the path. I kick off my flip-flops in the middle of the floor and crawl under the covers, shivering and half-soaked, hugging Kye's pillow to my chest.

Rose comes in less than an hour later, opens the door quietly—as she hasn't done since we moved into this smaller villa—and perches near my hip. "You okay?"

I shake my head, unable to speak, attempting to hold myself together with the aid of Kye's pillow.

"Word is that the empty bed in Alex's room has recently become occupied. Looks like I'm stuck here."

The only response I can muster is a sniffle. But I reach a hand out from under the blanket, gripping hers in a silent gesture of thanks.

She squeezes back. "You know he loves you, right? Everyone within a hundred miles can see it. In my whole life, I've never seen him so focused on anyone."

Sniffling again, I manage a strangled, "I know."

She plays with something on my finger—the new ring from Kye. I never took it off, never thought to give it back.

"You're too young to get married," she says.

My shoulders shake, more sobbing. *Happy birthday to me.*

Rose lets go of my hand and stands. "Did you eat?"

I don't respond.

"Do you want to?"

Again, no.

"Take a nap. I'll be back in a couple hours, then we're going to the club for a surprise birthday celebration a la Rose." She pauses with her hand on the door. "I'll bring another shot of tequila—this time with salt and lime."

In typical Rose fashion, when I most need someone, Rose sweeps in and picks up all my broken pieces, preparing to patch me back together like Humpty Dumpty. I only hope she has enough glue.

My dreams are fitful and disturbing. One in particular jerks me awake, shaking. In it, Morrigan, the goddess of love and fertility, tells me that I should stay with Kye because, although it appears we're killing each other, neither of us is capable of surviving alone.

Story of my life. But it's only a dream, rather than a vision. What I wish for, not necessarily what's best.

Another dream takes me to a funeral, one hand rubbing my large, round belly while I drop dirt on a coffin with the other. What I most fear, but not necessarily reality.

In a totally unrelated dream, Raina's guard, Liam comes to me and offers to sacrifice himself. I don't know for what.

Clearly, my brain has passed max capacity.

When the door opens, I look up expecting Kye, but it's Rose and Gabe. My throat clogs with disappointment. Rose whips my covers off. "Come on, get up." I don't move. Can't. "Abby, I brought your tequila, but you have to sit up to drink it."

"Leave me alone."

She fixes Gabe with a look. "Do it."

"Rose," he murmurs, voice filled with compassion. "She doesn't want to."

"Yes, she does," Rose insists. "She just needs a little help."

He leans over me. "You're not going to make this easy, are you?"

Again, I can't respond. Nothing in my life has been easy. How can he even ask that?

He scoops me up and carries me to the couch, forcing me to sit. "I'm only doing this because she's making me."

"Nobody makes you do anything." My voice sounds robotic.

His eyebrows shoot up as he crouches to my level. "You'd be surprised."

"Don't talk in riddles. My brain is hibernating."

Rose wraps my fingers around a glass, forcing the other hand into a fist. "Lick it so the salt will stick."

Too tired to bother, I close my eyes and down the shot, cringing as the bitter fire burns all the way down.

"Or just drink it. That's fine too." She offers me half a lime. "Softens the sting."

The taste brings tears to my eyes—or maybe they were already there?—and one escapes. Gabe wipes it away. "Not an ideal way to spend your birthday, is it?"

A knock sounds on the door, and Kye walks in, looking wrecked. He stops dead, eyes widening in pain as they land on Gabe. "Get. Away. From my fiancée."

Gabe stands, dropping his hands to his sides. "I'm just here to help."

"You've helped enough."

He steps aside, looking uncertain.

"What do you want?" I ask, staring at the floor.

"Can we please talk about this?" Kye glares at Rose, then shoots angry daggers at Gabe. "Alone."

Eyes closed, I lean against the cushion, trying to purge my brain of images of Kye kissing Crystal, and how he probably did it before I even left. *She wanted to do more.* How far did he go before he changed his mind? Was he with her before he came to tell me goodbye? Is that why he came in the middle of the night? "There's nothing to talk about. It's over. It has to be."

"No. No it isn't." He stalks to me. "Be reasonable, Abby. You have to listen to me."

Gabe steps between us. "No she doesn't. Not today."

They glare at each other. "Why are you still here?" Kye hisses. "This is my room, and my girlfriend, and my life. You have no right—"

"Abby," Gabe says, his voice deadly calm. "Do you want to talk to Kye right now?"

I swipe away another rogue tear. "No."

"Stop it," Kye shouts. "You've made your point, okay? Just tell him to go away so we can talk."

"No."

"Just go," Gabe says, a hint of sympathy in his voice. "Give her some space." The impact of a fist making contact echoes in my brain when Kye punches Gabe. Gabe doesn't fight back, but he does catch Kye's fist and avoid a second punch. "I only deserved one. Go."

"Fine." Kye glares at me. "Let me know when you're ready to be reasonable." He turns blistering eyes on Gabe, his voice cracking when he says, "You keep your hands off her. Your job depends on it." He storms out, slamming the door and letting in a gust of wind and the smell of more rain.

"Well that was fun." Rose plops next to me. "How long are you going to make him suffer?"

"Forever." It comes out as a whisper.

Gabe's eyes fill with pity and confusion. "Why?"

"Because I love him."

"The guy's a mess, Abby. And so are you. What happened?"

A hint of guilt tries to form, but I squash it. I would never have kissed Gabe if I hadn't believed Kye and me were over. "Go away, Gabe."

"Thanks for the help." Rose ushers him to the door. "We'll call room service and have a pity-slash-birthday-party here tonight. Catch up with you tomorrow."

Gabe hesitates, looking at me once more. "Are you—?"

"She'll be fine. I'll take care of her." Rose shoves him outside and flips the deadbolt. "Get dressed. We're sneaking out."

Meeting her determined eyes, I decide that Rose wins the award for best idea of the day.

An hour later, we sneak through the jungle on a somewhat elaborate path, hoping to avoid catching the attention of any Dragons. Alejandro is waiting with one of the resort golf carts. He welcomes Rose with a kiss. "Good evening, mi flor."

"Hiya, sexy," she says, climbing in next to him.

"Maybe we will perfect your Salsa tonight, yes, Abby?"

"Okay." I force a weak smile and accept Victor's steadying hand into the cart. The engine is surprisingly quiet as we zip to the club, barely protected from the rain. I hold out my hand, allowing drops to run down my arm, and wondering what good can possibly come from sneaking out with Rose?

Alcoholic numbness.

The ability to stop focusing on the bad things and smile.

Dancing until I feel like I can fly.

If I'm lucky, maybe I'll move out of my sad space and into one that involves more productive feelings—like anger.

After the first round of drinks, Victor invites me to dance. We shimmy around the room while I suppress vivid memories of being here with Gabe—how he held me close, even though he was angry. Even though he believed I was pregnant. How he was concerned about taking care of me, especially when he thought I wouldn't take care of myself. How he prepared to help me deal with my grief.

When I finally decide to sit one out, Victor finds another partner. Alejandro whirls Rose away, leaving me alone with three margaritas and a room full of strangers.

The cycle will never be broken.

I sip, contemplating Rose's theory about Theron and Raina. Though I know she has a valid point, something's bothering me. Theron was present when Raina had their baby—so obviously the curse hadn't killed him yet. But I've also seen visions of Raina alone, trying to protect her baby, without Theron's help—not knowing where he was.

If Theron was present for his daughter's birth, Raina couldn't have been missing, never to be seen again, as the story goes. Could Theron have kept her in hiding? Did they succeed in running away, sparking the rumors that Theron died?

I sit up straighter, calculating. Contemplating. Kye and I were both deathly sick when I left Jackson. And then we both got better for about a month, before Kye got worse again. And then I got worse.

What if the curse was meant to tear us apart—to keep us apart—in order to weaken us? To dull our powers, which are so much stronger when we're together. What if this second sickness is *because* of the distance between us, rather than in spite of it? When Kye is near, my Light is stronger, easier to access. Though I've learned to use it without him, when he's around it becomes a living glow, constantly alive inside me. And though he's been sick, physically, Kye looks stronger, healthier than he ever has before. His pallor is not yellow as it was when I left Jackson, the whites of his eyes not so gray. He's been training with the Dragons daily. I've seen him spar with several of them—Gabe included—and win more often than he loses.

And except for the night I was drunk, I haven't been sick since he came.

I'm not sick.

I'm not sick.

And Raina and Theron were together when she had the baby. She wasn't sick either. Because...

Because they were stronger together.

I need you like I need air.

Could it be that we've been thinking about this curse all wrong? I swallow the last of my drink and slam my glass on the table, stumbling to the dance floor. "We have to go."

Rose presses against Alejandro. "We just got here."

"I know, but I just figured out something important, and I have to go. Now." I have to talk to Eoin.

Alejandro's hand rests on the small of Rose's back. "Twenty minutes, Abby. And then we will take you home."

"Can you take me now? You can drop me off out front and come right back. I really need to go."

Rose sighs. "Fine. Can you at least let us dance to one more song? Just one?"

Her makeup-darkened eyes sparkle in the club lighting, and the way she clings to Alejandro reminds me of how tightly I sometimes hold onto Kye. She deserves this. "Okay. Just—please hurry."

On the other side of the dance floor, Victor works his magic on a local girl, and the grin he flashes makes me hesitant to interrupt, but I start toward him anyway. Before I can reach him, my danger instinct perks. Everywhere I turn, strangers. Again, I cut through the crowd, panic rising in my chest Victor has disappeared, and now I can't see Rose and Alejandro, either. When a meaty pair of hands captures me from behind, I'm not all that surprised.

I should have known this was coming. It always does.

THIRTY-SIX

Resurrected Enemy

My assailant hauls me outside through a back door. I scream, but no one can hear me above the music. Ribbons of fear slice my nerves when I notice I'm surrounded by the red-gray auras of the Dark Elen.

"We meet again." It's the same voice that has haunted my dreams for most of my life, the voice of the demon who took Kye from me in New York. The person I thought died of a bullet wound near the tomb in Yellowstone.

"Boone."

He's sporting a puckered red scar on one side of his face, but his eyes are still the same frightening violet that has terrified me for years. My heart plummets. "How are you alive?"

His evil cackle hasn't changed, and it still makes me shiver. "Do you not know what immortal means?"

I slide a hand in my pocket, hitting the touch screen on my cell phone and hoping I'm dialing Rose. "Living indefinitely doesn't mean you can't be killed," I point out. "Eric killed Juri." At least, I hope Juri died. If not, I'm in more trouble than I know.

Boone scowls, the scar wrinkling across his face. "Deserved what he got. So anxious to give away the power. Never considered that I could rule—without opening a tomb."

There's a frightening change in his aura since I saw him last. With the help of the demons, Boone has reached a new level of evil. Terror threatens to take over as I struggle to free myself from his grasp. "What do you want? I don't have the dagger, it was stolen."

Boone raises a brow, grinning a scary-clown-evil-joker grin, and removes a bundle from his pocket. He unwraps the sparkling handle with gentle precision. "You mean this dagger? Never trust a hotel housekeeper."

Oh no. Nonononono. This is not good. Not good at all. "But it's broken," I remind myself. "Valdemar drained its power."

His lips quirk, horror movie style, as he produces an onyx spear point and jabs it into the dagger's handle, creating a flash. The door behind us flies open. Victor and Alejandro step out, flanked by Rose and some other Dragons I didn't see when we came. "Looks like the real party is in the parking lot," Alejandro says.

Rose flexes her fingers. "I was worried you ditched us."

"Hardly."

Victor shakes his head, catching my eye. "Gabe was not kidding when he said trouble finds you."

Boone ignores them, still mesmerized by the glowing dagger. It illuminates his face, the light changing and covering him in a sheen of blue. As if noticing his own preoccupation, he rewraps the weapon. "The Arawn Dagger has been restored."

Alejandro mutters a stream of Spanish words (I assume he's swearing), and Victor joins him. But Rose focuses on the Dark Elen, centering energy into her throat chakra, preparing to power up her voice. She's about to buy us some escape time. Her Persuasive powers didn't quite work on Boone the last time she tried, but she's been training with Val. She knows how to use them now.

"Alex, you lied," she says, pouting. "The real party is inside. There's tequila inside, and dancing. Women." Her melodic Persuasion is like music that reaches down inside them, makes them yearn for an unidentifiable need, creates a throbbing ache in their chests and scrambles their brains. "Come inside. Come dance, and drink, and party with us." Her hips sway as if she's already dancing, and then she is, subtly drawing the Elen—including Boone—toward her. Her throaty, seductive voice eclipses all other sound until they're compelled to do as she says. "Come inside. We have a place for your pleasure. Dance. Drink. Touch. Come." The Dragons move aside as she opens the door, waving the Dark Elen ahead of her. "There's a private table in the corner. Meet me there."

I marvel at the level to which her skills have developed as the entire group of Elen file inside. At the last second, Boone—tucking the dagger inside his shirt—turns, looking as though he means to say something, but Rose lays a finger on his lips. "I'll be right behind you."

As soon as the door closes, the Dragons slide a crowbar between the handles. One of them barks into a cell phone as we tear around the building to where we left the golf cart. Alejandro starts the engine while Rose and I cram into the front, and the Dragons pile in the back. "I did it!" Rose squeals. "I can't believe it worked."

"How long will that last?" Alejandro asks.

"Minutes at most, so you'll need to floor this baby. I've never worked on so many boys at once."

He wiggles his eyebrows, growling. "I love a powerful mamacita."

Unfortunately, the cart's about as fast as a snail. Too soon, footsteps pound behind us, and a dark shadow rises, forming a barrier in front. Alejandro swerves and narrowly avoids plunging straight into it. "Go!" Victor and the others dive, energy-wands flashing as they hold the shadows back. Nearby, a massive tree splits down the middle, shaking the ground as each smoking log topples. Alejandro presses the pedal to the floor.

"Rose, they have the dagger—we can't let them catch us," I tell her.

"I know." She whips around, watching behind us.

"Maybe we should go on foot. Cut through the trees to the resort."

"We can't run this fast," she says, indicating her wedge sandals. "Alex?"

"I will protect you until reinforcements arrive," he says. "But it is more difficult on foot. We will drive as far as possible." As he says this, we hit a giant rock, and the cart is thrown violently; we nearly tip over. More shadows stretch, licking our feet with cold. "Hold on!" We turn into a narrow footpath and manage to squeeze between the trees with only minor damage to the cart, and none to the people. A sapling tumbles behind us, and the shadows fall back again. Alejandro's phone rings, and he answers—still driving—speaking rapidly in Spanish. When he hangs up, his smile is grim. "Sounds like we will be going into the cenote tonight."

"Great." Rose unbuckles her shoes. "Sounds about as fun as the club."

"We should not have gone there," he says.

"It's Abby's birthday," Rose counters. "She needed to get out."

The trees thin, and soon the black darkness of the jungle is broken by distant lights. Ahead, I hear shouting, yelling, thrashing of vines and trees, the hum of another engine. Above it all, a hoarse voice screams my name.

"Kye!" I yell. "I'm here. I'm coming. I'm here." The next two minutes pass like decades, but soon I catch sight of another golf cart, backlit by the floodlights surrounding the resort. "I'm here."

Alejandro stops the cart to let me out, and I'm caught in Kye's arms, blubbering like a childish, stupid baby. "I'm sorry. I love you so much, and I'm sorry."

He presses his lips against mine as Alejandro yells something about meeting us there and hits the gas again. "I'm sorry, too. Are you okay? Did they hurt you?"

"No. But Boone's here. He has the dagger, and he's alive, Kye. I thought you said he died?" The second cart is loaded with scuba gear and wetsuits. I get in next to Kye.

"He did. I swear. I saw him get hit and go down. He stayed down."

"Well, he must have gotten back up at some point, because he's right behind us."

"Great." The engine grumbles to life. "This day just keeps getting better." Kye sets his energy-wand on my lap, and we start through the jungle.

I know we've both apologized, but our fight, what we've both done, still weighs like an anvil on my chest. This isn't the most appropriate time, but I don't know when we'll be alone again. "I have to tell you something important."

He swallows, but offers no other response. My heart breaks. He thinks I'm about to confess something devastating. I've hurt him as deeply as he's hurt me.

"I think Theron and Raina ran away together. She must have gone into hiding, but he found her and joined her. She couldn't have died saving Theron, because they were together when the baby was born. There has to be more to the story than we know."

"I thought the same thing earlier," he says, clearly comforted by this topic. "Abby, I know you don't believe me, but I've been getting better since I came here, not worse. I never threw up before you left—only after. And hardly at all since I came here. I didn't mention it because I didn't want you to worry. I also don't want you trying to ease my symptoms—and don't tell me you wouldn't, because I know better. It's your instinct."

"I can't stand to see you suffer," I say.

"Ditto. So I kept it from you, and I'm sorry. I'll never keep anything from you again. Not ever." He reaches over, squeezes my hand. "You *can* trust me, Abby."

I'm still hurt. Unbelievably. And it'll take a while to get past that. But I've hurt him too. We'll have to work together to Heal each other of this one.

We circle around the resort, heading for the ruins. My throat tightens. I know I've had weeks, but I feel unprepared. A shadow shimmers to one side of us, and Kye plows past, gunning the gas so we fishtail in the dirt. I clutch the seat hard. When the ground levels, he chances a look at me, his expression wounded when he notices the way I'm dressed. "I wish you'd told me you were going to the club. I'd planned to take you tonight anyway."

"Rose made me."

"Are you drunk again?"

I shake my head, ashamed. "No, just buzzed. And not even much of that left, thanks to adrenaline."

His jaw tenses as he looks away. "Was Gabe there?"

"No, Kye." My voice wobbles with emotion. "I wouldn't do that to you. That night—I was just so angry at you, and lonely, and confused. And yes, that was the only time I've ever kissed Gabe, I swear."

"If I hadn't shown up ...?"

There's no way for me to give him an honest answer and not hurt him more. But there's also no way for me to truly know what would've happened between me and Gabe had Kye not shown up. I tell him the only thing I can, hoping it's the truth. "It wouldn't have happened again. It was a mistake."

He blinks, keeping his eyes closed a second longer than necessary. "This afternoon after you kicked me out, when I came in and he was there, I wasn't sure. I know you love me, Abby, but I've been tormented wondering if you might love him a little bit too. It haunts me."

Is that possible? "I'm scared, Kye. What if we're wrong? Being together could kill us."

"Being apart from you was already killing me." He squeezes my knee. "We're not wrong. I called Val this afternoon."

"You what? Why? What if he tries to separate us again?"

"My dad has a theory, and I had to ask Val about it. He's the only one who would know."

"Can we even trust what he says?"

"I don't know, but it's all we've got for now. It's a pure-love theory my dad found in one of his books. There are three scenarios, or trials, and we might have to survive all of them. First, sacrifice of self. We did that already last spring. Second, sacrifice of each other. No idea what that means. Val claims he has a theory, but wasn't forthcoming with it."

"Why?"

"Something about us needing to figure it out on our own."

"No wonder you don't trust him." I wait, but he doesn't offer the last scenario. "What's the third?"

"Val wouldn't discuss this one—at all. Neither would Dad. But I think I know." His silence worries me, but finally, he continues. "I love you. And I want to be with you in every way. Soon. I've been sharing a bed with you for a week and a half, but haven't tried anything more than actual sleep because of a phone conversation I heard between Dad and Val a while back. They were talking about sacrifice of the one we both love more than any other. In Theron and Raina's case, it was the baby. And they couldn't do it. But this time, we don't have a baby."

I swallow, thinking back on my conversation with Rose. "Nor even the possibility. How will that change things?"

He maneuvers around another tree. "I don't know. And I don't know how long we'll be forced to wait."

I have a moment of panic, wondering if this is Kye's way of backing out—taking his ring back. Before I can deliberate too hard, he changes the subject. "You haven't had much practice with the rappelling gear. Will you be okay going down yourself, or do you want to go tandem, the way we did in New York?"

I clutch the seat tighter as we bounce again. "I'm not ready for this, Kye. Can't we wait? Relocate again?"

"I wish." He glances at me, looking like he wants to give me any other answer than the one he has. "But as soon as we get through it, we'll make some decisions about our future." He wraps an arm around me. "I'm sorry if I pushed too hard earlier. I just—it's what I want, Abby. I'll never love anyone the way I love you. There's no way I ever could. So I want you to be mine, in all ways possible. I don't want to wait, but if you need a year, or two years, or even ten to decide ... I will. I hope I don't have to, but I'll wait as long as it takes."

"If we can beat this thing—the curse ..."

"Yes." He kisses my hair. "Of course."

We leave the jungle and come upon the ruins. Moonlight outlines the pyramids and surrounding buildings, making the landscape look like a scene in a movie. I hope it stretches into the sinkhole. There's no backup plan for going in during the night.

Several figures have gathered at the edge of the cenote, illuminated by solar powered spotlights. We lurch as Kye pulls to a stop. Gabe, wearing a wetsuit that covers him neck to ankle, stands very close to the edge, staring into the water like it's poisonous. "I can't believe we're jumping into that," he says as we approach.

"And yet, in Jackson, you and your dragon buddies jump into what appears to be a pool of acid every day," Kye shoots.

"Not even close to the same thing," Gabe says.

"If I'm lucky, maybe you'll drown," Kye mutters under his breath.

"What's the plan?" I ask, desperate to change the subject.

Kye sets a scuba tank at my feet and hands me my wet suit. "Put these on." He directs my attention to where Victor and another Dragon are securing rappelling ropes. "We'll head down when everyone's ready."

"And then?"

Kye whistles, and three sprites—Murtagh included—zoom to him. "Did you do it?"

Murtagh bobs, blinking. "The way. Murtagh found, yes. Ready to help *Calin*, princess-queen."

"Excellent." Kye offers Murtagh what has to be the biggest high five of his life. "Murtagh and his friends will show us where the tomb is located. We follow them in, clean up the mess, and get out as quickly as possible."

"You make it sound easy." I hope there's even a small chance things will happen that way.

He leans in, kisses the tip of my nose. "Not easy. But maybe simpler than last time."

From the corner of my eye, I catch Gabe narrowing his eyes as he watches us interact. I offer a weak smile and bend to pull on my wetsuit over my clothes.

"A ghrá, it's not going to zip that way. You'll have to take them off." Kye's raised eyebrows and suppressed grin suggest that he knew this would be the case. I take Kye by the shoulders, back to me, and use him as a shield. As I squeeze the form-fitting suit over my shoulders, Kye turns his head, eyes alight with mischief. "Can I help?"

I pull the zipper, scrunching my nose at him. "I'm capable of dressing myself, thank you very much."

"Just checking," he says. "Some things are more complicated than others."

"You ready?" Gabe calls from a few feet away. Unlike Kye, he kept his head respectfully turned, though I'm pretty sure he's seen me change before too.

"Not quite," Kye says, stripping off his shorts. I look away, but he murmurs, "It's okay. I promised I would never hide anything from you again. Nothing." I start to protest, but he's wearing boxers, and changes so fast there's almost nothing to see. Except, you know, his freakishly toned abs, and ridiculously ripped chest.

Gabe barely spares me a glance when Kye waves him over to help double check the rappelling lines, but as he passes, his fingers brush my hand, pausing just long enough to hook his pinkie around mine.

Apparently, he wasn't lying when he told me he wasn't going to let our kiss go. Now I just need to figure out what to do about it.

THIRTY-SEVEN

Stunned

Rose and Alejandro pull up in the other cart, explaining how they led Boone and the other Elen deep into the jungle before they circled back. I haven't even strapped on my scuba gear yet when the conversation near the edge gets loud and heated.

"It makes more sense for me to take her," Gabe tells Kye in a matter-of-fact tone. "I know you can do it, but you should reserve your energy for when we get to the tomb. Carrying a hundred extra pounds won't be anything for me."

"I told you to keep your hands off her, and I meant it." Kye huffs. "If she's going tandem with someone, it's going to be me. She's light. We've done this before. I was fine then, I'll be fine now. End of discussion."

"I know you're feeling possessive, but—"

"Don't go there. Don't even try to tell me how I'm feeling. Abby may be your job, but she's my life. As soon as this is over, you're getting reassigned somewhere on the other side of the world from wherever she ends up."

"What's your problem?"

Gabe steps forward, and Kye gets in his face.

"You," Kye says. "You're my problem."

Gabe's gaze catches mine, holds, his brow rising. *You told him?*

"Knock it off." I step between them. "We don't have time for this. I'm going down myself. I can do it myself."

Kye rests a hand at the small of my back, drawing me close. "Are you sure? Remember how scared you were last time?"

"I'm different now. Stronger. And there will be water—not land—beneath me this time."

We line up, preparing to go one after the other. First Kye, then me, Alejandro and Rose, last Gabe and Victor. Kye straps on his tank and lowers himself over the cliff. As his head disappears, a freezing, energy-charged wind swirls around the edges of the cenote, howling like hundreds of ghosts. I step back, fighting to keep calm as I shout, "They're here! The demons are here."

Clouds of darkness roll in, filling the sky with lightning and casting the same eerie glow that so frightened me in the cavern where the other tomb was located. Shadows snake around me, circling and howling until I'm directionally confused and sliding toward the edge. I dig my bare heels into the dirt, but it only earns me gravel-burned feet. The deafening wind roars. Through the dark, I can make out silhouettes. Rose, Gabe—clutching scuba gear in his fist—maybe Victor, Alejandro. They're focused on me, pounding at an invisible wall from far, far away. I can't hear them.

One shadow funnels, thickening and throbbing with life as it pours into a thick column of black, out of which walks Boone. He draws a symbol in the air. The force pushing me to the edge eases, but my limbs feel as heavy as lead. I can't move, no matter how hard I try. "I won't keep you long," he says. "Just need one thing." He whips out the dagger and slices the tip into the inside of my elbow. Blood streams down my arm and pools in his open palm.

Pain sears up my shoulder, down to my fingers, spreads across my chest, into my toes until the agony is so great that I can't hold back from screaming. Boone squeezes my blood into a glass vial. When he's satisfied, he removes the dagger and wipes it on his pants. "Juri's biggest mistake was not killing you the moment you walked into his casino. I am not as stupid as he." Boone shoves me to the edge until I teeter, prepared to beg. If only I could find my voice.

"I hope you can swim. Oh wait, you've been stunned. Guess not. Say goodbye to your friends."

Kye screams my name as I sail through the air, watching helplessly as the water rises up to greet me. The shock of cold steals my breath as I go under and continue sinking. Eyes open, I tip my head back. The water is clear, so I can see when Kye releases his harness and drops the remaining fifty feet. Someone else swan-dives from the top. *Stop it!* I want to yell. *You need your scuba gear first.*

A pink trail of blood marks my descent, so I have hope that they'll be able to recover my body.

Cold. So cold. My lungs scream for air, the pressure squeezing my chest tighter, tighter. *Take a breath, take a breath. No. Don't do it.* The urge to breathe becomes overwhelming, and when I can no longer fight it, I inhale water. Kye can't descend fast enough, so I close my eyes against the devastation I know he'll experience when he gets to me, and keep sinking.

And then something wraps around my wrist, halting my downward plummet. I still can't move, but warm lips press against mine, forcing something down my throat. I cough, knowing I've swallowed too much water. I'm a goner. But the lips press again, and again and again, offering relief as my lungs fill with air. Kye. The next time the lips press mine, I press back, taking the oxygen, as well as a taste of his lips—but something's different. Off. *Must be the water.*

A funny gurgling sound makes my eyes pop open, and as they focus, I'm horrified to discover that I've just kissed—not Kye—Alejandro. He's laughing. He takes another breath and presses his lips to mine again, filling my mouth with oxygen.

This isn't possible. People can't breathe underwater. Not like that.

But Alejandro's a Dragon, which means he has a very useful, and highly specialized Gift. *This must be it.* After each breath, Alejandro kicks us up a few feet, then stops to repeat the awkward process as we work toward the surface. To Kye.

First I kissed Gabe, and now Alejandro. This has M.E.S.S. written all over it. But considering that neither of us has a scuba tank, and I sank faster than I knew was possible, we really have no choice. Alejandro can breathe underwater, but I can't. And I need air to stay alive.

How will I ever explain this to Rose? She's in love with Alejandro. She hasn't said so, but she doesn't have to. I recognize the signs.

Alejandro presses his lips to mine, over and over again, offering the breath of life. After a long time, and a final hard tug, my head breaks the surface. Sputtering and choking, I inhale a breath for myself. He wraps my cold hands around a vine and props me against the steep rock of a hidden inlet. "Rest here, until the others come."

He swims to peer around the rocks, making hand signals.

As the water drains from my ears, I make out battle sounds. Howling, trees and foliage breaking, the clashing squeal of bending metal, the electric buzz of energy wands. Voices, screaming, and the staccato war-drum beat of thunder.

Alejandro returns. "You have not moved. Did not help swim before. Are you hurt?"

"I ... Boone cut me." I shake my head—the only movement I can manage. "I can't move my limbs."

"This is not good."

"No, it's not."

The water around us ripples. Kye rises up from beneath us, tearing off his goggles and wrapping his hand around mine—still secured by the vine. "You okay?"

"I kissed Alejandro—sort of," I blurt.

Alejandro winks at me.

"His helping you breathe is not the same thing as kissing," Kye says.

"If you say so, gringo," Alejandro teases. "But you would be wise to hold onto your lady, before someone steals her away."

Kye throws him a withering look, but then focuses on my arm and the pink-tinted water around it. "You're bleeding. What happened? Are you hurt anywhere else?"

Staring at the wide, deep cut, I murmur, "Stunned. Can't move. Boone came. He cut me with the dagger."

"He cut you? The dagger's broken. How is that possible?" Kye anchors himself to a vine and takes my hand, trying to hold my arm above the water high enough to examine.

"He fixed it with an onyx spear point. Took a vial of blood, but didn't go for my heart the way Tynan did. I don't know why." A fish bumps my leg and I catch a startled breath. "Do you think there are sharks in here?"

"Doubt it. It's fresh water," Kye mumbles, still examining my arm. "We need to bind this, put pressure on it."

The water ripples again, and Gabe emerges, followed by Victor. Both snap their masks onto their heads. Gabe has a diving tank strapped on each shoulder—his and mine. "How is she?" He closes the distance between us in two long strokes.

"Bleeding," Kye says. "So much for protecting her. You couldn't even keep her safe for two minutes once they showed up."

Something like shame flashes in Gabe's eyes. "I know. My strength doesn't mean squat against these demons." Worry etches lines around his eyes. "How bad is it?"

"I don't know," I say, my chin shaking. "I can't move. But it's still bleeding."

Kye glances at Gabe, speculating. "What are you wearing under your wetsuit?"

Gabe cocks his head, warily. "Why?"

Kye takes a pained breath, trying hard to be patient. "Because we need something to bind her wound, and Abby and I are both down to our underwear. Tell me you have on a T-shirt or something."

Gabe shakes his head. "Sorry. I can give her my swim trunks, but they're more likely to repel blood than absorb it."

Kye looks at Victor, eyebrow raised.

"I have a T-shirt." Victor hoists himself out of the water to his waist. Still holding onto the vine, he unzips his wetsuit. Gabe rips off the lower half of the cotton and hands it to Kye.

Kye takes the fabric, hesitating. "You're going to have to hold her up for me. I need my hands free."

Wordlessly, Gabe wraps an arm around my waist, lifting until my shoulders are above the water so Kye can get a better look at my wound. "Deep." He rubs his thumb over the cut, probing. "It's bad. Can you Heal it?"

I want to cry. "I can't even move. How would I Heal it? Besides, we don't have time. We have to get to the tomb before the demons come after us."

Kye winds the fabric around my elbow and ties it tightly. Already, a spot of red leaks through. "You can't go like this," he says. "Won't do us any good."

"You cannot send her back up," Victor says. "The ropes have been severed, and those above are busy fighting."

"What about Rose?" I ask. "Isn't she coming?"

Victor shakes his head. "The ropes were severed before she could be lowered down. It is only us now."

Alejandro makes a strangled noise and sinks underwater, swimming for the other side like his life depends on it. Seconds later, he's yelling, "Rosarita! Mi flor! Save yourself. Te amo."

"I will get him." Victor repositions his mask and swims after Alejandro.

"He's right," Gabe says. "We can't send her back up. She stands a better chance staying with us."

The muscle in Kye's jaw ticks the way it does when he's worried, but he nods. "Okay. It's going to be okay." He taps on Gabe's spare tank. "Let's get this on her so she can at least breathe."

Gabe straps on his own tank while Kye helps me into mine. His hands shake as he buckles the last strap, but he presses a steady kiss to my forehead. "Here we go."

A commotion on the other side has Gabe shooting out of our hidden alcove. Kye clutches my hand tight. Victor is screaming, yelling in Spanish. Battle sounds: thunder booms, rocks bounce off dirt, wood splinters, splashing, and then a high, keening yell—one of grief. My heart pounds. "What's happening?" I ask. "What's going on?"

Kye shakes his head. "I'll check." He swims out, and then returns, eyes wide, face chalky.

"What? What's happening?"

He secures his mask over his face, then reaches over to take care of mine. "We have to go. Now."

"Why?"

He takes a shaky breath. "Alejandro tried to climb up to help Rose. One of the shadows flew at him with a tree limb. It's bad, Abby. Really bad."

My next breath catches in my chest. "Maybe I can Heal him if you help move my hands. Take me to him."

Closing his eyes, Kye swallows. "Not this time, a ghrá. I think it's too late for Healing. We have a job to do."

"No, I–"

"Kye's right, Abby." Gabe, says, swimming around the corner. "You can't help him now. The best thing you can do is get that tomb sealed off so the demons can't hurt anyone else."

"What about Victor? Where's Victor?" My voice rises with panic. "Is Alejandro dead?"

"I am here." Victor floats in behind Gabe, his face raw with grief. "Put on your breathing apparatus, Abby. We must go now." He bites his own mouthpiece and sinks into the abyss, not bothering to wait for the rest of us.

"Are you sure I can't ...?" I start, glancing between Kye and Gabe, my brain refusing to comprehend this turn of events.

Gently, Kye presses my mouthpiece between my teeth and takes me away from the safety of the rocks. "He's gone, Abby. I'm sorry. Alejandro is dead."

THIRTY-EIGHT

Cold and Alone

I spit out my mouthpiece, struggling for air—real air that doesn't come from a tank. "How do you know? What if ..."

Gabe closes his eyes, urging me to move. "There's nothing any of us can do. We have to go now. Please stop arguing."

My mind creates hundreds of scenarios of what the demons have done to Alejandro, and how bad it must be for Victor to proclaim him definitely-dead. *Rose. Poor Rose.* How will I ever tell her? How will any of us? This is not the way things are supposed to go.

Kye presses the mouthpiece between my teeth again, and—blinking away tears—I take a practice breath, then another. Kye sinks under, dragging me behind. Gabe follows. We've only gone a few feet when Murtagh and two other sprites rocket past, leading the way. We find Victor forty feet down, staring into a cave. He shines his light on a second cave not far away. Kye makes a noise, some hand signals at the sprites, and Murtagh's blue-glowing friend directs us to the second cave. Murtagh blinks, a signal indicating we should go cautiously.

Red-eyed and grieving, Victor leads, and Kye drags me behind, dead weight.

How can I help seal the tomb when I can't even move?

As if he can read my thoughts, Gabe catches my foot. I turn my head, and he makes an OK sign with his fingers. I wish I could believe him. The cave narrows as we go, and unease skitters down my back until the toes on my left foot twitch. I wiggle them, hoping that whatever Boone did is temporary, and will wear off quickly.

Farther in, the darkness grows until we're completely dependent on our dive lamps. At one point, something slimy and long winds around my leg, startling a jerk from me. Gabe grabs hold of the enormous snake and flings it away. I shiver, finally able to move my right hand, and clumsily press it to my thumping heart, encouraged to realize that I can move a little.

After a while, we catch sight of a luminous green glow. As we come closer, the tunnel narrows, making it necessary for us to swim single file. Kye takes my face in his hands, forcing me to look into his eyes. Bubbles float out from his mouthpiece, but I can't understand his words. He closes his eyes and concentrates until a surge of energy sparkles in his fingers on my neck.

Use your Light. You're stronger than Boone. Heal whatever he did to you so you can swim. His voice. Inside my mind. This is new. He's never done this before, never told me he can. I shake my head to tell him I can't. I've been trying all along.

Try again. Concentrate and try again.

I can't.

Yes you can. Try, Abby. Just try. It's the only way. His hand trails down my uninjured arm to link with my fingers, and I can feel it, but not respond. Anger heats my blood, because I can't curl my fingers around his, can't respond to his touch, and it forms a Ping-Pong ball in my belly.

Kye's right. I do have to try.

That spark of heat spreads as I draw energy from Kye through our joined hands. I concentrate on the warm rush of power as it chugs through my veins like day-old ketchup, gradually bringing me back to life. Kye takes my other hand, and the heat spreads farther, moves faster. My pulse thrums, my breathing quickens, and when something brushes my calf, my eyes pop open with a start. Every part of me is sluggish. But when I try to move my limbs, they eventually obey. I couldn't swim far, but I might be able to get through the tunnel—I hope.

Kye signals for Gabe to make sure I don't get stuck, and leads us into the cave. *Here we go. Stay alert.*

As we navigate the rock and coral formations, the glow fades to darkest black, the temperature plummeting until I shiver uncontrollably. The water feels thick with an oppressive presence that swings like weights on my extremities. The water ripples, howling with a sound both familiar and foreboding. *We're close.*

Kye speeds ahead, and I follow until we pass into a cavern, blinded by an explosion of green light. The wailing moan is louder here. Kye presses his hands to my neck again. *Can you see anything? An opening? A door?*

I shake my head. The water is too cloudy.

Gabe taps my shoulder, wondering where the sprites have gone. I look around again, but the green has swallowed Murtagh's glow. Ahead of Kye, Victor stops, his grief seemingly eclipsed by dread.

He's kept a lead, but now hangs back, sticking close to us as if hesitant to go farther. Gabe's muscular arms cut through the muck, sending waves of gray silt rippling to either side of him. We follow as the muck thickens rapidly, boiling as if churned by propellers. My chest seizes when Kye's hand is ripped from mine and I lose sight of him. Panicked, I search for him, for anyone, but we've all been separated.

When the swirling calms, the sludge settles enough that I can make out silhouettes moving to form a circle around me. Melodic silence fills the cave, that of ebb and flow, of dark and light, from a flight of soprano to a rich chocolate baritone, and every note between. The harmony of the rising moon, the powerful sun, the ever-moving ocean, and the beating heart, the living core of life-sustaining earth. It vibrates, presses against my ears, shivers into bone and muscle, and flows into my veins, threatening to drown out thoughts of anything and everything except the all-consuming music.

Murtagh and his friends cower behind my tank, shaking so violently I can feel their quivering in my back. Whatever caused the upset in the water has them terrified.

Kye's back is to me, his gaze focused on a point in the distance, jaw clenching. He signals for Gabe and Victor to squeeze in tighter. I squint into the dark abyss as shapes come into view. The music swells. Overwhelming. Hypnotizing.

Terrifying.

A never-ending line of creatures. Everywhere we turn, they glide closer, showing off sharp claws and row upon row of razored fangs.

Forget the tomb. The four of us are facing an army of unfriendly mermaids.

It takes all my will-power to continue to breathe, slow and even, the way our scuba instructor continually stressed. I've faced a demon prince, fought the most powerful of shadow monsters, and sacrificed myself to Heal the person I love, but the mermaids are a hundred percent more terrifying.

The creatures wear no clothing or adornments, other than the seaweed caught in their long, tangled hair. But neither are their upper bodies built in the same way as humans. Long and sleek, with shimmery blue-green skin, and sharp dorsal fins protruding from their backs. The larger ones scowl, showing off shark-like teeth.

One mermaid seems to be in charge. Inky hair swirls around her shoulders, and the muscles in her scaled abdomen crunch with each flip of her fin. She opens her mouth and lets forth a hypnotic melody.

Beautiful. Simply beautiful. And peaceful.

Tired. My eyes ... so heavy. Heavy. Heavy. I close them. My body ... numb. Numb and heavy and tired. I relax, drifting, sinking, and let the warm, soft water embrace me in a cocoon.

The water rises up to greet Liam, stealing his breath upon impact. For the first time ever, he doesn't fight, choosing instead to fix his eyes on Raina, watching her shrink as he rockets toward the bottom. When he can no longer see her, even as a pinprick on the edge of the precipice, his lids fall closed as he allows the darkness to claim him.

But he does not die, as expected.

He awakes, surrounded by frighteningly beautiful water-beings who draw him into their circle. As black spots fill his vision, a timid-looking maid seizes his shoulders and crushes her mouth to his, filling his lungs with ... something. Not oxygen, but not water, either. His head buzzes pleasantly when their lips part, and he offers her a grateful smile, indescribably happy.

The maid takes his hand, drawing him farther into the deep, dark water. A mile, two miles, three miles down, over, away—until Liam has no idea where they're going, or from which direction they started. Each time he begins to struggle for air, the maid stops to again press her lips to his and fill his lungs, offering sheer pleasure.

After hours, days, months, or maybe only minutes, they reach a cave bathed in a glow of soft green. His escort kisses him once more, and then shoves him through a dark portal. A stone door closes between them.

When his eyes adjust he perceives the shape of a large fish-man, who speaks in a language Liam has never heard before, but over which he marvels because he can suddenly understand.

"Welcome to the realm of Sea Children. The souls who pass through this portal will be rededicated, ever more to belong as a Child of the Sea."

Liam tries to respond, but only manages to release bubbles of air. To be imprisoned and enslaved in an underwater kingdom is not in his plan. When he finds his voice, "My life and soul have long been dedicated to Queen Raina of Dryden. I can serve none other for the rest of eternity."

"You are not given to choose," announces the merman. "Once you've entered into the bosom of the Sea Colony, you may never leave. By accepting Aniya's help, you have accepted my help, and as such, belong to me."

Liam's heart plummets. "Please, sir. I am ever and always enslaved solely to Queen Raina, unto and after my life and death."

"You would rather die than to become a Sea Child?"

Liam closes his eyes, allowing peace in as he prays again for Raina and the babe. "Yes. Please, if you must sacrifice me, have mercy and make it swift." When he dares open his eyes again, the merman appears *thunderstruck, but resolute.*

"Granted. But it will not be swift." He waves at finned guards hiding *in the shadows. "Take him to the shark cave."*

Cold.

So, so cold.

The right side of my cheek and most of my body is pressed against a slab of unforgiving, solid ice. Shivering to my core, I open my eyes, wondering where I am and how I got here. The dark is absolute.

A moan escapes when I try to move. I'm no longer under water, nor am I wearing my scuba tank or mask. My hand flies to the control on my headlamp, but it, too, is gone. A deep, anxiety-ridden breath knifes down my throat and into my lungs, the cold that follows unlike anything I've felt before.

"Kye?" I croak. "Gabe? Victor?"

But the echo of my rusty voice is the only reply, the only stirring of life. With a great deal of effort, I pull my knees into my chest and wrap my arms around them, attempting to get warm, but already violently shaking.

My wet hair has dried in places, frozen painfully to my cheeks and neck, and it crunches when I peel it away. Light. I need Light. And hopefully a source of heat to unthaw the parts of me I can't feel—like my fingers. "Kye?" I murmur again.

Still no response.

I rub my hands together, my movements sluggish with the after effects of Boone's cut, and try to dig down to find the power hidden in my center. My Gift. The reason I'm here. In this hole. In this country. In this existence at all, I suspect. Finding the ball of heat takes all my energy, but finally, my Light, my power begins to warm my core, working out and down until it reaches my fingertips and glows soft blue.

I squint into the darkness, attempting to make out something other than the cold stone floor. Ten feet away, movement. A flicker reflects, refracts, spirals around and back into itself before starting the process over again. I inch forward and realize that my Light is reflecting off a large, black pool of water.

Panicking, I stand, turn until I'm dizzy. Full circle. Despair wells in my chest, threatens to steal my breath, overwhelm my functioning abilities.

Trapped in a dark cave.

On a slab of frozen stone maybe ten feet wide by eight feet long.

And

I

Am

Alone.

THIRTY-NINE

Death

I crash to my knees, skinning my hands on the rough edges of the rock, and barely avoid toppling head-first into the water. My Light goes out, plunging me back into cold, lonely darkness. I curl into a ball, terrified and freezing, until my thoughts align.

Eyes closed, concentrate, focus. Open third eye chakra, spiral the spotlight on ... who?

Kye. Of course Kye. Our connection will make him easiest to See.

But what about the others? Using my Sight will take lots of energy. I've never forced multiple visions. Who is most able to help me save the rest? Who has the training, the ability, and the skills that will ensure the best chance of survival for everyone else, even if I become dead weight?

Gabe. Something whispers inside me. *I should find him first. Gabe. Find Gabe. Gabe.*

But Kye will strengthen my power. We're better together. And if something happens to him, how will I go on fighting? How will I survive?

Even as I think it, something deep down whispers that I could do it, if I had to. I've spent most of the summer learning to function without him. If he hadn't come when he did, I would have proceeded.

No. Nothing bad is going to happen to Kye. I'll find him. Look for him first. No, next.

I should get to Gabe first. He can help me save the others. My nerves coil, tying into tight, hard knots. I close my eyes, concentrating the way Kye did when he spoke to me underwater.

Kye? Can you hear me?

Nothing, nothing, nothing.

Kye? Please? Please listen. Where are you? I don't know what to do.

The sensation comes again, stronger this time. *Find Gabe.* It isn't Kye's voice, but a female one.

"Gram?" I whisper. "Is that you?"

Gabe. Find Gabe.

Maybe it isn't Gram. I don't know who's trying to help me, or why, but my instincts, my guts, tell me that finding Gabe is our best chance. I refocus on Gabe, his mellow voice calming me, his strong arms protecting me, his smooth logic teaching me.

A glimmer of Light opens in my brain, disappearing as fast as it came. "Gabe, where are you?" I whisper to the dark. "Where?"

His arms around me, holding me, embracing me, cradling me as he takes me away from danger. His hands ... how they held my hair back when I was sick, poured water down my throat when I couldn't do it myself, how they smoothed the covers over my shoulders when he tucked me in—

Wait.

When did he tuck me in?

I shake away the question. I'll have to figure that out later.

His finger catches mine. The flood of relief when he realized I'm not pregnant. The shape of his mouth when he smiles. Our fingers entwined, the salty citrus taste on his lips when I kissed him ...

Bright white, but nothing more than a pinpoint. Again, I concentrate on the kiss, trying hard to not analyze why this is the incident that opens our connection.

The way his arms wrapped around me when I leaned into him, different from all the times he's carried me out of duty. He kissed me back. Not sweet or tender, but rough, hungry like he was determined to swallow every last drop of me before doing the right thing—because I was drunk and depressed, and he didn't want me to rebound. Because he wanted to ensure he could make me as happy as Kye does. Or because he knew Kye was coming and worried I'd regret kissing him so thoroughly. Or ... what? Why *did* he push me away?

Do I regret it? The question floats, hangs in the air, suspended, as if it needs to be answered before I'll be able to really See. After everything, all the anxiety it's given me, the pain it has caused—and I do regret the pain—I can't wish it undone.

Because the thing is, I do love Gabe a little.

I love Gabe.

This can't be happening. I can't love Gabe. Not like that. Not when Kye overwhelms every part of me. When Kye's near, he's all I see, all I need. Everything. But somehow Gabe has become part of me, too. Not the river-rush of emotion I have for Kye, but soft, like wind. Constant. Steady. Never-ending.

He helped me survive what could have been the toughest months of my life. He has protected and sheltered me, given up his personal life to be here to guard me. How can I not care about him? How can I not love him?

My Sight explodes again, sending searing pain through my forehead. When the Light dims, and the pain dulls to a low-grade throb, I see him. My Gabe.

Through a foggy haze, I distinguish the outline of a body sprawled on a cold stone floor. The contours of his shoulders, arms bulging with strength, leaves me no questions that it is indeed Gabe. With a thrust of energy, I distinguish subtle details: the shadow of stubble dotting his jaw, the curve of closed eyes, the gentle slope of his nose. The rapid rise and fall of his chest, the way he curls his arms around his knees, indicates that he's cold. But those same things also indicate he's alive. A trickle of relief drips through me as I stretch my Sight up and out, wondering how to get to him.

He too is without his scuba gear, and—from what I can tell—surrounded by water.

Those mermaids knew what they were doing.

The only difference is that his cave is lit with a soft green glow. Expanding my vision, I search for a way in or out—a tunnel, a skylight, anything. But there's nothing.

I swear, and Gabe's eyes pop open as if he hears me. His eyes meet mine. *Can he actually See me?* My vision shimmers, the window shrinks, fading into black. Slivers of cold slice my body, crawling up to nestle in my head. I need to move, force my blood to pump harder, but the vision has left me weak, nauseated, and confused.

Under my wetsuit, the diamond around my waist warms, reminding me that it's still there. All hope is not lost. But if I use it, my life very well might be. The Morrigana warned me that I will not have the same choices should I call them a second time.

Still. If it comes to survival, I have a way to save the others. The knowledge calms me somewhat. If I die, Kye can close the tomb. Gabe and Victor will protect him.

When the weakness passes and I'm able move, I sit up, ignoring my stinging palms as I cup my hands and force another feeble ball of Light. It takes some time, but when the Light is stable, I hold it steady in one hand and test the water temperature with the other. Biggest. Mistake. Yet.

Five seconds. I'm blinded by bright flashes, deafened by a long, shrill screech that grates my nerves until I curl onto the ground, covering my head with my arms. Something latches onto my ankle and yanks me off the platform, plunging me into the icy water. I kick for the surface, fighting, struggling against knives of pain that shoot up my legs, and manage to get my head above the water long enough to catch a mouthful of air before I'm sucked down again. This time, struggling does me no good. I continue moving through the dark water, sinking lower, farther away from any chance of taking another breath.

Somehow I manage to keep Light glowing in my fingertips, and I keep my eyes open, praying to find an escape.

The cave walls stretch far into the water. The mermaid doesn't look at me as she shoves me through a dark spot in the hard rock. I struggle harder, losing precious bubbles of air, and brace myself for an impact that never comes. It's a short, dark, tunnel. I kick hard, lungs screaming, squeezing until I see spots, but the mermaid wrenches me back. She wraps webbed fingers around the front of my wetsuit and yanks me up. Up. Up. More spots, and now my head pounds like it's been crunched between stones. *I'm going to die. And no one will ever find my body.*

We're too deep, the surface out of reach. Desperate for sweet air, I inhale, choking, because there is none. The mermaid thrashes, shoves me hard ahead of her, swimming faster than I've ever moved. I feel like a tug boat cutting through the wake of a tanker. I know I'll never make it, so I close my eyes and surrender to the blackness.

Then my head breaks free, and my cheek scrapes against another rock platform.

I can't remember how to breathe. Choking, gagging, I somehow manage to cough up the water blocking my airway. The world seems fuzzy, so I lie flat, fighting to pull in a breath. Something is different. A familiar, rhythmic sound that my befuddled brain struggles to compute.

Breathing. But not mine. My eyes fly open as oxygen—stale, heavy, cold—re-inflates my lungs. The same eerie green light from my vision is present here. Much better than complete dark.

My eyes focus, fix on the mermaid, watching from a few feet away. The breathing must be hers. I wonder how deep we were. Hope I don't end up with the bends after the rapid ascent. "Any idea what happened to my scuba gear?"

Her green eyes gleam, but give away no sign of comprehension. She turns her head, fixing her gaze on something. My eyes struggle to adjust, but near the wall is a shallow cove, where a dark lump rests not far from the ledge.

Fear consumes me. *What if it's not one of us? What if it's not human? What if it's a trap? I wish I could talk to her, the way Kye can...*

And then it hits me: maybe that's why the mermaid brought us together.

"Kye!" I slide into the water, cutting across to the alcove. "Kye? Kye. Please be okay. Please." The lack of response from my ring terrifies me. I heave myself onto the rock with fingers so frozen I can scarcely feel them and crawl to him, nerves crackling. My gut bubbles with a too-familiar sick sensation as I reach out to prod his shoulder. "Kye?" The figure flops onto his back with a sickening, liquid crunch.

I'm staring into Alejandro's misshapen face—battered, blue, one side caved in, vacant eyes staring at nothing. Some underwater thing has already taken residence in one of his ears, enveloping half of his head, including an eye. Other parts of him have been nibbled away. Chunks of flesh and tissue are missing in his cheeks, his forehead, shoulder, arm, torso.

A scream crawls up my throat, erupting over and over, as I scramble to the wall—as far from the body as possible—tears gushing. That it isn't Kye doesn't matter. I've already been stuck here for an eternity, unable to get out, unable to help Alejandro, unable to do anything more than cry.

And scream.

FORTY

Slave

After what feels like hours of incoherent mumbling, I remember the mermaid.

"What do you want?" I shriek, pointing at the deteriorating body. "Why did you bring me here? I can't fix that. No one could." My voice cracks as I fall apart, sobbing again.

She tilts her head, opening her mouth to emit a piercing screech. Startled, I cover my ears, begging, "Stop. Please, stop. I can't understand you." In the dim light, I try reading her energy, hoping to figure out what she wants. Fear. Nerves. Defiance—but not directed at me. Anger. Longing. Hunger. Intelligence. Desire. More anger.

It's clear she isn't supposed to be here. So why is she?

The screeching stops, and we size each other up. *She wants something.*

I reach out my hand, and she swims over to sniff my knuckles, and then, frowning, licks my palm. I yank it away and dip my hand in the water, wiping it on my wetsuit. "Gross."

She swims to Alejandro, but I can't look again, so I slam my eyes shut, knowing I'll forever be haunted by his face.

A touch on my foot has my eyes popping open, and then I'm sobbing unintelligible words of anguish. The mermaid witnesses me falling apart in a way I haven't since I last thought Kye was dead.

Maybe he really is dead this time, and Gabe too. And Victor. Maybe the mermaids killed them, and I'm the only one left. Maybe.

But I'm alive, and I need to find a way to stay that way. If the others are dead, I can't save them. The first lesson Gram taught me was that you can't Heal a dead person. End of story. That's that. As long as someone's heart is still beating, there's a chance. But once it stops—once they're dead—I can't do anything for them. They have no energy left to fix.

If I'm the only one of us still alive, I have to see this through. Close the tomb, destroy the demons, and eradicate the mess if for no other reason than to finish what we started in honor of those who are lost.

Clamping down my heartache, I wipe my face and press my lips together, filling my cracks with determination. When the mermaid sees that I am truly done crying, she knocks on the rock. The empty reverberating indicates that these walls are either very thin or hollow. She flips, dives deep, and comes up, pointing.

I scoot closer to the edge only to have her seize my ankle again. This time, I have the presence of mind to inhale. And because I get that she's taking me somewhere, rather than fighting, I follow her lead, hoping to get there faster than the last time.

When she shoves me through another gap, I figure out the tunnels are connected. By the time we reach the surface, my lungs are squeezed so tight, I think they'll collapse. My movements are sluggish to the point of non-existent. Without the mermaid's help, I'd never make it. She shoves me none-too-gently onto another ledge. This time, before my eyes adjust, I feel the warmth of a presence.

"Gabe?" I murmur, hoping.

"No," Kye croaks from behind me. "It's me."

Relieved, I throw myself at him, sobbing as his arms envelop me in comfort. I bury my face in his neck. His skin is warm, his breath in my hair soothing, his cheek on my forehead the strongest form of reassurance. Kye's alive. Maybe the others are too. Except

Alejandro. The memory of his vacant stare burns my throat, but I swallow past it. "Are you hurt?"

Kye squeezes me tighter. "Cold. And terrified. I'm better now that I'm holding you. How did you get here?"

I blink, forcing my eyes to adjust to the dim light, and point at the mermaid. "Her. We found Alejandro." My voice cracks. "He's dead. Really, really dead."

He mutters a string of swear words. "You saw him?" I nod, swallowing grief and burying my face in his neck. He rubs his hands up and down my arms, whispering, "Do you trust this mermaid?"

"What other choice do we have?"

"I'm going to talk to her," he says. "It's easier underwater. We won't go far, but stay aware. If you sense danger ... I want you to do whatever you have to."

He unsheathes his dive knife, but I stop him, replacing the blade. "Take it with you." I hold up my ringed hand. "I have my own weapons."

He kisses my knuckles, and his lips turn up when all the gems illuminate—including the new ones. "You're still wearing it."

I pull my hand away, uncomfortable. How can I love Kye so completely and still have an inexplicable longing for Gabe?

Kye frowns as he turns away. "Wish me luck."

Fear coils in my belly as the dark water sucks him down and the mermaid follows. Seconds tick by, becoming minutes that seem like hours. I've nearly chewed a hole in my lip by the time he bubbles to the surface—alone.

I breathe a sigh of relief, unable to speak.

Shivering, Kye hauls up next to me, his dripping hair and sopping wetsuit leaving a puddle. "Still not sure if we can trust her, but she's our only chance."

"What does she want?"

He scrubs his hands over his face and slicks back his hair. "Freedom. Problem is, I'm not sure we can promise her that. And *she's* not sure she can promise *us* that, either."

I huddle closer, summoning some warmth for us to share. "Freedom from what? From whom?"

"The demons. Get this—the mermaids used to be human. Lived in a city with a thriving economy until an earthquake dumped the community underwater." He makes a plopping noise, demonstrating with his hands. "The people who lived were taken captive by demons and given a choice between death or an eternity of servitude. Those who didn't want to die were given Gifts to help them survive in their new environment. Fins, gills, webbed fingers. They became slaves to demon kings. Malina has been helping guard this tomb for five hundred years. They all have. But she wants the open ocean, the sunlight, the sky. I think she hopes we'll destroy the tomb entrance so she can break free."

"If they want to help us, why did they take us captive? Separate us?"

Kye squeezes more water out of his wetsuit. "I don't think they all want out, Abby. Just Malina. We have no reason to trust her, but by being here, by bringing you to me, she risks retribution. I think we have to risk something too. She'll help us find the others, so that's our first priority. We need all the strength we can get. But it'll be taxing without our tanks. No way to breathe in between."

"Tell her to let us catch our breath before she brings us down. That will help."

He scoots forward, sinking his feet into the water. "Ready?"

I run through the breathing techniques I learned from the dive instructor and open my eyes to accept Kye's outstretched hand. And then we plunge in, trusting a mermaid who could very likely be leading us to our deaths.

Two caverns later, we find Victor, passed out, barely breathing in the cold. I want to Heal him, give him a smidgen of warmth to get him going, but Kye won't let me. He thinks I don't have enough strength to risk it.

I hate knowing he's right.

Kye slaps Victor's cheeks, yells at him, unzips his wetsuit and yanks chest hairs before Victor finally comes around. We give him time to orient himself while we explain what's happening, and then the three of us set out to find Gabe.

The next two caverns are empty except for the green glow that seems brighter each time we surface. The third time we come up in an empty cave, the alarm that's been gnawing on me since I Saw Gabe in the vision blooms into full-fledged panic. Something's wrong. Something must be wrong.

"What if we don't find him? What if they've done something to him? Killed him the way they did Alejandro? What if—"

Kye covers my quivering lips with his fingers. "Don't. We'll find him."

Still bobbing in the water, I turn, and turn, and then turn again. "And how are we ever going to find our way out? It's like a labyrinth. We can't see. We can't breathe. We can't find Gabe or Murtagh or the tomb. We're on the brink of hypothermia—Victor, don't shush me, your lips are blue—and I don't know about either of you, but I haven't eaten in like, two days. What if we die here?"

"That is not going to happen—" Victor starts.

"It's reality," I insist.

Sighing, Kye ducks underwater again, communicating with the mermaid in a language I stopped trying to decipher when I realized how badly mermaid language hurts my ears. When he resurfaces, he swims with long, smooth strokes toward a rocky ledge and boosts himself up, then offers me a hand. Victor joins us, and we all huddle together.

"What did she say?"

Kye holds me close, re-establishing his territory. "I told her we need to rest, but I'm not sure she understands. Mermaids don't take breaks."

"They do not sleep?" Victor rubs his hands together. They're purple. Worried, I cover his hands with mine and summon some warming Light.

"Well, they do." Kye frowns at our joined hands. "But there's no underwater distinction for night and day. I'm gathering that they sleep seasonally—a hibernation-type deal. So when they're awake, it's for a really long time."

Wishing I could hibernate, I yawn, leaning against Kye's shoulder as Victor's hands turn a more healthy pink. "Must be nice to be able to sleep for an entire season."

Kye kisses my hair. "Nah. I love night. Holding you, watch you sleep, feeling your heart beat in rhythm to mine. I'd do anything to preserve that."

Victor tips his head in thought. "I agree. Sleep is a luxury to be enjoyed. There is nothing better than the comfort of a cozy bed, cool, soft sheets, and the whir of a fan blowing all thoughts away."

"Night sleeping *is* better, even without a bed." I smile at Victor. "We once slept on a bench in a shopping mall in Las Vegas."

Kye groans. "Those metal slats left patterns on our backs for like, two days. My neck has never been so stiff."

"Mine either," I agree, an idea trying to surface, but not quite reaching the conscious part of my brain.

"I have spent many nights with my back in the sand," Victor says, "and others in lounge chairs not made to be used as beds. Those left lasting marks. But worse were the bug bites. Once, I fell asleep near a sand hive of bees and was stung three times before I could move."

Victor's words tickle my brain again, leaving me reaching. Pattern. Bees? Something.

"I am a night person," Victor continues. "Right, Abby? We first met when she took a late night run to my yard."

Kye stiffens. "You were running in the middle of the night?"

I squirm, uncomfortable. "It was our first day here. I slept the whole trip and when I woke up, I had all this energy to expel. Didn't intend to go out alone. It just sort of happened."

Kye glances at Victor, then back at me. "Where was Gabe? My mom?"

I can't meet his eyes. "Asleep."

"And you went running in a strange country all by yourself? Abby!"

Finally sensing he's said something wrong, Victor amends, "Not by herself. No. With Murtagh. She came to save him from a sprite-eating lizard."

Kye drops his arms from around me, baffled. "What?"

"Long story," I mumble. "He was looking for the sprite colony—did you know they build their communities like beehives? A kind of honeycomb ..." I trail off as the idea that's been struggling to get through finally gels. "What if the mermaid colony is built like a honeycomb? In a repeating circular pattern. Me in the first, Alejandro in the second, Kye in the third, Victor in the fifth, then six, seven," I count off my fingers. "This is eight. So if this place is built the way the bees do it, number nine might be the last cave before we go back to number one again."

"If that is true," Victor says, "there must be a tunnel that leads to a central location."

"What if Gabe's in the middle?" I wonder aloud.

"That wouldn't make any sense," Kye says. "But I bet there's something else important there. Like a tomb. If there's a middle, and the passages are cut into each cave of the pattern, then there must also be more tunnels on the outer rim, right?" He stands, running his hands along the rock wall behind us and knocking. It makes a similar hollow sound.

My heart sinks. "If there's an outer rim, there are a lot more caves. It could take us weeks to find Gabe."

"Yes, it could," Kye agrees, and for the first time since I brought up the kiss thing, I sense that he's worried about Gabe. "Might be faster to find the tomb."

"But we need Gabe," I say. "We planned to hit the tomb with six people, not three. We're already down ..." I stop, not wanting to bring up Alejandro. None of us needs to be reminded what we've lost. "At the last tomb, we needed strength to close the door. Way too many shadows escaped while we struggled with it. Gabe could prevent that."

"I know, Abby," Kye says. "But how much farther can we swim? We're already exhausted. What good will we be at the tomb if we use all our energy searching for Gabe?"

"You're not suggesting we leave him!"

"I do not think that is what he means, Abby," Victor cuts in. "And I must agree. We could look for Gabe until we drop with exhaustion, or we can find the tomb and get to work."

"A ghrá, I promise we won't leave Gabe behind. I just think we need to focus on one task at a time. We haven't found Gabe, but we might know where to look for the tomb. I think we need to do that before we collapse from exhaustion."

I want to argue, want to convince them that they are so wrong because we need Gabe. We *need* him. But I can't, because the truth is that Victor and Kye don't need Gabe. The only person who really needs him is me.

Kye asks Malina to take us to the middle of the colony, inciting an underwater wail that echoes off the walls. I worry that she'll back out, leaving us trapped here, but Kye surfaces and signals that we're ready.

Without a word, Victor pushes forward.

And somehow, I do too.

FORTY-ONE

Bloody Tomb

After another half hour of exhaustive swimming, I realize Kye was right that we should look for the tomb first. The subzero water has ceased to keep me going, and is now slowing me down. I'm completely numb. We do find Murtagh, which makes me feel a little better, but when we emerge in the fifth empty cave, I begin to doubt my beehive theory.

The light is brighter here, and eerie, glowing through the thick fog that hovers on the water. There is a nearly palpable evil in this place.

We find a ledge, but it's narrow, so Kye and I stay in the water while Victor scopes out the cave. My muscles ache, and my head throbs from hunger, exhaustion, and from holding my breath for too long.

"Here," Victor says. "There is a tunnel here, and it is not underwater."

We find a place where the ledge is wider and hoist ourselves onto the rock. I follow Victor, running my hands along the muddy walls where water slides in sheets. Occasionally, clods of dirt rain from the ceiling. I've done this before, and it wasn't all that long ago. Only this time, Kye is with me.

As the cold numbness wears off, my wounded arm throbs, blood pressing against the makeshift bandage. I flex my fingers to stretch the muscle, not wanting to consider how deep the laceration or how extensive the damage. We can't afford the time required to Heal it, even enough to stop the bleeding, nor will I borrow energy from Kye or Victor and weaken them before we face the demons. So I bear the pain in silence.

Eventually the tunnel branches off from the main hall. Here, light pulses with energy so black that a bubble of it throbs. Ribbons of darkness slither along the floor, up the walls, snaking back to reach through the air, only to be sucked in again. Despite the dark fog, I'm disoriented by blinding light, and one step nearly plunges me into more water. I stumble backward, flailing. "End of the road."

When my eyes adjust, I see that we've reached another ledge.

Victor says, "I do not see a tomb here."

"Where else is there to look?" I murmur.

Kye scrubs his hands over his face. "What now?"

"I don't know I—"

"*Calin* friend!" Murtagh's light blinks rapidly as he emerges from the water and lands on my shoulder. "Find Dragon guy, I did. Right away needs help. A Healer. Soon, very soon."

Relief pours into me. Murtagh has found him.

"Abby. Help. Please, help." It's Gabe's voice, but I can't see him—can't see anything.

"Gabe?"

Kye grips my hand, holding me in place.

"Here. Over here. Need your help."

"We can't see anything," Kye says. "Are you in the water?"

"No," Gabe says. "On a lip near it. You might have to swim to me."

"This is not right," Victor whispers.

I agree. But it's Gabe, and I can't risk leaving him. "Are you hurt?"

"Yes." His voice is weak. "My leg—it's broken. Maybe some ribs. I need your help. Need you to Heal me."

My heart sinks. Gabe could have twenty broken bones, but he would never ask me to Heal him. Ever. My voice shakes. "Which leg?"

"Maybe both," he says. "Hurry. I'm in so much pain."

"That's not Gabe," I tell Kye.

Murtagh blinks in agreement. "Not Dragon guy, *Calin*."

"I know, Murtagh," I whisper. "But I have to pretend—it's the only way to find the tomb."

"He wants you to get in the water," Victor says. "So you must not."

"He also wants her to come to the other side of this cave," Kye says, agreeing with Victor. "Which means that's probably where we need to go."

"I will jump in," Victor says, his expression hardening. "There will be a disturbance. And if there is not, I will make one." He points at Kye and Murtagh. "You go with Abby along the ledge and find the tomb. When we are through, we will find the real Gabe."

"Abby?" Gabe's voice says again, sounding strained. "Abby, hurry. It hurts. I'm in so much pain."

"I'm coming." My chest squeezes. The voice sounds so much like him, I wonder if it could really *be* Gabe. "Victor, we don't know what's waiting in the water—it's too risky."

Victor's eyes are still red, but there's a fire in them I've never seen before. "Those demons killed my best friend. Now I must destroy them."

Kye claps him on the shoulder. "You sure about this?"

He nods. "I am sure."

Worried that I might not have another chance, I throw my arms around Victor and hug him tight, kiss his cheek. "Thank you for being a true friend."

Victor signals a countdown. Murtagh perches on my shoulder, and Kye slides his hands along the wall, ready to move. "Kye, what if it's really Gabe?" I whisper, not wanting Victor to hear.

He frames my shoulders like he's squaring me for a punch to the gut. "Then we're in big trouble, because it probably means he's working for Boone." Kye gives Victor a nod and Victor leaps, shouting profanities. His splash sprays us head to toe. We scoot along the edge, quickly and cautiously, waiting for Victor to resurface.

Waiting. And waiting. And waiting.

Halfway around the cave, Kye finds another opening. "Call Gabe," he whispers.

"Gabe?" My voice echoes. "You still there?"

"Abby," the voice says again. "I'm here. Please hurry."

We're close. Kye steps into the dark, gesturing for me to call again.

"Gabe?"

"Abby, I'm in so much pain." There's a patch of space where the light doesn't reach, and it sounds like Gabe's voice comes from there. Kye inches forward, cautious. I am about to enter as well when Victor finally resurfaces, yelling unintelligible words. Kye and I both whip around, realizing that Victor is surrounded by mermen—angry, large mermen with talons and sharp teeth. One holds him captive, jabbing a sharp piece of bone against his throat.

"Abby," Gabe says again.

Fighting his captor, Victor yells, "Save yourselves and seal the tomb!"

I've never been so torn. I have to be sure the voice isn't really Gabe's, but I can't just stand here while Victor fights for his life. Kye glances between me and the water, looking torn himself. "What do we do?"

After a moment of indecision, I take Kye's hand and brush Murtagh into it. "Help him. Both of you. I got this."

"It's a trap." Kye checks his knife again, sounding petrified.

"I know," I agree. "They both are."

He nods, accepting that this is how the battle has to go, and dives in to help Victor.

"Abby, hurry," Gabe begs.

My arm throbs with every beat of my racing heart, the inside of my wetsuit sleeve growing wet and sticky. I approach the shadow cautiously, and as my eyes adjust, make out Gabe's outline. I know his build well.

It's really him.

My throat constricts. How could he? How could he betray me?

"I'm so glad you're here," he moans. I want to scream and yell and beat on him, tell him exactly how much I hate him in this moment, but I can't let on that I know. Cunning is my best weapon against Gabe's strength. My only weapon. I'm no match for him.

I approach, forming a ball of Light in my fist. "What happened?"

"Fought with some mermen," he says, sounding more pathetic than ever. "One of them sent me through the rapids and over a waterfall. There were boulders at the bottom. I didn't have a chance. Half my body is broken."

I can't Heal him. It would be suicide. But I have to pretend to try, because that's what he expects. "I don't have the pendant, or my crystals."

"You have the ring," he says.

The knife twists. Of course. It's always about the ring. "Lie flat," I tell him. "Let's see what I can do." He does as I ask, and I want to stomp on him, really break his leg. Both of them. Instead, I swallow hard, preparing to do something truly horrible to my best friend. I take my position near his waist. "Which leg?"

"Left," he says, writhing in pain.

I run my hands through his energy field, spinning chakras, but as I near his leg, I encounter a solid wall of nothingness. It's as if he has no leg at all. My eyes pop open, and I verify that Gabe's leg is, in fact, still there. Then I close them and try again. This time the block pops up near his torso, in his core chakra. I break through, wondering how I'm supposed to even pretend. He's so blocked. When I get to his third eye chakra, it's wide open, and the things I See in it are not things from Gabe's life, but someone else's. Sinister memories, thoughts.

It's not really Gabe.

My hands shake as I go through the motions, wondering if he knows I'm spinning backwards, slowly sucking away his energy. He captures my wrist, eyes bright and anxious. "Now use the ring," he insists. "I need the power of the ring."

"I ... I don't think it will help," I start.

"Try." Gabe-not-really-Gabe sits up, and now I can see his face. Everything about him looks like Gabe—my Gabe—except his eyes. They're so violet that in this light they appear red.

"Boone."

He grins, a long, wide grin that splits his face with an evil edge. "I knew you'd come for me someday," he says. "Women are such fickle creatures. One day kissing one man, the next moving in with another."

He's been watching us.

The sounds of battle continue behind me, muffled by the water. "The question is," Boone continues in Gabe's voice, "which one will you choose when the drama dies down?"

Boone-who-looks-like-Gabe's gaze shoots to the water as he stands—on legs that are clearly not broken—and cuffs my wrists in his hand. "Let's go. We have work to do." Behind him, the dark space opens into another cave and he takes me there, where the faintest hint of the green light shimmers in streaks along the walls, shooting jolts of energy into the crevices and casting the room in a dull glow. On my left, a tall stone door leans slightly open. Not enough so a person could fit through, but enough for shadows to come and go. There is no pulsing energy, nor ghostly howling here, but I know—know—that Boone has at last brought me to the tomb. Just past the door, the tunnel curves around, a deep, dark crypt.

"You do see that it's already open?" I point out a shadow as it squeezes through and screams away.

"Needs to be closed," he says. "Having shadows wreak havoc around the world, creating mischief, is not helping my cause. They're in my way."

"That makes two of us," I mutter. And then, "I don't have the Keys this time."

"You have the ring," he says, his Gabe façade fading rapidly.

"The ring isn't enough. I need them all." His face contorts, reshaping into its original non-Gabe form. I notice his energy is still trickling out—unbeknownst to him. It's a very small leak, but a leak nonetheless. It may take a while for him to feel it, but he will. Eventually. And I hope I'm ready to strike when he does.

"I've watched you," he says, shoving me forward. The façade is completely gone now, replaced by Boone's face—the scarred one that has always frightened me to the point of hysteria. "You came here to do this, to seal it. You and the Dragons have spent weeks planning. I'm not holding the dagger to your throat the way Juri did, not forcing you to do something against your will. I helped you find the tomb so you can fulfill your purpose."

This is not what I've ever expected from Boone.

"How did they say you should close it?"

Before I can answer, the shadow that has been trying to squeeze out flies at my face, screeching and wailing like an injured bat. It hurls at me, pelting me with shards of water and dirt until I drop on the ground and cover my head to protect my eyes. Boone shrieks, swatting the shadow away.

I run.

He catches me around the waist and shoves me forward, pressing my hands against the door. I heave, trying to close it, but my wound pulses, the bandage so soaked that blood trickles down my arm and drips like little sparks of power on the floor. I press the cloth, feeling like a baby for wanting to cry over pain, not realizing until later that both my hands are now coated with blood. When Boone sees me attempting to shove the tomb closed manually, he helps. We manage to get the door sort-of in place.

There are two dark-red hand prints on the stone, between which is a cutout I would never have seen except that it's at my eye level, and is now sparkling with crimson flecks. There's another cutout, bigger. I can't imagine what should fit inside it. I fit my ring into the smaller one, summoning my Light, relieved that it comes more easily now than an hour ago.

Again, the earth quakes and cracks, debris rains on our heads, and the ground pitches me forward as if trying to beat me against the wall. My arm gushes, and the shadows writhe as if my blood is exactly what they crave. There is no loud and scary voice this time, just the empty hollow howl of what some would call ghosts.

It starts with one, and is soon joined by another, and another, until a chorus swells. There are more shadows here than can be seen. Their energy circles the tomb, some scrambling back inside, while others slither out, screeching and wailing and moaning in anger. They press against me, sucking at my energy as if waiting for something.

Now I know what they want.

Shivering, I remove my bandage, and rub a circle of blood around the cutout, reciting an incantation I must know from a past life. Green light snakes around the edges of the door as another dirt clod falls from the ceiling. I recite again, over and over, rubbing blood around the cutout while holding my ring in the slot. It is only when Boone presses his hand against the stone that the upper hole opens, and I can feel air being sucked inside it with a loud whoosh.

The shadow that just came for me becomes the first victim, but it is not the only one. Boone and I watch as six or seven shadows are sucked through. Boone drops his hand, but the vacuum remains open, taking with it the evil presences I have felt for so many days. When I'm certain there's nothing more I can do, short of personally recruiting the shadows to follow me to the tomb, I turn to him.

"Where's the real Gabe?"

"Is it closed?" Boone asks, ignoring my question.

"Yes," I tell him, though I'm not sure. This part was too easy, and it leaves me uncomfortable.

"You positive?"

There's a new light in his eyes, one I recognize. This is the Boone I've experienced in the past. "I'll answer your question when you answer mine."

"I'll take that as a no," he says, his voice gruff. He shoves me on the ground, his knee digging into my arm as he holds me in place. He removes the dagger from his shirt and lays the blade against my cheek, the red-stained tip coming ridiculously close to my mouth. "Must need more blood."

It's not my blood you need, idiot. But telling him that would put the others at risk, and I can't do that. His knee on my arm sends shockwaves of pain across my chest, causing my vision to blur. Boone lifts his knee as blood pools beneath me, and he rubs his hands in it, presses them against the stone door.

The moment he can tell it's not going to work, I see the bulb click on in his brain. He stands and walks deeper into the tunnel, where there is only inky blackness. I sit up, dizzy from blood loss, and lean against the door. Though the green light still pulses, everything is now tinted gray around the edges. Pressing my hand against my wound, I start forward, refusing to let Boone win. I've only taken a few steps when the world tilts, my shoulder hitting the wall as I begin to slide down.

Whatever battle is happening with the mermaids has quieted significantly, leaving only the wailing shadows to keep my mind moving—however sluggishly.

I. Will. Not. Pass. Out.

Not today. Not now. The light I kept at my fingertips has faded, so I summon it again, pulsing energy into my damaged flesh and hoping to slow the bleeding, even temporarily. The Light is weak and drains what little warm energy I have left, but does help some.

By the time I start forward, Boone has returned. "He told me I needed it. I thought he was lying. That Dragon really will do whatever it takes to save you."

His words paralyze me. "What do you mean, whatever it takes?"

He holds up a vial filled with dark-red blood and uncaps it. "This is Dragon blood. It will help complete the seal. I had hoped to use this to increase my powers, but these demons make the cost necessary." He dribbles a line of it into the open cutout, muttering about not knowing the chant, and grabs my arm, yanking me up and hauling me back to the door. "Say the words."

"Whose blood is that?"

"Just say them."

"They're different for someone else. I need to know who is helping form the seal."

His violet eyes light with vengeance. "One last gift from your guardian Dragon."

"What did you do to him? Where is he?"

"I took him out of the equation." He shoves me again, presses my face against the stone door. "Say the words."

My throat constricts, shock draining my ability to think.

"Say. The words." Boone repeats.

My voice cracks, and tears break free and run down my cheeks as I mutter the necessary incantation. I can't concentrate on sealing this tomb if Gabe is dead. Gabe, who took care of me when I was drained, who protected me from strangers and friends alike, who tucked me in bed when I couldn't function through my pain. Gabe—the Gabe I love.

The Gabe I love.

When the tomb is sealed, Boone drops his hand from my neck, watching as I slide to the ground, sobbing. His scar puckers as he looks me over. "You're quite useful to have around, Abby. Maybe it's better to leave you alive. For now."

It's the first time I've heard him use my actual name. I want to spit on him, but am too busy sobbing.

"I'll see you next time. If you make it out of here." Footsteps. I open my eyes in time to see him turn to look back as he goes white, falling to his knees near the water, and watch as his energy is syphoned out and much of it is sucked into the tomb. Knowing this might be my only chance, I crawl toward him. His face is ash gray. I plant a foot in the small of his back and shove. He topples into the water, where a swarm of mermaids rush the sinking body, followed by two tiny balls of light.

My fingers are frozen from blood loss, and I need to go to Gabe—the real Gabe. I stare into the water, wondering where Kye and Victor have gone. I hope they're all right. There are no more battle sounds, no more splashing or thunder. Nothing but silence.

Panic grips my chest. What if they're all dead? What if Gabe was right that this is a suicide mission, and I'm the only one still breathing? The cold has left me numb, and I can feel remnants of Boone's dark energy soaking into me. Powerless to stop it, I let it happen, collapsed on the ground, fingers trailing into the water as my Light fades.

FORTY-TWO

Freedom

Clanking metal reverberates in my head, an explosion of pain, and light shines in my eyes. My body convulses as if it really, really wants to get rid of something, but can't.

Can't be in heaven, so I must not be dead.

"Abby, come on. Come on. Wake up."

It's Kye. He's alive. My eyes flutter. "You're not dead?"

"No," he says, sprinkling water over my face. "But you will be soon if we don't get you to a Healer."

"I am a Healer," I mumble, closing my eyes again.

"Abby, come on. You have to stay awake."

"We've found the tanks," Victor says from a distance. "And also ..."

"Bad, very bad." Murtagh's voice is faint, but I'm relieved to hear it. "*Calin* happy, not."

I try opening my eyes again. Victor looks like he has more to say, but is hesitant. "Gabe's dead, isn't he?"

Victor doesn't respond. Kye's hand is on my cheek and he turns my head, forcing me to look at him. "Stay with me. Listen. We have to get you out of here. You've lost way too much blood, and we can't help you without getting you out of here. Victor and I both have important things to carry. How do we give you some extra strength so you can swim?"

They'll be carrying bodies. And I'm glad. I can't bear the thought of leaving Alejandro or Gabe down here forever.

"I need my crystals," I croak, wondering what happened to them. Was I wearing crystals when I zipped on my wetsuit?

"We don't have crystals, Abby. Only your ring."

It's not enough. But I'm wearing the cuff bracelet Kye gave me for my birthday, and that will help. "My ..." It takes more energy than I have to speak, to even think. "My arm."

Kye cradles my head on his lap. "I know, babe. I know it hurts. I'm sorry. I'm so sorry."

"No," I mumble. "Bracelet. Suit."

He shakes his head, confused, until Victor stalks over and starts to unzip my wetsuit. "She wants you to get her bracelet, gringo."

Kye slaps Victor away. "I'll do it. Turn your head." He braces me against his chest and peels the suit over my shoulders, down around my waist, and then goes to work freeing my arm. Blood has caked around the wound, gluing the neoprene to my skin. Removing it would be painful if I weren't so numb. Kye's intake of breath, tells me that it's worse than we realized. He continues to work, faster now, as if desperate, and finally manages to expose my bracelet. He then goes to work unbending it, until I tell him to stop. "Leave it on. I just need to touch it with my fingers. But you'll have to lift my hand to it."

"Abby, you don't have any energy to spare."

"I'll be fine," I lie. Because he's right. These stones will do little good in my current state.

"Take some of mine," he begs. "Please. You'll never make it out of here if you don't."

And because I know he's right, I let him help me rub the stones, accept the energy that flows through his fingers into mine, and breathe deeply. I won't be Healed, but I will be well enough to stand on my own, and I will find the strength to swim.

Victor straps a scuba tank over my shoulders, careful to avoid my injured arm. "I am glad you are still here with us, Abby. I did not want to return to the resort without you." I nod, unable to speak. We've lost too many friends today.

Kye won't let me see Gabe, but I know they've found him and are waiting until the last minute to bring him to the ledge. I'm afraid to look. Afraid to see his last expression and know that he died protecting me.

Wordlessly, I slide into the water, testing my mask and mouth piece, making sure my equipment works. When I've given the thumbs-up, the guys disappear into the tunnel to retrieve Gabe. Malina floats silently underwater, ready to take us to Alejandro, and then to freedom.

Tears fog my mask as I float in Malina's wake. Now that we have our scuba tanks, there's no need to surface in each cavern, and it speeds our journey significantly. It takes only minutes for Murtagh to show us the way. Victor insists on a moment alone with Alejandro, though I don't want him to see, don't want this to be his last memory of his best friend. But we respect his request and let him go alone, knowing there's no easing his grief.

I risk a glance at Kye, who has Gabe's large form slung over his shoulder, still wearing his scuba gear. I can't see his face, but considering the damage to Alejandro's, I decide that's for the best. Kye sees me looking and caresses my jaw, urging me to turn my head, his eyes alight with sympathy. *You don't want to see.*

We're at least fifteen feet below the cave, but can still hear Victor's grief. This isn't the way my birthday should be ending. This isn't the way any day should end. We shouldn't be saying goodbye to our friends.

Victor enters the water, the weight of Alejandro's body creating a wave that reaches us. Malina leads us out and I follow with Murtagh, resisting the urge to glance behind me at the others as I struggle to keep my mask clear.

What feels like hours later, we emerge into another cave. Confused, I glance back at Kye.

It's the way out. There's a tunnel. We can walk the rest of the way.

I don't have the energy to walk. And I know Kye and Victor can't carry the bodies that far. They're strong guys, very strong, but Gabe and Alejandro are heavy, and soaked, and we're all exhausted. I can't help but think how easy it would be for Gabe to carry two people, if only he were not one of them. As if he can read my thoughts, Kye's voice explains, *We'll leave them here and go get help to bring them out.*

When we surface, Kye and Victor hoist their loads onto a path that is much wider than the ones in the other caves. Sunlight streams in from an opening above our heads and I swim to a patch, relieved to feel he natural warmth. Before I can emerge, Malina grabs my wrist and pulls me down again, her eyes pleading.

Kye speaks to her and she replies, gesturing with her arms and swishing her tail.

Freedom.

She holds out her arms, and I notice—for the first time—that they're scarred, tattooed. It's as if she's bound by shackles.

Can you Heal them without shackling yourself in her place? Is that possible?

I don't have my Healing crystals, or herbs, but I'm bleeding. If blood can seal a tomb, it can—theoretically—free a mermaid. I nod, hoping it's true. Malina risked a lot to save us. She deserves for me to at least try.

Pink ribbons of blood swirl in the water when I unbind my cut. The bleeding has slowed significantly, thanks to the cold water, but what's left of Alejandro's T-shirt is bright red with it. I wrap the shirt around Malina's damaged wrists and hum, bubbles of sound floating away. My ring glows as I summon my Light, growing brighter, warming my hands as I circle the scars, and fading the black rings to gray. Spots sparkle in my eyes as I transfer the small amount of energy Kye gave to me into Malina. I'm slipping. But he's there, holding me up, his hands joining mine as we remove the darkness that keeps her bound. With Kye's help, the last of the gray lifts and dissolves in the water, leaving her grinning from ear to ear.

My own wrists burn like they're on fire, but I do my best not to acknowledge that as she hugs me, her mouth awkwardly struggling to form the words, "Thank you."

We join Victor on the path. He has removed Gabe's scuba gear and laid him flat on his back, eyes closed. A line of blood trickles from a cut on his head and more blood gushes from a wound on his arm that looks suspiciously like mine. But Gabe is not mangled. He's not even horribly bruised. He appears peaceful and innocent, like he's taking a trip to dreamland and will wake again in the morning.

Swallowing hard, I bend to brush his hair out of his eyes. "Abby ..." Kye starts.

And then Gabe coughs.

Startled, I hold my hand under his nose, check the pulse in his neck. It's faint, but there. Gabe is still alive. Relief flows like a cool river. "He's not dead. I can help him, because he's not dead."

"I know." Kye kneels next to me, helping me roll Gabe on his side as he coughs up water.

He knew? "Then why? Why would you let me believe he was dead? Do you have any idea how devastated I've been?"

He tries to offer a hug of apology, but I shrug him away. "I didn't want you trying to Heal him while you were already energy deficient. I still don't want you trying. Gabe didn't either. Before we left, he made me promise that I wouldn't let you risk yourself for him, and he promised me the same thing."

"He could have died, Kye! While we were swimming, he could have died, and then I wouldn't have a chance to help him. I can't Heal a dead person."

"No. I wouldn't have let that happen. Why did you think we took the time to make sure he was breathing through his mouthpiece? He's not dead, Abby. Not even close. Just unconscious from loss of blood, same as you were."

Anger turns my blood to lava. "You have no right to take away my choice to Heal someone. No right, Kye."

Gabe coughs again, spitting water and wheezing. His eyes roll as if he's trying to open them. "No," he says.

I lean closer, caressing his shoulder. "Gabe?"

"No," he says again. "I don't need you to Heal me."

I sit back, feeling like I've been punched. "Gabe, I—"

"Don't need it. Only suffering from a cut, same as you." But his eyes roll back in his head and he falls unconscious again.

My muscles tighten, anger overflowing. "Too bad. That's just too damn bad." And though I know it's stupid, I call forth my Light—weak as it is—and begin to spin his chakras.

After everything that has happened today, I'm positive about two things: Gabe's blood has been poisoned—same as mine—and Kye lied to me. Again.

I drown out the sound of Kye's objections, and Victor's, and hum the blood Healing tones, realizing that the damage caused by the dagger is deeper than what we can see. Gabe's power is slowly draining, his energy dying cell by cell. Boone has cut him in seven places. Once on each arm, twice on his chest, once above each knee. But the worst is the deep stab into his abdomen, just below his belly button. The cold water has kept him from bleeding to death, but if I don't Heal him, his intestines will wither up, followed by his colon and other organs. The poison will spread through his bloodstream, and Gabe will die a slow and painful death.

My ring hums to life as the desperation of the situation hits me.

"Abby, you can't do this." Kye pleads. "You're not strong enough."

The knot of fury in my core burns hot, clearing my head and keeping me focused. "I was born to do this. He's dying," I sob. "I'm not going to let him."

Kye's hurt, angry, but resolute as he settles next to me. Victor flanks my other side, and each of them rests a hand on my shoulder to lend me additional energy to get this done.

Murtagh lands on my hand, holding my index finger to help me keep my hands moving.

The stones in my bracelet aren't nearly as powerful as the pendant I used when I Healed Kye, but I have the ring, and my blood. Lots of that. However disgusted I was to learn that blood can be used as a tool and a weapon, I'm remarkably grateful that it can also be used as a Gift. I will give Gabe back his life.

I remove my rings and place them on his torso, above the worst of his wounds, and Murtagh helps me continue to rotate his chakras. The gems flicker, their power diminished by my lack of energy. I've only just started and already my arms ache with exhaustion.

Gabe's eyes pop open again, his lips bowing into a frown. "I said no."

I ignore him, still humming, calling on energy I don't have, desperate to save this person who has risked everything to save me. I spin, and sing, and focus my Light, my energy, until Gabe's energy shifts, forcing his sluggish to heart pump harder and all his broken parts to rise to where I've called them. As Gabe's energy funnels, my own drains, and my vision goes hazy. I must sway, because Kye's hands brace my back; he holds me up. He's saying something, but his words are jumbled and nonsensical.

Desperate to stay conscious, I call Gabe's energy into me, knowing I've only touched the worst parts of his injuries, and then I tug a small amount of energy from Victor, hoping it's enough. When it's not, I borrow some from Kye, swirling the three together, using our combined strength to mend Gabe's most devastating fissures before I send his energy back.

He won't be one hundred percent, but he'll live, and that's what's most important for now.

I work hard, relieved to feel the transfer of pain, the now-familiar building of pressure, and keep spinning, singing, mending, until my control escapes, and it's time to send his energy back. My completion is abrupt, but the energy continues to flow from me into Gabe, weighing my eyes and limbs and head down. When the transfer is complete, I collapse into Kye, eyes closed, desperate for a nap.

Someone's talking. I can't tell who, nor can I decipher what they're saying. I only know there are lots of voices, and they're loud. I force my eyes open, expecting to be in bed, having lost more days of my life, but I'm not. I'm lying on a patch of grass, surrounded by jungle and trees. The setting sun casts a red-gold light, turning the sky a brilliant orange I worried I'd never see again.

Kye, Victor, and Gabe are nearby, obscured from view by enormous jungle leaves. They're arguing.

"... don't know how long."

"... promised you'd stop her."

"... she didn't have the strength."

"... can't just take her. She has to wake up."

"... too long. Might be days."

I blink, ignoring the sharp, burning pain in my abdomen, and croak, "I'm awake."

The three of them whip around, eyes wide with shock. Both Gabe and Kye fall to their knees next to me. "How do you feel, babe?" Kye murmurs.

At the same time, Gabe says, "Why are you so determined to kill yourself?"

I blink again, ignoring the useless questions, and focus on Victor. "How long have I been out?"

"About two hours." His smile spreads into a grin. "I have never seen a Healer work before. Good job, gringa."

"Thanks." *Two hours? That can't be right. Last time it was days. Nine of them.* "Will someone help me up? We should find the others, see how the battle went. Where's Murtagh?"

"He went to get help." Kye slides his hands under my arms and lifts until I'm standing. Gabe's not at his best since some of the poison still lingers inside him, so Kye and Victor each brace one side of me. I don't tell them that I have no feeling in my feet—just focus on moving them. Before long, we come upon an abandoned golf cart, probably left behind by our team. Victor drives us back to the hotel, where—according to the plan—the Dragons are supposed to have regrouped. There are signs of battle everywhere. Downed tree limbs, broken ruins, crumbled rocks, shattered pieces of life. I don't want to know how many friends we've lost today, so I'm beyond glad when we don't come across any bodies—demon or human.

When we reach the main building, Gabe and Victor insist on informing Enrique that we're back so they can send someone to recover Alejandro's body.

I'm not sure why I'm already conscious rather than lapsed into the Healer's sleep, but I know I need lots of Healing herbs and rest. I don't want to talk to anyone, but I have to tell Rose about Alejandro because I don't want her to find out from someone else. Rather than go inside to be debriefed, I wait for Gabe to look inside and wave at me to indicate that Rose isn't there.

Kye starts the engine and drives to our bungalow, wordlessly. Something has changed between us, and I'm afraid it might take a while before we figure out what to do about it.

Rose isn't in there, and so, exhausted, the two of us head for Christine and Eoin's. As the adrenaline wears off, my mind grows foggy and sluggish. My arm throbs, pulsing with a mixture of heat and cold that should be at odds, and yet spreads a pleasant sensation of detachment through me. Kye knocks on the door, and we wait for an eternity before deciding that no one is here, either.

"You need to rest," he says. I can't bring myself to respond. I love Kye, I do, but I don't know if I can forgive him for taking away my choices—for not trusting me with my own power, my own Gifts. I don't know if I can forgive him for other things, either. And so, rather than speak, I follow him to our room, knowing I need to talk to Rose, but unable to continue for another second, and fall, face-first, on the bed, never more relieved to be lying horizontal. Kye gingerly wraps a hand towel around my arm, tying it tight enough to cut off my circulation, and then falls next to me, his fingers wrapping around mine, eyes closed. He doesn't try to enfold me in his arms, and I'm glad. I think we both just need some sleep. I hope.

FORTY-THREE

Facing Destiny

It feels like only minutes have passed when Gabe shakes me awake. "Hey," he murmurs, obviously trying not to disturb Kye— who is breathing deeply and heavily beside me. "Rose is back. And so is Christine. She needs to look at that wound."

I scarcely have the energy to nod. Gabe notices without my having to tell him, and scoops me into his arms. Kye sits up rapidly, his croaky voice a mixture of anger and exhaustion. "What are you doing? Where are you taking her?"

"Relax. Your mother's here. She needs to look at Abby's arm."

"Oh. I'll take her." Kye jumps up, immediately awake—far more than me, anyway—and makes an awkward attempt to wrestle me from Gabe.

"I already have her," Gabe says, sounding amused. "Go back to sleep. I promise I'll bring her back soon."

But Kye follows anyway, looking like an angry puppy. Gabe takes me to the sitting room in Christine's villa, where Rose is curled up in a recliner, sobbing into a pillow.

"Who told her?" I ask Gabe.

"No one. We didn't need to," Gabe murmurs. "He's not here, and we are. The Dragons are in body recovery mode."

He sets me in the chair next to hers and I reach out, rest a hand on her shoulder, because I don't have the strength to stand. "I'm so sorry, Rose. So sorry."

"Did ... did you try?" she asks, her words pleading. "Please tell me you tried."

Every part of me wants to lie, tell her that I did try, that I tried hard. I want her to know that I would have tried if I had the opportunity. But I think she already knows, and I'm not good at lying. "I couldn't. By the time we got to him—"

"You didn't try?" she shouts. "My boyfriend died and you couldn't even try to save him? Why Abby? Isn't he good enough? Important enough? I'm your best friend—aren't I important enough? I love him!"

"Yes, Rose, of course you are. Of course. You're my best friend and I love you, and I know you love him and I would have done anything, anything to have been able to Heal him and save you this grief. But I couldn't Heal Alex. There was nothing I could do."

"Why?" she shouts again. "Why not, Abby?" She's sobbing, hysterical, clutching the wet pillow as if she could rip it to shreds—which she might. "I'll never forgive you for not trying. I can't believe you didn't even try."

My eyes burn with tears and I let them fall, aching for the person I couldn't save. "Rose, I would have. I swear I would have. But when we got to him, he was already dead. The energy had already left his body."

"Noooo!" Her gasp is so deep, so wrenching that I can feel the energy in the room shift with her grief. I try to sit up, needing to hug her, to be there for her, but as soon as I move, I see spots, feel the world tilt. Kye stands instead, crouching in front of Rose to murmur words of comfort, while Christine enters with a basket of dried herbs and cloths and begins to poke at my already festering wound. She gasps. "Is this from the dagger?"

I nod, remembering what I saw when I Healed Gabe, the end result of a dagger wound. "It's draining me, isn't it?"

She doesn't respond, but her hands shake as she digs through her basket, looking lost.

"Why don't you start with black pepper?" I suggest. "Make a poultice using juniper berries and lavender. Also, I have a good detoxifying crystal somewhere." Nodding, Christine goes to work creating the poultice, with me throwing in suggestions as I think of them. My cut is packed and bandaged, the crystal taped on top, and infused with Healing energy from Christine. When the door opens behind us, I don't turn around—that would require too much energy. But then an arm comes around the chair to hug me. It's accompanied by a familiar smell, and the words, "Happy birthday, baby doll." I jerk my head back to see for myself. "Mom." I whisper. "Mom!"

As promised, my mother came. Just because I needed her.

It's nearly midnight and Rose is tucked in bed, having taken a handful of customized sleep aids that include heavy doses of valerian root and melatonin. We lost six Dragons to the demons, but Alejandro was the only one we all knew personally, and the one whose face will continue to haunt me forever. The rest of them came in force and are currently cleaning up the aftermath of battle.

Eoin and Christine have called me and Kye to their room, along with my mother and Akers—who came with her—for a private meeting. At nine a.m., Kye and I are expected to give a full report of everything we saw, did, or experienced in regards to the tomb and its mermaid guards. I'm hoping I'll somehow fall into a Healer's sleep before then, because I don't want to talk about it. Ever again.

Unfortunately, since that sleep hasn't come already, it's probably not going to.

Eoin gets right to the point, focusing on Kye and me. "There's a lot of information to share, but we don't have much time. Val and Zane know Marian and Landon are here, which tells me they also know that Kye and I have come. I'm still not certain why they're so determined to keep the two of you apart, but as I continue to research, everything I'm finding indicates that though Theron and

Raina suffered from a curse, that wasn't necessarily the thing that killed them. In fact, we aren't positive how they died."

"What are you saying?" Mom asks. And I'm grateful she asked so I don't have to.

"This is just a theory," he says, his voice measured and slow. "But it's possible that the curse has become a tool used to control your choices—regardless of right or wrong. It's possible that Val is making you both sick in order to keep you apart. It's possible he believes that keeping you apart is the best way to prevent you from producing a child, while still utilizing your abilities to help bring down the demons he's been trying to vanquish for so many years. And I'm not going to lie. I believe he's playing the part of a puppeteer, timing things according to his will, including if and when another child is produced to carry on the royal lineage." He pauses at my gasp of alarm. "Don't look so shocked, Abby. We're all adults now, and the royal child has been the catalyst to bring Theron and Raina down every time."

"I don't understand," I murmur, swallowing around a completely different lump. "Are you saying ... are we supposed to make ... to do ... to have a baby, then? Is that what they want?"

My mother squeezes my hand, already shaking her head. "No. Abby's not a pawn. We're not going to play that game. She's eighteen years old. Barely. I don't care how much they may love each other—that's way too young. She's too young to get married, to have a baby, to save the damn world."

I can't look at Kye right now. Can't. I do love him, but I'm still so hurt by all the things that have happened recently. And now we're talking family as if I don't even have a choice? This doesn't sit well with me. I'm still wearing his ring, but I have a sudden intense urge to give it back. Now. Right now.

"Actually, no," Eoin continues. "Quite the opposite. I think my niece hit on a real point when she shared her theory about past patterns and what might be necessary to break them."

He looks pointedly at Kye, who actually blushes. My own cheeks heat. We haven't done *that*. But the only people who can be sure are me and Kye. Everyone else can only guess.

"It's absolutely essential that the two of you understand how much is at stake. You cannot, under any circumstances, make that risk a reality."

I'm shaking my head, still not quite getting it when Christine chimes in with a quiet, but firm, "Birth control methods are not enough. There's only one absolute way to prevent pregnancy, and that's abstinence."

I want to die. Want to melt into a puddle on the floor and slide around the tile until I find a deep, dark corner where I can hide and never come out again. I settle for hiding my face in my mother's sweater.

"Since you're both responding by hiding, I'm going to assume you understand that part," Eoin says, tapping his pen against the little pad of hotel paper. "So back to Val and Zane. They're coming. And since you're strongest together, I prefer not to have them tear you apart again." He sends a semi-questioning glance to Kye, who nods slowly. "It's time for you to run."

And so, at three-something a.m., at a resort in the jungles of Mexico, I find myself in a room I've been sharing with the boy I once hoped to marry. We pack in silence, nerves on edge, because I've just been told to do the thing I avoided doing a week ago. Despite my feelings for Gabe, or the anger and confusion I feel toward Kye, despite the fact that my best friend in the world just lost the boy she loves in a horrific demon battle, or the fact that even the smallest slip up in the bedroom could bring the world crashing down, I'm running away with Kye.

After my mother calmed down, Landon managed to convince her that this really is the best thing for me, so she has come to help me pack. "Baby, you don't have to go. You have choices. I don't care what these people say—you will always have lots and lots of choices."

"I know," I tell her, zipping the last of my things into a suitcase. "I wish I knew which choice was best."

"Me too," she says, double-checking the bathroom, the closet, under the bed. "But after talking to Landon, I think I'd rather know that you're in control of your circumstances instead of having people we hardly know calling all your shots."

I nod. She's right. Beyond everything else, beyond reason or ruin or absolute rapture, leaving now with Kye will give me the chance to decide for myself where I'd like my future to go.

So I wheel my ginormous suitcase to the car Eoin rented at the airport. Kye's already there, his things loaded in the trunk. I'm not sure how to look at him now that things have changed so drastically, so I don't. I hug my mother, Landon, Christine, and Eoin. This decision has been made in the dead of night, and the six of us are the only ones who know. I cannot say goodbye to Gabe, or to Rose or Victor. I can't even say goodbye to Murtagh, who has spent the night helping clean up the mess.

Eoin hands Kye a thick envelope. "New accounts, new identities. Check in only in extreme emergency, and only as you're leaving a place to which you will not be returning, or if either of you gets too sick to function. Please don't take chances we can't afford."

He hugs us both, and then Mom hugs me again, slipping a folded piece of paper into my hand. "You have more choices than you know. Be a broad thinker. I love you, baby."

There's no moon tonight, and even the stars seem extra far away as I buckle my seatbelt and Kye starts the car. Once we've left the lot and can no longer see those we're leaving behind, I unfold the paper my mother slipped into my hand:

Spencer Johnson
Box 203
Clontarf Road Post Office
64 Clontarf Road
Dublin 3

My gasp of surprise makes Kye cast a furtive glance in my direction, and I meet his eyes for the first time since I Healed Gabe. "What is it?" he asks.

"It's an address," I manage, heart racing, thoughts colliding. "For my dead father."

Kye hits the brakes, his eyes as wide as mine must be. I swallow. Swallow. Swallow again. Blink, because I'm frozen. This is huge. Everything I've believed about my family has just been ripped to shreds. And Kye, who must sense the way I am shaken to the core, puts his foot on the gas and presses down.

It's up to us where we go from here.

Nichole Giles was born in Nevada and has lived in a number of cities in and around the Midwest. Her early career plans included becoming an actress or a rock star, but she decided instead to have a family and then become a writer. Writing is her passion, but she also loves to spend time with her husband and four children, travel to tropical and exotic destinations, drive in the rain with the convertible top down, and play music at full volume so she can sing along.

Acknowledgements

Some people claim that writing is a solitary endeavor, but if that were true, this section wouldn't be necessary. It doesn't seem possible, but I have even more people to thank this time around.

My writing village is more like a city, at the center of which is my family—Gary, Brayden, Brittany, Madison, and McKay—who are not only the solid ground where my feet are planted, but also the people who keep my world spinning. Your love and support gives me every tool I need to succeed, and a net to catch me if ever I fall. I love you through time and space and all eternity.

I would never survive the publishing universe without Elana Johnson, who supports me in a thousand different ways, and who recently reminded me exactly why I'm in this business. Also, my remarkable critique group, whom I have grown to appreciate even more since I moved away: Keith Fisher (whose hugs I miss tremendously), Kim Job, (whose enthusiasm always spurs me on), Tristi Pinkston (my editing guru), and Heather Justesen, (a formatting/publishing genius who deserves a medal for always coming to my rescue). Rachelle Christensen is not only a great friend, but a gem who jumped in to help edit this book (along with all the above mentioned people). Photography goddess, Erin Summerill, is responsible for both my author photo and also my beautiful cover. A thousand thank-yous to you all for sharing your prowess with me.

I will always have a soft spot for my Rhemalda team—Rhett and Emmaline Hoffmeister, Dianne Dalton, and Michelle Davidson Argyle. Without all of you, DESCENDANT wouldn't have been published, and BIRTHRIGHT would remain an outline for an idea on an old computer file. I miss working with you, and will be forever grateful for everything I learned from being part of your publishing family.

Special thanks to my marvelous, talented agent Sarah Negovetich, who is cool enough to invite me to hang out at book festivals, will read for me even though she's crazy busy, and has enough faith to keep us both going. I'm glad you're in my writing city.

L.T. Elliott, Jenn Johanson, Debbie Davis, Windy Aphayrath, Karen Hoover, David McDonald, Erik Kluth, Kellie Peterson, Cindy and Russ Beck, and Connie Hall each deserve their own notes of thanks, along with my people at Authors Incognito and LDStorymakers. Sports teams have cheerleaders in the bleachers. I have all of you.

Success and love to Tova Heaton at TheWayOfTheWitch.com, my holistic healing source, for helping me keep my herbs and crystals straight, and for a lifetime of friendship more valuable than any precious stone.

Special loves to my FABs, Jennifer Brown, Tiffany Wood-McCarthy, Raylene Long, and Lori Smith, for always knowing I need you without knowing why, for holding me together when I might otherwise fall to pieces, and for supplying me with more laughter than most people have in a lifetime. Whoever said slumber parties are for little girls never had a sleepover with us!

Kisses to my siblings: Ryan, Matt (and Nicole), James, Jodi (and Nick), Chandi, Zack, Justin, Cameron, Daeton, and Troy. Also to my parents, Joe and Pam Petersen, Steve and Deanne Hechtle, and Kay and Carol Giles. And the rest of my extended family—naming you all would take another full novel, but I love every one of you.

The thing about villages that turn into cities is that they continue to grow. There is no way to name all the wonderful people who have influenced, supported, and loved me through this process. Just because your name isn't listed here doesn't mean I don't recognize or remember your contribution. I do. And I will never forget. Sending you all my most heartfelt love. Thanks for reading.

www.ingramcontent.com/pod-product-compliance
Lightning Source LLC
Chambersburg PA
CBHW072128250626
47159CB00007B/2612